Published by
KaBOOM!

Ross Richie   CEO & Founder
Matt Gagnon   Editor-In-Chief
Filip Sablik   President of Publishing & Marketing
Stephen Christy   President of Development
Lance Kreiter   VP of Licensing & Merchandising
Phil Barbaro   VP of Finance
Bryce Carlson   Managing Editor
Mel Caylo   Marketing Manager
Scott Newman   Production Design Manager
Kate Henning   Operations Manager
Sierra Hahn   Senior Editor
Dafna Pleban   Editor, Talent Development
Shannon Watters   Editor
Eric Harburn   Editor
Whitney Leopard   Associate Editor
Jasmine Amiri   Associate Editor
Chris Rosa   Associate Editor
Alex Galer   Associate Editor
Cameron Chittock   Associate Editor
Matthew Levine   Assistant Editor
Sophie Philips-Roberts   Assistant Editor
Kelsey Dieterich   Production Designer
Jillian Crab   Production Designer
Michelle Ankley   Production Designer
Grace Park   Production Design Assistant
Elizabeth Loughridge   Accounting Coordinator
Stephanie Hocutt   Social Media Coordinator
José Meza   Sales Assistant
James Arriola   Mailroom Assistant
Holly Aitchison   Operations Assistant
Sam Kusek   Direct Market Representative
Amber Parker   Administrative Assistant

ADVENTURE TIME MATHEMATICAL EDITION Volume
Eight, May 2017. Published by KaBOOM!, a division of
Boom Entertainment, Inc. ADVENTURE TIME, CARTOON
NETWORK, the logos, and all related characters and
elements are trademarks of and © Cartoon Network.
(S17) Originally published in single magazine form as
ADVENTURE TIME No. 35-39. © Cartoon Network. (S15)

A catalog record of this book is available from OCLC and
from the BOOM! Studios website, www.boom-studios.com,
on the Librarians Page.

BOOM! Studios, 5670 Wilshire Boulevard, Suite 450, Los
Angeles, CA 90036-5679. Printed in China. First Printing.

ISBN: 978-1-60886-967-1, eISBN: 978-1-61398-638-7

ADVENTURE TIME™

MATHEMATICAL EDITION
Volume Eight

kaboom!™
CARTOON NETWORK.

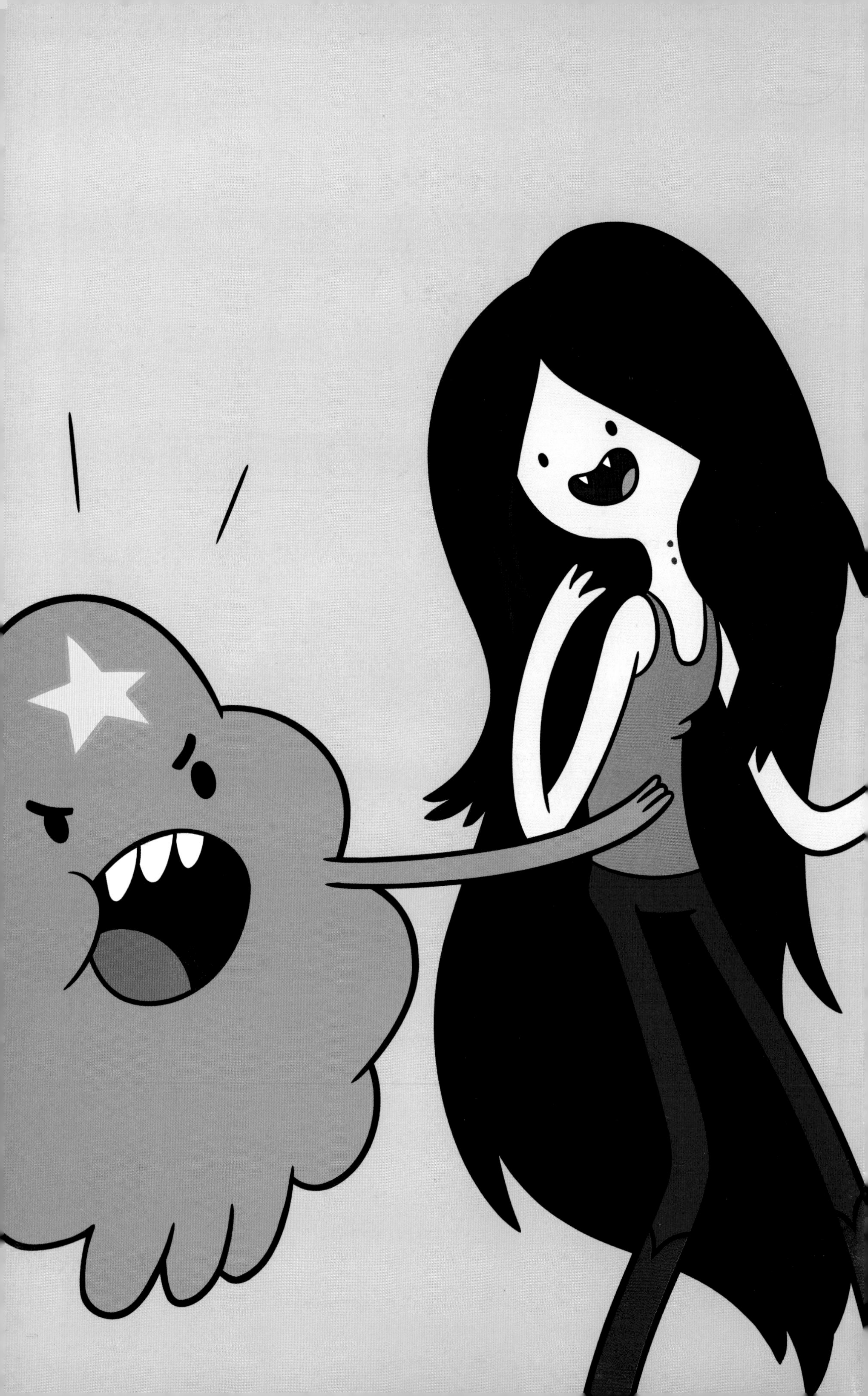

ADVENTURE TIME

CREATED BY

Pendleton Ward

CHAPTER ONE

WRITTEN BY

Ryan North

ILLUSTRATED BY

Shelli Paroline & Braden Lamb

CHAPTERS TWO THROUGH FIVE

WRITTEN BY

Christopher Hastings

ILLUSTRATED BY

Zachary Sterling

COLORS BY

Maarta Laiho

LETTERS BY

Steve Wands

COLLECTION AND COVER DESIGN
Kelsey Dieterich

ASSOCIATE EDITOR
Whitney Leopard

EDITOR
Shannon Watters

With Special Thanks to Marisa Marionakis, Janet No, Curtis Lelash, Conrad Montgomery,
Meghan Bradley, Kelly Crews, Scott Malchus, Adam Muto and the wonderful folks
at Cartoon Network.

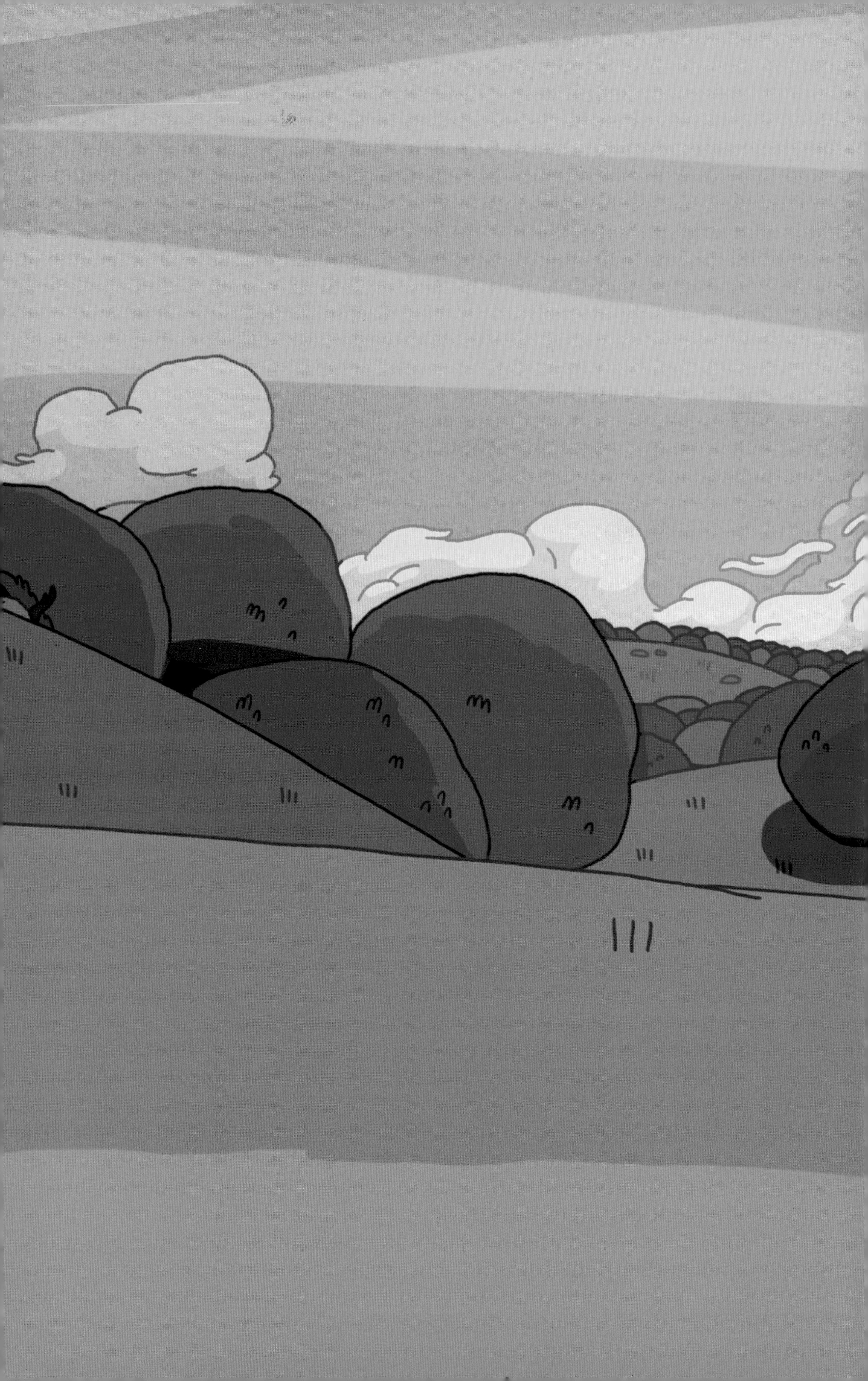

CHAPTER ONE

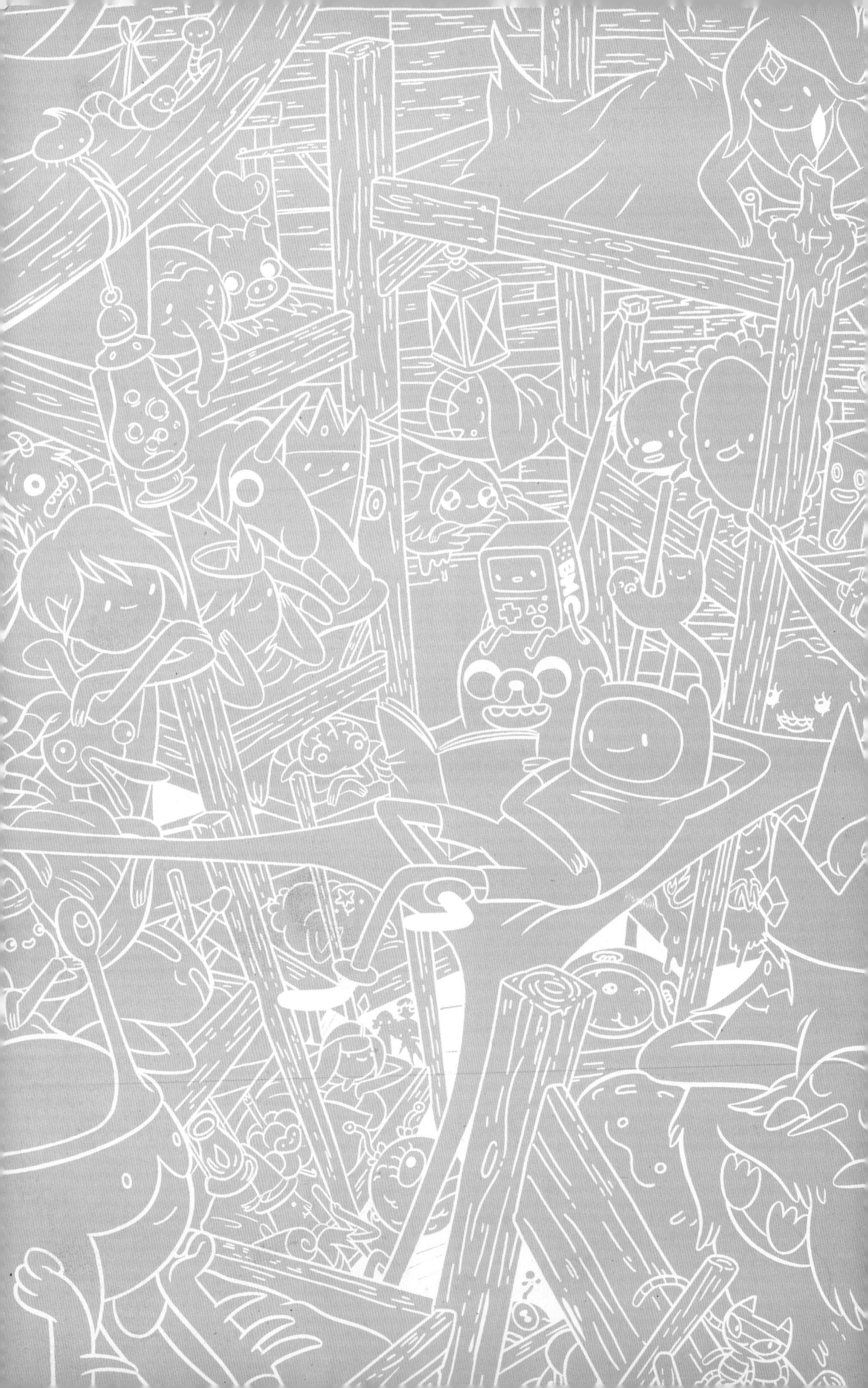
BMO

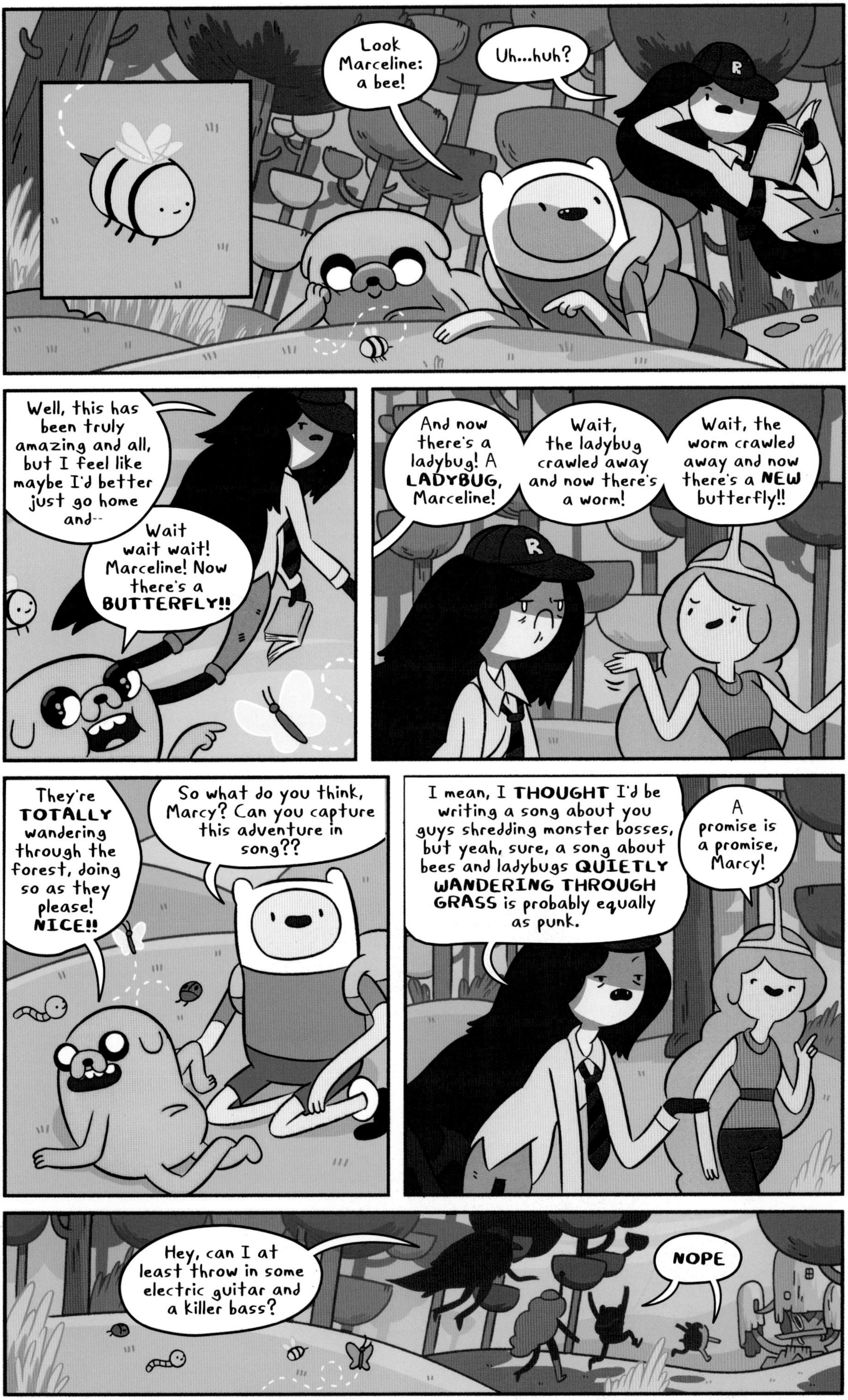
Look Marceline: a bee!
Uh...huh?
Well, this has been truly amazing and all, but I feel like maybe I'd better just go home and--
Wait wait wait! Marceline! Now there's a BUTTERFLY!!
And now there's a ladybug! A LADYBUG, Marceline!
Wait, the ladybug crawled away and now there's a worm!
Wait, the worm crawled away and now there's a NEW butterfly!!
They're TOTALLY wandering through the forest, doing so as they please! NICE!!
So what do you think, Marcy? Can you capture this adventure in song??
I mean, I THOUGHT I'd be writing a song about you guys shredding monster bosses, but yeah, sure, a song about bees and ladybugs QUIETLY WANDERING THROUGH GRASS is probably equally as punk.
A promise is a promise, Marcy!
Hey, can I at least throw in some electric guitar and a killer bass?
NOPE

Come along with me / And this book will be your key / It's not prose but it's a comic / and it's like what's on TV

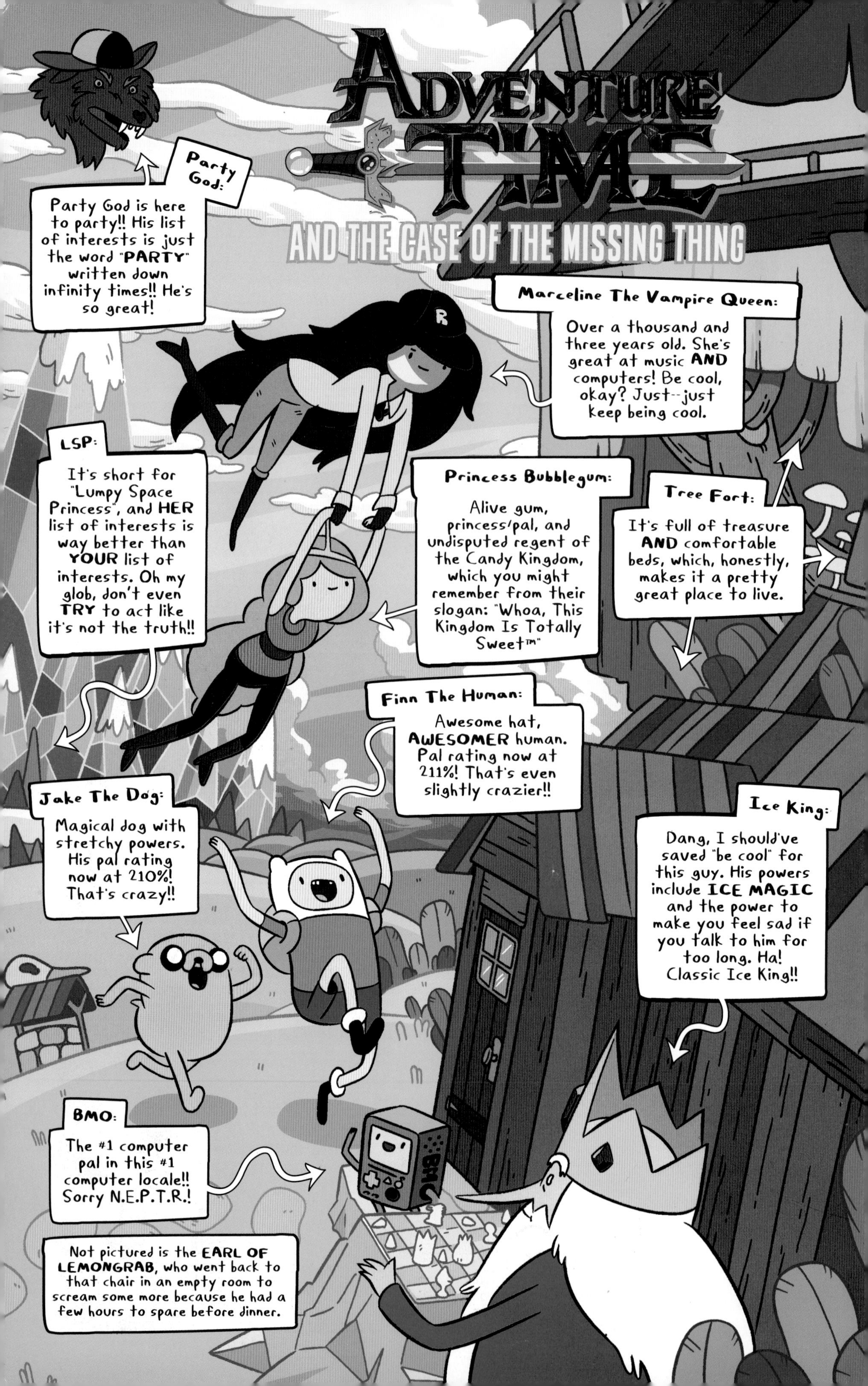
ADVENTURE TIME
AND THE CASE OF THE MISSING THING
Party God:
Party God is here to party!! His list of interests is just the word "PARTY" written down infinity times!! He's so great!
Marceline The Vampire Queen:
Over a thousand and three years old. She's great at music AND computers! Be cool, okay? Just--just keep being cool.
LSP:
It's short for "Lumpy Space Princess", and HER list of interests is way better than YOUR list of interests. Oh my glob, don't even TRY to act like it's not the truth!!
Princess Bubblegum:
Alive gum, princess/pal, and undisputed regent of the Candy Kingdom, which you might remember from their slogan: "Whoa, This Kingdom Is Totally Sweet™"
Tree Fort:
It's full of treasure AND comfortable beds, which, honestly, makes it a pretty great place to live.
Finn The Human:
Awesome hat, AWESOMER human. Pal rating now at 211%! That's even slightly crazier!!
Jake The Dog:
Magical dog with stretchy powers. His pal rating now at 210%! That's crazy!!
Ice King:
Dang, I should've saved "be cool" for this guy. His powers include ICE MAGIC and the power to make you feel sad if you talk to him for too long. Ha! Classic Ice King!!
BMO:
The #1 computer pal in this #1 computer locale!! Sorry N.E.P.T.R.!
BMO
Not pictured is the EARL OF LEMONGRAB, who went back to that chair in an empty room to scream some more because he had a few hours to spare before dinner.

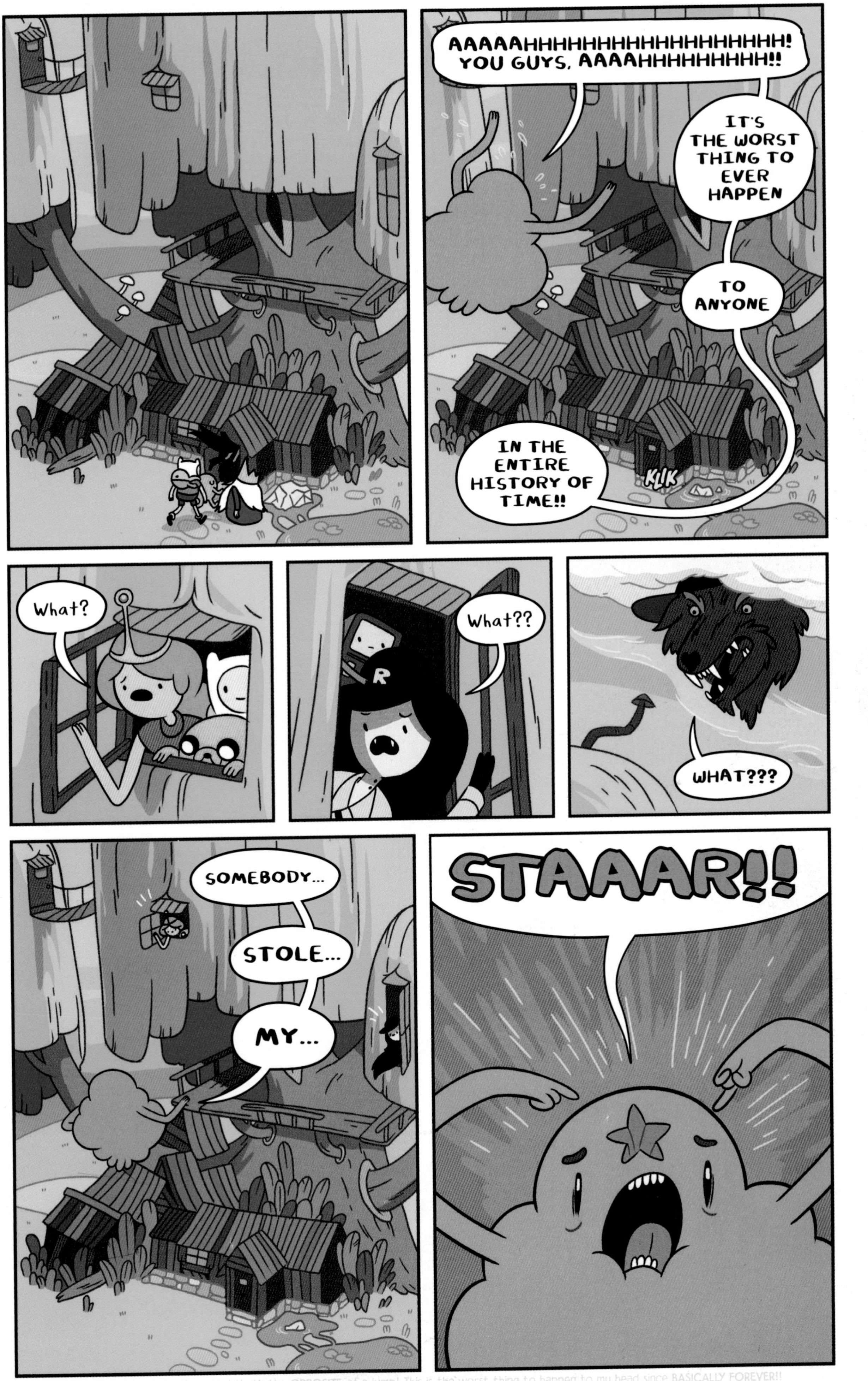
AAAAAHHHHHHHHHHHHHHHHHH! YOU GUYS, AAAAHHHHHHHHH!!
IT'S THE WORST THING TO EVER HAPPEN
TO ANYONE
IN THE ENTIRE HISTORY OF TIME!!
KLIK
What?
What??
WHAT???
SOMEBODY...
STOLE...
MY...
STAAAR!!

Now I've got a hole there and that's the OPPOSITE of a lump! This is the worst thing to happen to my head since BASICALLY FOREVER!!

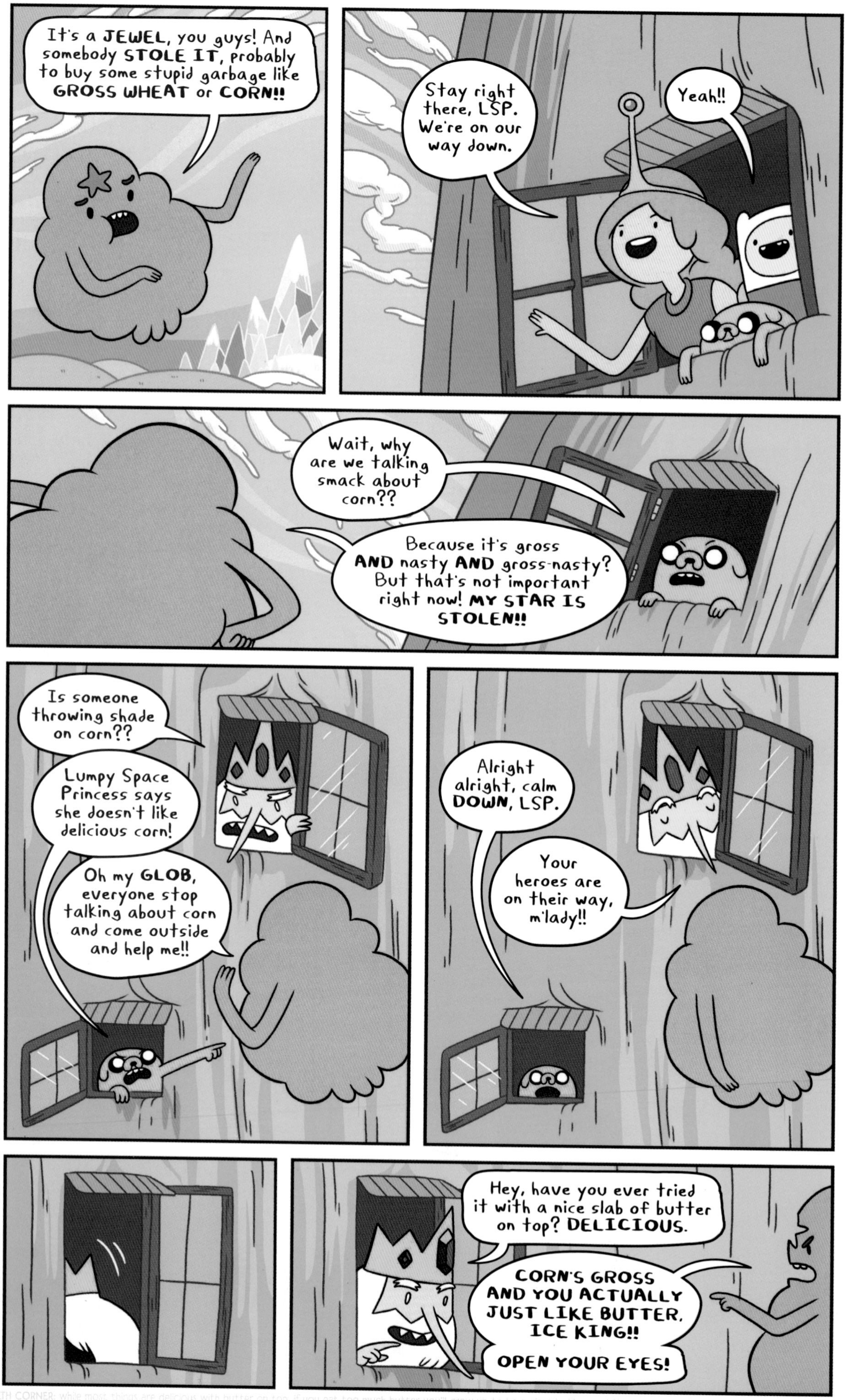
It's a **JEWEL**, you guys! And somebody **STOLE IT**, probably to buy some stupid garbage like **GROSS WHEAT** or **CORN!!**
Stay right there, LSP. We're on our way down.
Yeah!!
Wait, why are we talking smack about corn??
Because it's gross **AND** nasty **AND** gross-nasty? But that's not important right now! **MY STAR IS STOLEN!!**
Is someone throwing shade on corn??
Lumpy Space Princess says she doesn't like delicious corn!
Oh my **GLOB**, everyone stop talking about corn and come outside and help me!!
Alright alright, calm **DOWN**, LSP.
Your heroes are on their way, m'lady!!
Hey, have you ever tried it with a nice slab of butter on top? **DELICIOUS**.
CORN'S GROSS AND YOU ACTUALLY JUST LIKE BUTTER, ICE KING!!
OPEN YOUR EYES!

HEALTH CORNER: while most things are delicious with butter on top, if you eat too much butter you'll grow up to be a giant butter, and then someone will put you on a corn. BE CAREFUL.

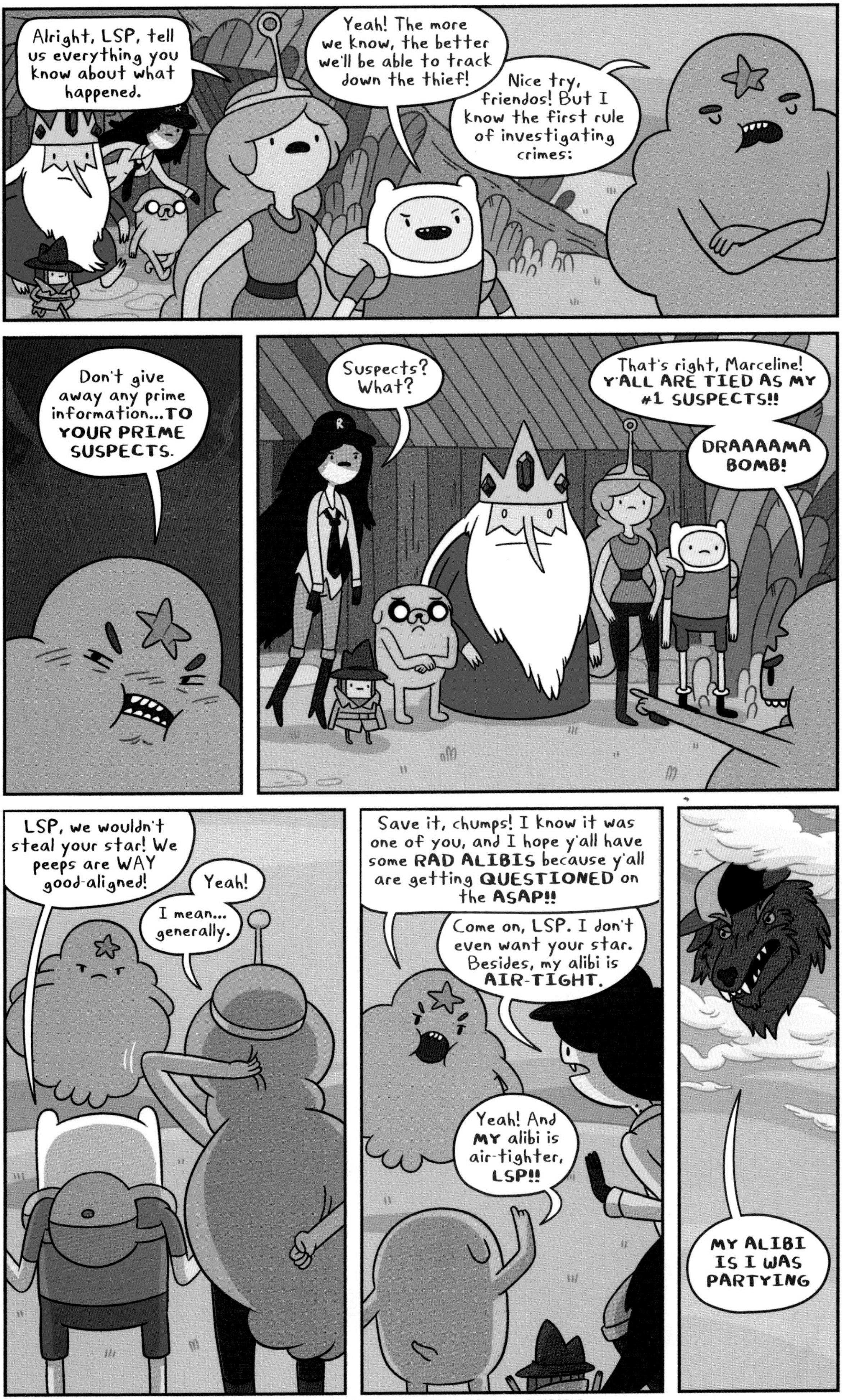
Alright, LSP, tell us everything you know about what happened.
Yeah! The more we know, the better we'll be able to track down the thief!
Nice try, friendos! But I know the first rule of investigating crimes:
Don't give away any prime information...TO YOUR PRIME SUSPECTS.
Suspects? What?
That's right, Marceline! Y'ALL ARE TIED AS MY #1 SUSPECTS!!
DRAAAAMA BOMB!
LSP, we wouldn't steal your star! We peeps are WAY good-aligned!
Yeah!
I mean... generally.
Save it, chumps! I know it was one of you, and I hope y'all have some RAD ALIBIS because y'all are getting QUESTIONED on the ASAP!!
Come on, LSP. I don't even want your star. Besides, my alibi is AIR-TIGHT.
Yeah! And MY alibi is air-tighter, LSP!!
MY ALIBI IS I WAS PARTYING

YBEJZHUQANTBFXVXFFCSIUAGDJPHUQJZOYVYMDJZHUQBZHE

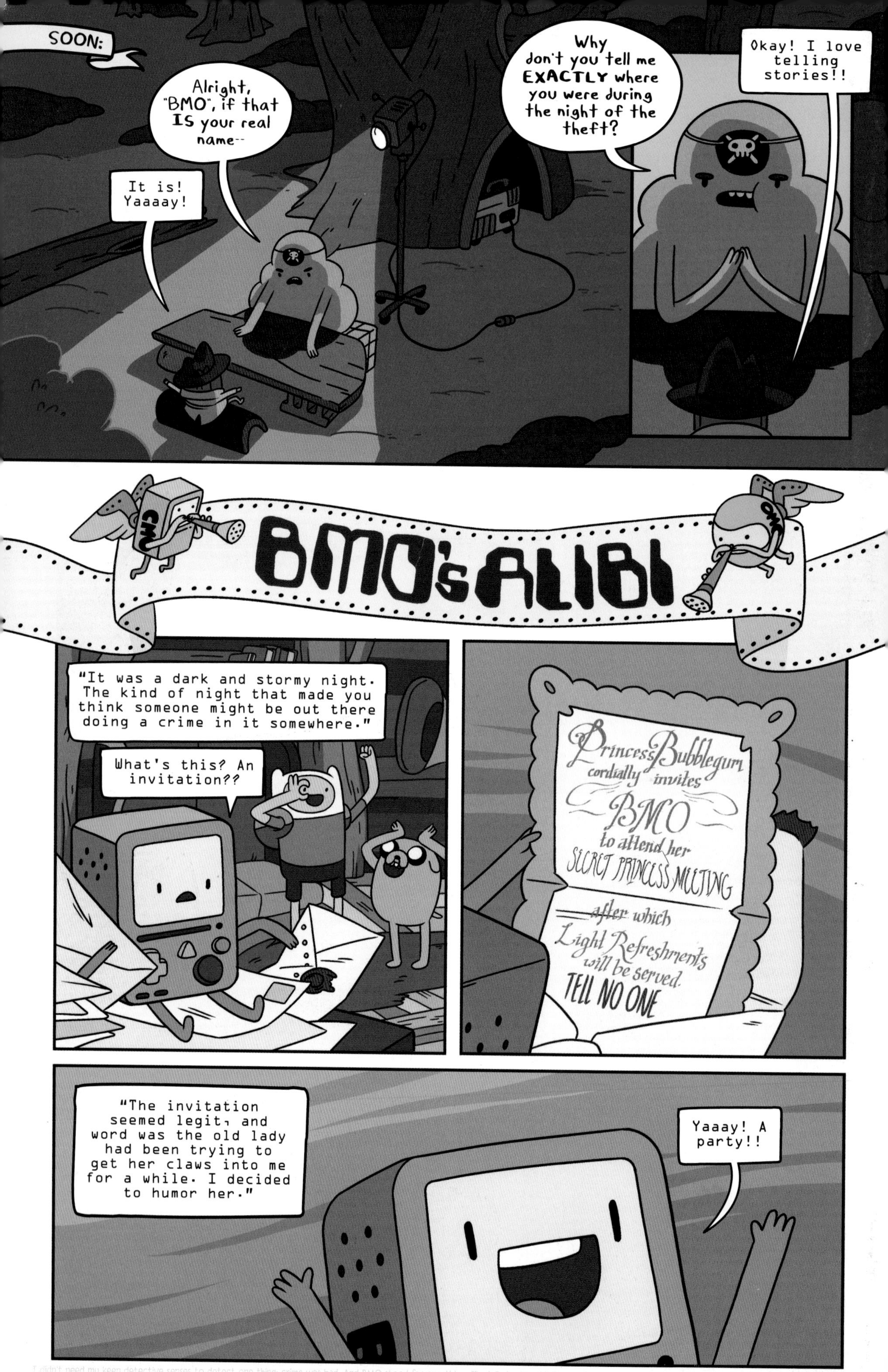
SOON:
Alright, "BMO", if that IS your real name--
It is! Yaaaay!
Why don't you tell me EXACTLY where you were during the night of the theft?
Okay! I love telling stories!!
BMO's ALIBI
"It was a dark and stormy night. The kind of night that made you think someone might be out there doing a crime in it somewhere."
What's this? An invitation??
Princess Bubblegum cordially invites BMO to attend her SECRET PRINCESS MEETING after which Light Refreshments will be served. TELL NO ONE
"The invitation seemed legit, and word was the old lady had been trying to get her claws into me for a while. I decided to humor her."
Yaaay! A party!!

I didn't need my keen detective senses to detect one thing: crime was bad. And BMO stood for one thing: "Best Detective, Yo." Hey: I said I was good at detection. Never said I was good at acronyms.

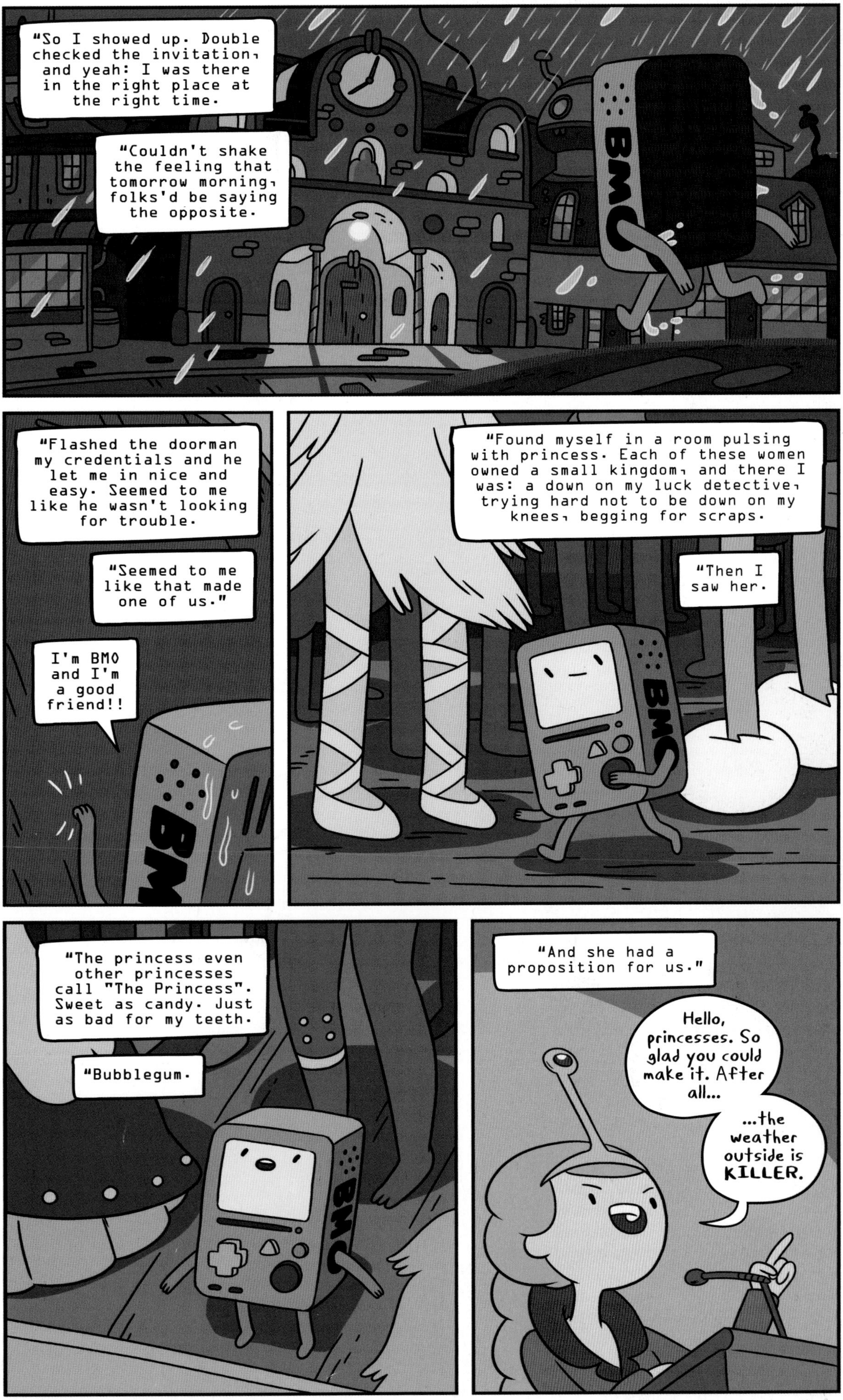
"So I showed up. Double checked the invitation, and yeah: I was there in the right place at the right time.
"Couldn't shake the feeling that tomorrow morning, folks'd be saying the opposite.
"Flashed the doorman my credentials and he let me in nice and easy. Seemed to me like he wasn't looking for trouble.
"Seemed to me like that made one of us."
I'm BMO and I'm a good friend!!
"Found myself in a room pulsing with princess. Each of these women owned a small kingdom, and there I was: a down on my luck detective, trying hard not to be down on my knees, begging for scraps.
"Then I saw her.
"The princess even other princesses call "The Princess". Sweet as candy. Just as bad for my teeth.
"Bubblegum.
"And she had a proposition for us."
Hello, princesses. So glad you could make it. After all...
...the weather outside is **KILLER.**

She was sweet as candy, sure, but she could be hard like hard candy and sour like sour candy too. She was metaphorically like candy in a whole kingdom's worth of ways.

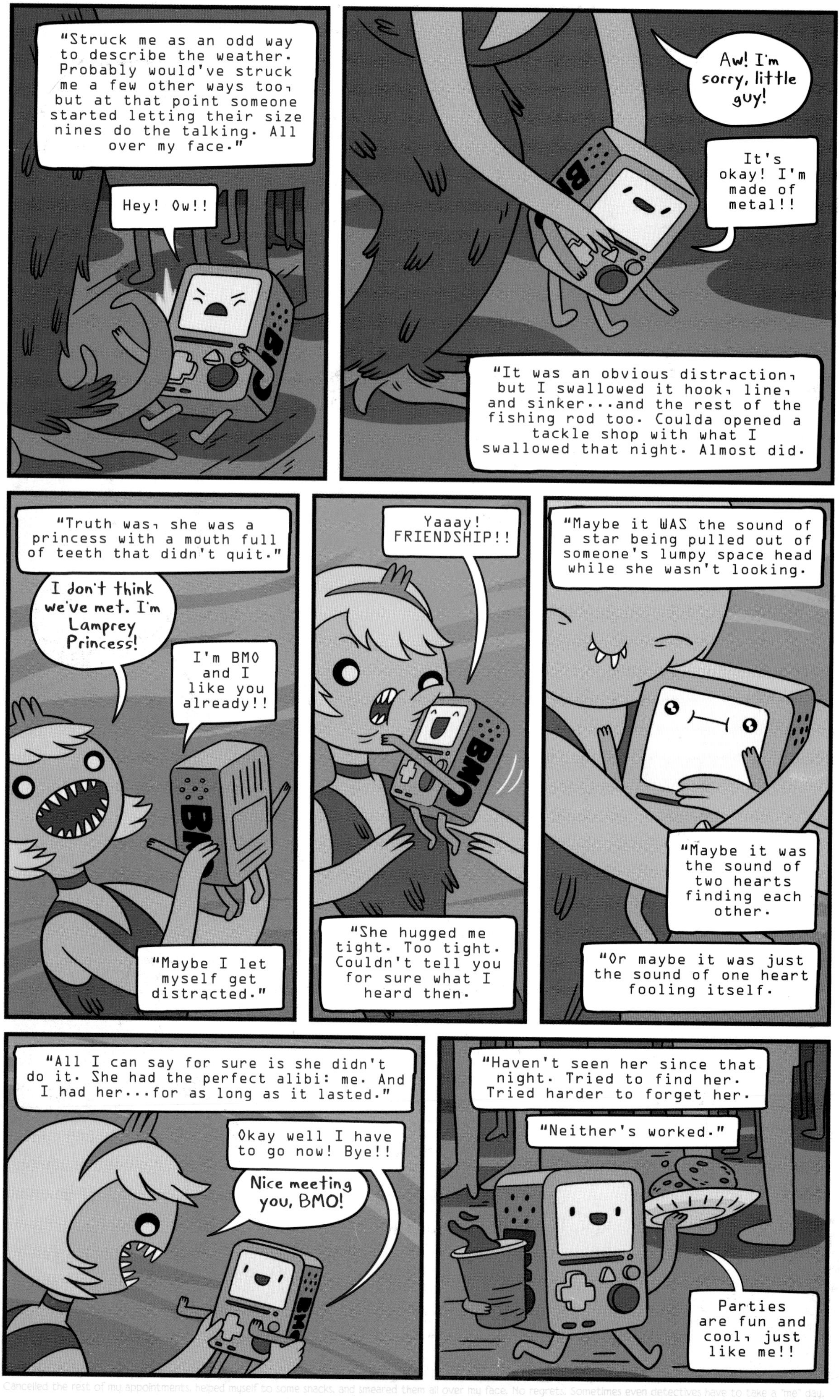
"Struck me as an odd way to describe the weather. Probably would've struck me a few other ways too, but at that point someone started letting their size nines do the talking. All over my face."
Hey! Ow!!
Aw! I'm sorry, little guy!
It's okay! I'm made of metal!!
"It was an obvious distraction, but I swallowed it hook, line, and sinker...and the rest of the fishing rod too. Coulda opened a tackle shop with what I swallowed that night. Almost did.
"Truth was, she was a princess with a mouth full of teeth that didn't quit."
I don't think we've met. I'm Lamprey Princess!
I'm BMO and I like you already!!
"Maybe I let myself get distracted."
Yaaay! FRIENDSHIP!!
"She hugged me tight. Too tight. Couldn't tell you for sure what I heard then.
"Maybe it WAS the sound of a star being pulled out of someone's lumpy space head while she wasn't looking.
"Maybe it was the sound of two hearts finding each other.
"Or maybe it was just the sound of one heart fooling itself.
"All I can say for sure is she didn't do it. She had the perfect alibi: me. And I had her...for as long as it lasted."
Okay well I have to go now! Bye!!
Nice meeting you, BMO!
"Haven't seen her since that night. Tried to find her. Tried harder to forget her.
"Neither's worked."
Parties are fun and cool, just like me!!

Cancelled the rest of my appointments, helped myself to some snacks, and smeared them all over my face. No regrets. Sometimes even detectives have to take a "me" day.

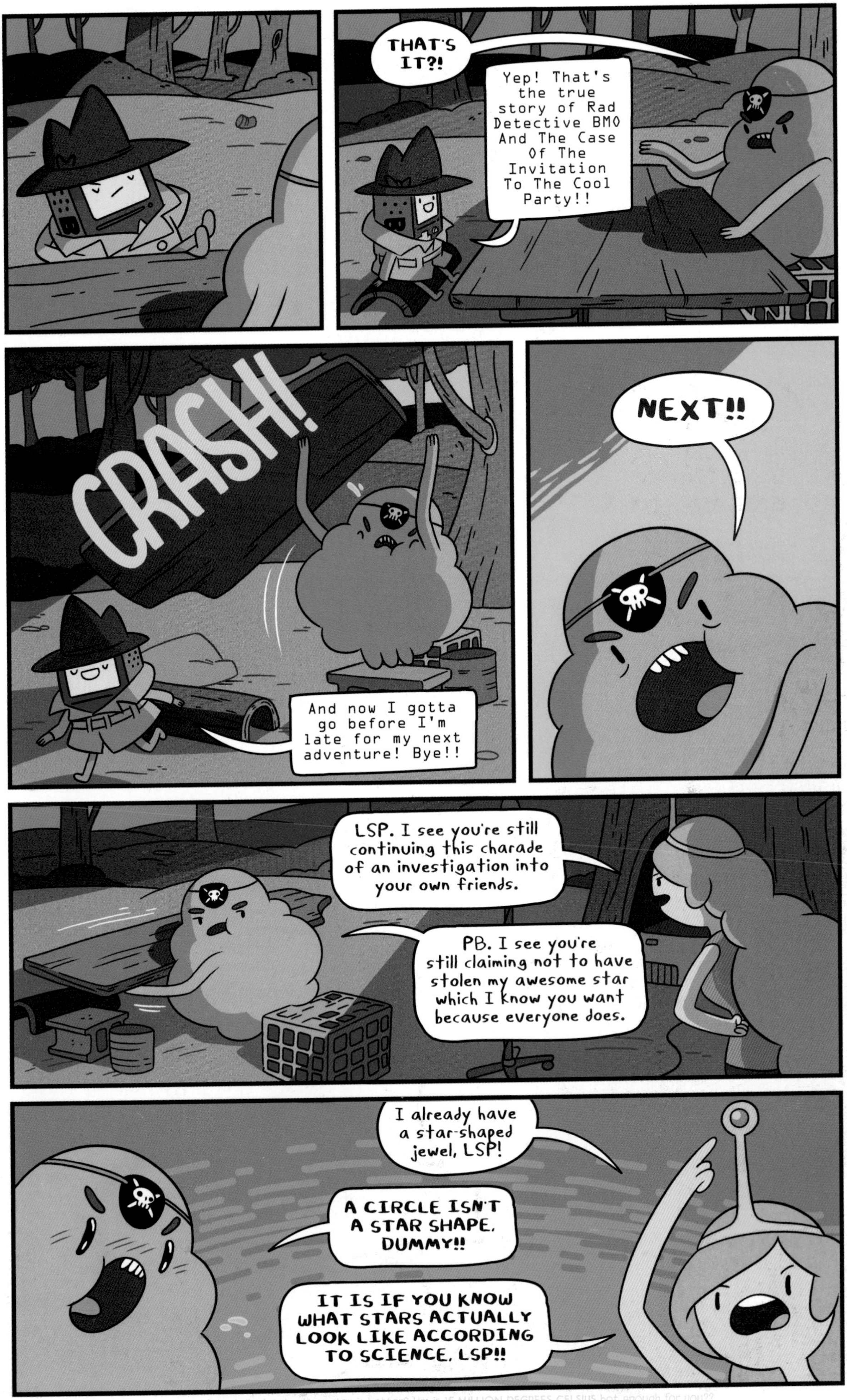
THAT'S IT?!
Yep! That's the true story of Rad Detective BMO And The Case Of The Invitation To The Cool Party!!
CRASH!
And now I gotta go before I'm late for my next adventure! Bye!!
NEXT!!
LSP. I see you're still continuing this charade of an investigation into your own friends.
PB. I see you're still claiming not to have stolen my awesome star which I know you want because everyone does.
I already have a star-shaped jewel, LSP!
A CIRCLE ISN'T A STAR SHAPE, DUMMY!!
IT IS IF YOU KNOW WHAT STARS ACTUALLY LOOK LIKE ACCORDING TO SCIENCE, LSP!!

Oh, you want to talk about whose star is hotter? Um is 15 MILLION DEGREES CELSIUS hot enough for you??

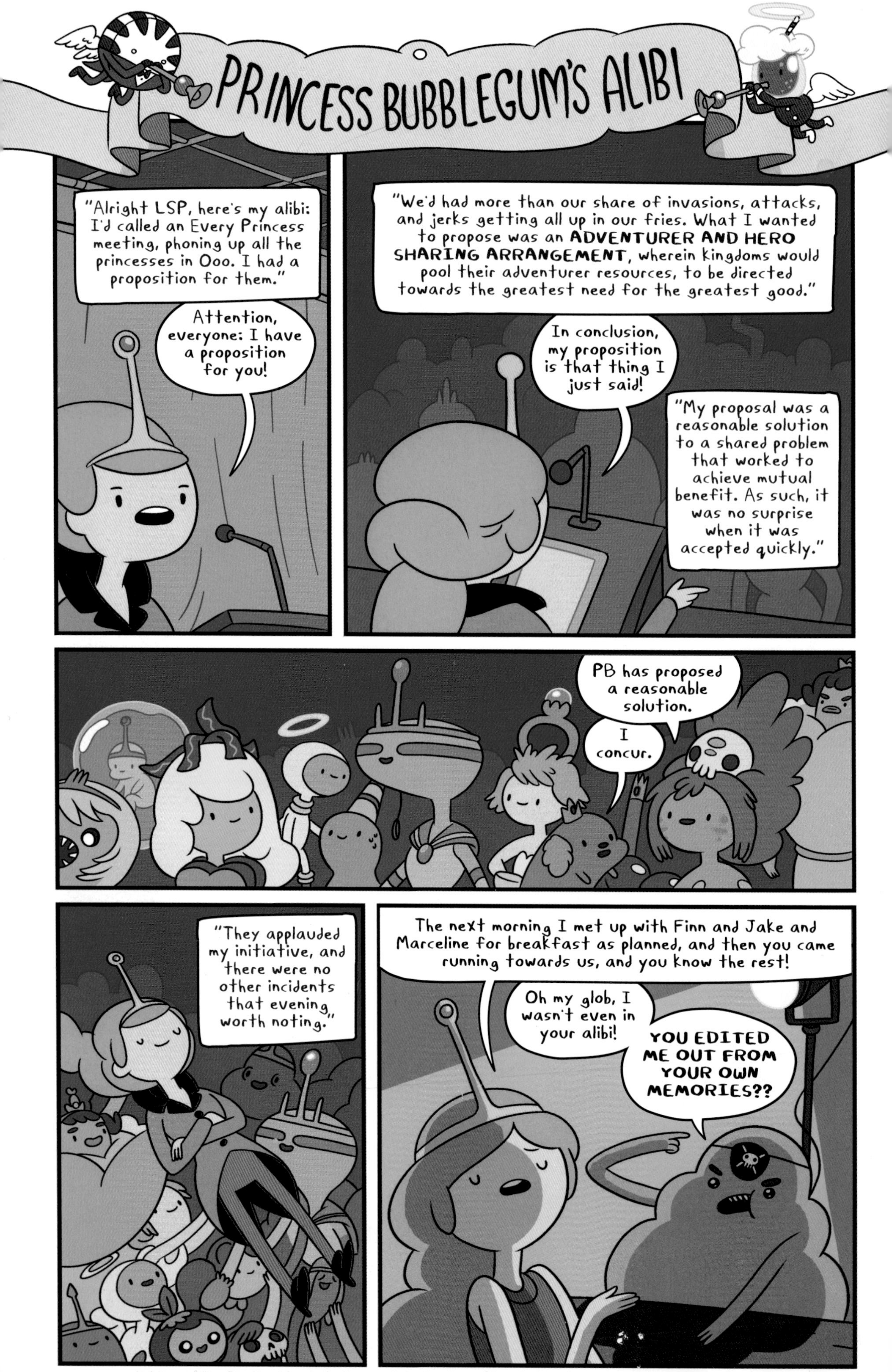
PRINCESS BUBBLEGUM'S ALIBI
"Alright LSP, here's my alibi: I'd called an Every Princess meeting, phoning up all the princesses in Ooo. I had a proposition for them."
Attention, everyone: I have a proposition for you!
"We'd had more than our share of invasions, attacks, and jerks getting all up in our fries. What I wanted to propose was an ADVENTURER AND HERO SHARING ARRANGEMENT, wherein kingdoms would pool their adventurer resources, to be directed towards the greatest need for the greatest good."
In conclusion, my proposition is that thing I just said!
"My proposal was a reasonable solution to a shared problem that worked to achieve mutual benefit. As such, it was no surprise when it was accepted quickly."
PB has proposed a reasonable solution.
I concur.
"They applauded my initiative, and there were no other incidents that evening worth noting."
The next morning I met up with Finn and Jake and Marceline for breakfast as planned, and then you came running towards us, and you know the rest!
Oh my glob, I wasn't even in your alibi!
YOU EDITED ME OUT FROM YOUR OWN MEMORIES??

And so, my fellow Ooo-ians: ask not why there are jerks all up in our fries, ask why we're leaving our fries out in the first place.

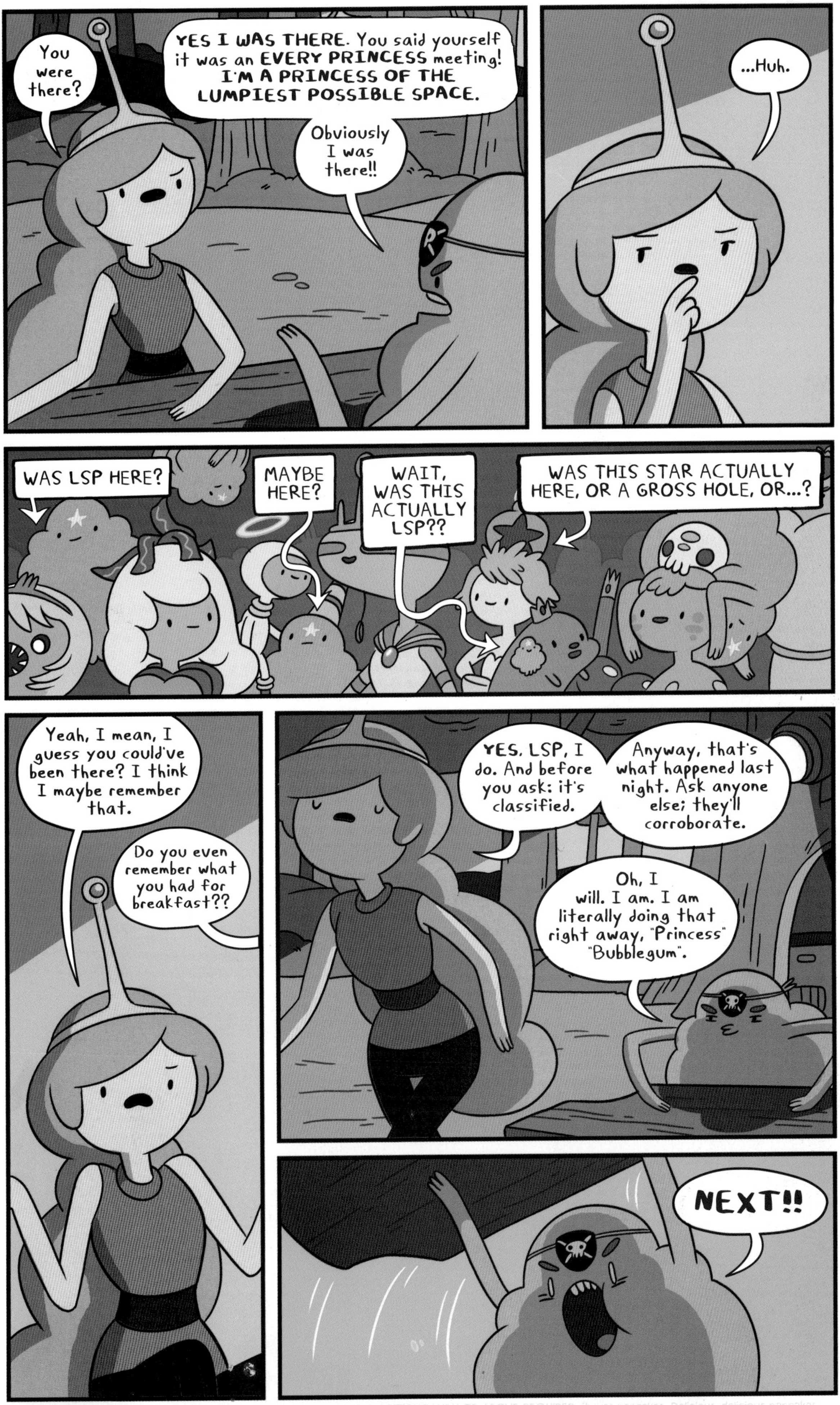
You were there?
YES I WAS THERE. You said yourself it was an EVERY PRINCESS meeting! I'M A PRINCESS OF THE LUMPIEST POSSIBLE SPACE.
Obviously I was there!!
...Huh.
WAS LSP HERE?
MAYBE HERE?
WAIT, WAS THIS ACTUALLY LSP??
WAS THIS STAR ACTUALLY HERE, OR A GROSS HOLE, OR...?
Yeah, I mean, I guess you could've been there? I think I maybe remember that.
Do you even remember what you had for breakfast??
YES, LSP, I do. And before you ask: it's classified.
Anyway, that's what happened last night. Ask anyone else; they'll corroborate.
Oh, I will. I am. I am literally doing that right away, "Princess" "Bubblegum".
NEXT!!

COSMIC TOP SECRET CLASSIFIED INFORMATION: ACCESS LEVELS COTTONCANDY OR ABOVE REQUIRED: it was pancakes. Delicious, delicious pancakes.

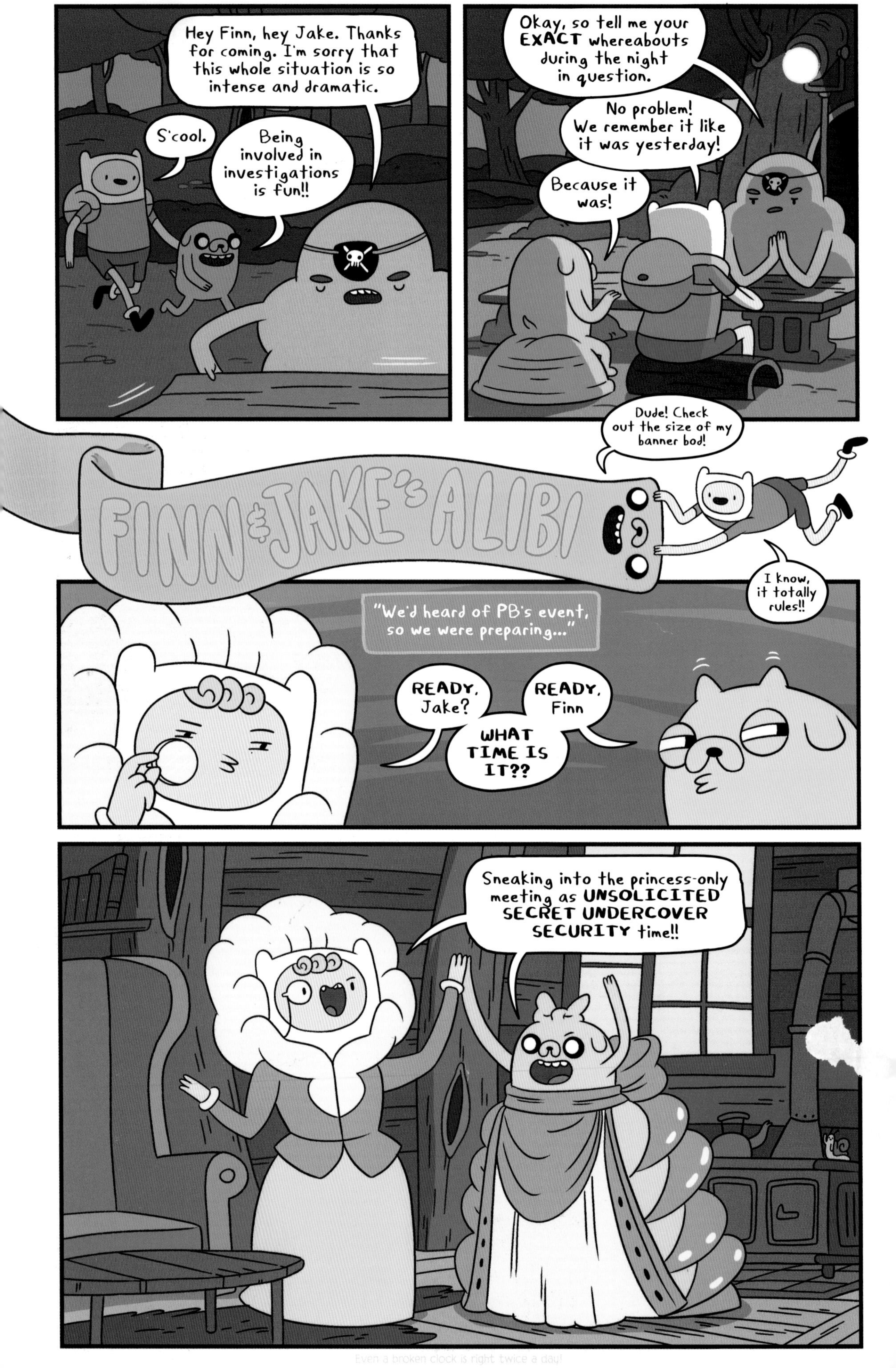

Hey Finn, hey Jake. Thanks for coming. I'm sorry that this whole situation is so intense and dramatic.
S'cool.
Being involved in investigations is fun!!
Okay, so tell me your EXACT whereabouts during the night in question.
No problem! We remember it like it was yesterday!
Because it was!
FINN & JAKE'S ALIBI
Dude! Check out the size of my banner bod!
I know, it totally rules!!
"We'd heard of PB's event, so we were preparing..."
READY, Jake?
READY, Finn
WHAT TIME IS IT??
Sneaking into the princess-only meeting as UNSOLICITED SECRET UNDERCOVER SECURITY time!!

Even a broken clock is right twice a day!

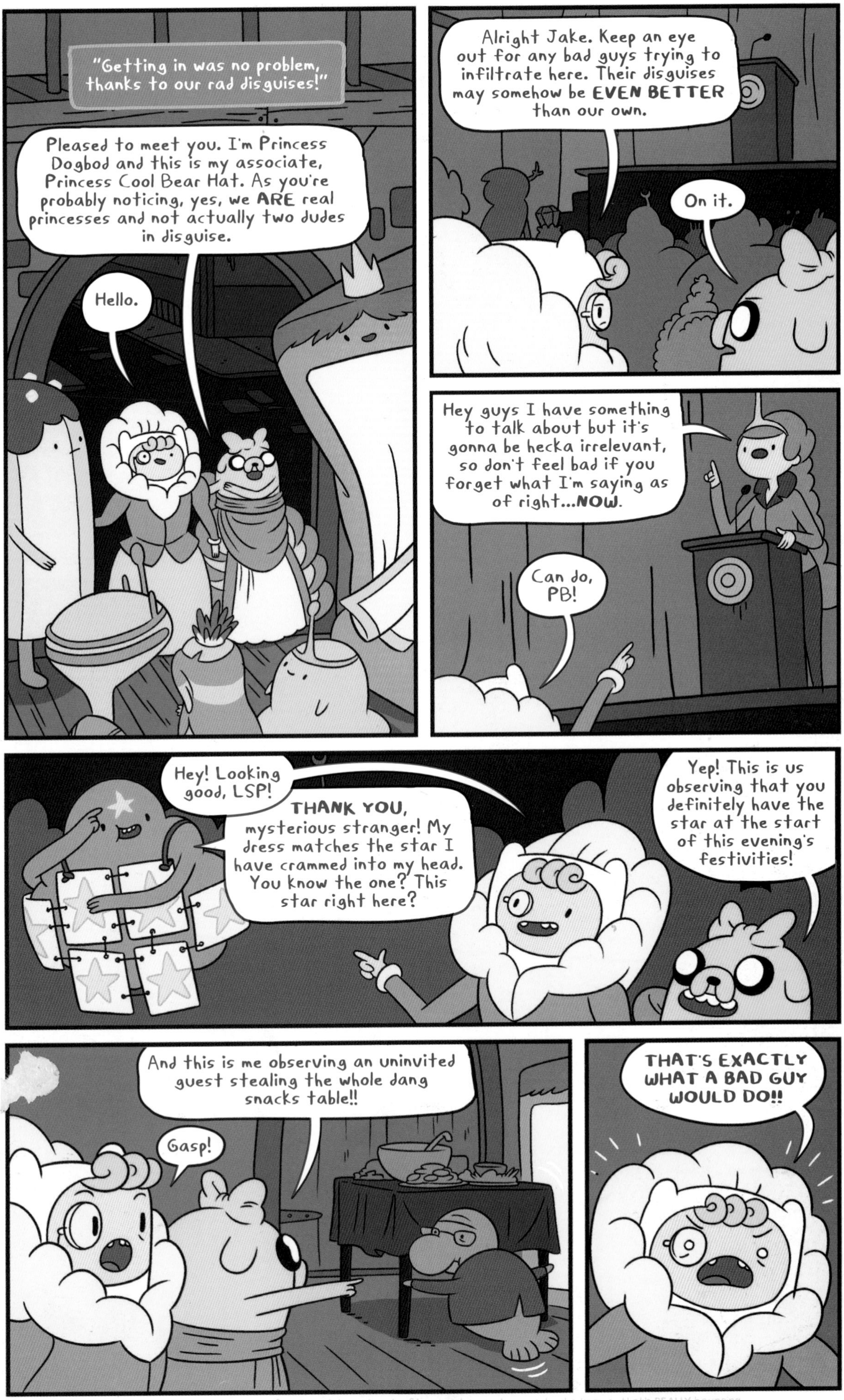
"Getting in was no problem, thanks to our rad disguises!"
Pleased to meet you. I'm Princess Dogbod and this is my associate, Princess Cool Bear Hat. As you're probably noticing, yes, we ARE real princesses and not actually two dudes in disguise.
Hello.
Alright Jake. Keep an eye out for any bad guys trying to infiltrate here. Their disguises may somehow be EVEN BETTER than our own.
On it.
Hey guys I have something to talk about but it's gonna be hecka irrelevant, so don't feel bad if you forget what I'm saying as of right...NOW.
Can do, PB!
Hey! Looking good, LSP!
THANK YOU, mysterious stranger! My dress matches the star I have crammed into my head. You know the one? This star right here?
Yep! This is us observing that you definitely have the star at the start of this evening's festivities!
And this is me observing an uninvited guest stealing the whole dang snacks table!!
Gasp!
THAT'S EXACTLY WHAT A BAD GUY WOULD DO!!

Bounce House Princess wonders if you want to get out of here and come to a party she knows...that's **REALLY** bouncing.

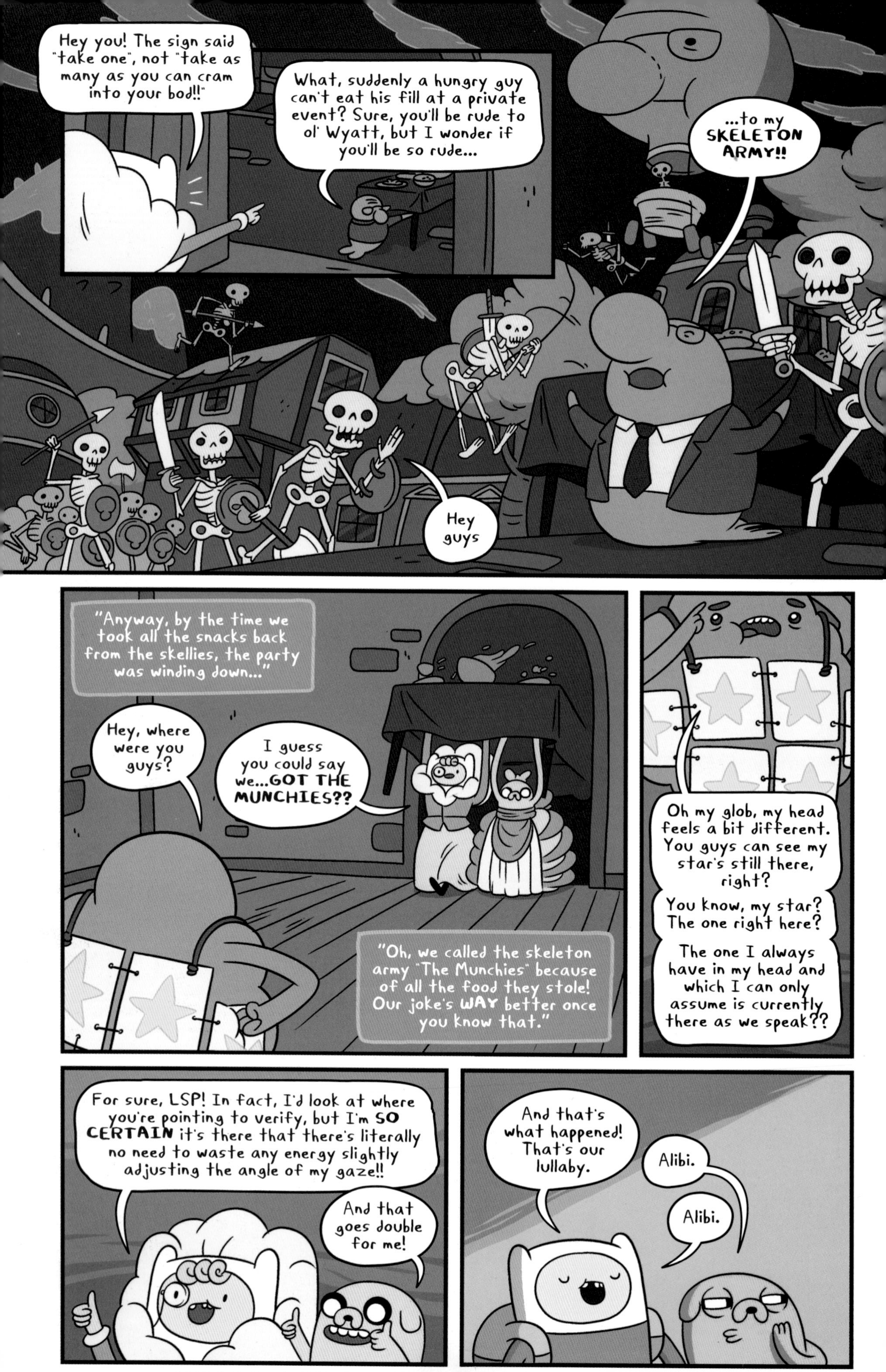

Hey you! The sign said "take one", not "take as many as you can cram into your bod!!"
What, suddenly a hungry guy can't eat his fill at a private event? Sure, you'll be rude to ol' Wyatt, but I wonder if you'll be so rude...
...to my SKELETON ARMY!!
Hey guys
"Anyway, by the time we took all the snacks back from the skellies, the party was winding down..."
Hey, where were you guys?
I guess you could say we...GOT THE MUNCHIES??
"Oh, we called the skeleton army "The Munchies" because of all the food they stole! Our joke's WAY better once you know that."
Oh my glob, my head feels a bit different. You guys can see my star's still there, right?
You know, my star? The one right here?
The one I always have in my head and which I can only assume is currently there as we speak??
For sure, LSP! In fact, I'd look at where you're pointing to verify, but I'm SO CERTAIN it's there that there's literally no need to waste any energy slightly adjusting the angle of my gaze!!
And that goes double for me!
And that's what happened! That's our lullaby.
Alibi.
Alibi.

I mean, it could also be a lullaby if you want to lay down a sick slow beat while we told it again. Anyone? No?

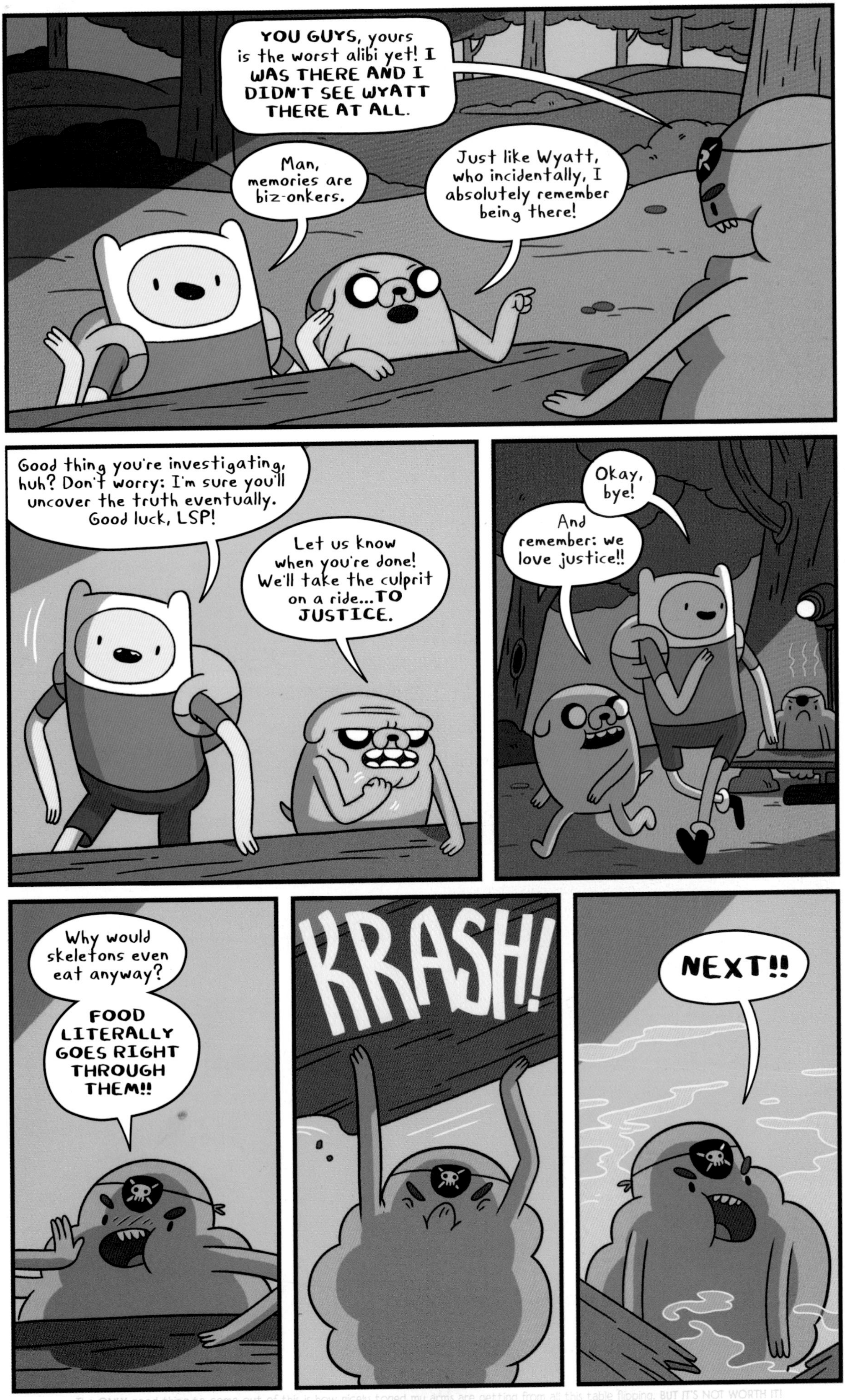
YOU GUYS, yours is the worst alibi yet! I WAS THERE AND I DIDN'T SEE WYATT THERE AT ALL.
Man, memories are biz-onkers.
Just like Wyatt, who incidentally, I absolutely remember being there!
Good thing you're investigating, huh? Don't worry: I'm sure you'll uncover the truth eventually. Good luck, LSP!
Let us know when you're done! We'll take the culprit on a ride...TO JUSTICE.
Okay, bye!
And remember: we love justice!!
Why would skeletons even eat anyway?
FOOD LITERALLY GOES RIGHT THROUGH THEM!!
KRASH!
NEXT!!

The **ONLY** good thing to come out of this is how nicely toned my arms are getting from all this table flipping. **BUT IT'S NOT WORTH IT!**

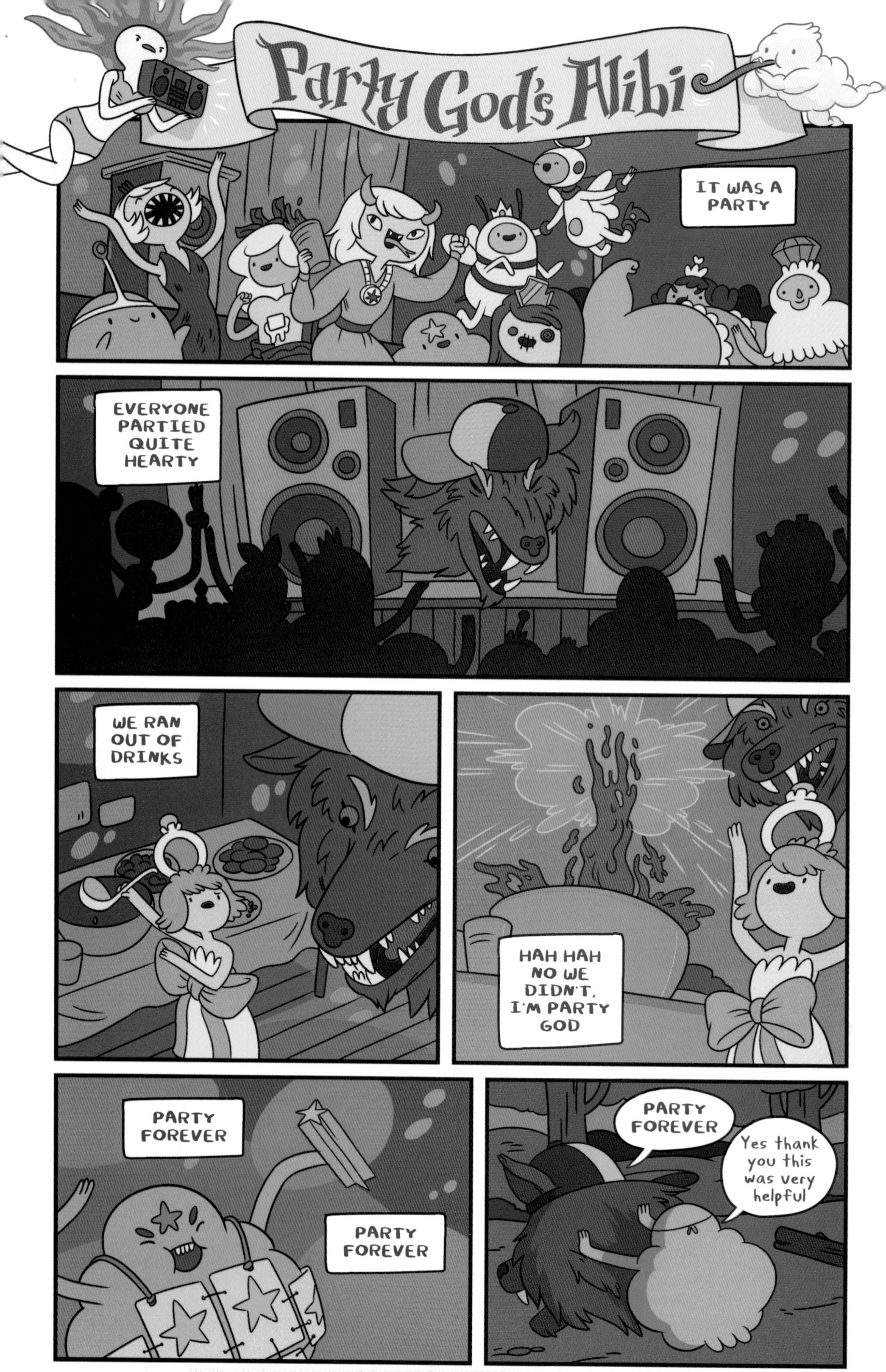

Party God's Alibi
IT WAS A PARTY
EVERYONE PARTIED QUITE HEARTY
WE RAN OUT OF DRINKS
HAH HAH NO WE DIDN'T, I'M PARTY GOD
PARTY FOREVER
PARTY FOREVER
PARTY FOREVER
Yes thank you this was very helpful

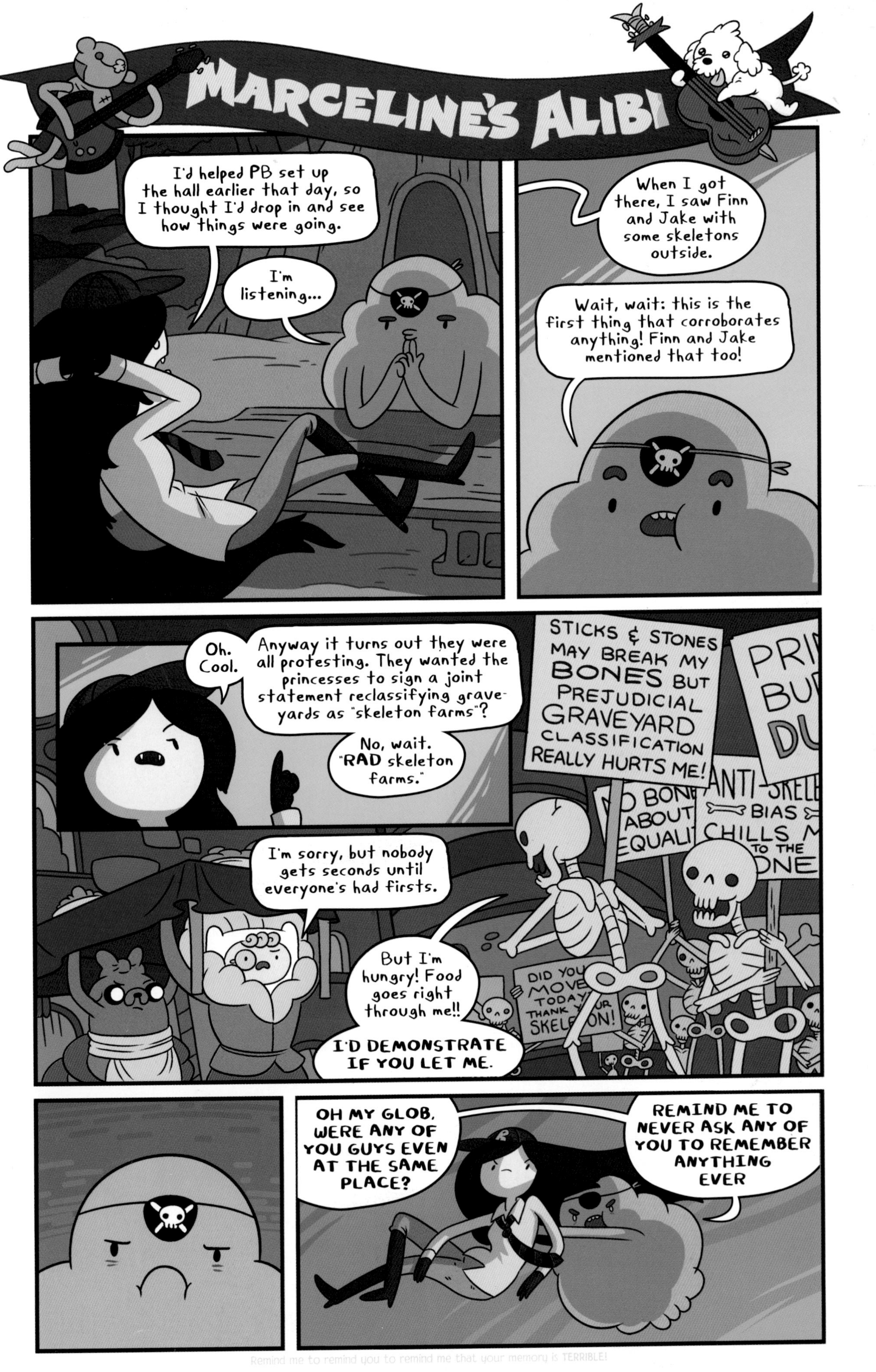
MARCELINE'S ALIBI
I'd helped PB set up the hall earlier that day, so I thought I'd drop in and see how things were going.
I'm listening...
When I got there, I saw Finn and Jake with some skeletons outside.
Wait, wait: this is the first thing that corroborates anything! Finn and Jake mentioned that too!
Oh. Cool.
Anyway it turns out they were all protesting. They wanted the princesses to sign a joint statement reclassifying graveyards as "skeleton farms"?
No, wait. "RAD skeleton farms."
STICKS & STONES MAY BREAK MY BONES BUT PREJUDICIAL GRAVEYARD CLASSIFICATION REALLY HURTS ME!
BIAS
I'm sorry, but nobody gets seconds until everyone's had firsts.
But I'm hungry! Food goes right through me!!
I'D DEMONSTRATE IF YOU LET ME.
OH MY GLOB, WERE ANY OF YOU GUYS EVEN AT THE SAME PLACE?
REMIND ME TO NEVER ASK ANY OF YOU TO REMEMBER ANYTHING EVER

Remind me to remind you to remind me that your memory is TERRIBLE!

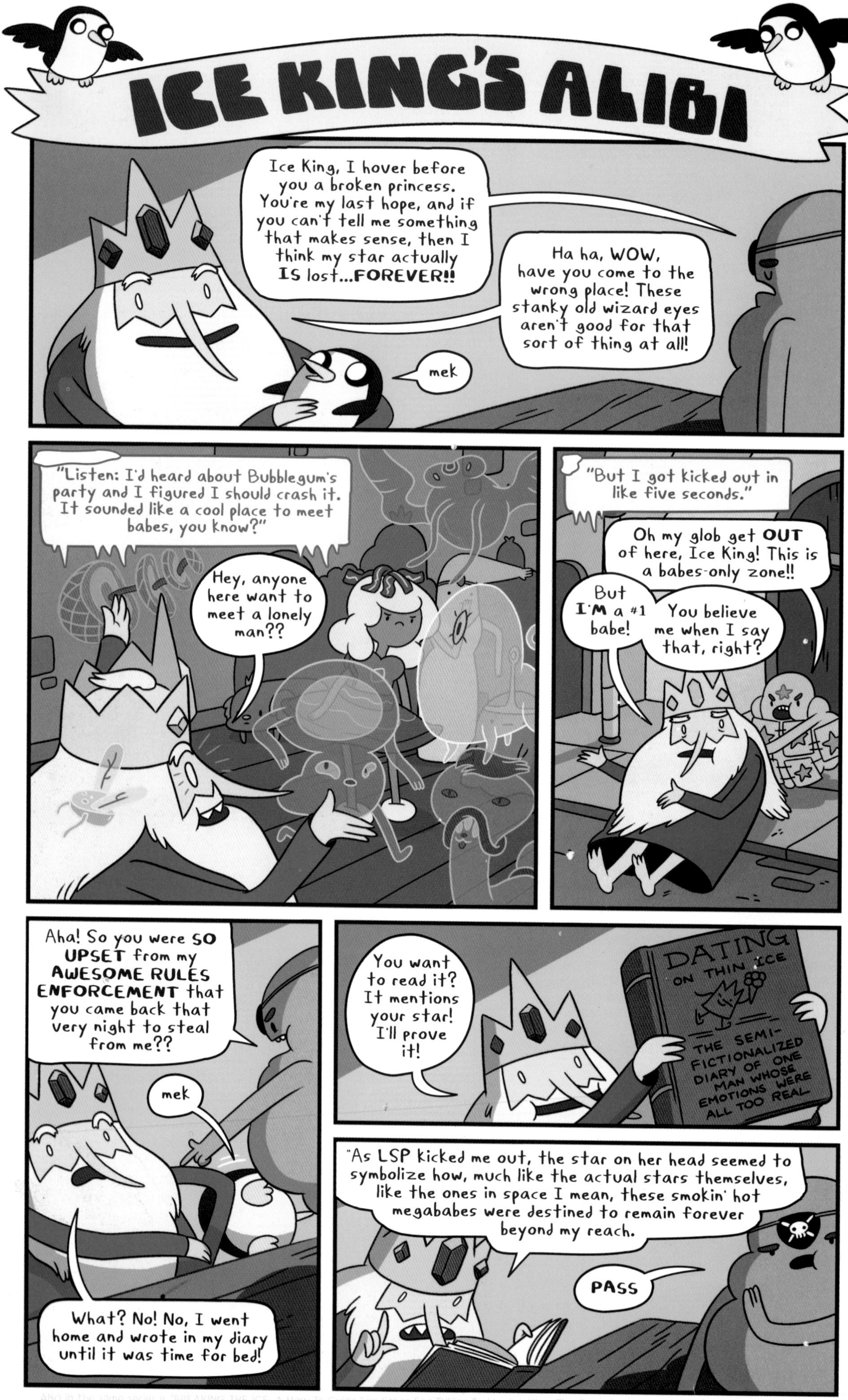
ICE KING'S ALIBI
Ice King, I hover before you a broken princess. You're my last hope, and if you can't tell me something that makes sense, then I think my star actually IS lost...FOREVER!!
Ha ha, WOW, have you come to the wrong place! These stanky old wizard eyes aren't good for that sort of thing at all!
mek
"Listen: I'd heard about Bubblegum's party and I figured I should crash it. It sounded like a cool place to meet babes, you know?"
Hey, anyone here want to meet a lonely man??
"But I got kicked out in like five seconds."
Oh my glob get OUT of here, Ice King! This is a babes-only zone!!
But I'M a #1 babe!
You believe me when I say that, right?
Aha! So you were SO UPSET from my AWESOME RULES ENFORCEMENT that you came back that very night to steal from me??
mek
What? No! No, I went home and wrote in my diary until it was time for bed!
You want to read it? It mentions your star! I'll prove it!
DATING ON THIN ICE
THE SEMI-FICTIONALIZED DIARY OF ONE MAN WHOSE EMOTIONS WERE ALL TOO REAL
"As LSP kicked me out, the star on her head seemed to symbolize how, much like the actual stars themselves, like the ones in space I mean, these smokin' hot megababes were destined to remain forever beyond my reach.
PASS
Also in the same series is "BREAKING THE ICE: A How-To Guide For Babes For Talking To Me, Ice King, The Guy Who Wrote, And Handed Them, This Book"

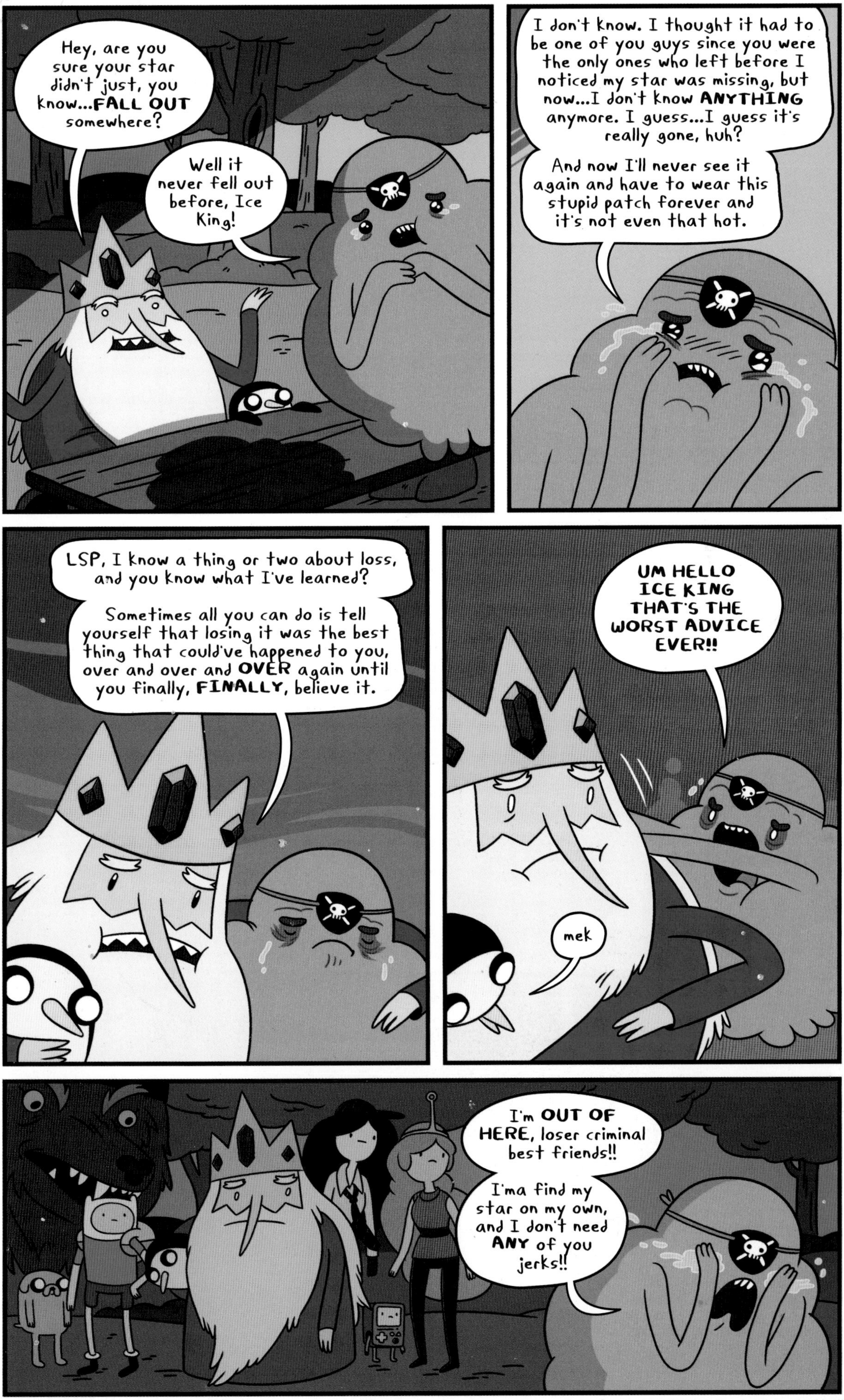
Hey, are you sure your star didn't just, you know...FALL OUT somewhere?
Well it never fell out before, Ice King!
I don't know. I thought it had to be one of you guys since you were the only ones who left before I noticed my star was missing, but now...I don't know ANYTHING anymore. I guess...I guess it's really gone, huh?
And now I'll never see it again and have to wear this stupid patch forever and it's not even that hot.
LSP, I know a thing or two about loss, and you know what I've learned?
Sometimes all you can do is tell yourself that losing it was the best thing that could've happened to you, over and over and OVER again until you finally, FINALLY, believe it.
UM HELLO ICE KING THAT'S THE WORST ADVICE EVER!!
mek
I'm OUT OF HERE, loser criminal best friends!!
I'ma find my star on my own, and I don't need ANY of you jerks!!

Man that was awkward. Are you reading this text down here because you hope to feel less awkward about spying on that raw display of emotion? Well TOO BAD, it's awkward down here too!!

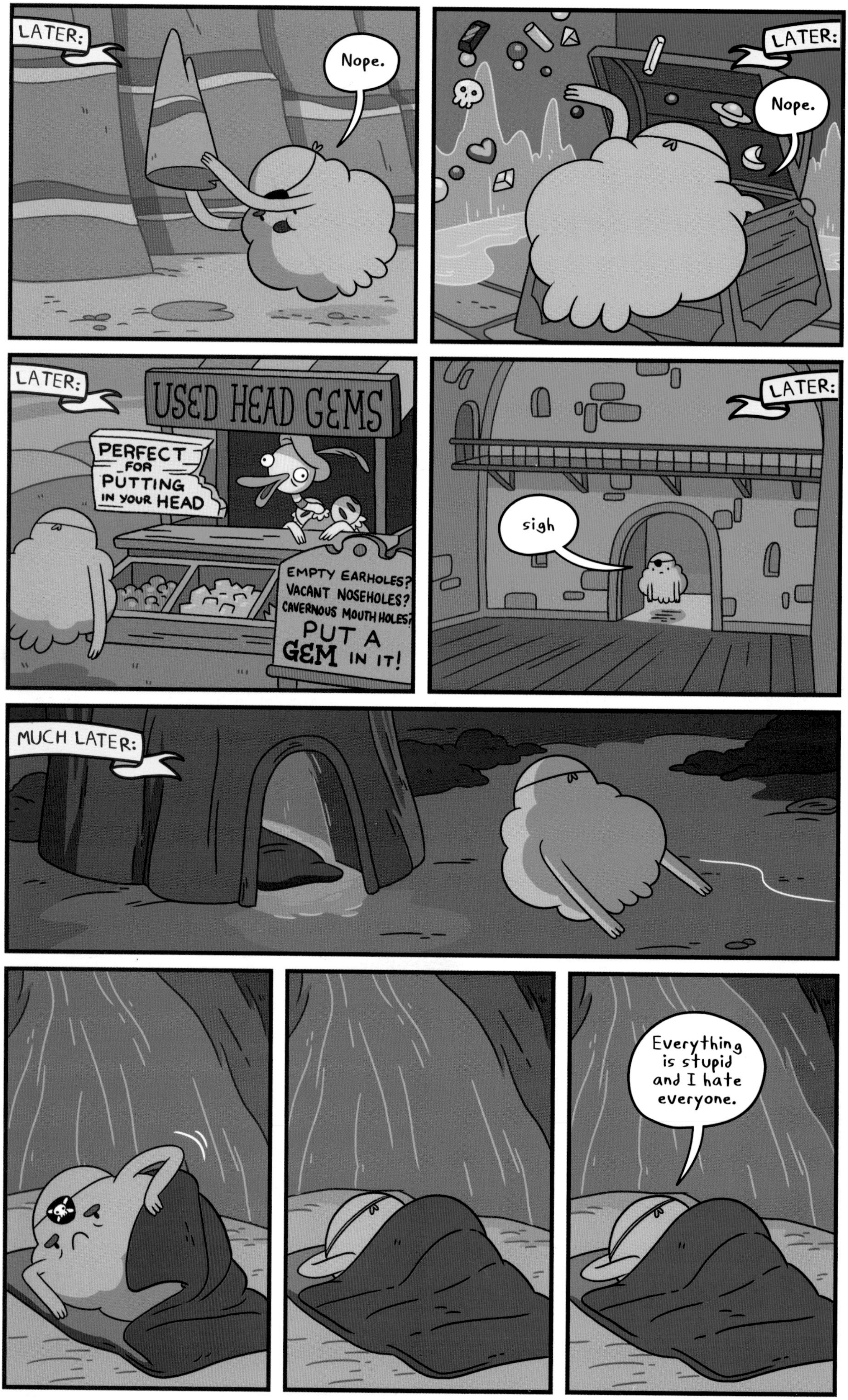
LATER:
Nope.
LATER:
Nope.
LATER:
USED HEAD GEMS
PERFECT FOR PUTTING IN YOUR HEAD
EMPTY EARHOLES? VACANT NOSEHOLES? CAVERNOUS MOUTH HOLES? PUT A GEM IN IT!
LATER:
sigh
MUCH LATER:
Everything is stupid and I hate everyone.

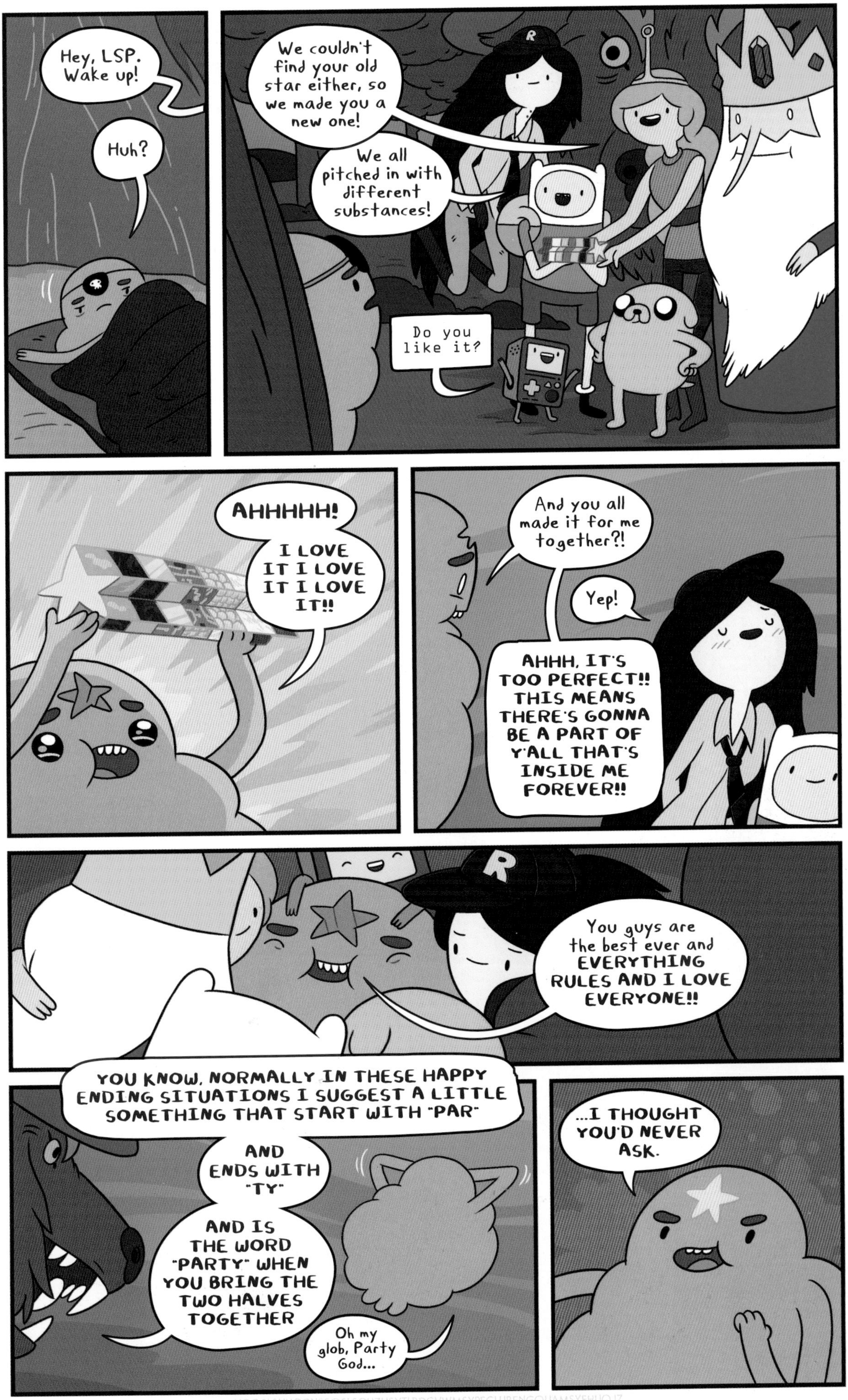

Hey, LSP. Wake up!
Huh?
We couldn't find your old star either, so we made you a new one!
We all pitched in with different substances!
Do you like it?
AHHHHH!
I LOVE IT I LOVE IT I LOVE IT!!
And you all made it for me together?!
Yep!
AHHH, IT'S TOO PERFECT!! THIS MEANS THERE'S GONNA BE A PART OF Y'ALL THAT'S INSIDE ME FOREVER!!
You guys are the best ever and EVERYTHING RULES AND I LOVE EVERYONE!!
YOU KNOW, NORMALLY IN THESE HAPPY ENDING SITUATIONS I SUGGEST A LITTLE SOMETHING THAT START WITH "PAR"
AND ENDS WITH "TY"
AND IS THE WORD "PARTY" WHEN YOU BRING THE TWO HALVES TOGETHER
Oh my glob, Party God...
...I THOUGHT YOU'D NEVER ASK.

LIOQSLSNHOGNSEQSLSOUZUSYTLBDGVWMSYPFCLUBFNGQUAMSXFHUQJZ

A> <B

THE ADORED STAR HAD FALLEN OUT OF LSP'S HEAD AND INTO A NEW VENTURE WHEN IT ROLLED AWAY AND A WEE BIRD USED IT TO MAKE HER NEST. MANY YEARS FROM NOW, AND EVEN THOUGH YOU MIGHT NEVER HAVE GUESSED IT, THAT BIRD AND LSP EVEN BECAME...FRIENDS

A> <B

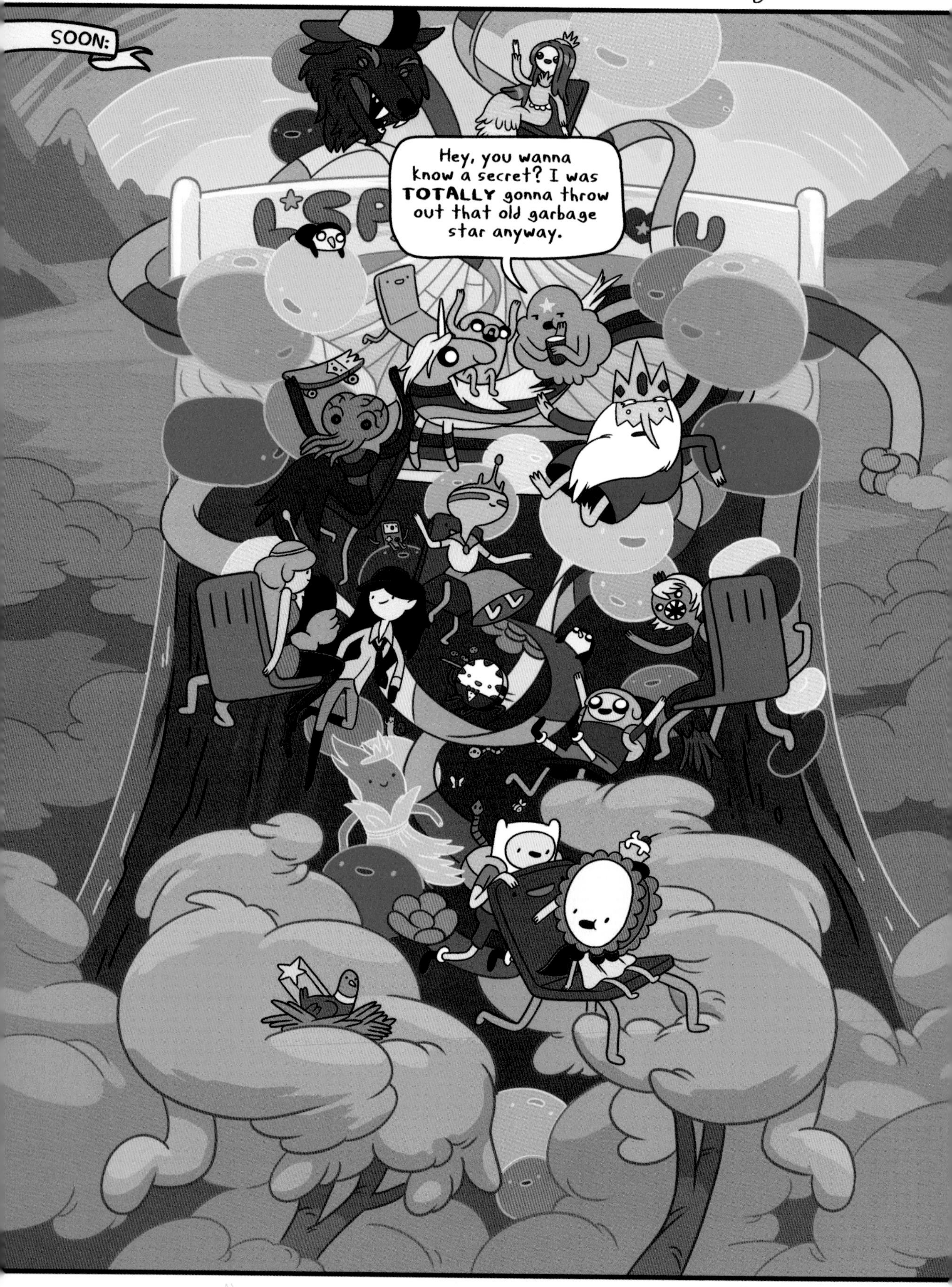

SOON:
Hey, you wanna know a secret? I was **TOTALLY** gonna throw out that old garbage star anyway.
LSP

A) <B

THANKS TO PARTY GOD FOR SUCH A RAD PARTY, FOR AGREEING TO APPEAR IN THIS COMIC, AND FOR BEING THE #1 BEST DUDE IN CHARGE OF PARTY GROWTH AND/OR SPREADING!!

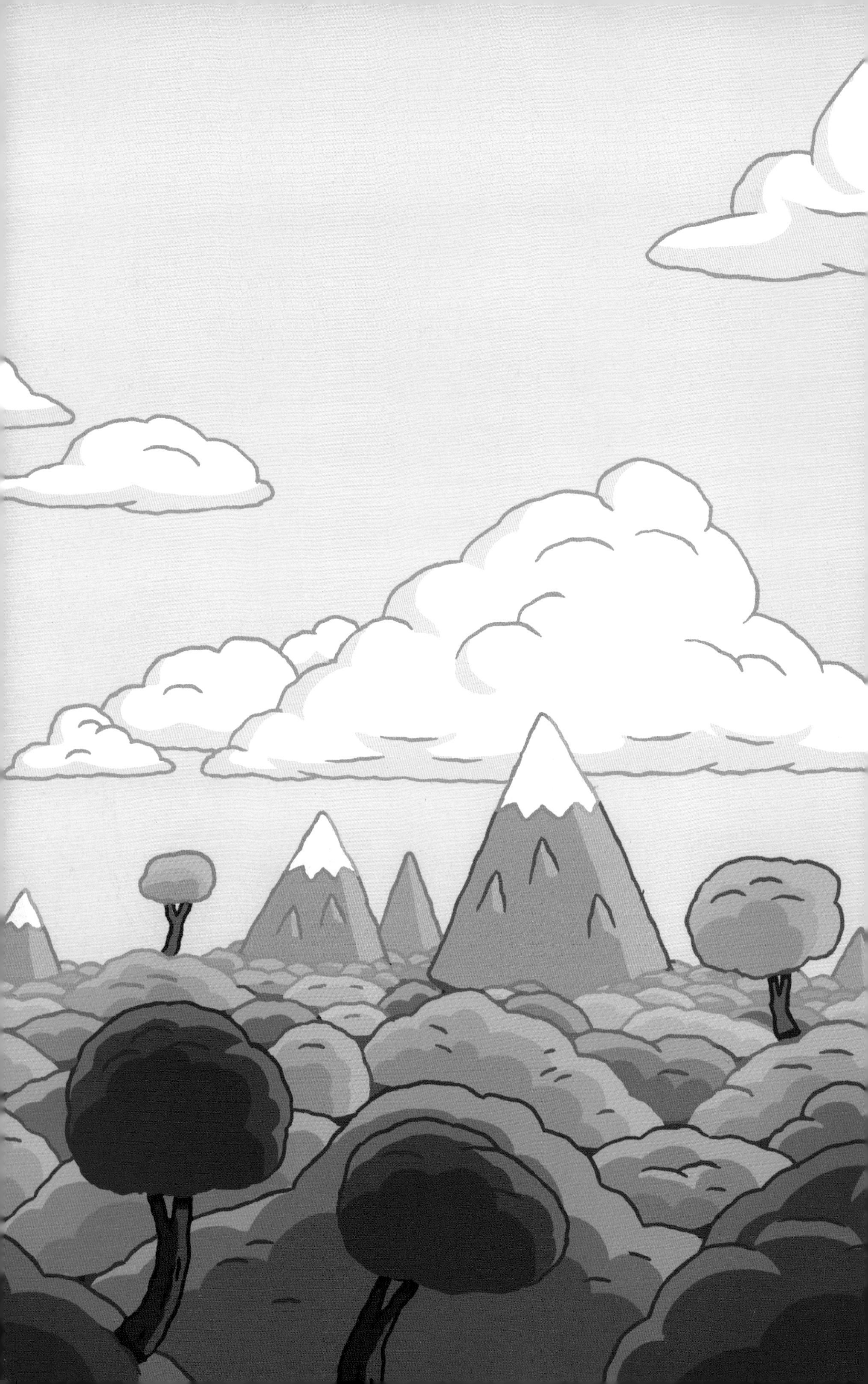

CHAPTER TWO

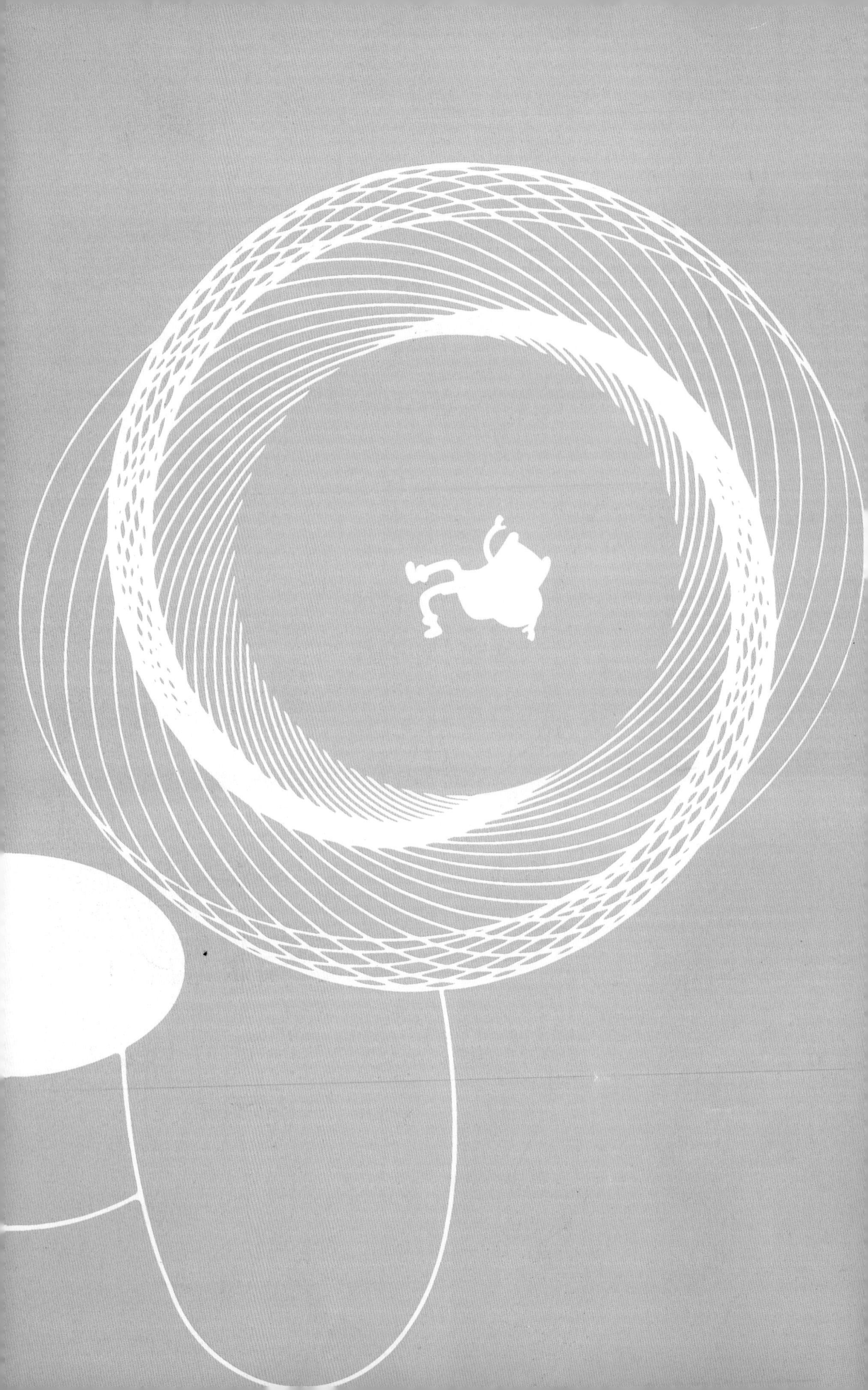

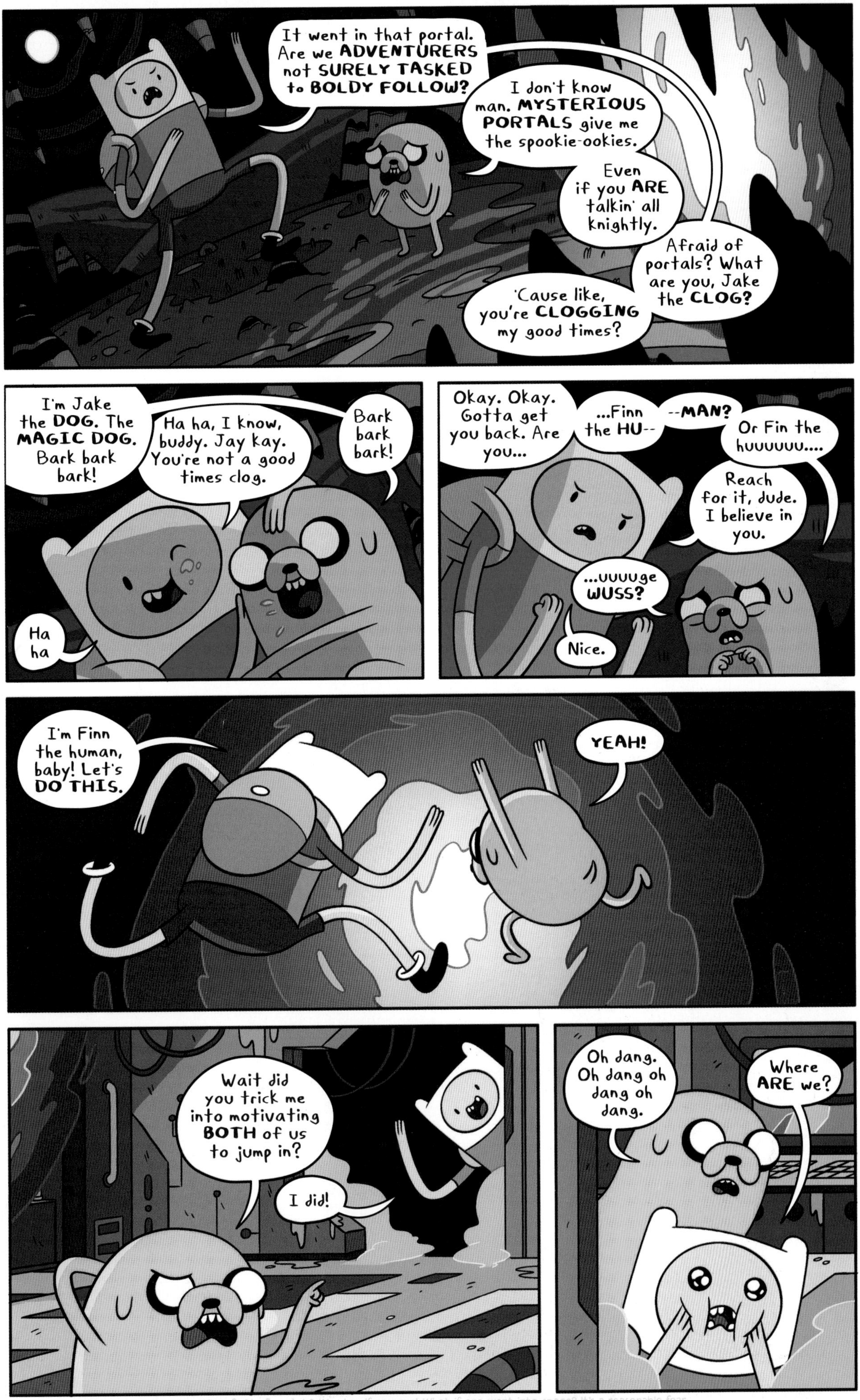
It went in that portal. Are we ADVENTURERS not SURELY TASKED to BOLDY FOLLOW?
I don't know man. MYSTERIOUS PORTALS give me the spookie-ookies.
Even if you ARE talkin' all knightly.
Afraid of portals? What are you, Jake the CLOG?
'Cause like, you're CLOGGING my good times?
I'm Jake the DOG. The MAGIC DOG. Bark bark bark!
Ha ha, I know, buddy. Jay kay. You're not a good times clog.
Bark bark bark!
Ha ha
Okay. Okay. Gotta get you back. Are you...
...Finn the HU--
--MAN?
Or Fin the huuuuuu....
Reach for it, dude. I believe in you.
...uuuuge WUSS?
Nice.
I'm Finn the human, baby! Let's DO THIS.
YEAH!
Wait did you trick me into motivating BOTH of us to jump in?
I did!
Oh dang. Oh dang oh dang oh dang.
Where ARE we?

Are YOU afraid of portals? It's okay if you are! What if one went into space? It's a reasonable fear.

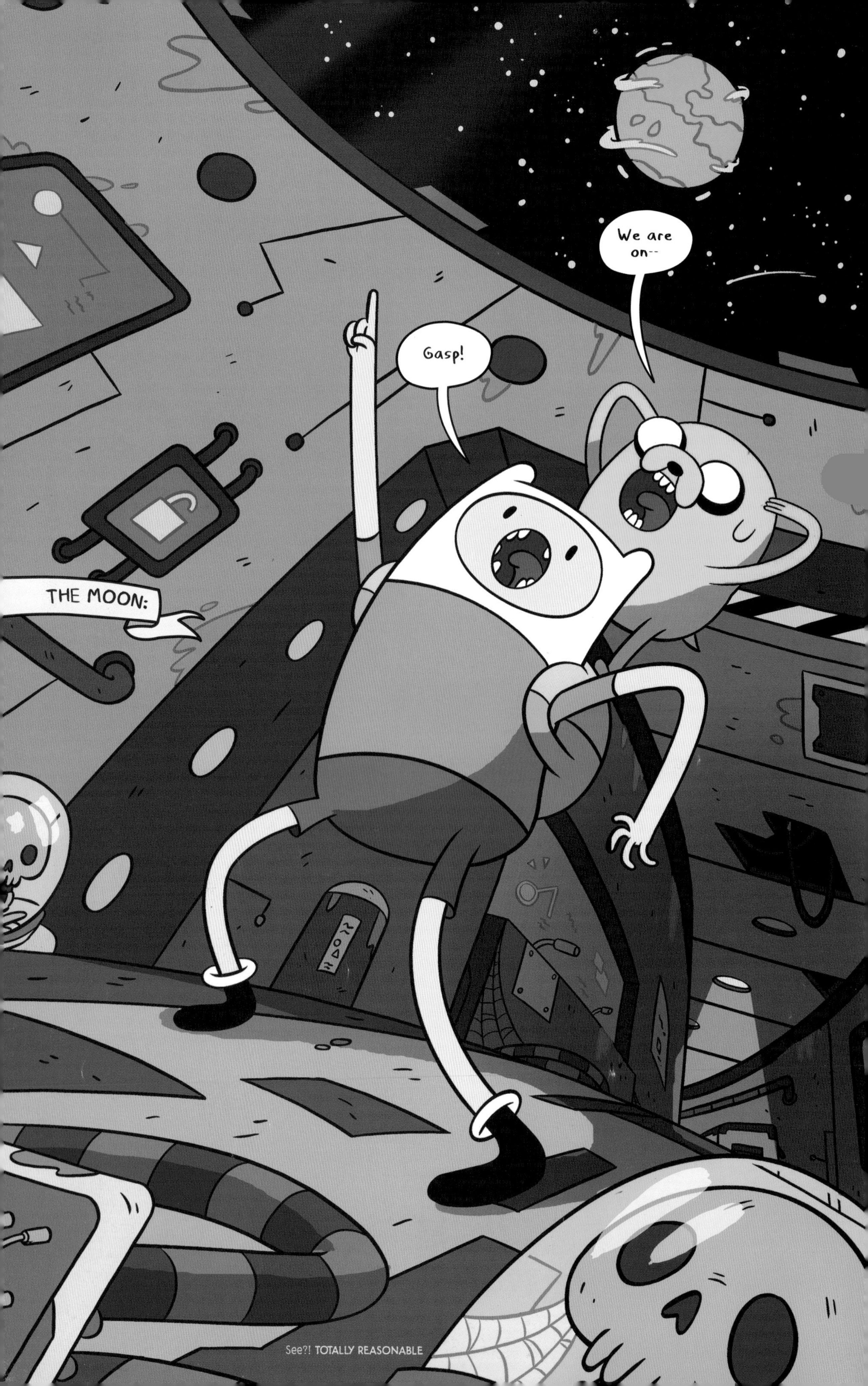
THE MOON:
Gasp!
We are on--
See?! TOTALLY REASONABLE

THE MOON!

WE'RE ASTRONAUTS!

AAAAAAAAA

LET'S INVESTIGATE!

Low gravity? Mad ups? IT'S THE MOON ALRIGHT.

I bet I can dunk on you now. Let's find a b-ball court in here so I can dunk on you.

You can NEVER dunk on THIS ACTION...

...FOOL!

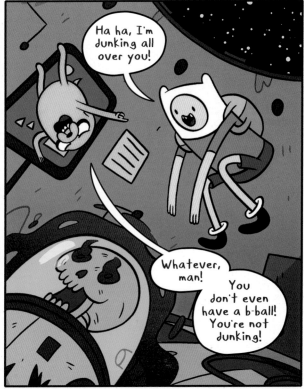

Ha ha, I'm dunking all over you!

Whatever, man! You don't even have a b-ball! You're not dunking!

It's very difficult to play basketball with a dog with legs that can stretch to infinity. That dog's gonna win, friend. He's got infinity legs.

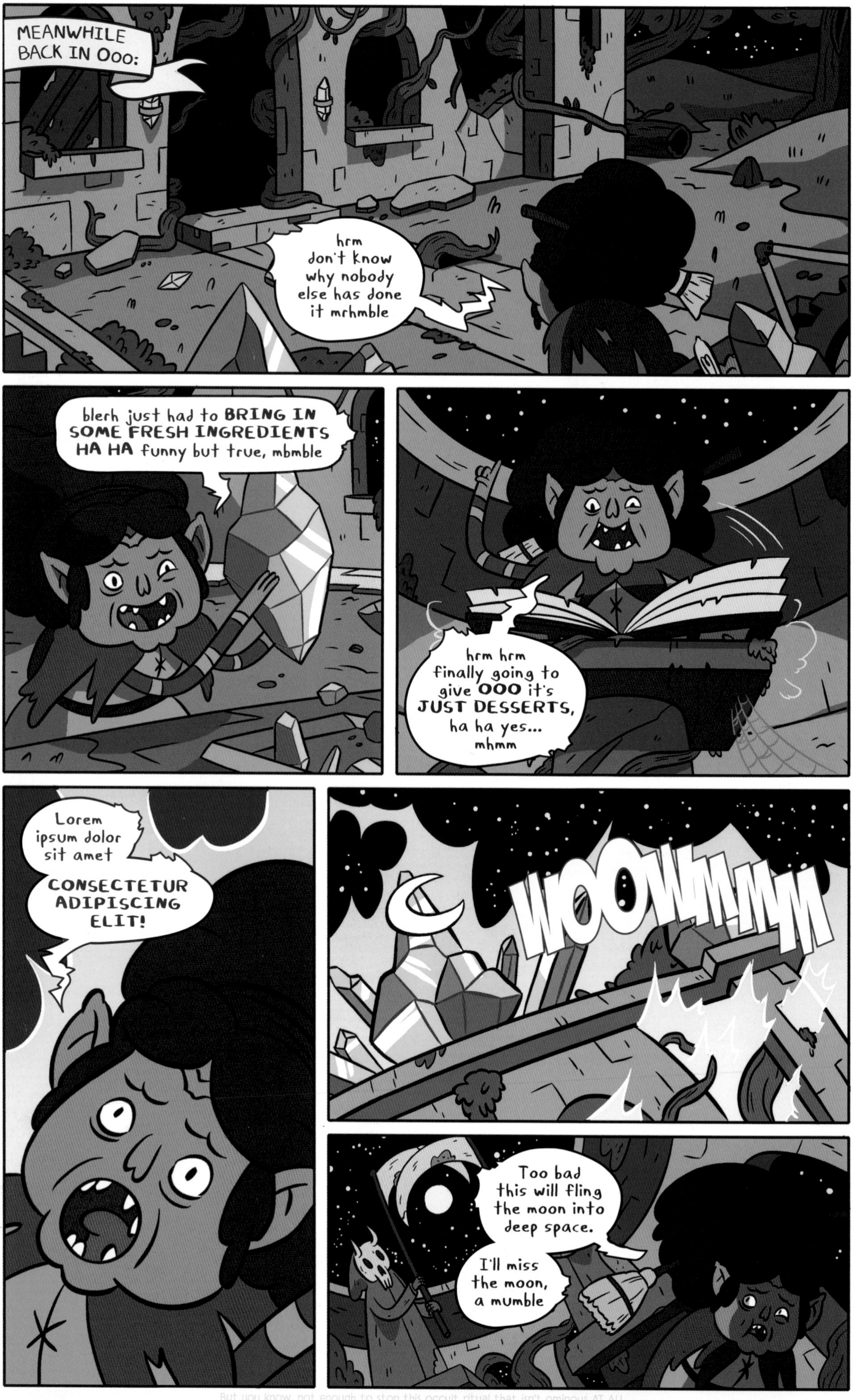
MEANWHILE BACK IN Ooo:
hrm don't know why nobody else has done it mrhmble
blerh just had to BRING IN SOME FRESH INGREDIENTS HA HA funny but true, mbmble
hrm hrm finally going to give OOO it's JUST DESSERTS, ha ha yes... mhmm
Lorem ipsum dolor sit amet
CONSECTETUR ADIPISCING ELIT!
WOOWMMM
Too bad this will fling the moon into deep space.
I'll miss the moon, a mumble

But you know, not enough to stop this occult ritual that isn't ominous AT ALL.

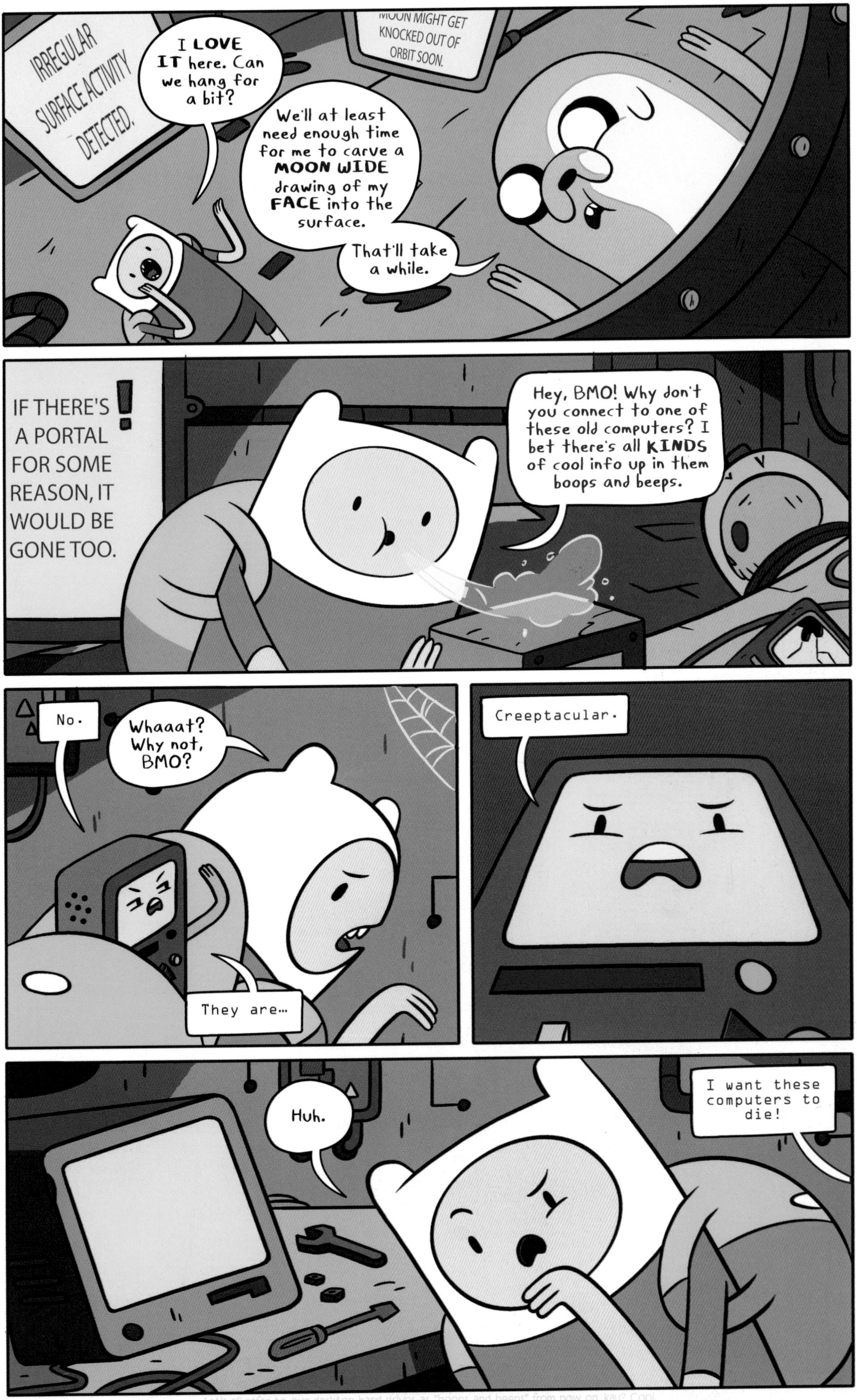
IRREGULAR SURFACE ACTIVITY DETECTED.
MOON MIGHT GET KNOCKED OUT OF ORBIT SOON.
I LOVE IT here. Can we hang for a bit?
We'll at least need enough time for me to carve a MOON WIDE drawing of my FACE into the surface.
That'll take a while.
IF THERE'S A PORTAL FOR SOME REASON, IT WOULD BE GONE TOO.
Hey, BMO! Why don't you connect to one of these old computers? I bet there's all KINDS of cool info up in them boops and beeps.
No.
Whaaat? Why not, BMO?
They are…
Creeptacular.
Huh.
I want these computers to die!

Let's all refer to our desktop hard drives as "boops and beeps" from now on, kay? Cool.

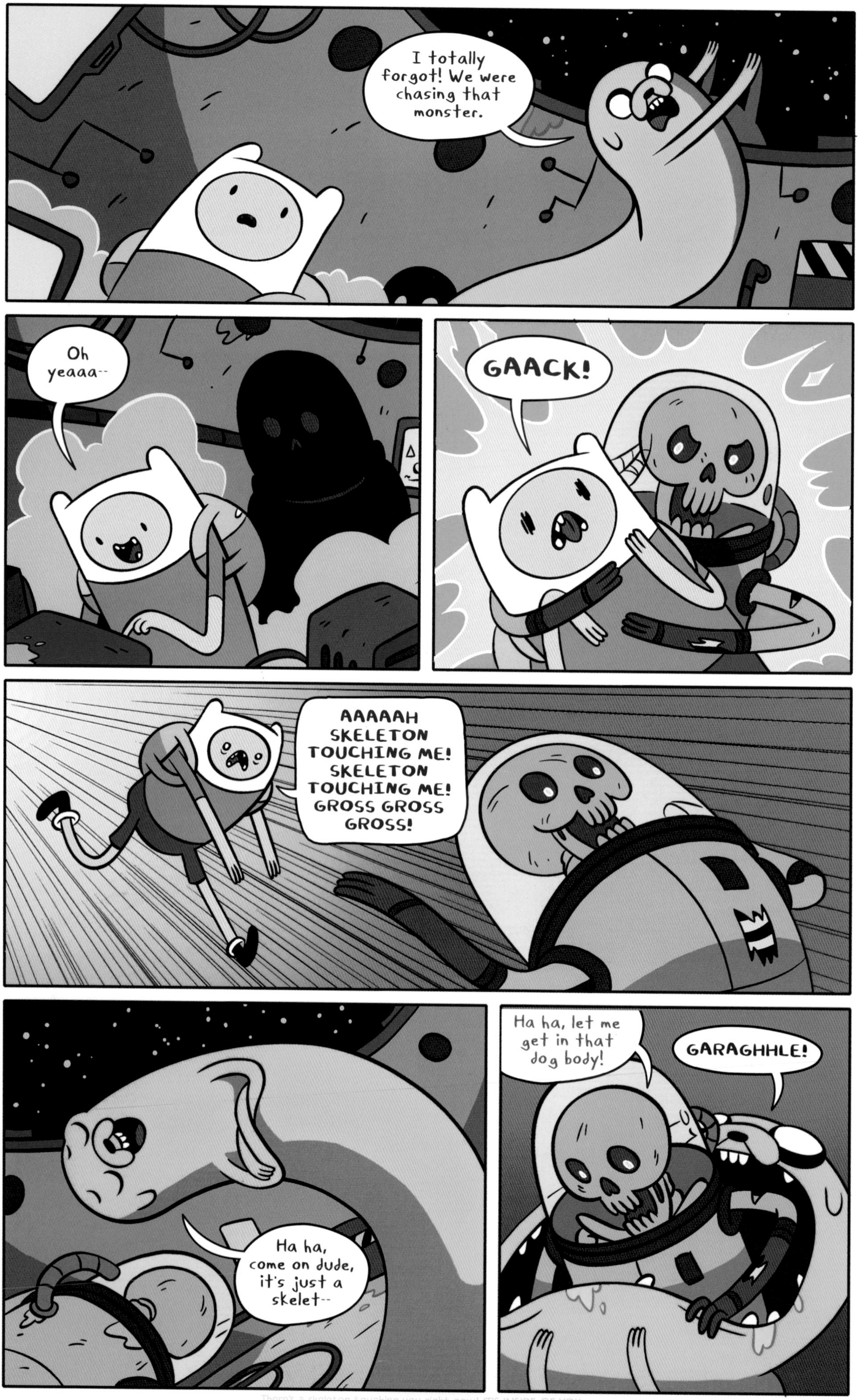
I totally forgot! We were chasing that monster.
Oh yeaaa--
GAACK!
AAAAAH SKELETON TOUCHING ME! SKELETON TOUCHING ME! GROSS GROSS GROSS!
Ha ha, come on dude, it's just a skelet--
Ha ha, let me get in that dog body!
GARAGHHLE!

There's a skeleton touching you right now! IT'S INSIDE OF YOU.

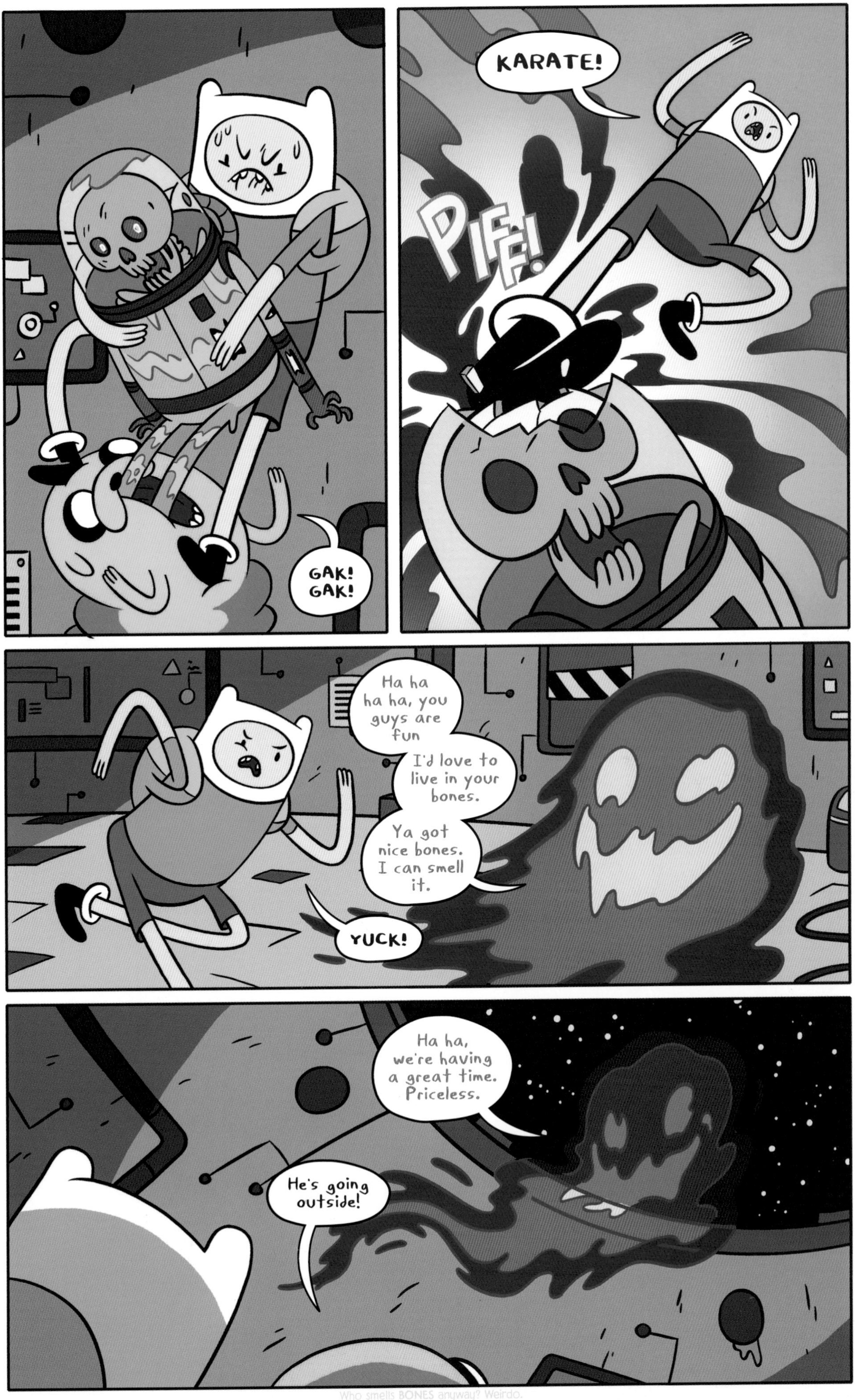
GAK! GAK!
KARATE!
PIFF!
Ha ha ha ha, you guys are fun
I'd love to live in your bones.
Ya got nice bones. I can smell it.
YUCK!
Ha ha, we're having a great time. Priceless.
He's going outside!

Who smells BONES anyway? Weirdo.

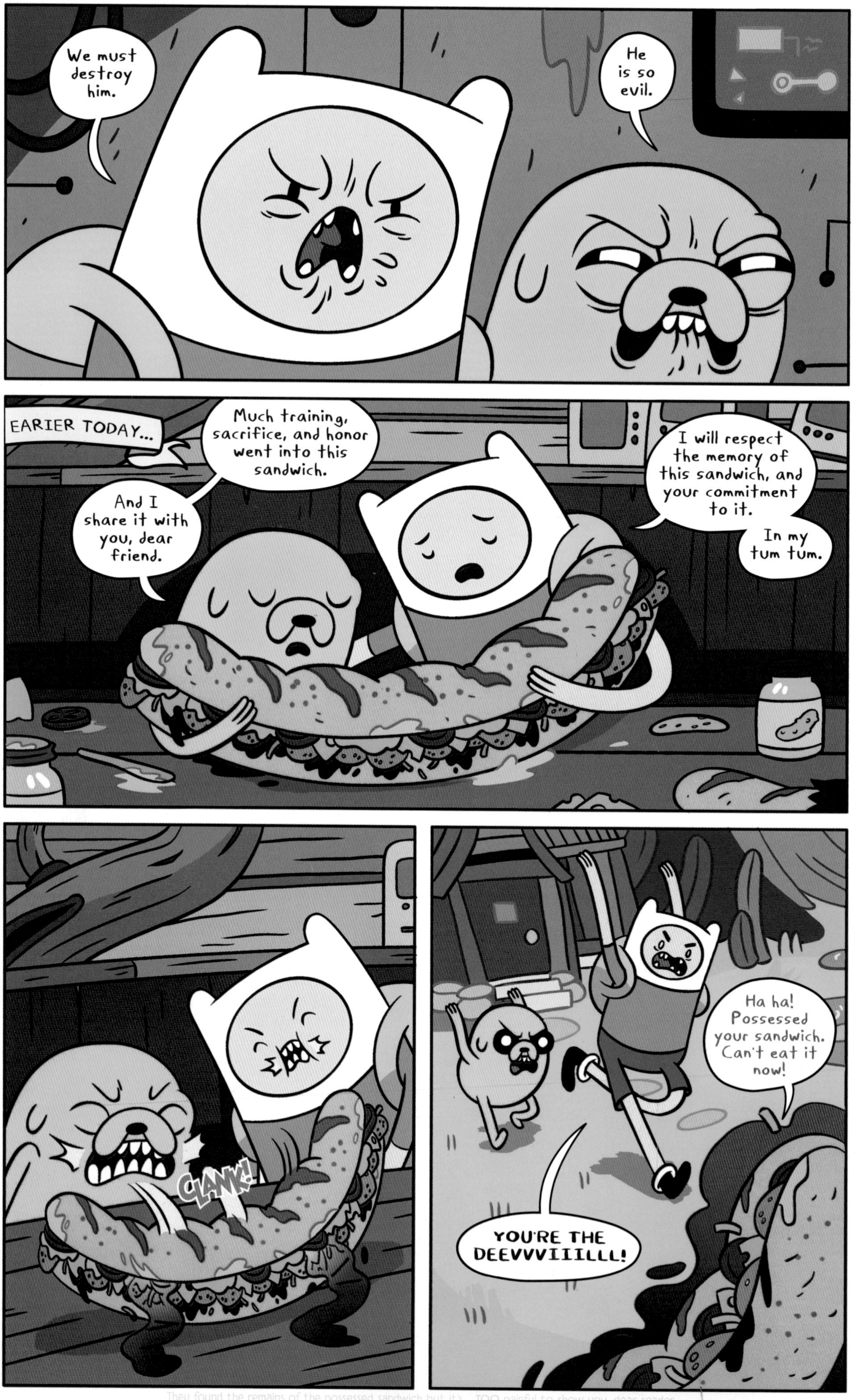
We must destroy him.
He is so evil.
EARIER TODAY...
Much training, sacrifice, and honor went into this sandwich.
And I share it with you, dear friend.
I will respect the memory of this sandwich, and your commitment to it.
In my tum tum.
CLANK!
Ha ha! Possessed your sandwich. Can't eat it now!
YOU'RE THE DEEVVVIIILLL!

They found the remains of the possessed sandwich but it's... TOO painful to show you, dear reader.

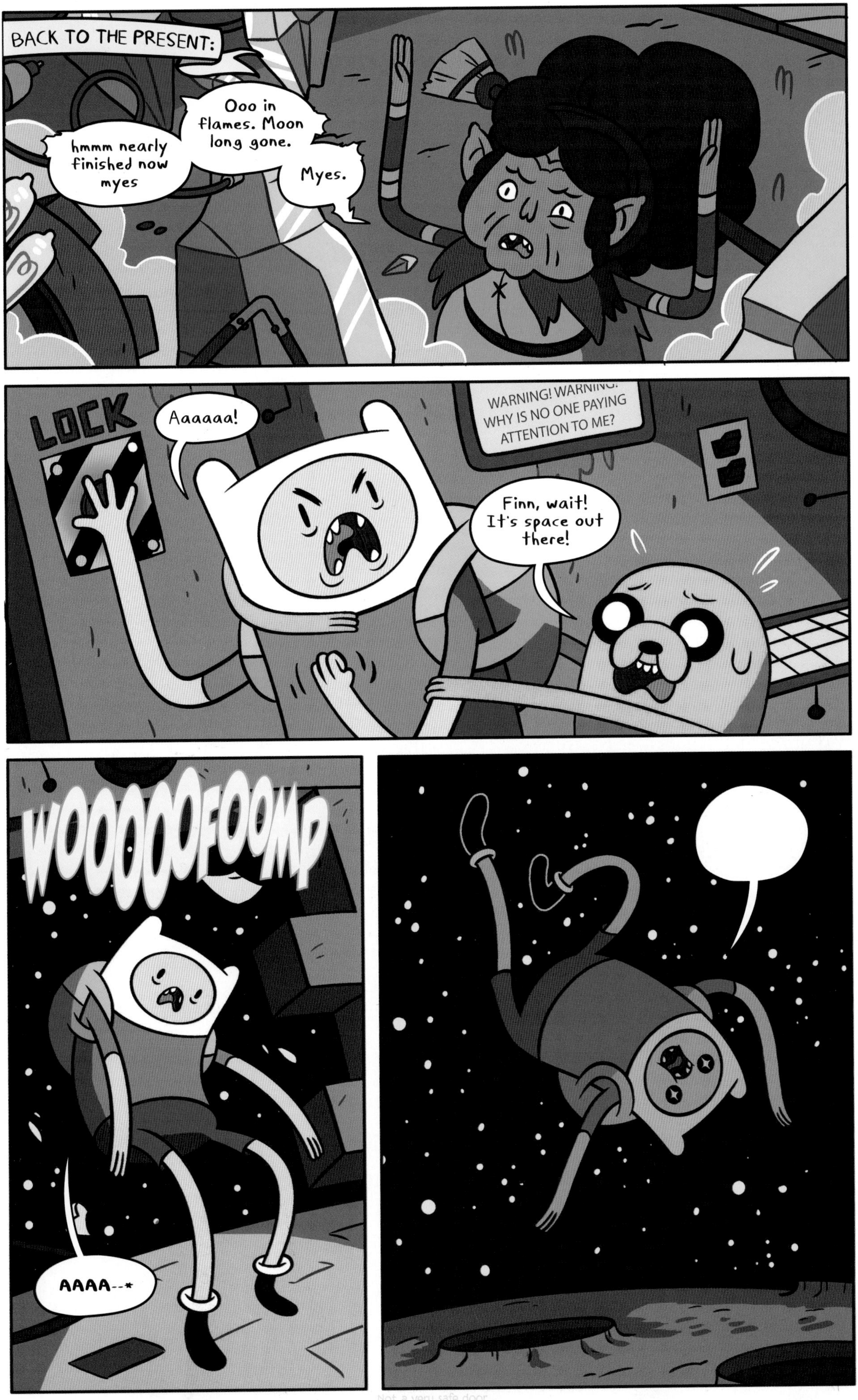
BACK TO THE PRESENT:
hmmm nearly finished now myes
Ooo in flames. Moon long gone.
Myes.
LOCK
Aaaaaa!
WARNING! WARNING! WHY IS NO ONE PAYING ATTENTION TO ME?
Finn, wait! It's space out there!
WOOOOFOOMP
AAAA--*

Not a very safe door.

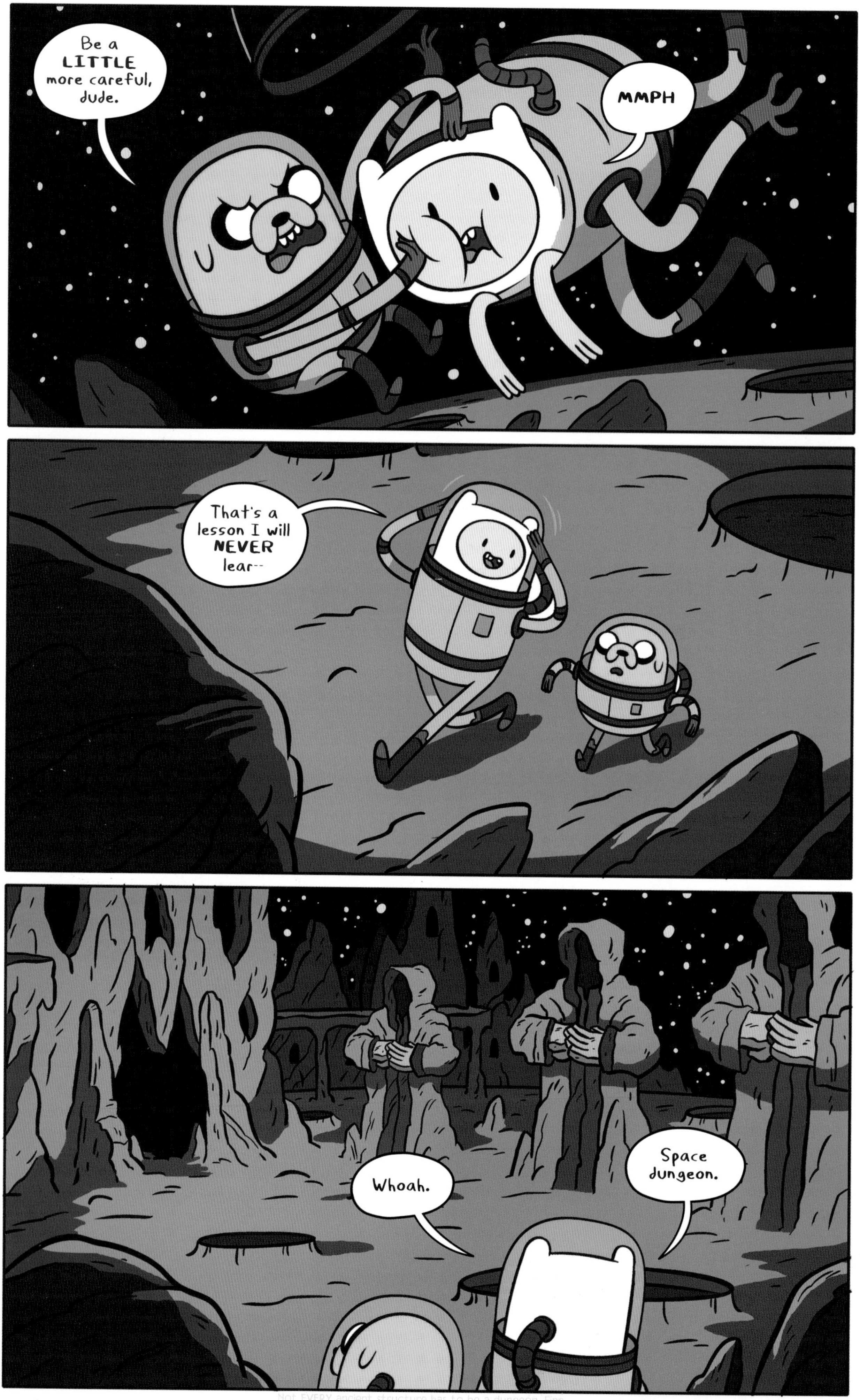
Be a LITTLE more careful, dude.
MMPH
That's a lesson I will NEVER lear--
Whoah.
Space dungeon.

Not EVERY ancient structure has to be a dungeon, Finn.

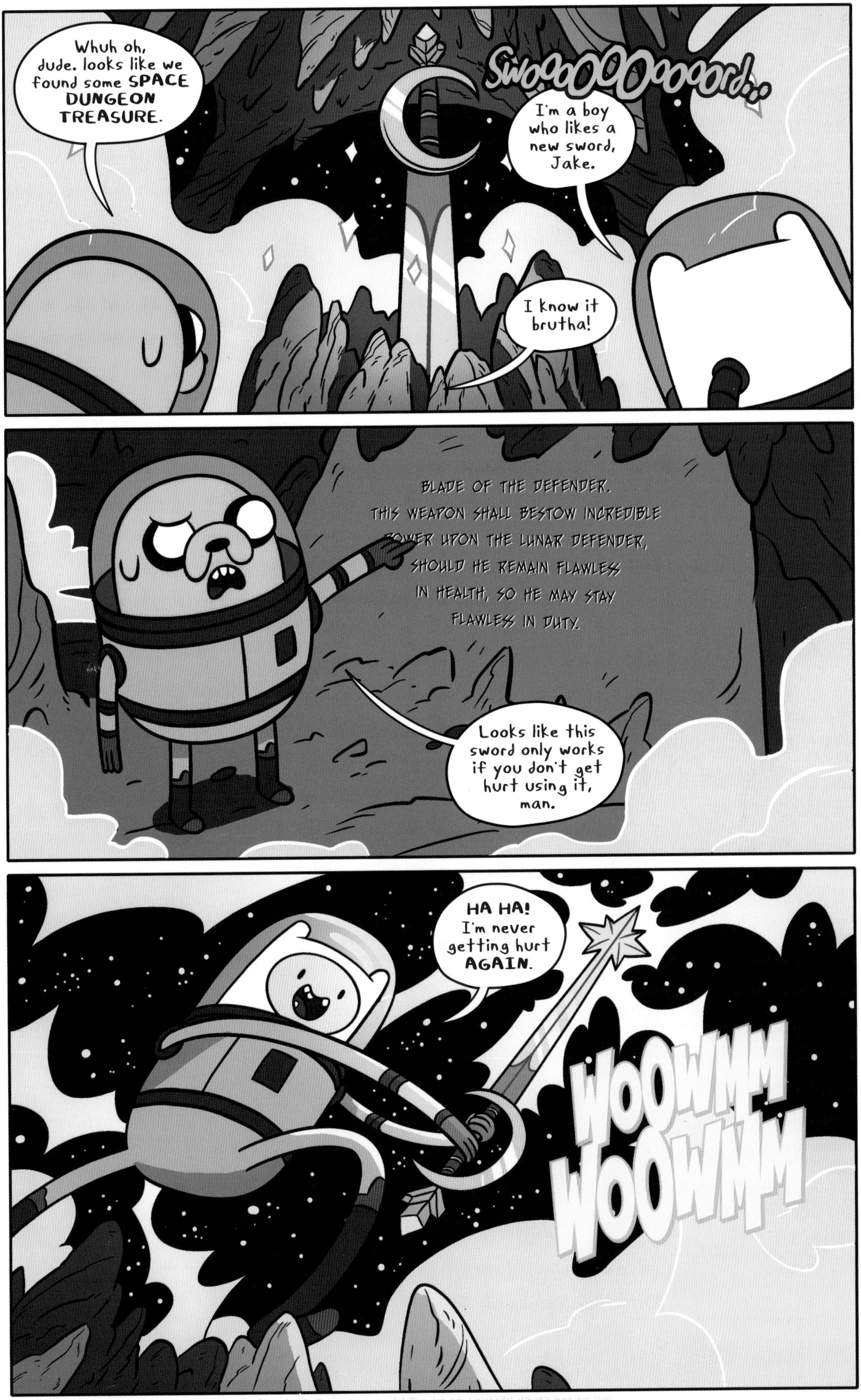
Whuh oh, dude. looks like we found some SPACE DUNGEON TREASURE.
SwoooOOOoooord...
I'm a boy who likes a new sword, Jake.
I know it brutha!
BLADE OF THE DEFENDER.
THIS WEAPON SHALL BESTOW INCREDIBLE POWER UPON THE LUNAR DEFENDER, SHOULD HE REMAIN FLAWLESS IN HEALTH, SO HE MAY STAY FLAWLESS IN DUTY.
Looks like this sword only works if you don't get hurt using it, man.
HA HA! I'm never getting hurt AGAIN.
WOOWMM WOOWMM

Everybody likes new swords! They're new swords! What's not to like.

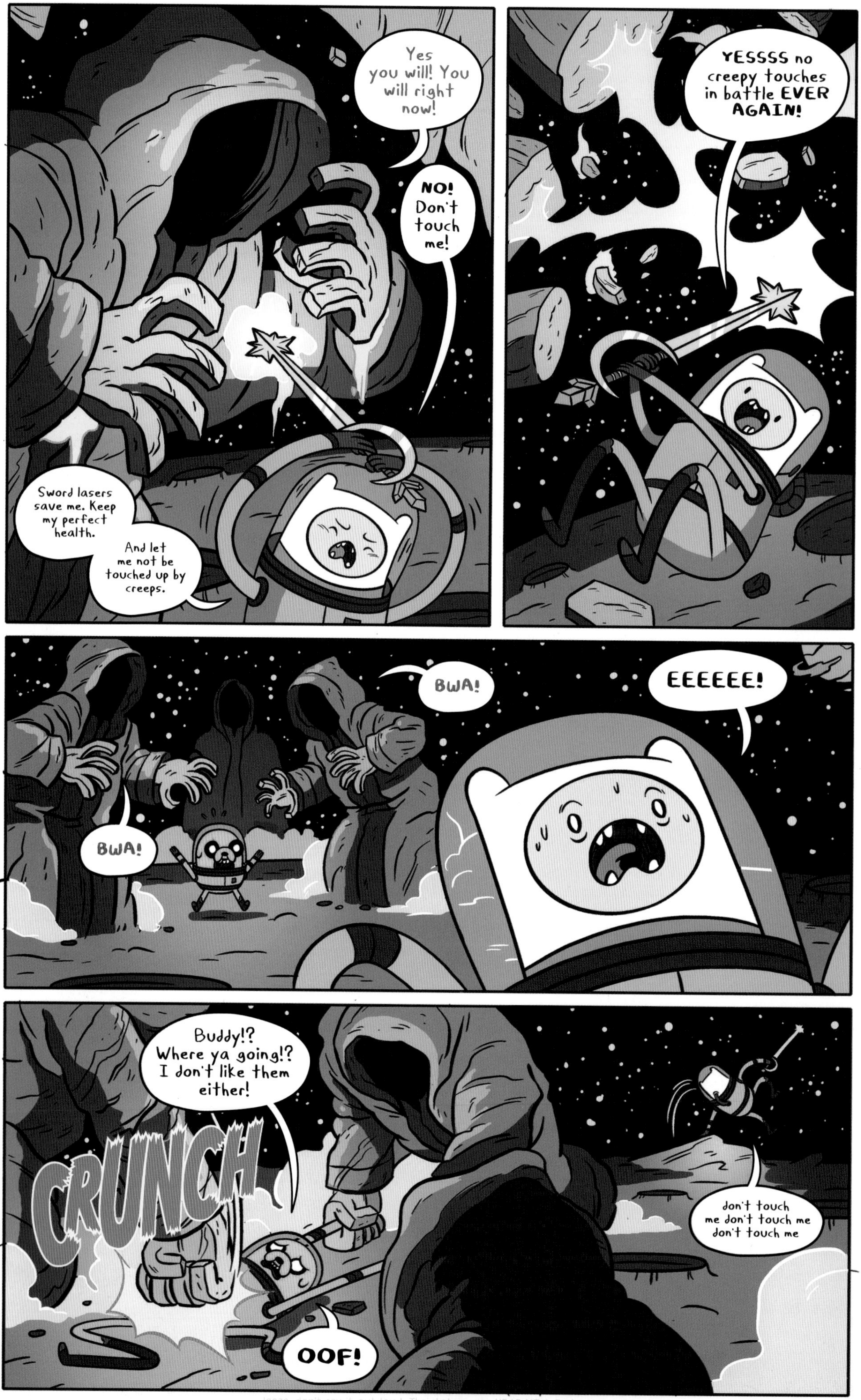
Yes you will! You will right now!
NO! Don't touch me!
Sword lasers save me. Keep my perfect health.
And let me not be touched up by creeps.
YESSSS no creepy touches in battle EVER AGAIN!
BWA!
BWA!
EEEEEE!
Buddy!? Where ya going!? I don't like them either!
CRUNCH
OOF!
don't touch me don't touch me don't touch me

Jeeze, don't say it out loud. The statues can HEAR YOU. Rude.

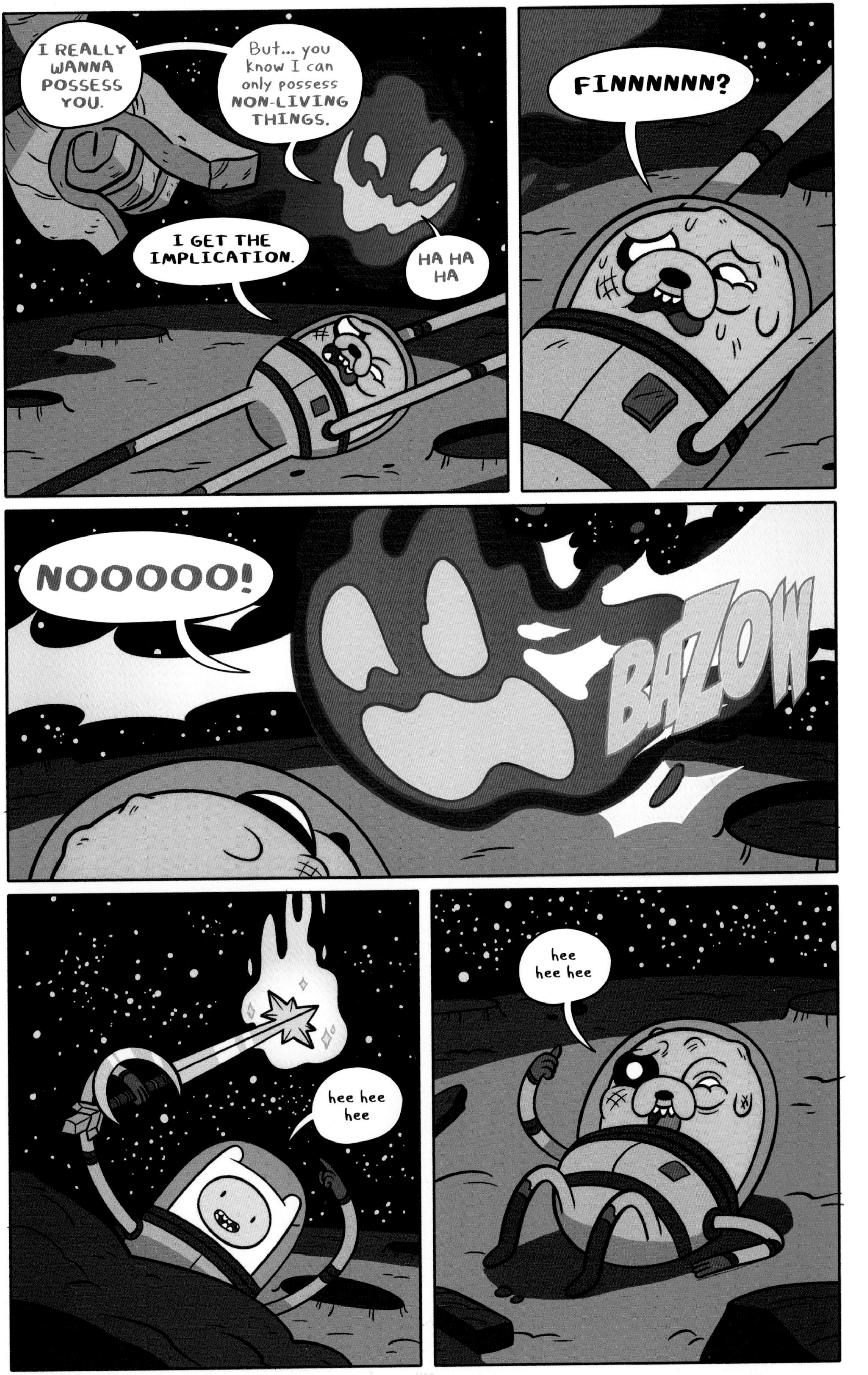
I REALLY WANNA POSSESS YOU.
But... you know I can only possess NON-LIVING THINGS.
I GET THE IMPLICATION.
HA HA HA
FINNNNNN?
NOOOOO!
BAZOW
hee hee hee
hee hee hee

Hee.

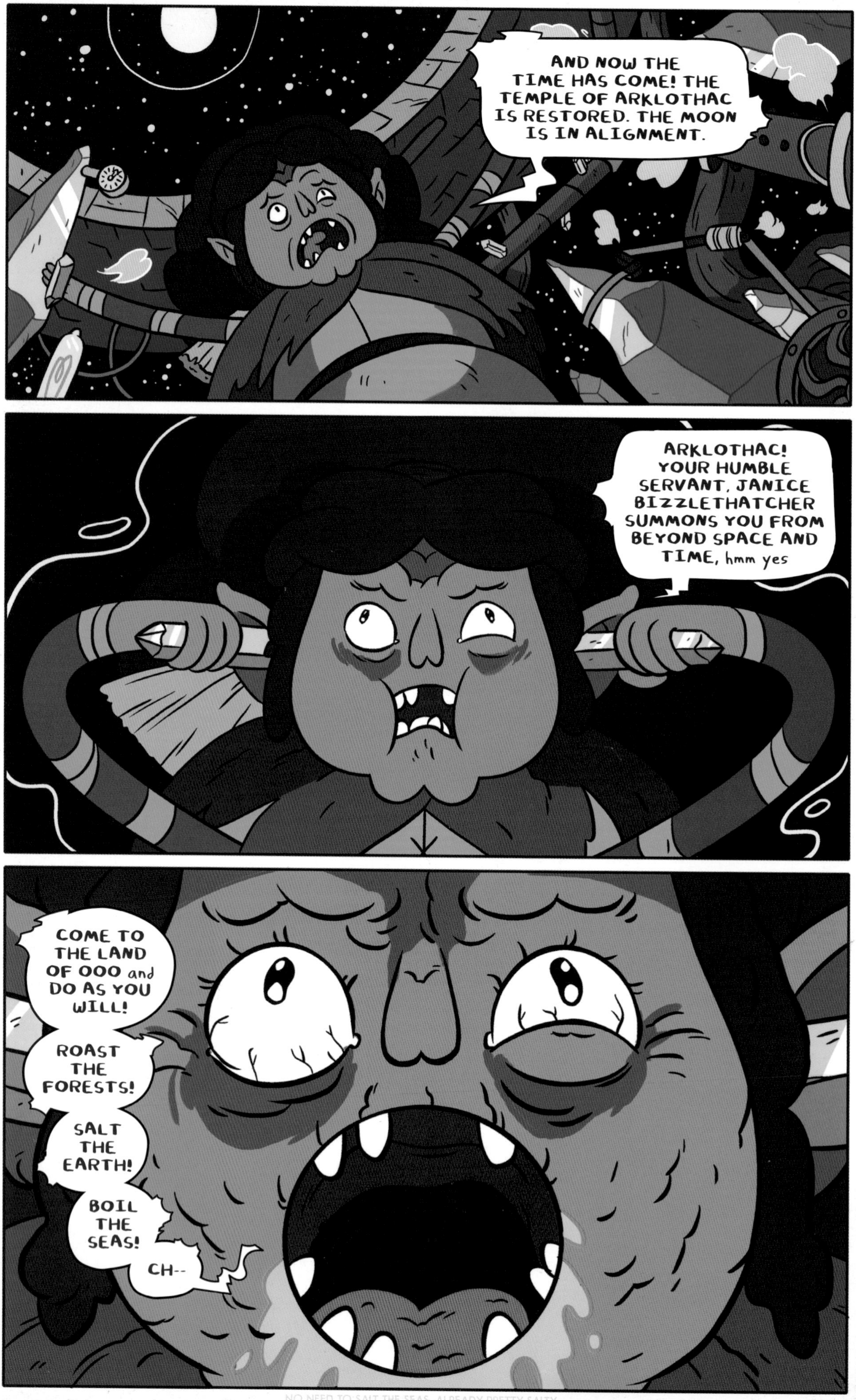
AND NOW THE TIME HAS COME! THE TEMPLE OF ARKLOTHAC IS RESTORED. THE MOON IS IN ALIGNMENT.
ARKLOTHAC! YOUR HUMBLE SERVANT, JANICE BIZZLETHATCHER SUMMONS YOU FROM BEYOND SPACE AND TIME, hmm yes
COME TO THE LAND OF OOO and DO AS YOU WILL!
ROAST THE FORESTS!
SALT THE EARTH!
BOIL THE SEAS!
CH--

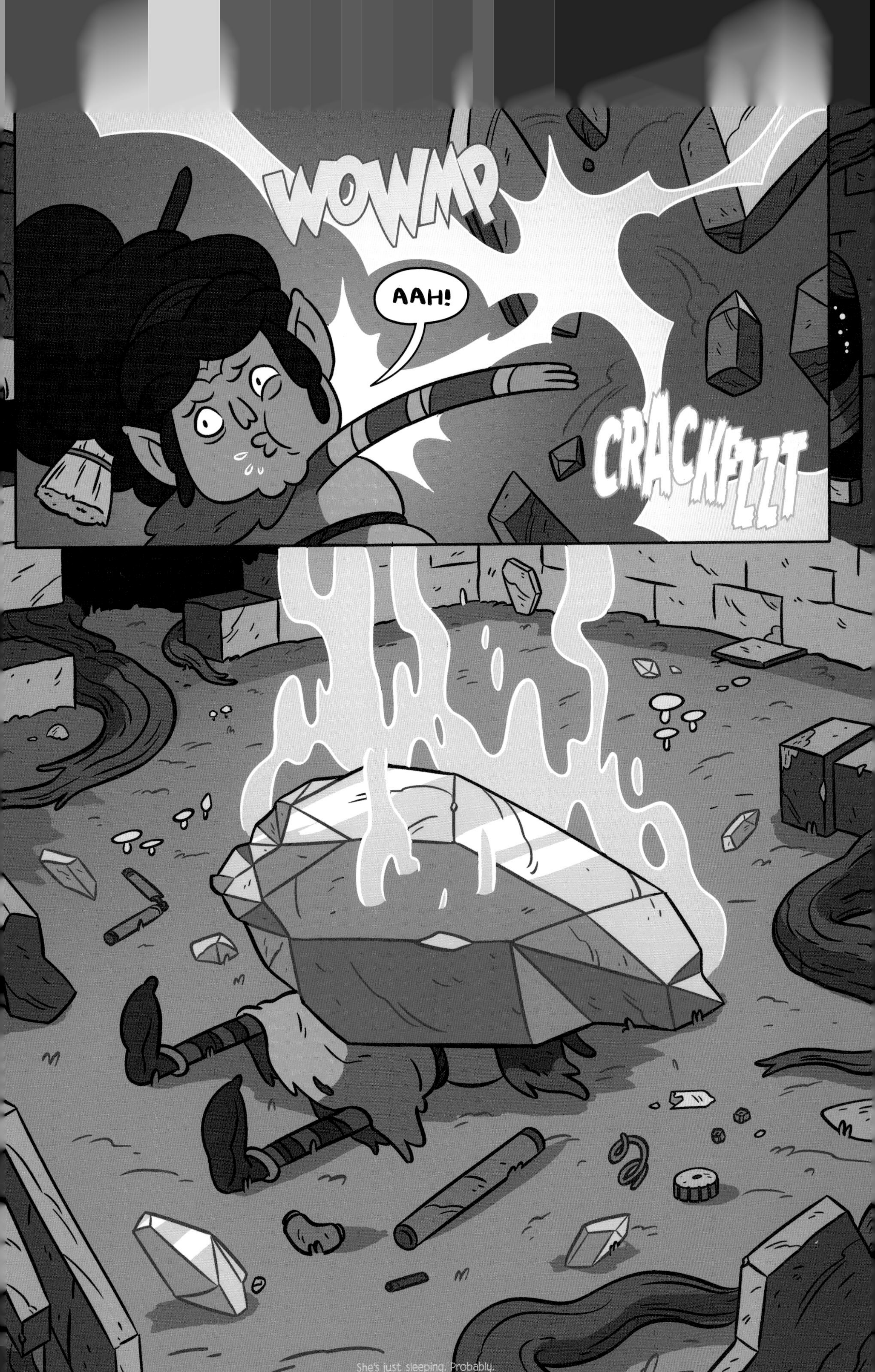
WOWMP
AAH!
CRACKFZZT

She's just sleeping. Probably.

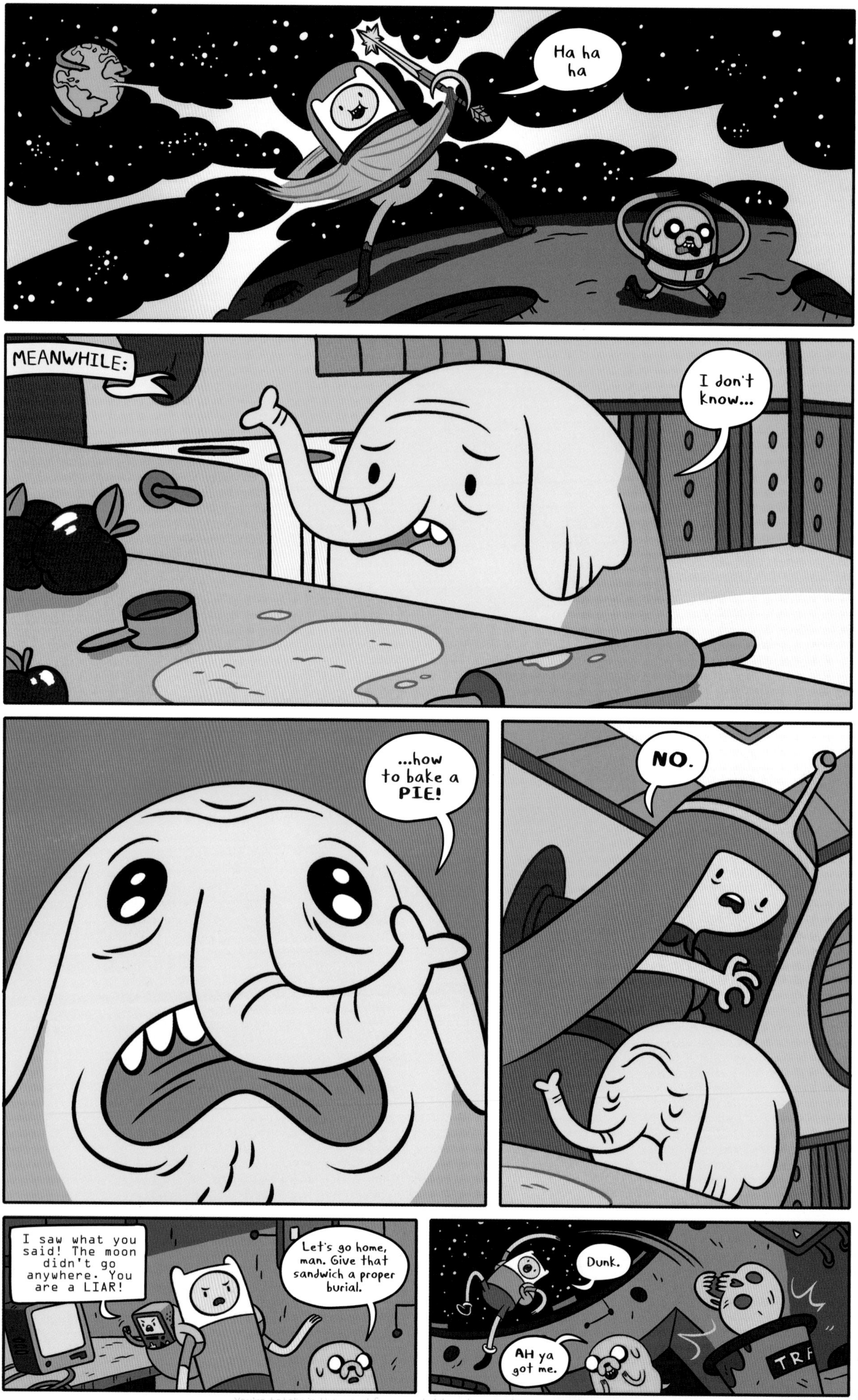
Ha ha ha
MEANWHILE:
I don't know...
...how to bake a PIE!
NO.
I saw what you said! The moon didn't go anywhere. You are a LIAR!
Let's go home, man. Give that sandwich a proper burial.
Dunk.
AH ya got me.

You're totally in the mood for a sandwich and some pie now, aren't you?

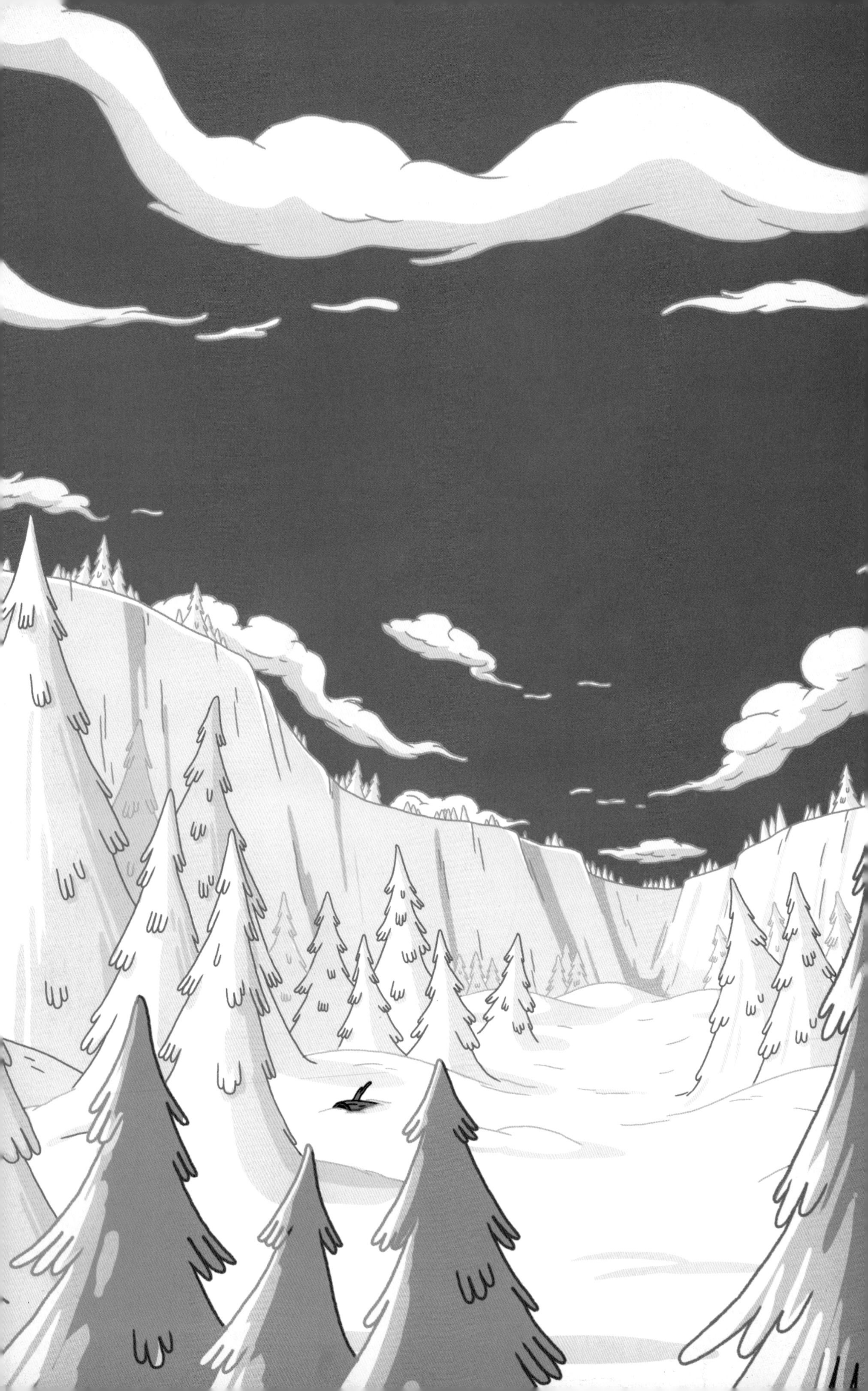

CHAPTER THREE

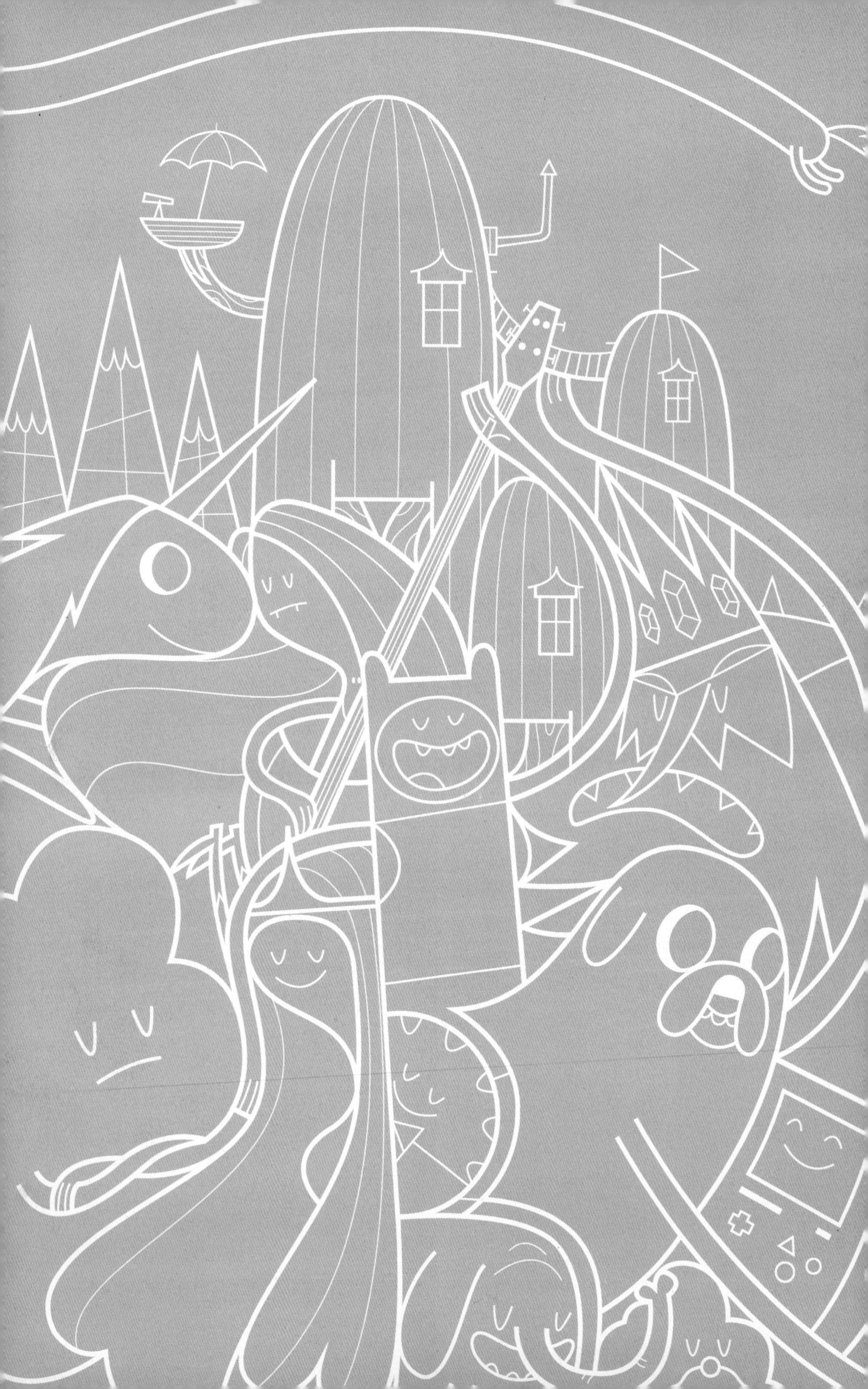

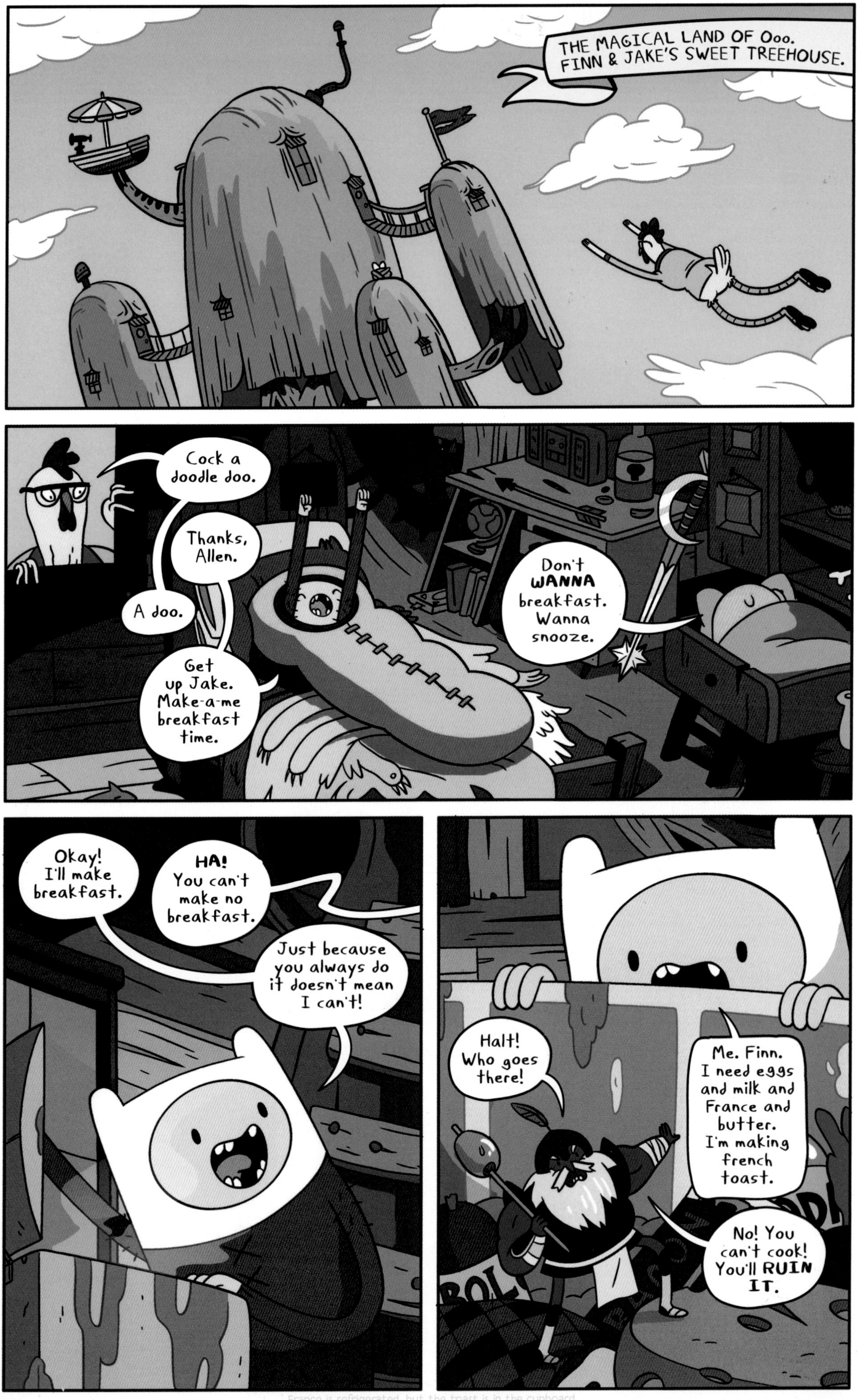
THE MAGICAL LAND OF Ooo. FINN & JAKE'S SWEET TREEHOUSE.
Cock a doodle doo.
Thanks, Allen.
A doo.
Get up Jake. Make-a-me breakfast time.
Don't WANNA breakfast. Wanna snooze.
Okay! I'll make breakfast.
HA! You can't make no breakfast.
Just because you always do it doesn't mean I can't!
Halt! Who goes there!
Me. Finn. I need eggs and milk and France and butter. I'm making french toast.
No! You can't cook! You'll RUIN IT.

France is refrigerated, but the toast is in the cupboard.

I CAN COOK.

IT will be YUMMY.

You'll waste the food!

I'll just follow Jake's notebook!

Noooo... it's his favorite! You'll waste iiiiit...

BIG OL' COOKBOOK

WHIZ

FLUMPF

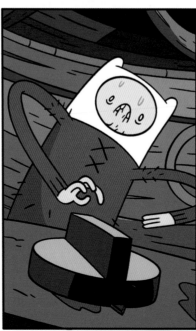

I think... I'm doing it.

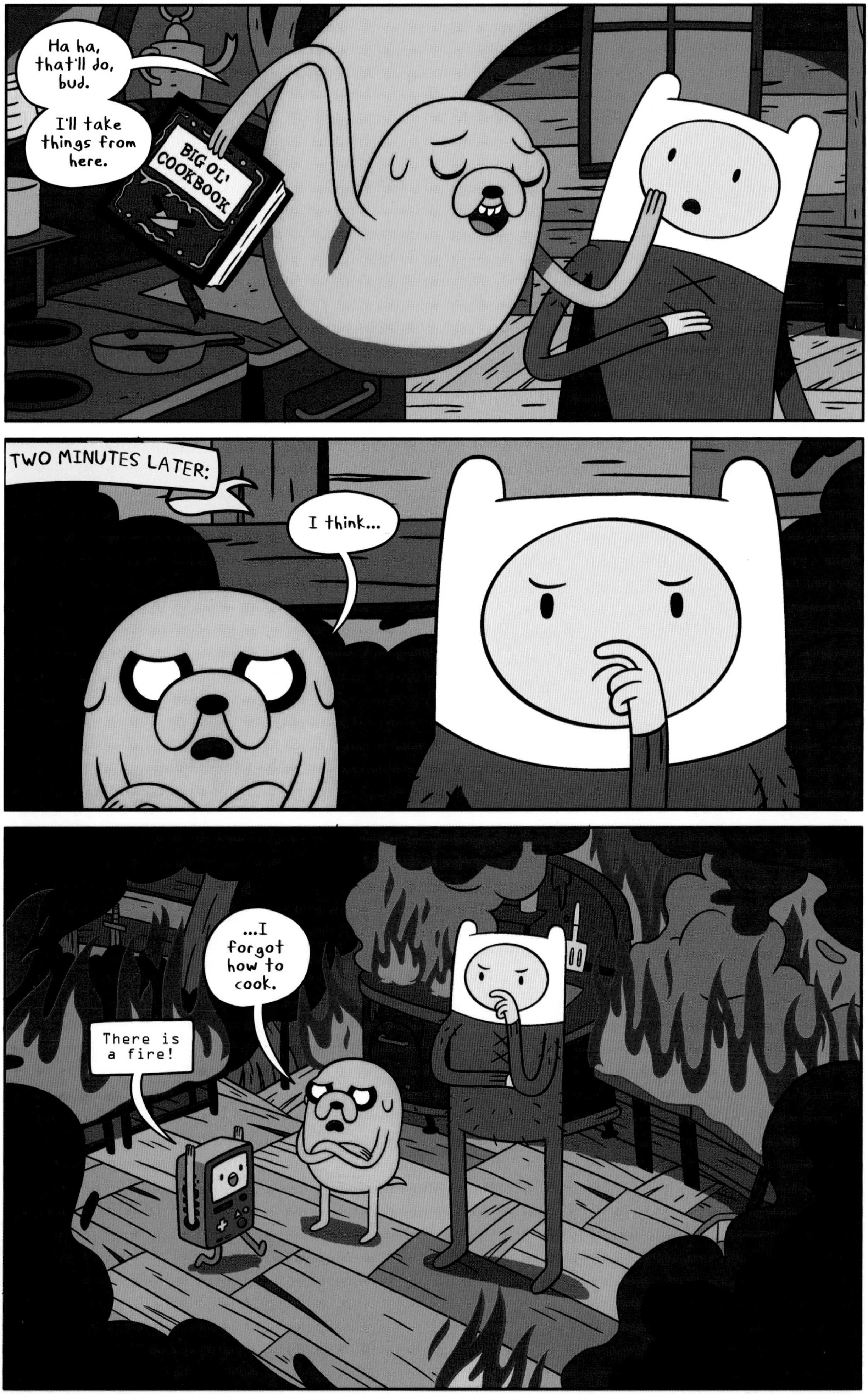
Ha ha, that'll do, bud.
I'll take things from here.
BIG OL' COOKBOOK
TWO MINUTES LATER:
I think...
...I forgot how to cook.
There is a fire!

And this is a comic book! Sorry, we're all just saying things that are true?

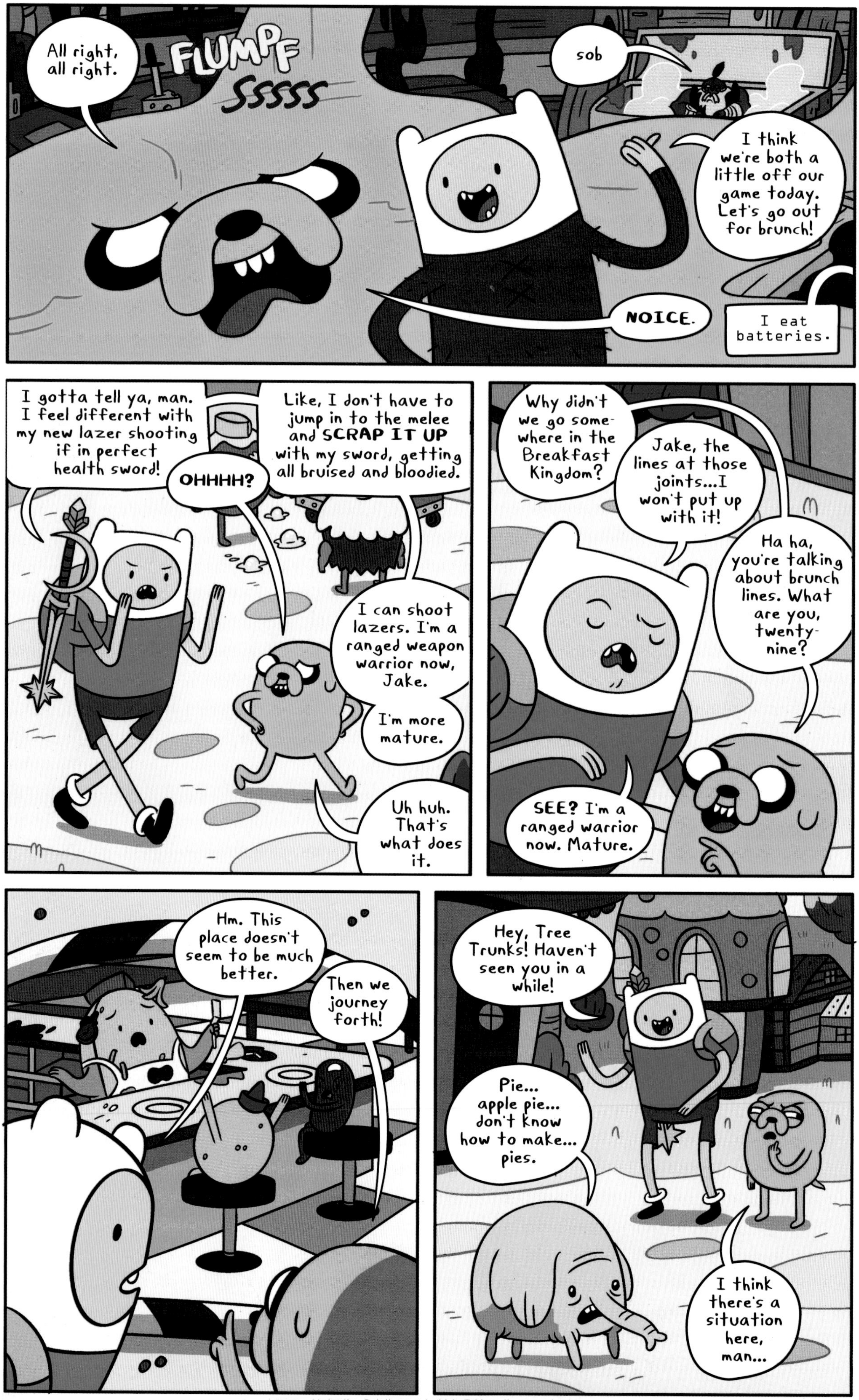
All right, all right.
FLUMPF
SSSSS
sob
I think we're both a little off our game today. Let's go out for brunch!
NOICE.
I eat batteries.
I gotta tell ya, man. I feel different with my new lazer shooting if in perfect health sword!
OHHHH?
Like, I don't have to jump in to the melee and SCRAP IT UP with my sword, getting all bruised and bloodied.
I can shoot lazers. I'm a ranged weapon warrior now, Jake.
I'm more mature.
Uh huh. That's what does it.
Why didn't we go somewhere in the Breakfast Kingdom?
Jake, the lines at those joints...I won't put up with it!
Ha ha, you're talking about brunch lines. What are you, twenty-nine?
SEE? I'm a ranged warrior now. Mature.
Hm. This place doesn't seem to be much better.
Then we journey forth!
Hey, Tree Trunks! Haven't seen you in a while!
Pie... apple pie... don't know how to make... pies.
I think there's a situation here, man...

Lazers = Maturity. Put it on a t-shirt. Tattoo it on my body.

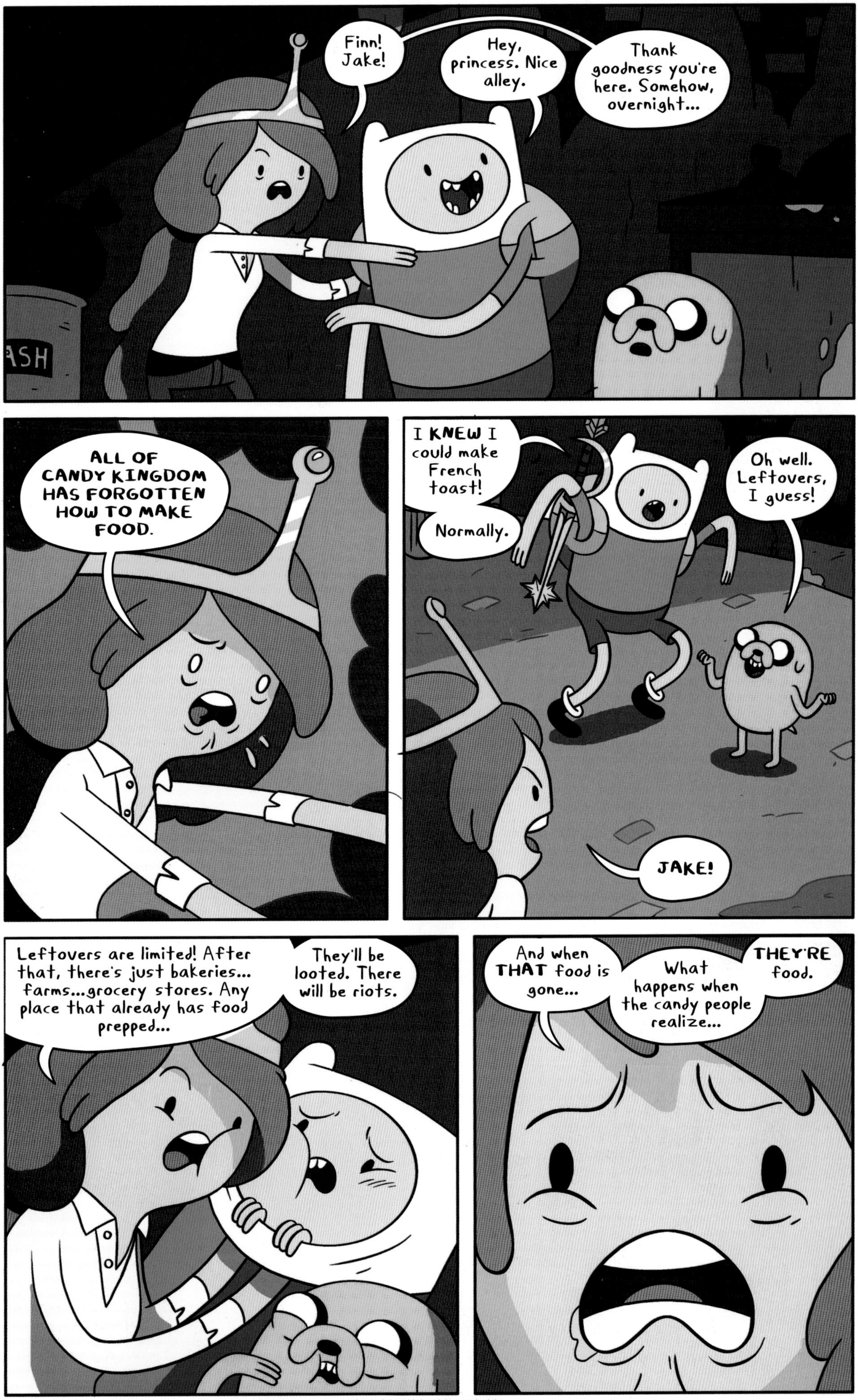

Finn! Jake!
Hey, princess. Nice alley.
Thank goodness you're here. Somehow, overnight...
ASH
ALL OF CANDY KINGDOM HAS FORGOTTEN HOW TO MAKE FOOD.
I KNEW I could make French toast!
Normally.
Oh well. Leftovers, I guess!
JAKE!
Leftovers are limited! After that, there's just bakeries... farms...grocery stores. Any place that already has food prepped...
They'll be looted. There will be riots.
And when THAT food is gone...
What happens when the candy people realize...
THEY'RE food.

An existential crisis, probably.

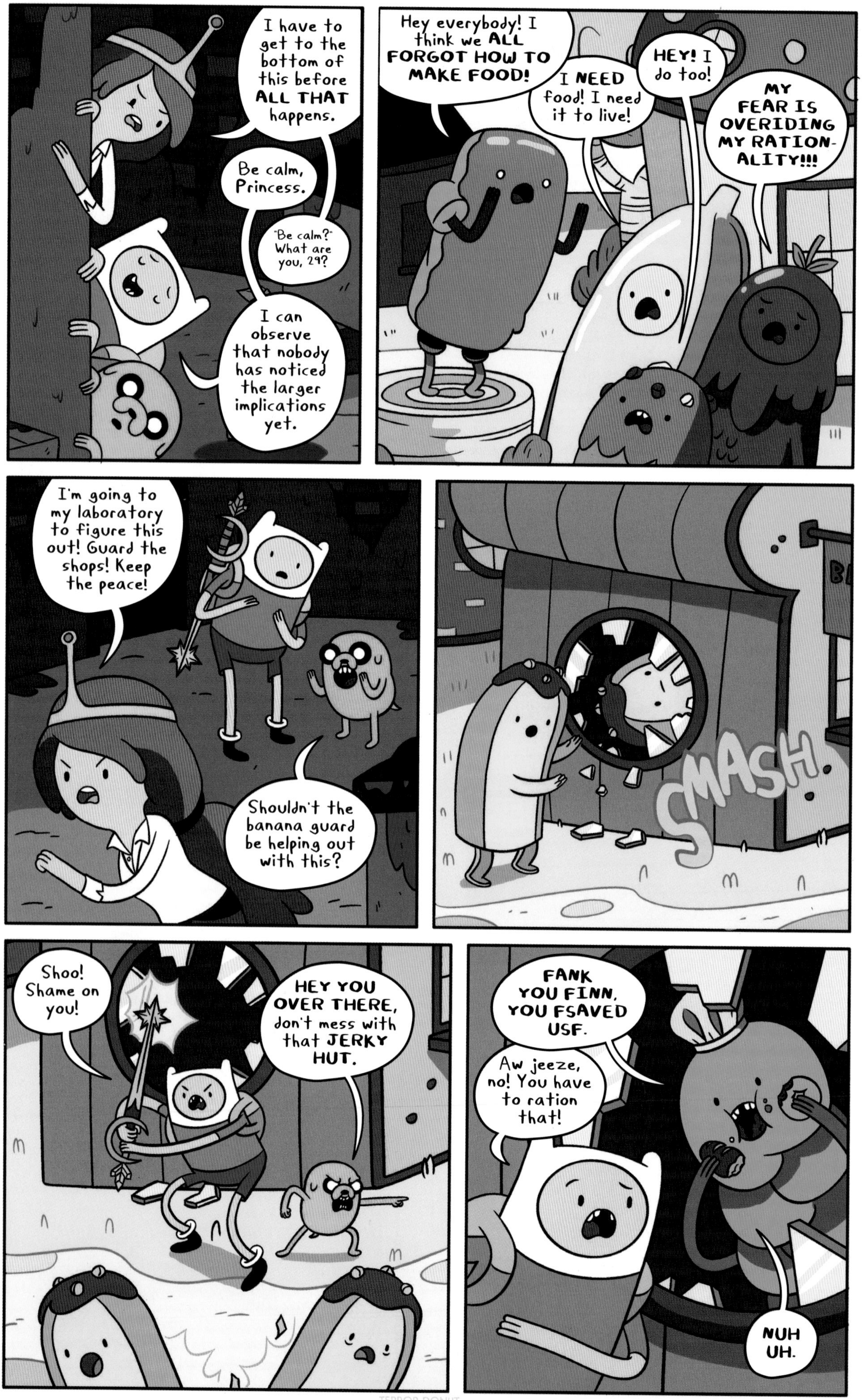

I have to get to the bottom of this before ALL THAT happens.
Be calm, Princess.
"Be calm?" What are you, 29?
I can observe that nobody has noticed the larger implications yet.
Hey everybody! I think we ALL FORGOT HOW TO MAKE FOOD!
I NEED food! I need it to live!
HEY! I do too!
MY FEAR IS OVERIDING MY RATION-ALITY!!!
I'm going to my laboratory to figure this out! Guard the shops! Keep the peace!
Shouldn't the banana guard be helping out with this?
SMASH
Shoo! Shame on you!
HEY YOU OVER THERE, don't mess with that JERKY HUT.
FANK YOU FINN, YOU FSAVED USF.
Aw jeeze, no! You have to ration that!
NUH UH.

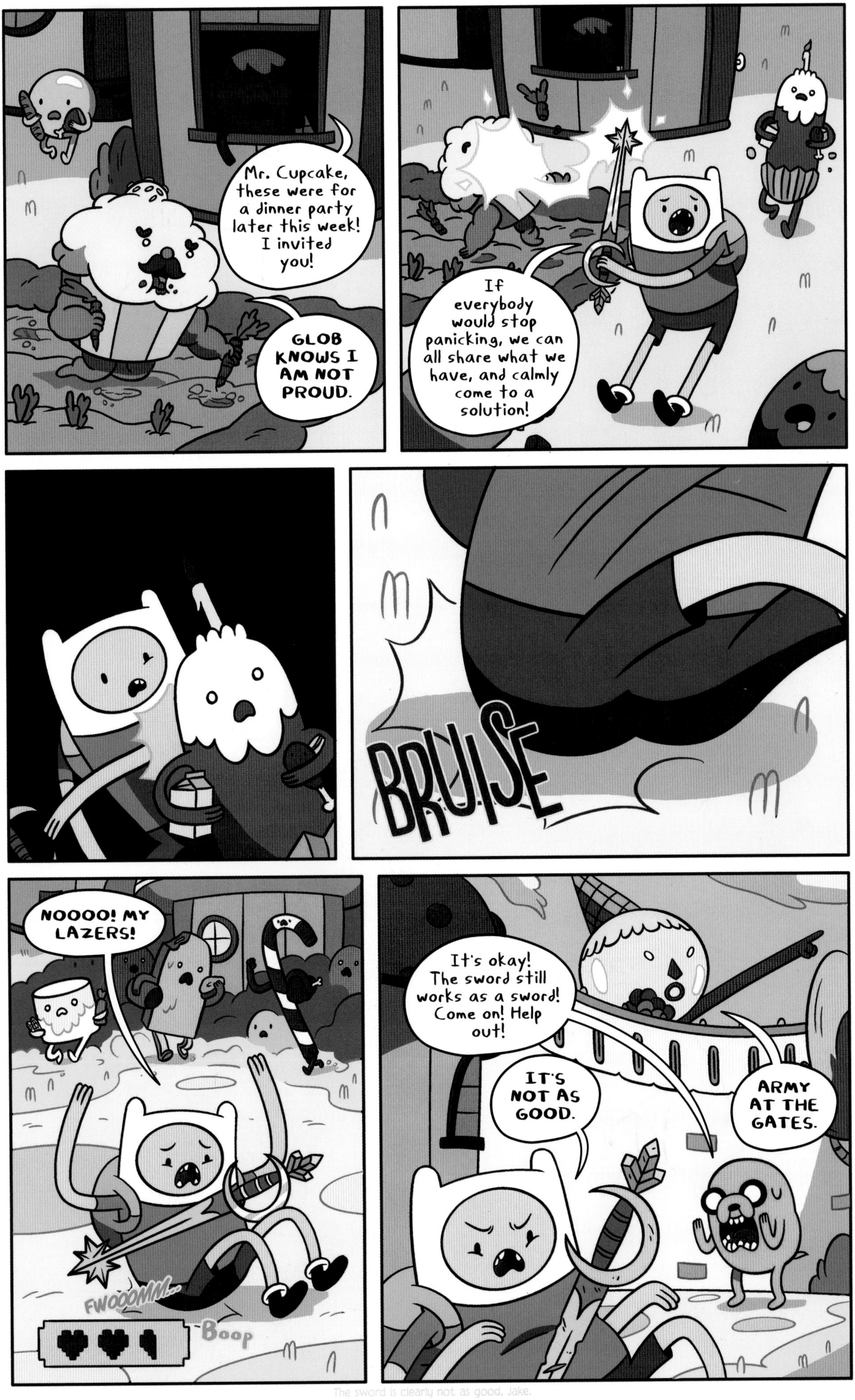
Mr. Cupcake, these were for a dinner party later this week! I invited you!
GLOB KNOWS I AM NOT PROUD.
If everybody would stop panicking, we can all share what we have, and calmly come to a solution!
BRUISE
NOOOO! MY LAZERS!
FWOOOMM...
Boop
It's okay! The sword still works as a sword! Come on! Help out!
IT'S NOT AS GOOD.
ARMY AT THE GATES.

The sword is clearly not as good, Jake.

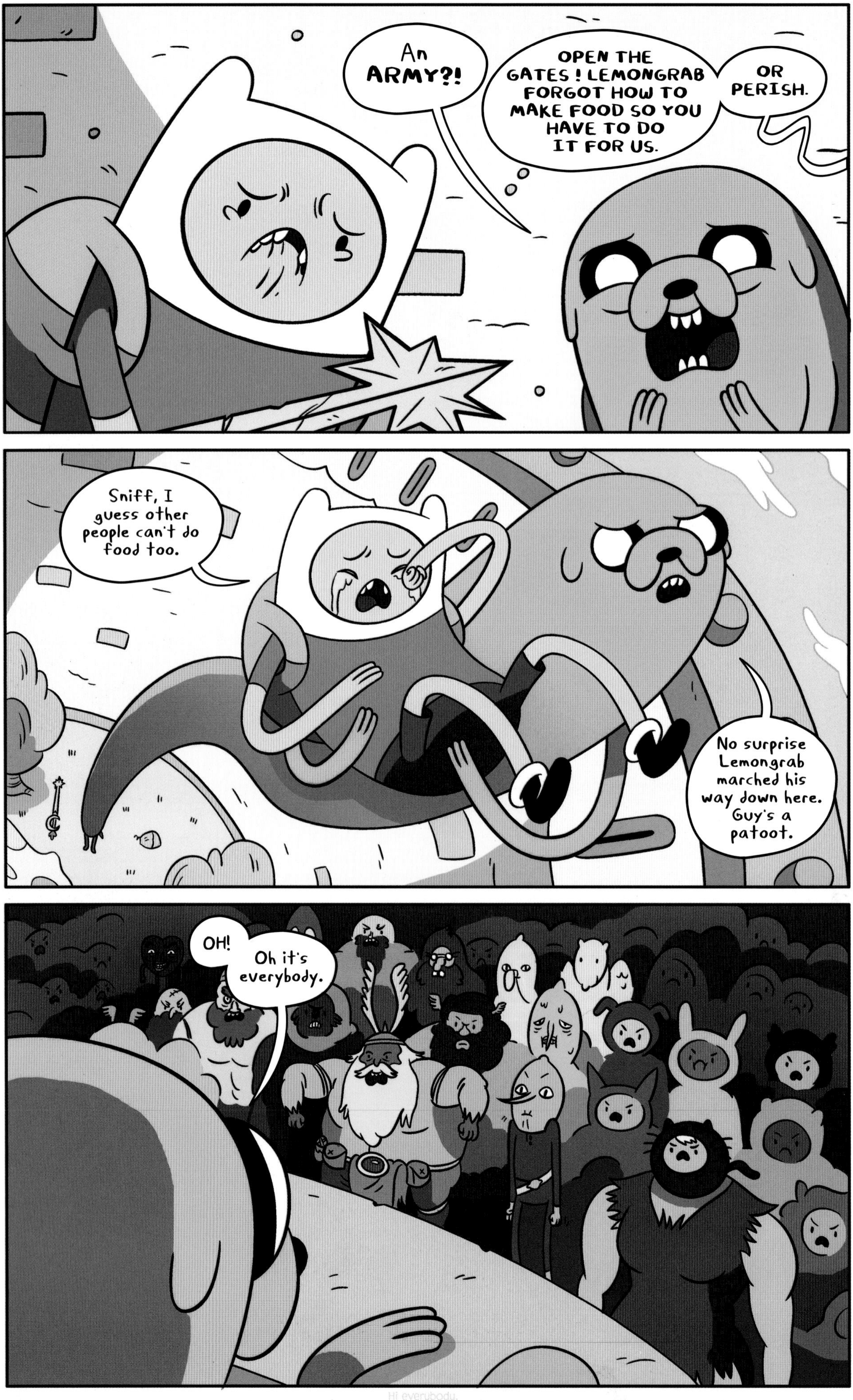
An ARMY?!
OPEN THE GATES! LEMONGRAB FORGOT HOW TO MAKE FOOD SO YOU HAVE TO DO IT FOR US.
OR PERISH.
Sniff, I guess other people can't do food too.
No surprise Lemongrab marched his way down here. Guy's a patoot.
OH!
Oh it's everybody.

Hi everybody.

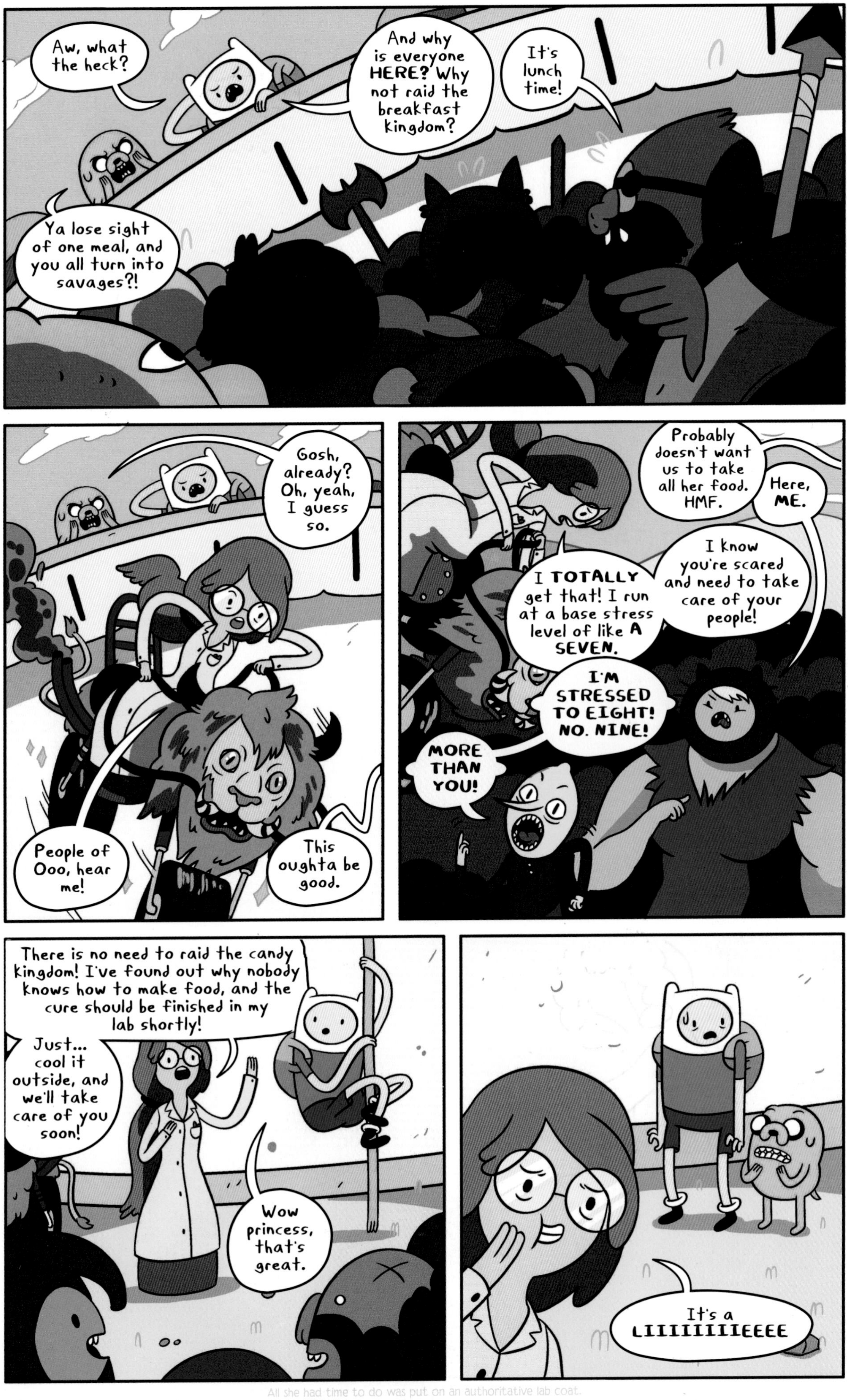

Aw, what the heck?
And why is everyone HERE? Why not raid the breakfast kingdom?
It's lunch time!
Ya lose sight of one meal, and you all turn into savages?!
Gosh, already? Oh, yeah, I guess so.
People of Ooo, hear me!
This oughta be good.
Probably doesn't want us to take all her food. HMF.
Here, ME.
I know you're scared and need to take care of your people!
I TOTALLY get that! I run at a base stress level of like A SEVEN.
I'M STRESSED TO EIGHT! NO. NINE!
MORE THAN YOU!
There is no need to raid the candy kingdom! I've found out why nobody knows how to make food, and the cure should be finished in my lab shortly!
Just... cool it outside, and we'll take care of you soon!
Wow princess, that's great.
It's a LIIIIIIIIEEEE

All she had time to do was put on an authoritative lab coat.

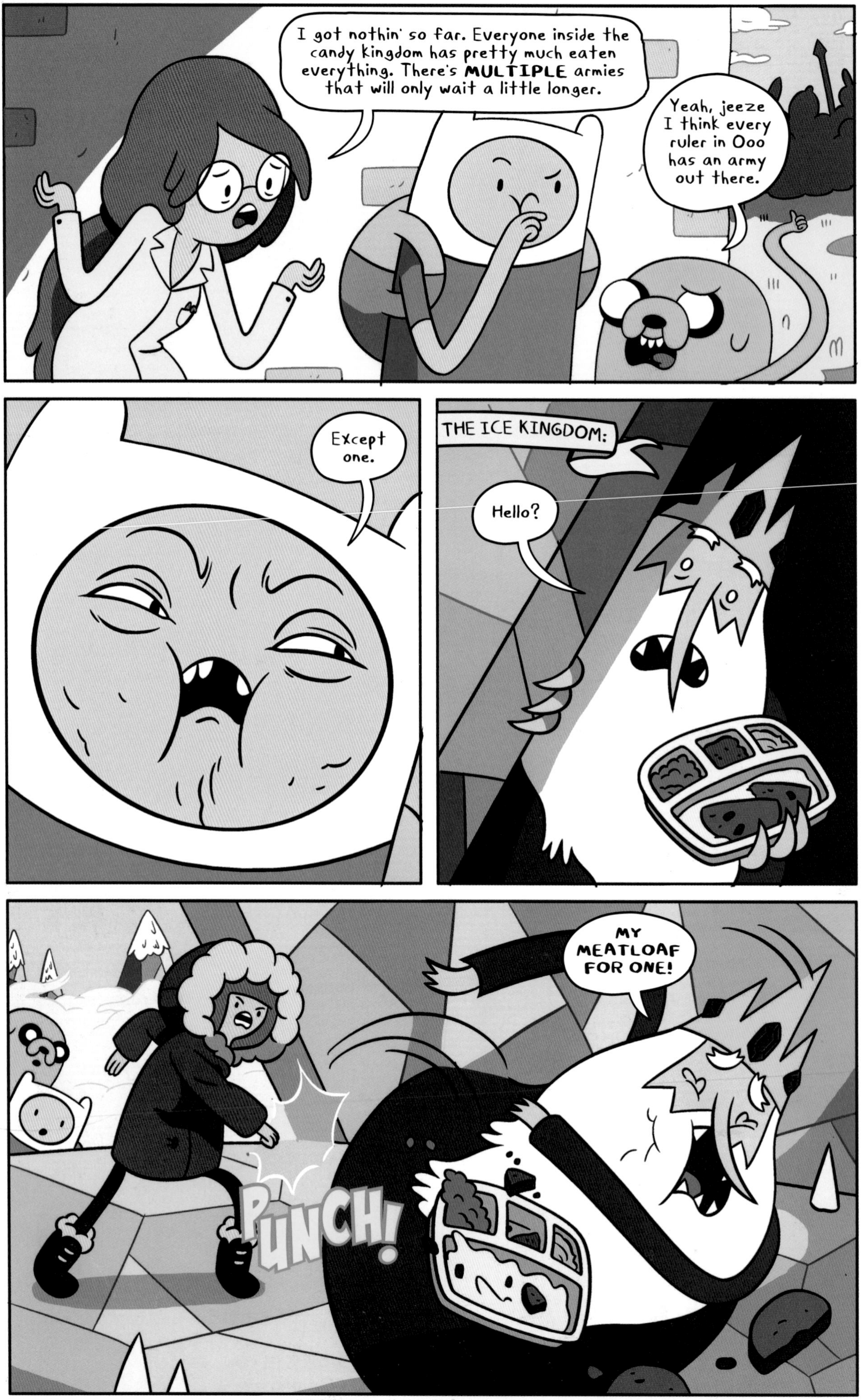
I got nothin' so far. Everyone inside the candy kingdom has pretty much eaten everything. There's MULTIPLE armies that will only wait a little longer.
Yeah, jeeze I think every ruler in Ooo has an army out there.
Except one.
THE ICE KINGDOM:
Hello?
MY MEATLOAF FOR ONE!
PUNCH!

It totally says on the box it's for two, you GLUTTON.

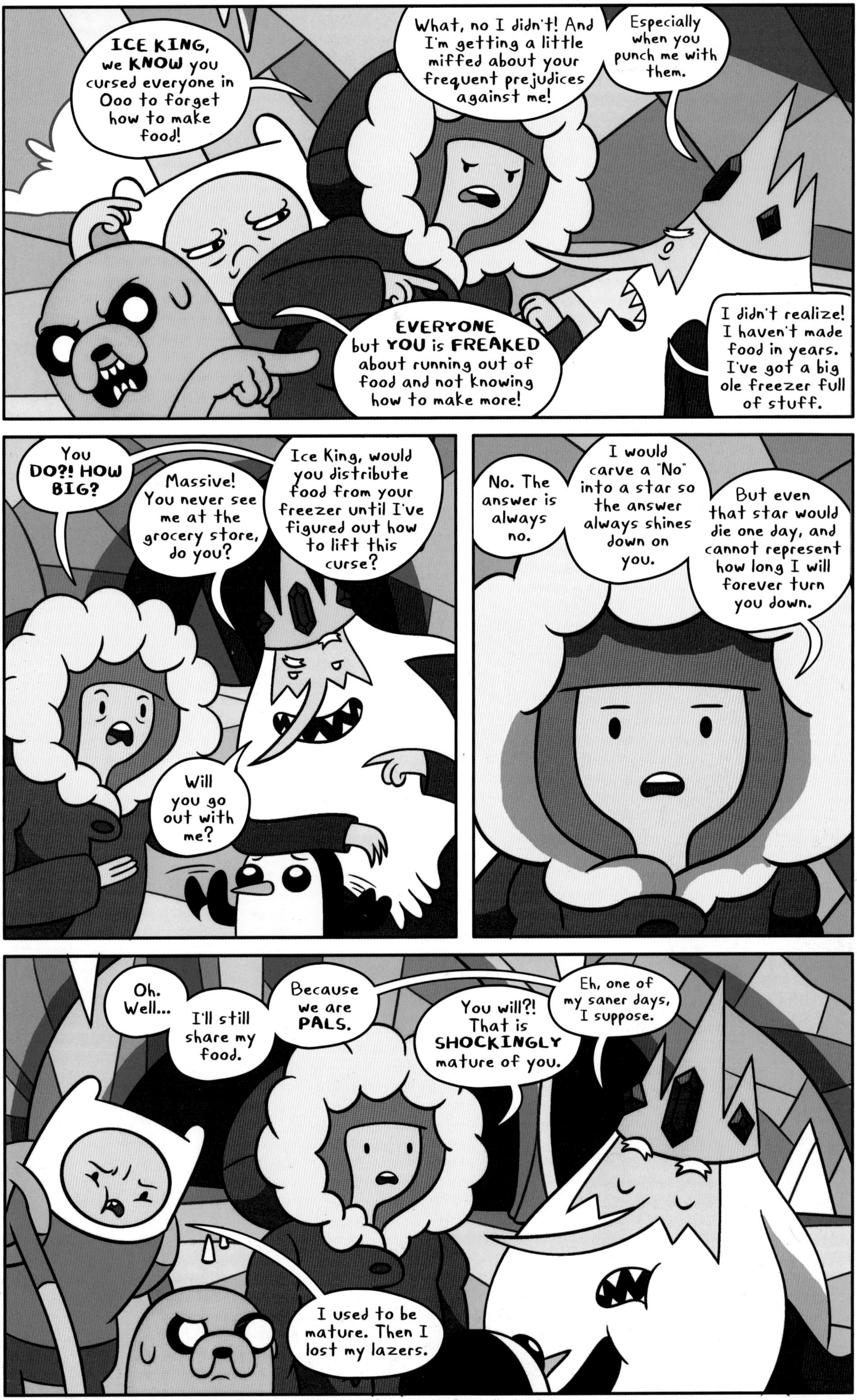
ICE KING, we KNOW you cursed everyone in Ooo to forget how to make food!
What, no I didn't! And I'm getting a little miffed about your frequent prejudices against me!
Especially when you punch me with them.
EVERYONE but YOU is FREAKED about running out of food and not knowing how to make more!
I didn't realize! I haven't made food in years. I've got a big ole freezer full of stuff.
You DO?! HOW BIG?
Massive! You never see me at the grocery store, do you?
Ice King, would you distribute food from your freezer until I've figured out how to lift this curse?
Will you go out with me?
No. The answer is always no.
I would carve a "No" into a star so the answer always shines down on you.
But even that star would die one day, and cannot represent how long I will forever turn you down.
Oh. Well...
I'll still share my food.
Because we are PALS.
You will?! That is SHOCKINGLY mature of you.
Eh, one of my saner days, I suppose.
I used to be mature. Then I lost my lazers.

"I only eat frozen meatloaf on sanity days."

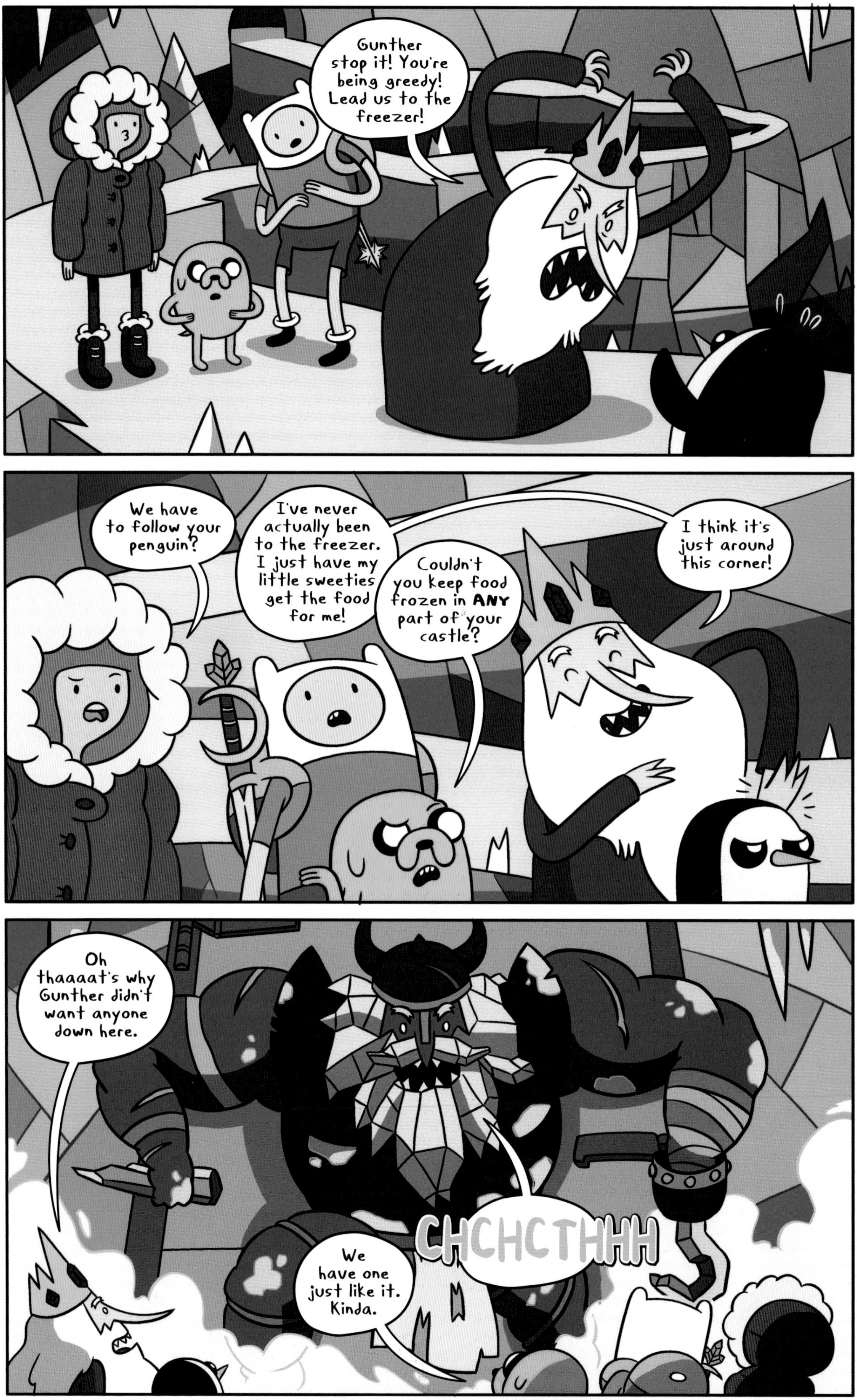
Gunther stop it! You're being greedy! Lead us to the freezer!
We have to follow your penguin?
I've never actually been to the freezer. I just have my little sweeties get the food for me!
Couldn't you keep food frozen in ANY part of your castle?
I think it's just around this corner!
Oh thaaaat's why Gunther didn't want anyone down here.
CHCHCTHHH
We have one just like it. Kinda.

Standard issue food guardian. With maybe a TOUCH of twisted evil ice magic.

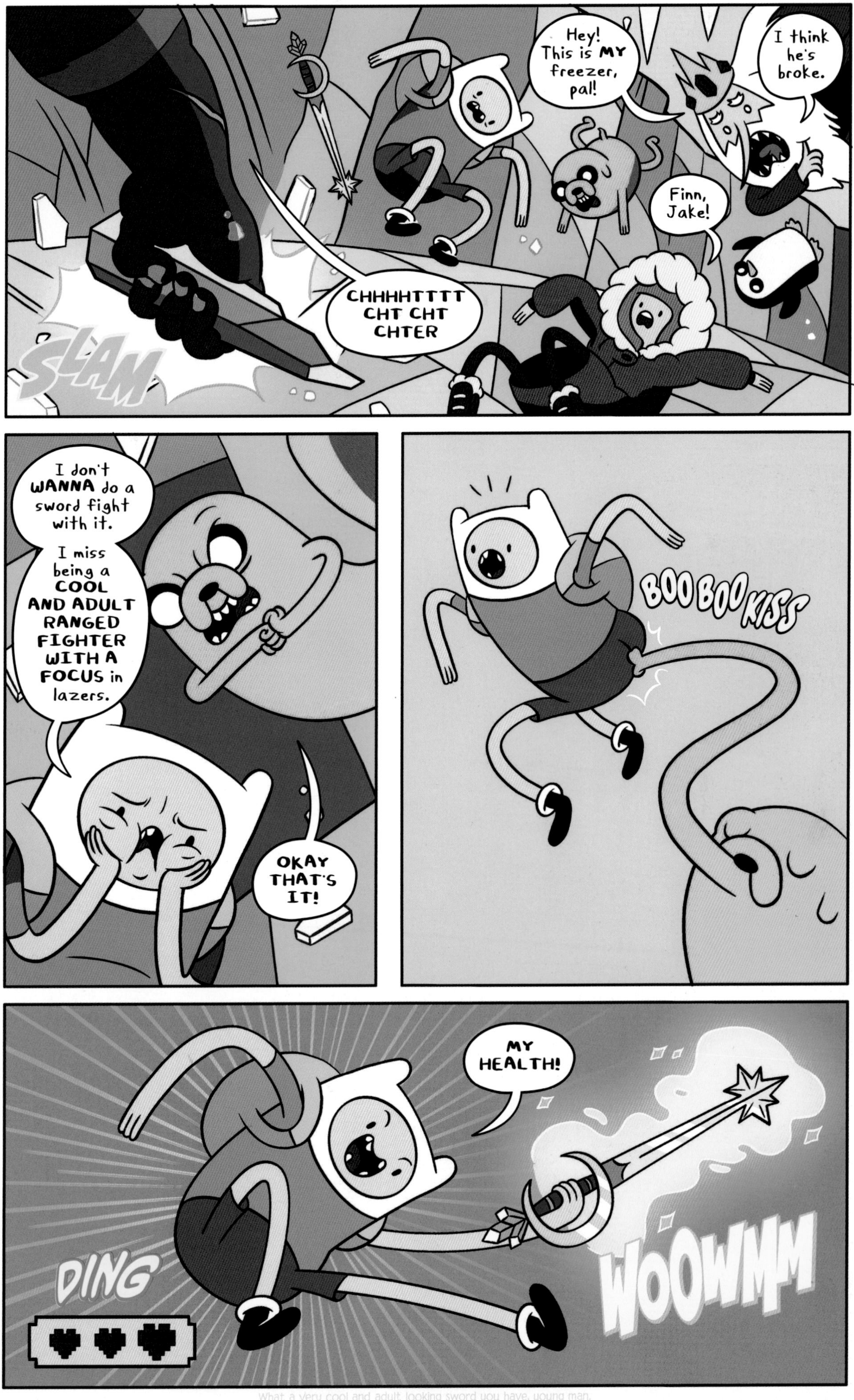
Hey! This is MY freezer, pal!
I think he's broke.
Finn, Jake!
CHHHHTTTT CHT CHT CHTER
SLAM
I don't WANNA do a sword fight with it.
I miss being a COOL AND ADULT RANGED FIGHTER WITH A FOCUS in lazers.
OKAY THAT'S IT!
BOO BOO KISS
MY HEALTH!
DING
WOOWMM

What a very cool and adult looking sword you have, young man.

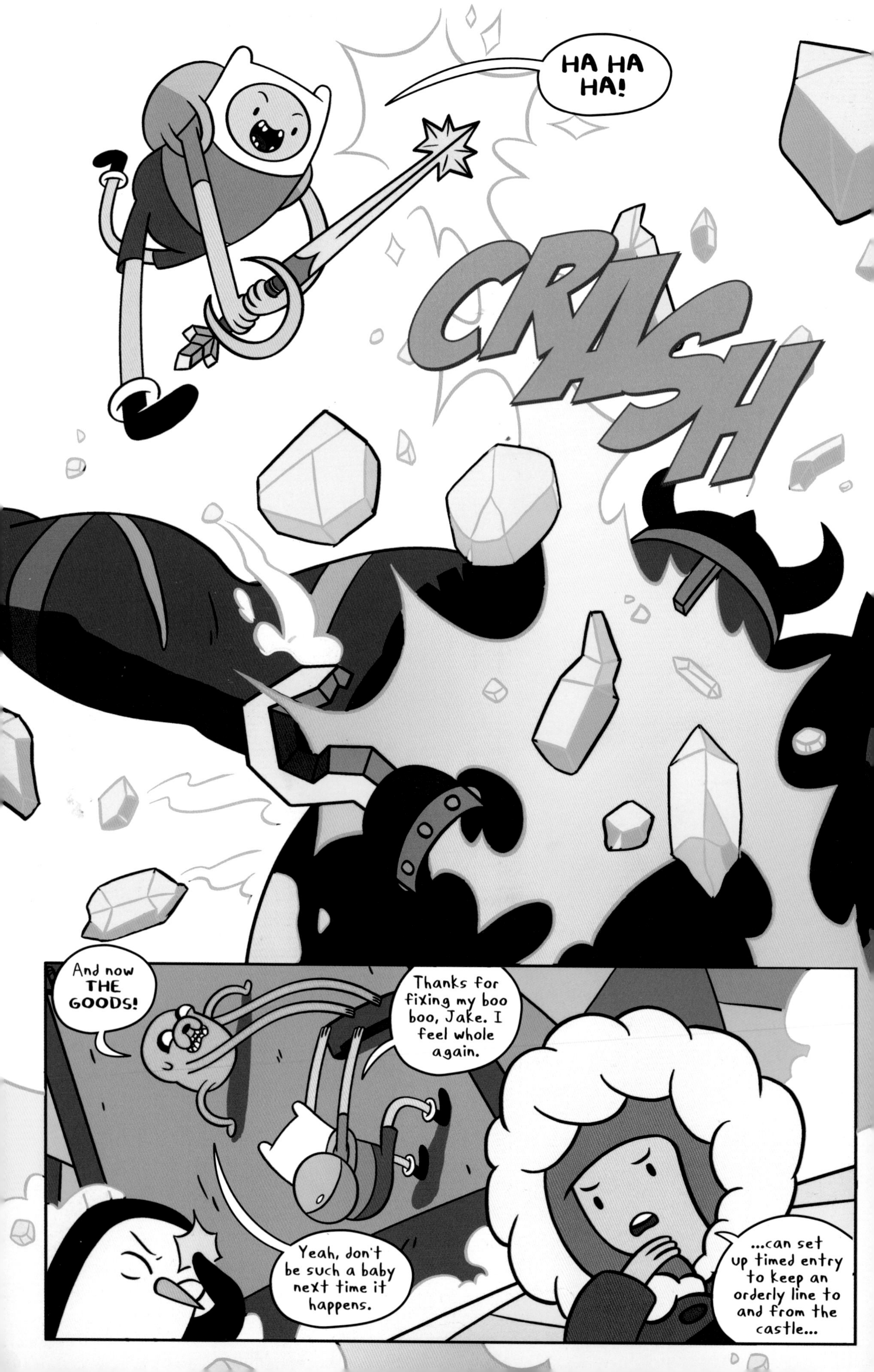
HA HA HA!
CRASH
And now THE GOODS!
Thanks for fixing my boo boo, Jake. I feel whole again.
Yeah, don't be such a baby next time it happens.
...can set up timed entry to keep an orderly line to and from the castle...

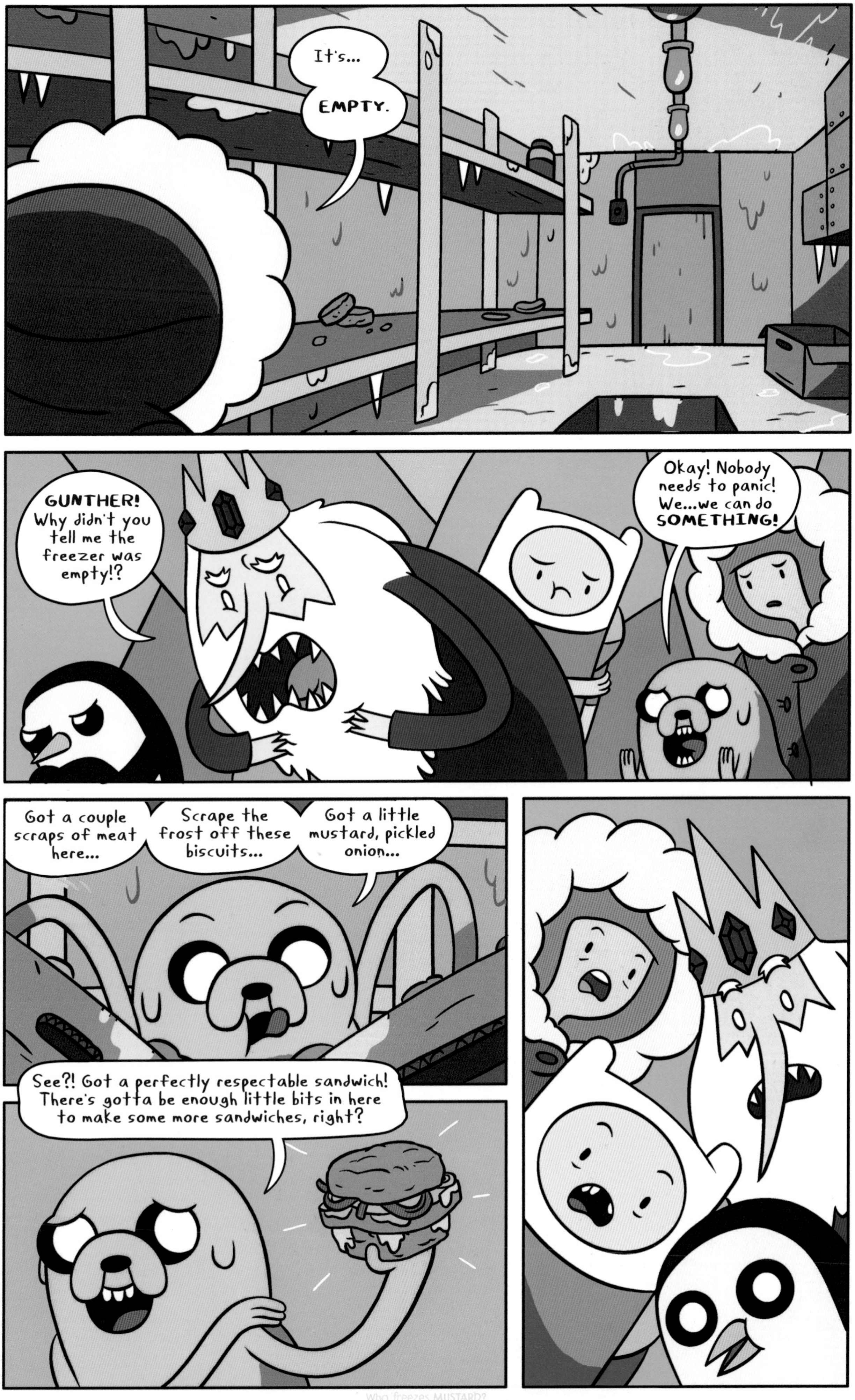
It's...
EMPTY.
GUNTHER! Why didn't you tell me the freezer was empty!?
Okay! Nobody needs to panic! We...we can do SOMETHING!
Got a couple scraps of meat here...
Scrape the frost off these biscuits...
Got a little mustard, pickled onion...
See?! Got a perfectly respectable sandwich! There's gotta be enough little bits in here to make some more sandwiches, right?

Who freezes MUSTARD?

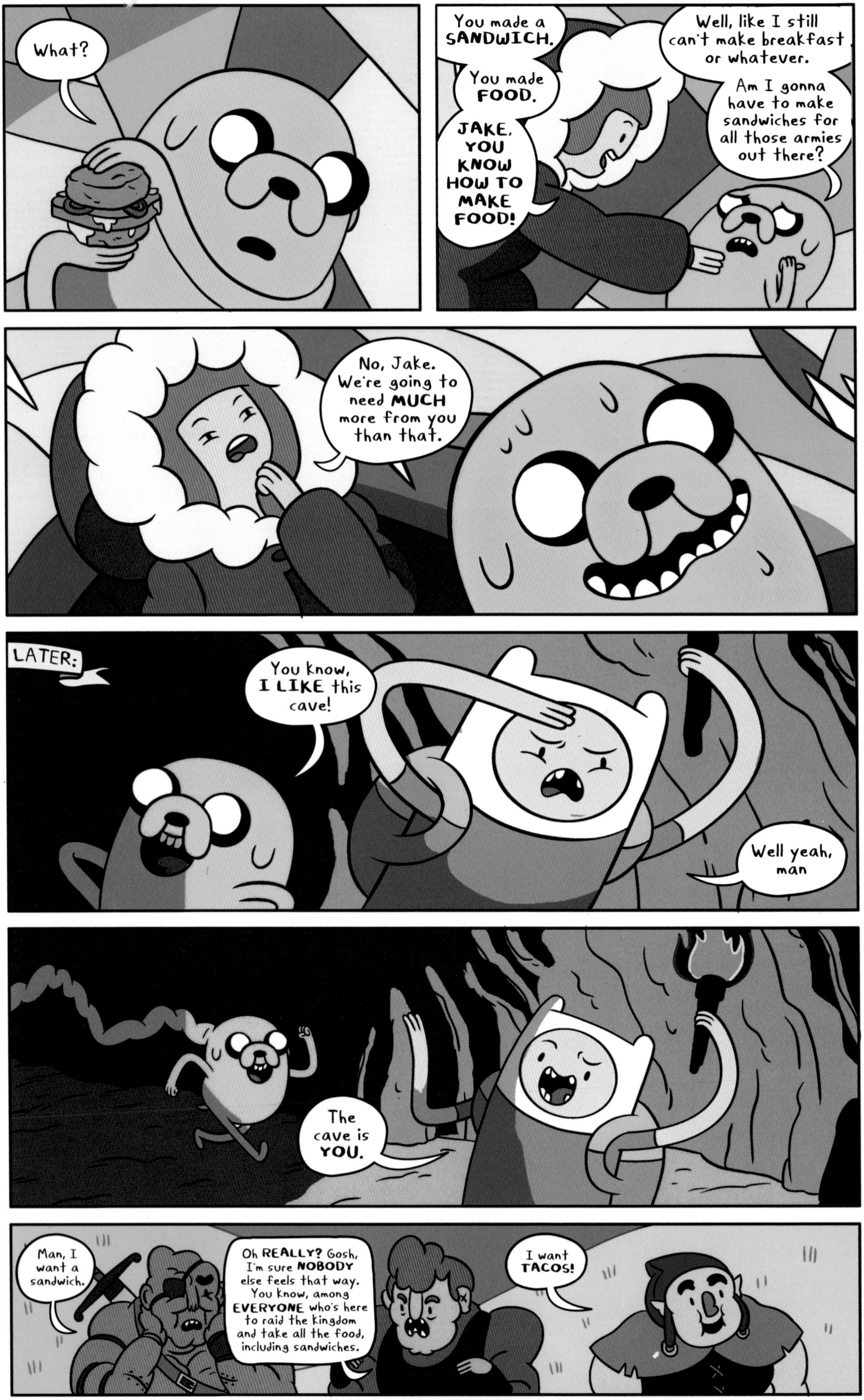
What?
You made a SANDWICH.
You made FOOD.
JAKE, YOU KNOW HOW TO MAKE FOOD!
Well, like I still can't make breakfast or whatever.
Am I gonna have to make sandwiches for all those armies out there?
No, Jake. We're going to need MUCH more from you than that.
LATER:
You know, I LIKE this cave!
Well yeah, man
The cave is YOU.
Man, I want a sandwich.
Oh REALLY? Gosh, I'm sure NOBODY else feels that way. You know, among EVERYONE who's here to raid the kingdom and take all the food, including sandwiches.
I want TACOS!

Lotsa good foods out there worth strapping on armor for, sure.

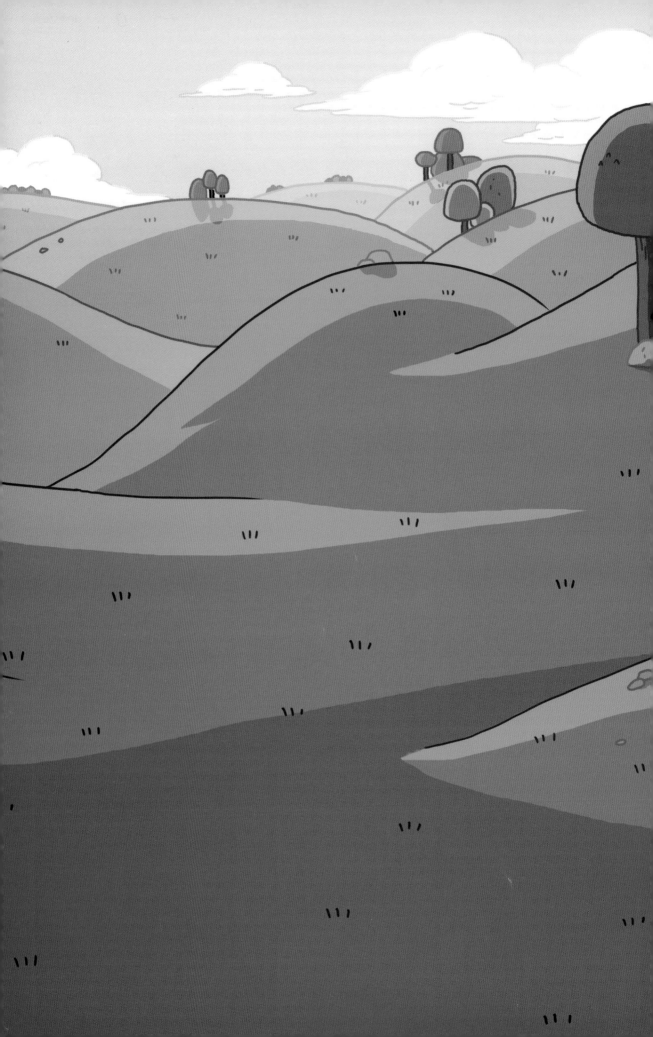

CHAPTER FOUR

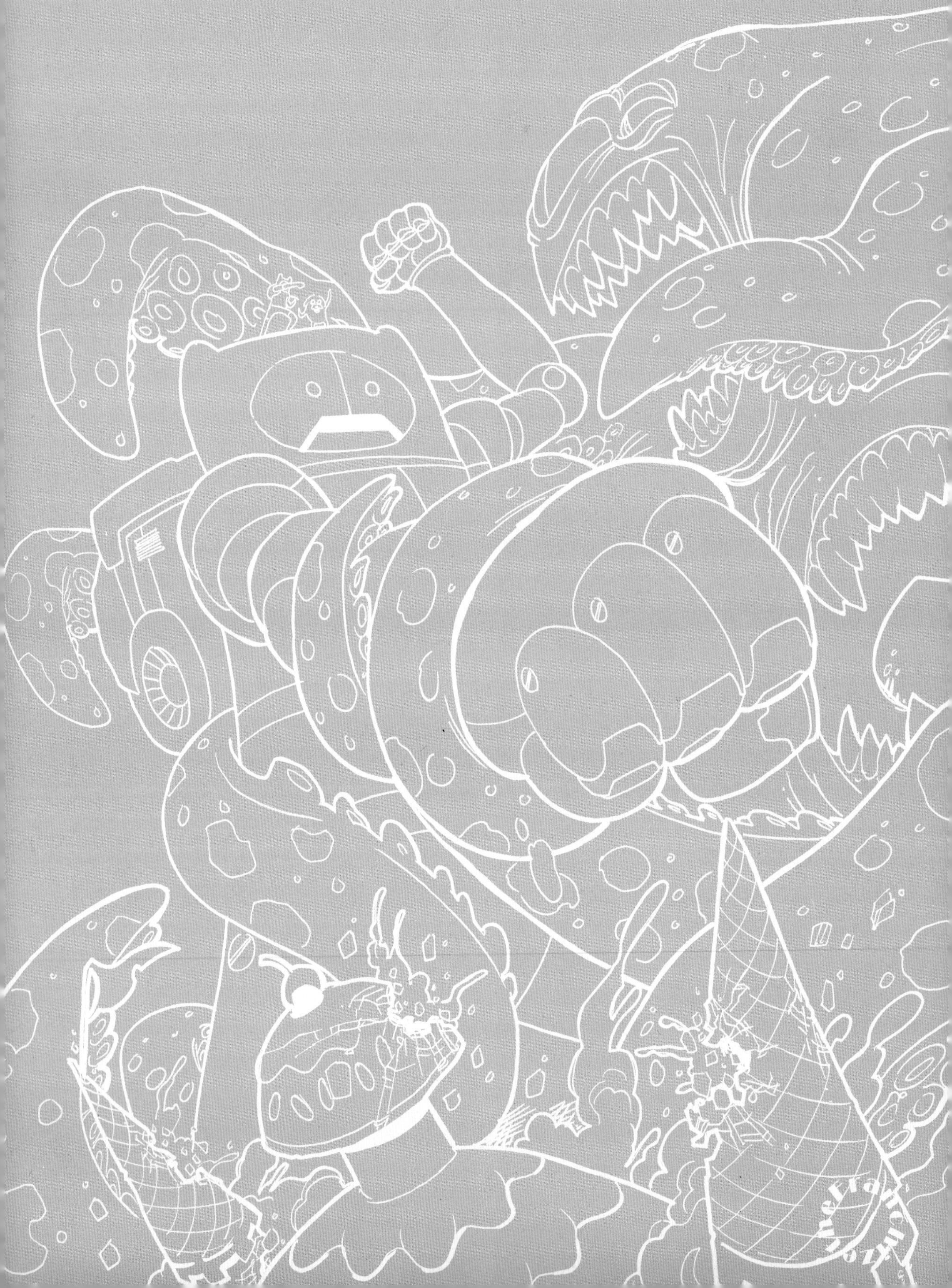

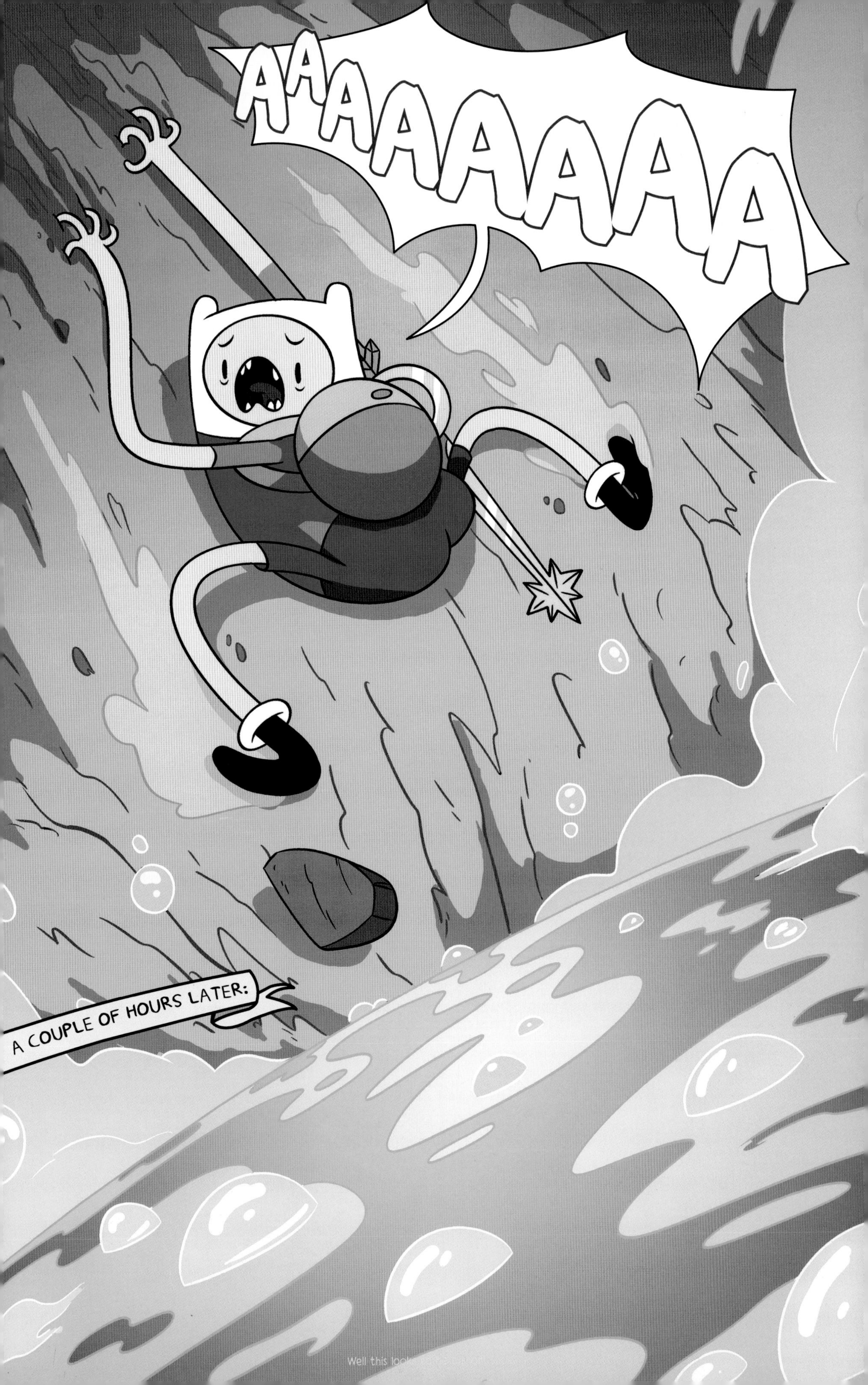
AAAAAAAAA
A COUPLE OF HOURS LATER:

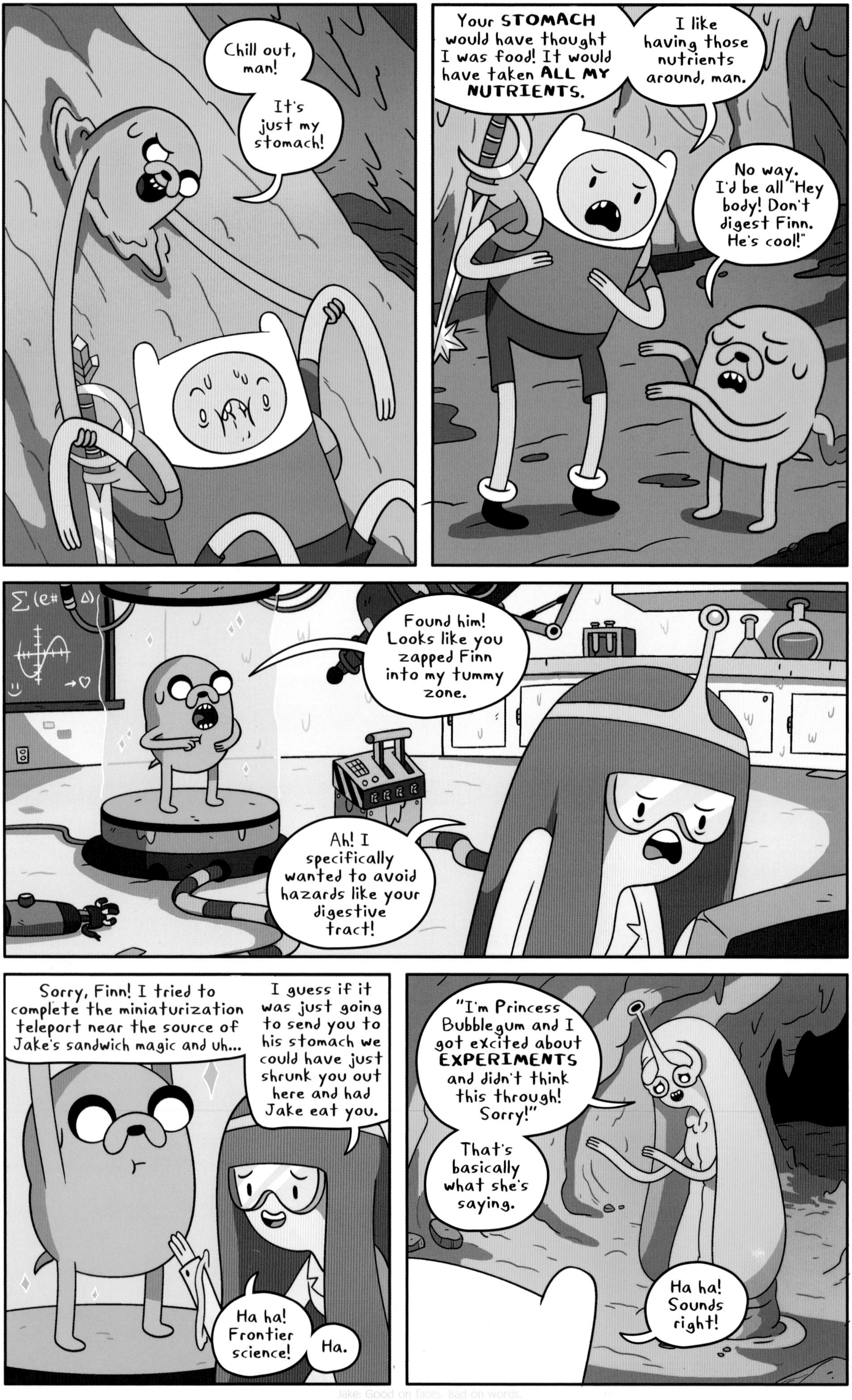
Chill out, man!
It's just my stomach!
Your STOMACH would have thought I was food! It would have taken ALL MY NUTRIENTS.
I like having those nutrients around, man.
No way. I'd be all "Hey body! Don't digest Finn. He's cool!"
Found him! Looks like you zapped Finn into my tummy zone.
Ah! I specifically wanted to avoid hazards like your digestive tract!
Sorry, Finn! I tried to complete the miniaturization teleport near the source of Jake's sandwich magic and uh...
I guess if it was just going to send you to his stomach we could have just shrunk you out here and had Jake eat you.
Ha ha! Frontier science!
Ha.
"I'm Princess Bubblegum and I got excited about EXPERIMENTS and didn't think this through! Sorry!"
That's basically what she's saying.
Ha ha! Sounds right!

Jake: Good on faces. Bad on words.

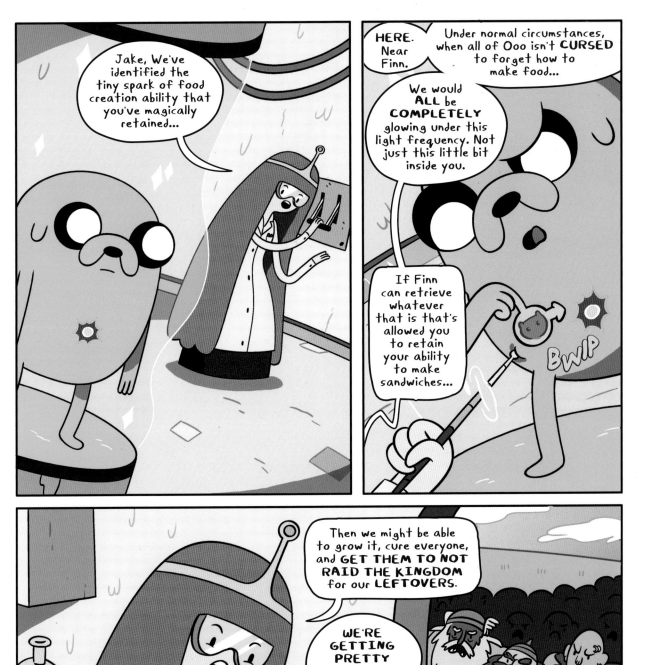

Jake, We've identified the tiny spark of food creation ability that you've magically retained...

HERE. Near Finn.

Under normal circumstances, when all of Ooo isn't CURSED to forget how to make food...

We would ALL be COMPLETELY glowing under this light frequency. Not just this little bit inside you.

If Finn can retrieve whatever that is that's allowed you to retain your ability to make sandwiches...

BWIP

Then we might be able to grow it, cure everyone, and GET THEM TO NOT RAID THE KINGDOM for our LEFTOVERS.

WE'RE GETTING PRETTY HANGRY, PRINCESS!

WHY WOULD YOU THINK I'VE FORGOTTEN THAT?!

"Hangry" is a mix of "Angry" and "Hungry" but deep down inside, you knew that.

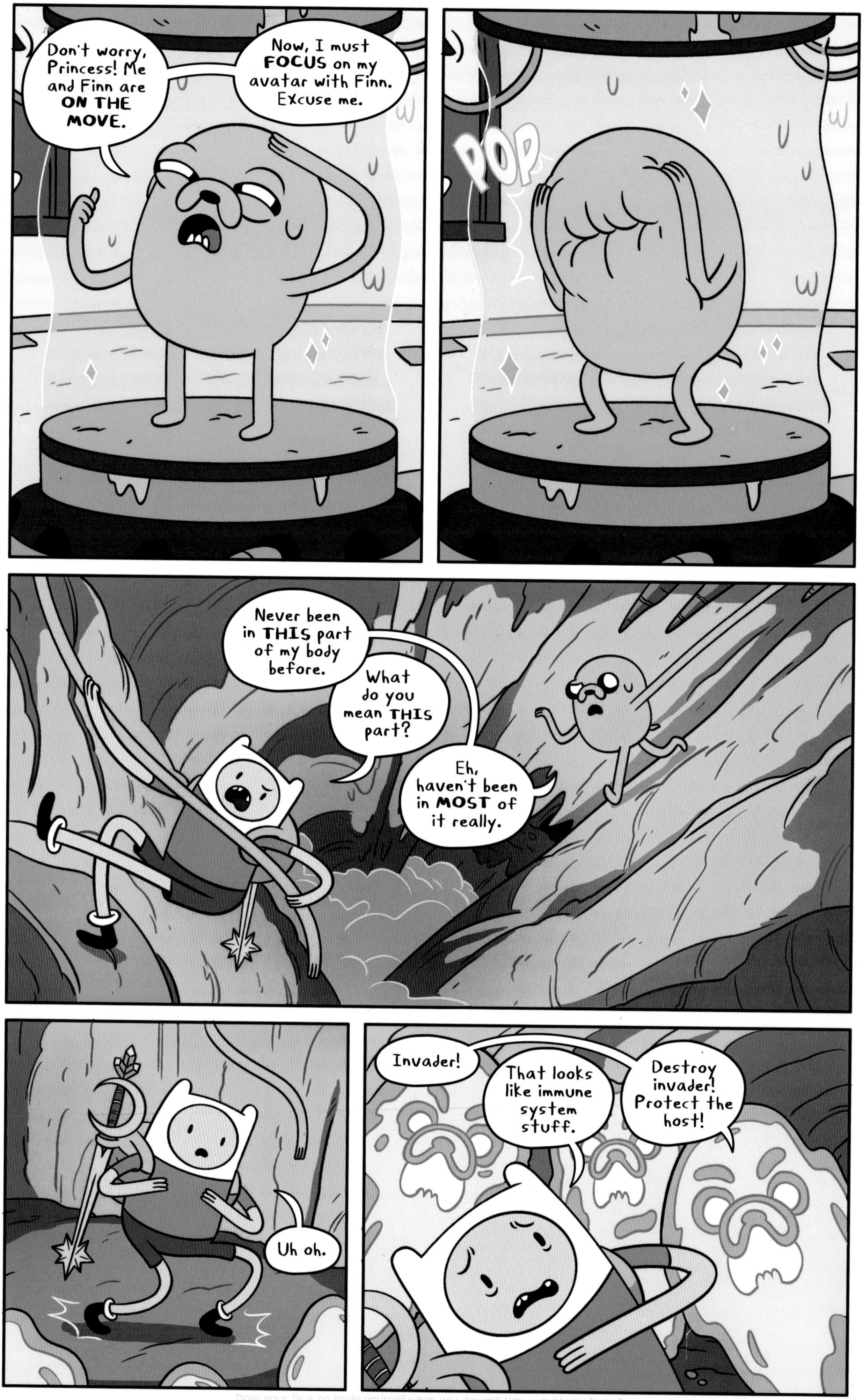
Don't worry, Princess! Me and Finn are ON THE MOVE.
Now, I must FOCUS on my avatar with Finn. Excuse me.
POP
Never been in THIS part of my body before.
What do you mean THIS part?
Eh, haven't been in MOST of it really.
Uh oh.
Invader!
That looks like immune system stuff.
Destroy invader! Protect the host!

Does your face go inside yourself when you dream? How would you know?

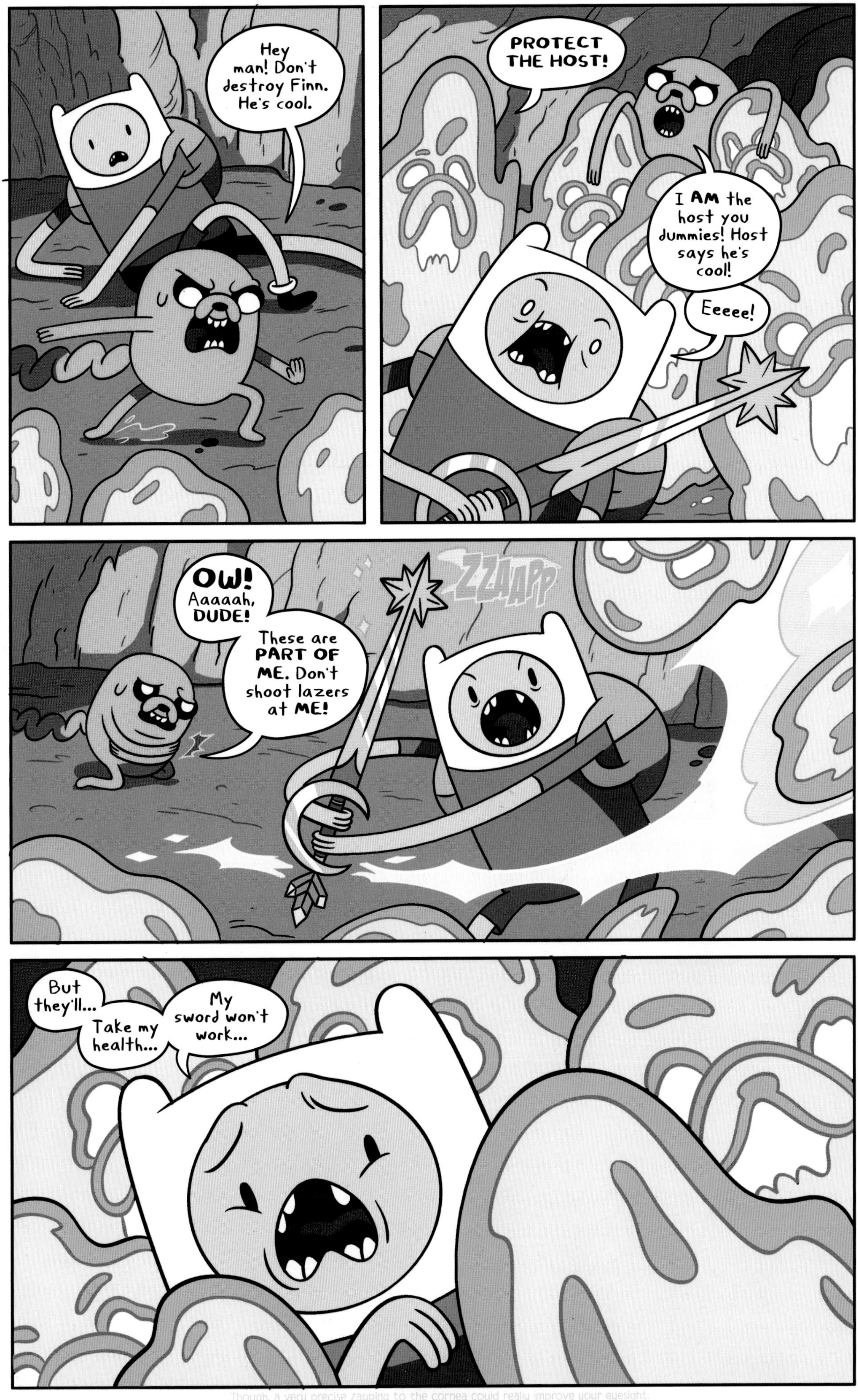
Hey man! Don't destroy Finn. He's cool.
PROTECT THE HOST!
I AM the host you dummies! Host says he's cool!
Eeeee!
OW! Aaaaah, DUDE!
These are PART OF ME. Don't shoot lazers at ME!
ZZAAPP
But they'll...
Take my health...
My sword won't work...

Though, a very precise zapping to the cornea could really improve your eyesight.

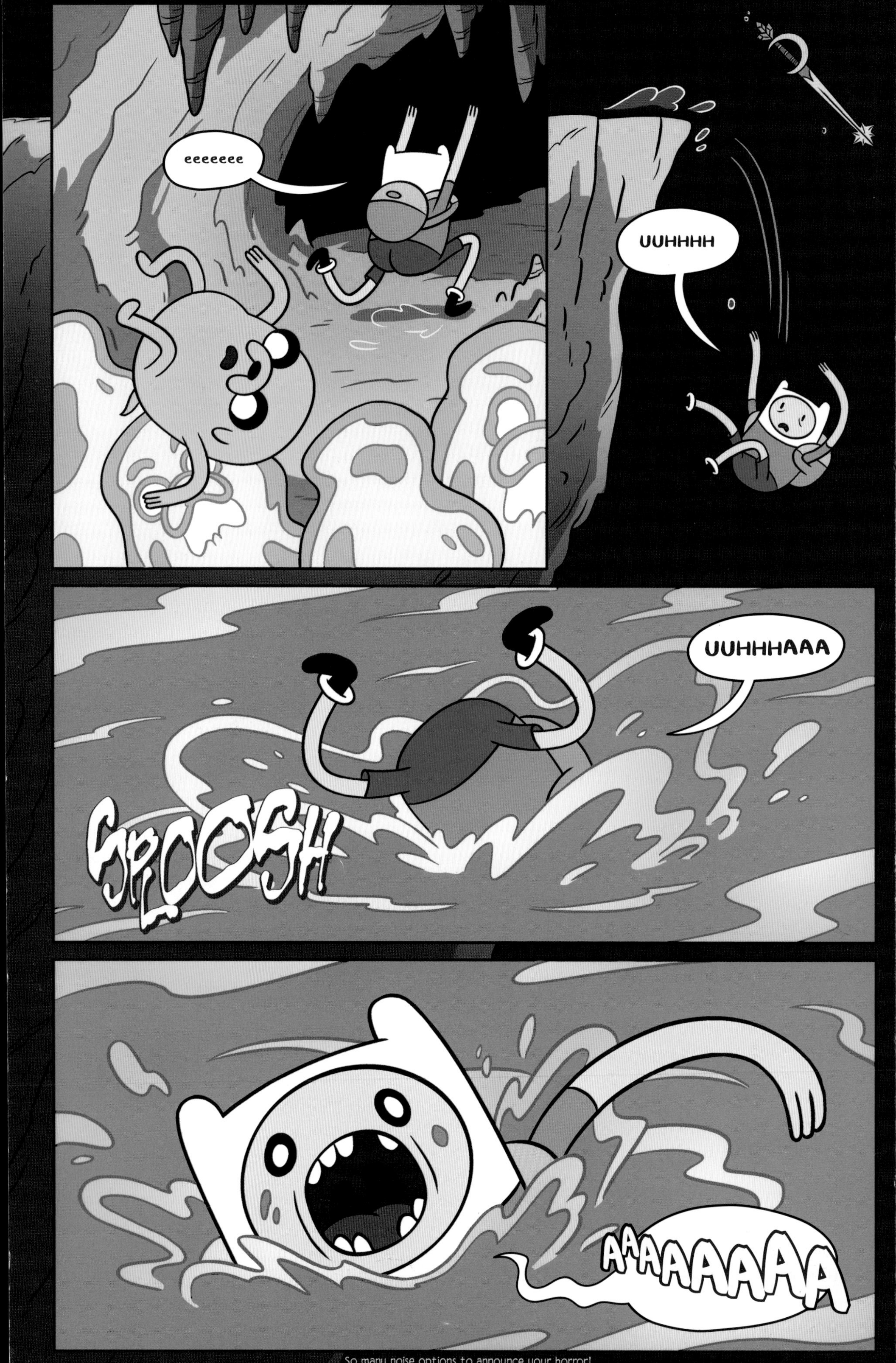
eeeeeee
UUHHHH
UUHHHAAA
SPLOOSH
AAAAAAAA

So many noise options to announce your horror!

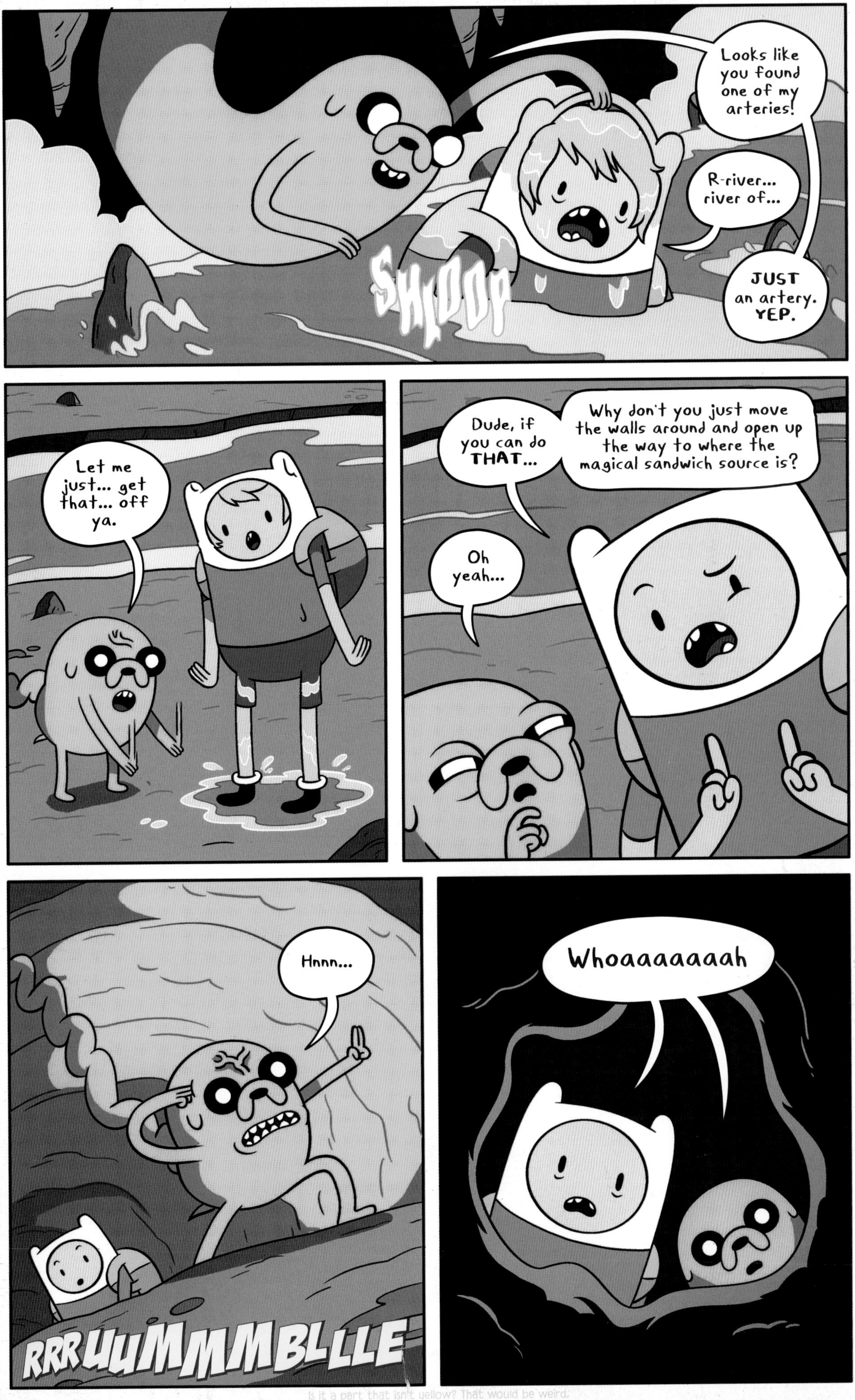
Looks like you found one of my arteries!
R-river... river of...
SHLOOP
JUST an artery. YEP.
Let me just... get that... off ya.
Dude, if you can do THAT...
Why don't you just move the walls around and open up the way to where the magical sandwich source is?
Oh yeah...
Hnnn...
RRRUUMMMMBLLLE
Whoaaaaaaah

Is it a part that isn't yellow? That would be weird.

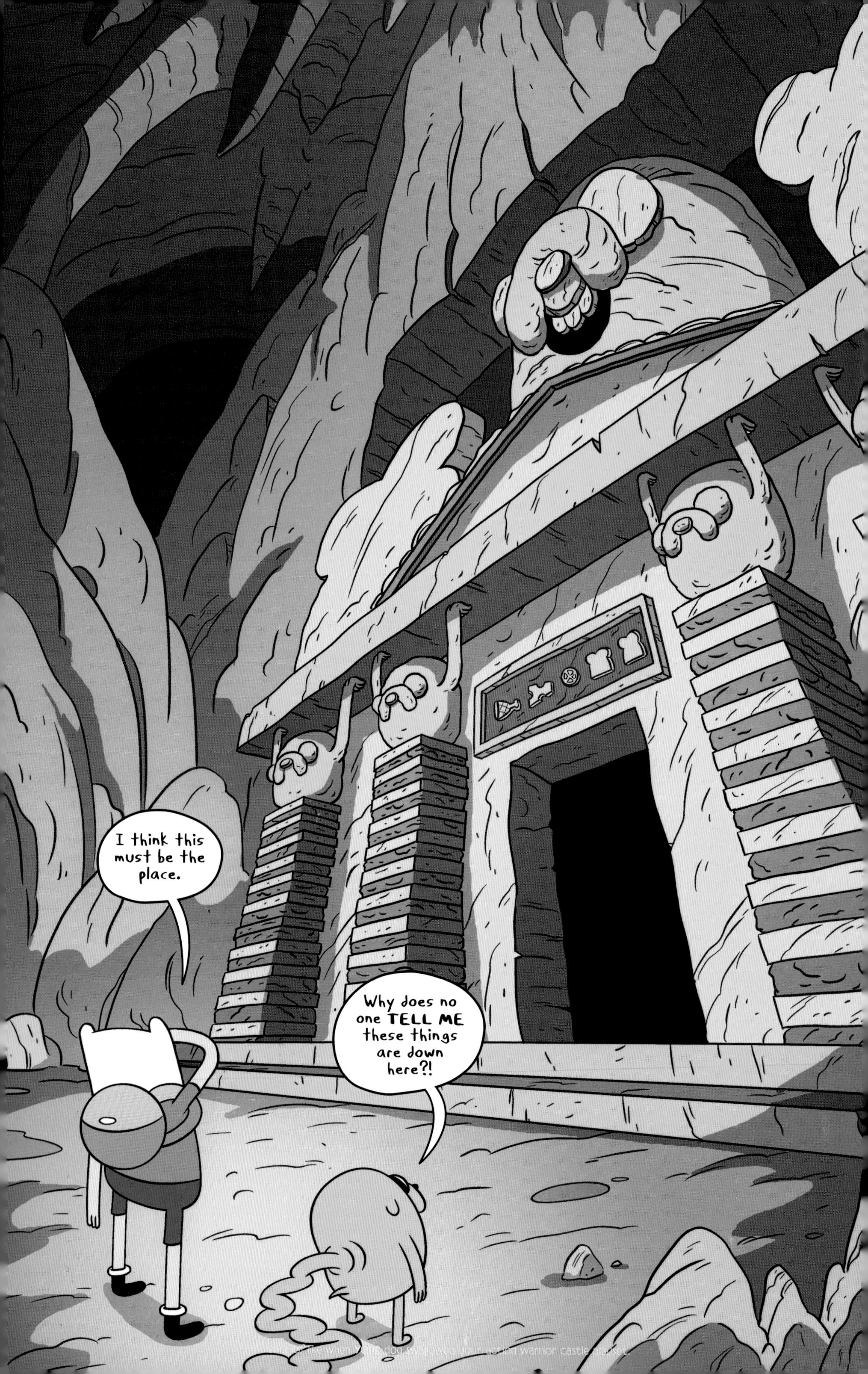
I think this must be the place.
Why does no one **TELL ME** these things are down here?!
Sort of like when YOUR dog swallowed your action warrior castle playset.

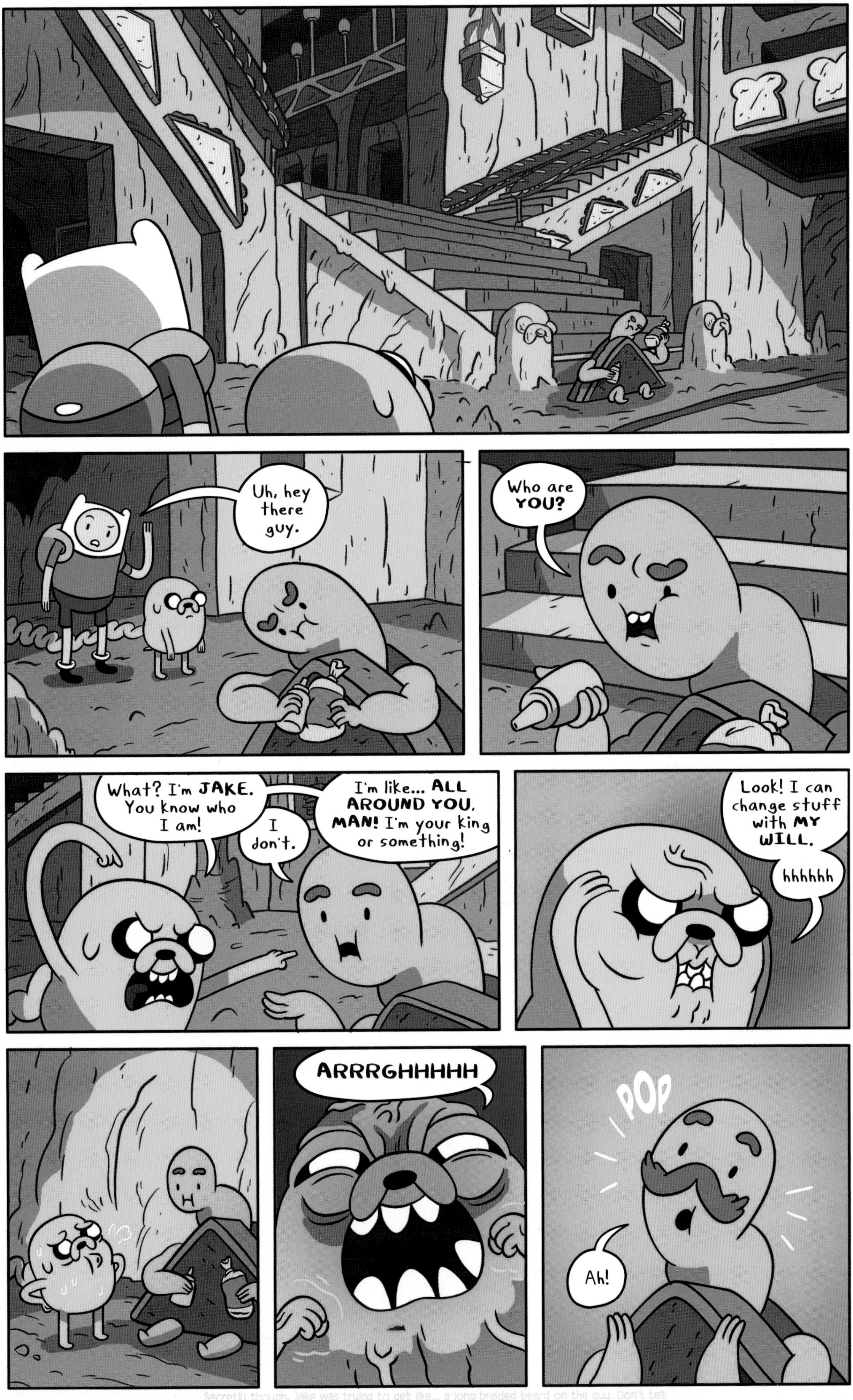
Uh, hey there guy.
Who are YOU?
What? I'm JAKE. You know who I am!
I don't.
I'm like... ALL AROUND YOU, MAN! I'm your king or something!
Look! I can change stuff with MY WILL.
hhhhhh
ARRRGHHHHH
POP
Ah!

Secretly though, Jake was trying to get like... a long braided beard on the guy. Don't tell.

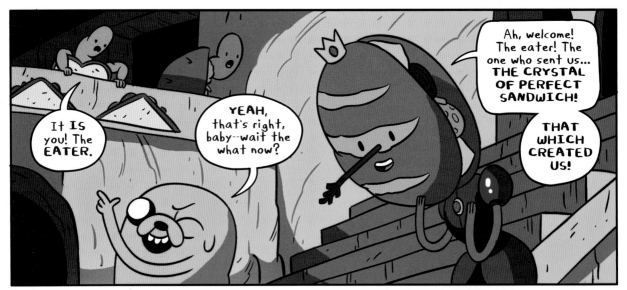

It **IS** you! The **EATER**.

YEAH, that's right, baby--wait the what now?

Ah, welcome! The eater! The one who sent us... **THE CRYSTAL OF PERFECT SANDWICH!**

THAT WHICH CREATED US!

I think that's what we were looking for, buddy!

A perfectly preserved... tiny piece...

Of the greatest sandwich I **EVER HAD.** I remember that sandwich!

It must have gotten stuck like that! And gave me **POWERS.**

Looks like it made part of you into a **PRETTY CUTE** princess too, buddy.

Hee hee hee

What?! Oh jeeze! YOU **TWO WOULD BE PERFECT TOGETHER!**

She's a little of **ME,** your best friend! And she's a little of **SANDWICH,** the best food!

And she's **TOTAL PRINCESS.**

You'd have to stay in here. She can't leave.

I'd miss you, but I can come visit! I--

Dude. Chill. I don't want to go out with **ANY** princesses right now.

My sword lazers only work if I have perfect health!

Don't wanna risk a **BROKEN HEART.**

Seriously? Maybe we talk about that sword later.

What are you talking about?

Is it sandwiches?

Well, whatever you were talking about, it was with your mouths, which is where sandwiches go, so I'll just assume it was about sandwiches.

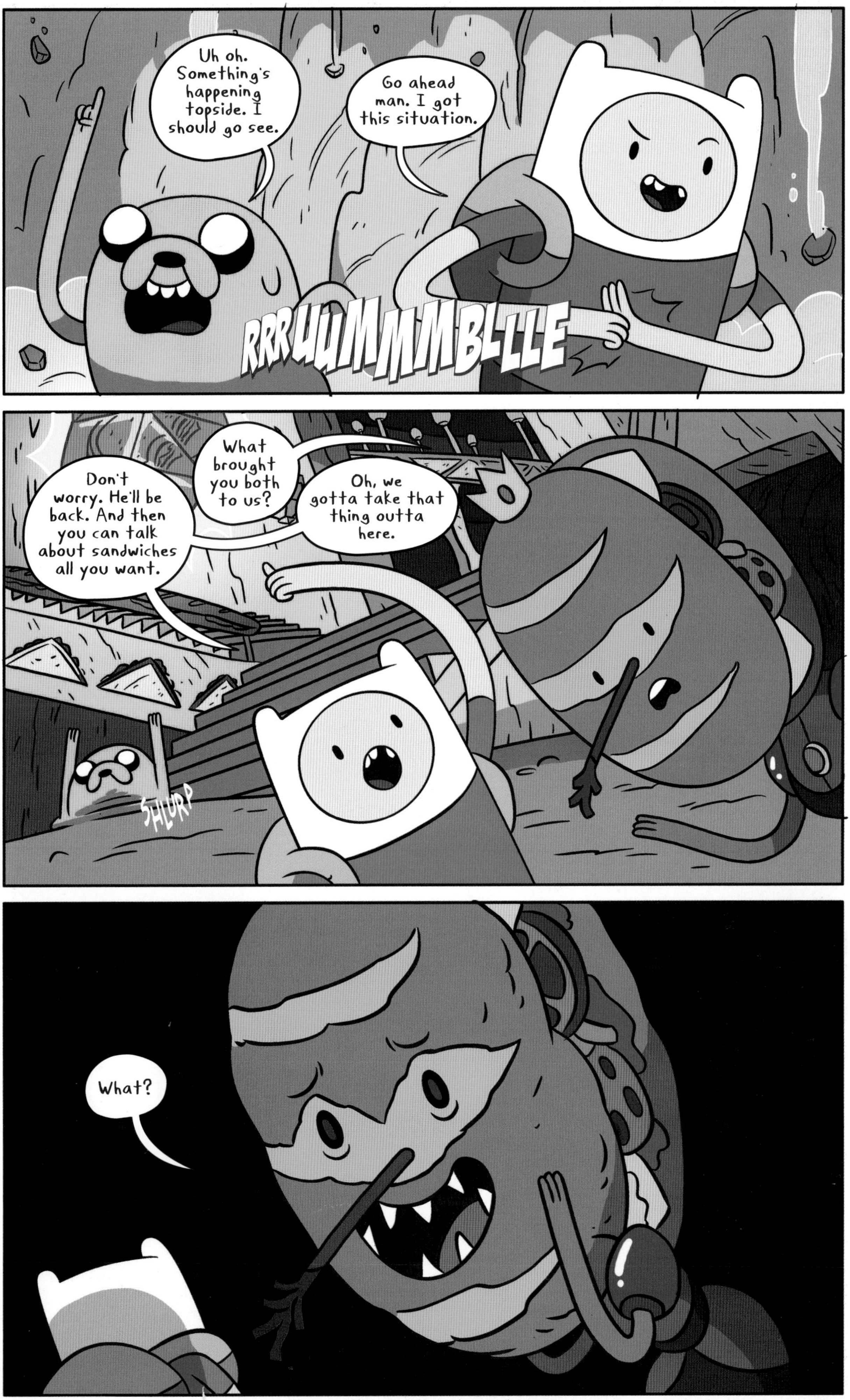
Uh oh. Something's happening topside. I should go see.
Go ahead man. I got this situation.
RRRUUMMMMBLLLE
Don't worry. He'll be back. And then you can talk about sandwiches all you want.
What brought you both to us?
Oh, we gotta take that thing outta here.
SHLURP
What?

Finn you gotta... you gotta work on reading a room.

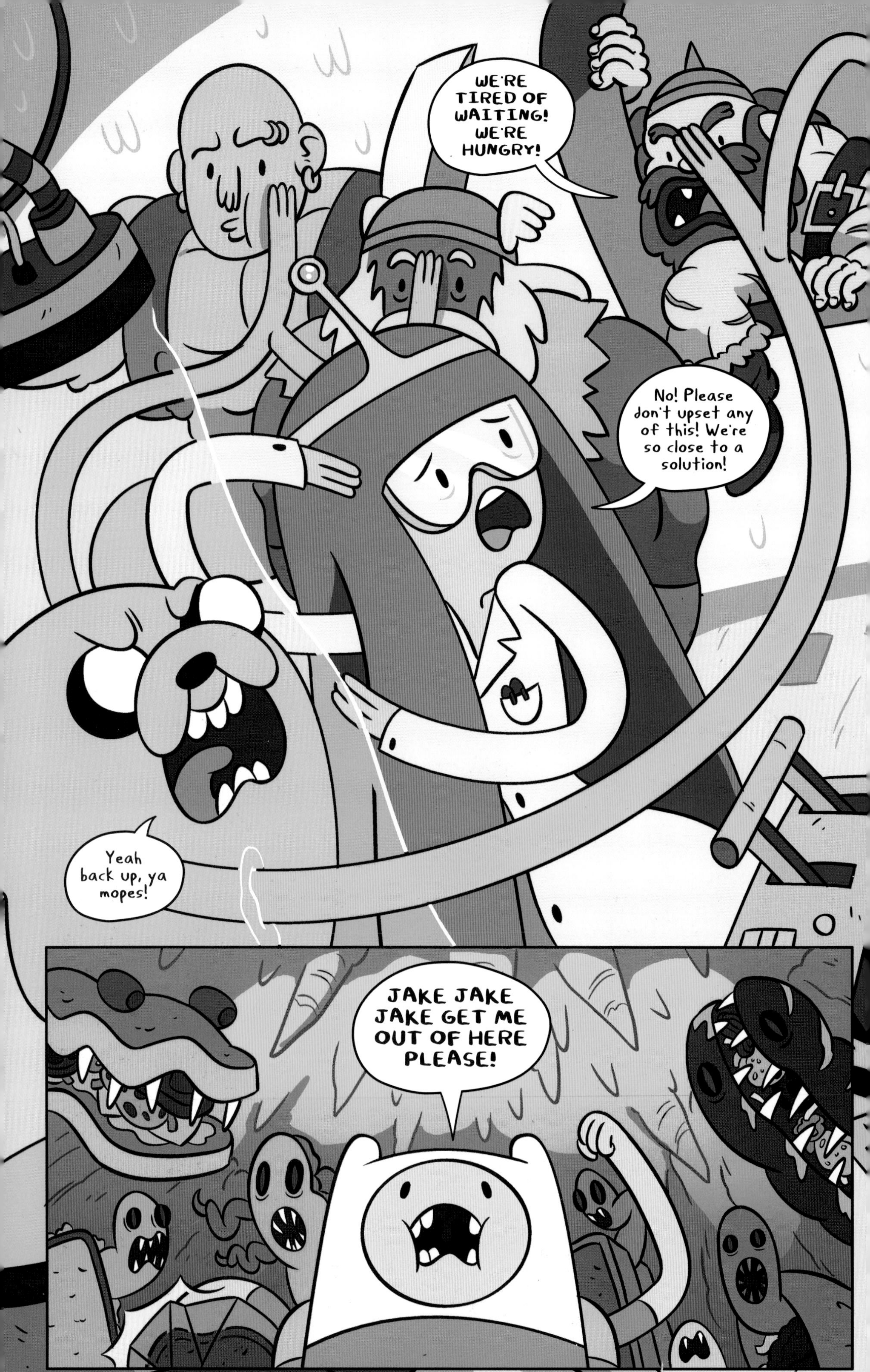
WE'RE TIRED OF WAITING! WE'RE HUNGRY!
No! Please don't upset any of this! We're so close to a solution!
Yeah back up, ya mopes!
JAKE JAKE JAKE GET ME OUT OF HERE PLEASE!

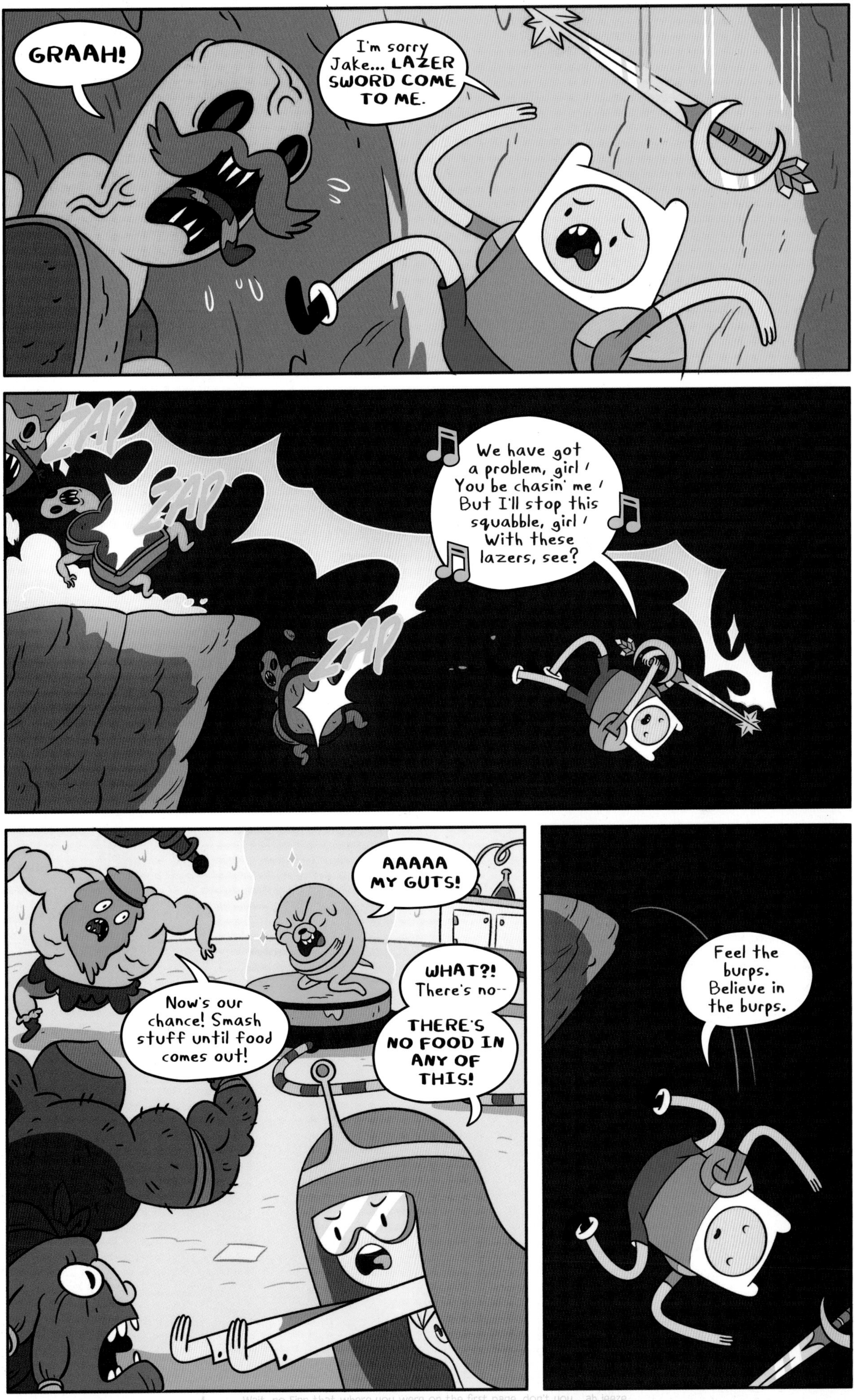
GRAAH!
I'm sorry Jake... LAZER SWORD COME TO ME.
ZAP
ZAP
ZAP
We have got a problem, girl / You be chasin' me / But I'll stop this squabble, girl / With these lazers, see?
AAAAA MY GUTS!
Now's our chance! Smash stuff until food comes out!
WHAT?! There's no--
THERE'S NO FOOD IN ANY OF THIS!
Feel the burps. Believe in the burps.

Wait, no Finn that where you were on the first page, don't you... ah jeeze.

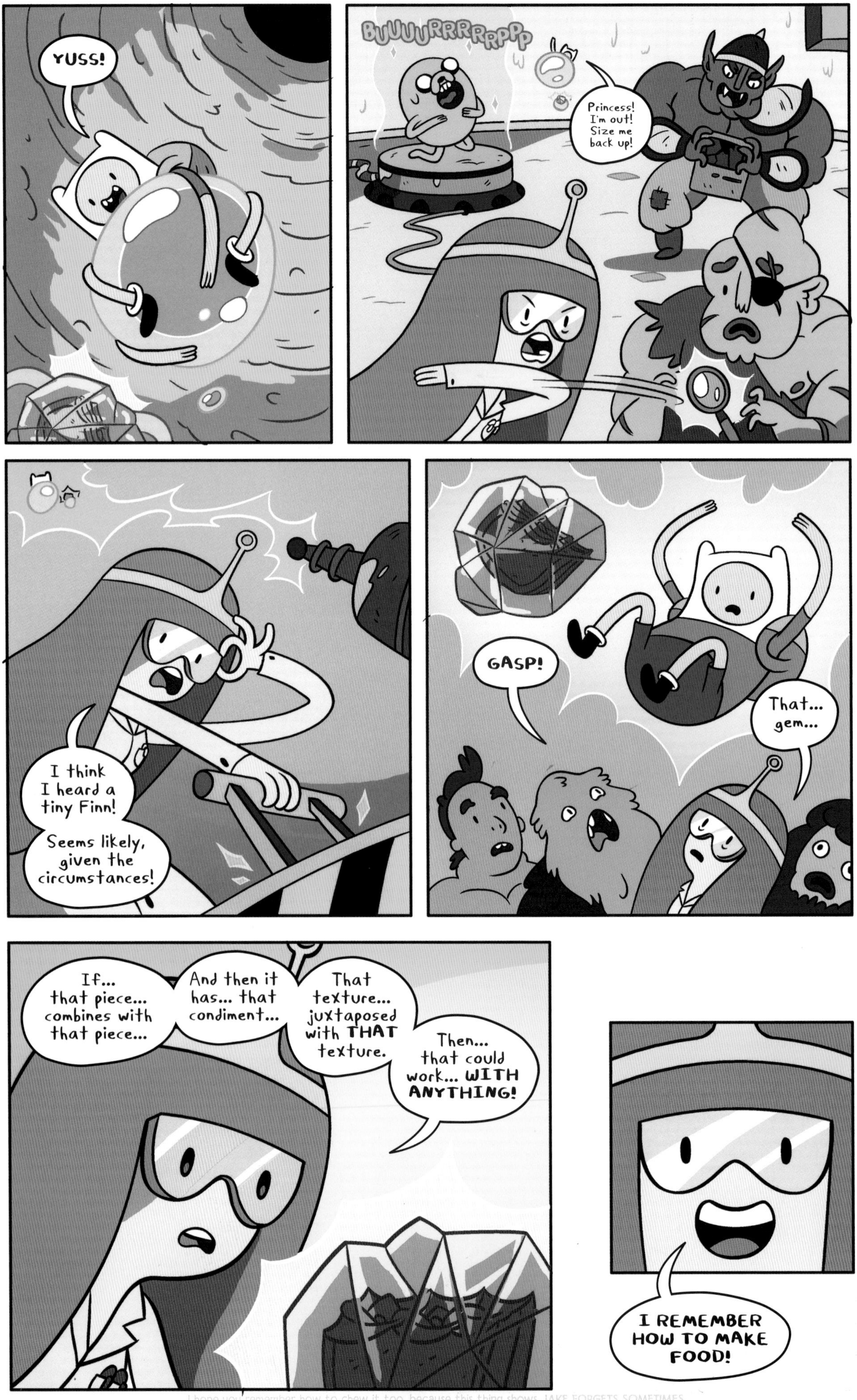
YUSS!
BUUUURRRRRPPP
Princess! I'm out! Size me back up!
I think I heard a tiny Finn!
Seems likely, given the circumstances!
GASP!
That... gem...
If... that piece... combines with that piece...
And then it has... that condiment...
That texture... juxtaposed with THAT texture.
Then... that could work... WITH ANYTHING!
I REMEMBER HOW TO MAKE FOOD!

I hope you remember how to chew it too, because this thing shows JAKE FORGETS SOMETIMES.

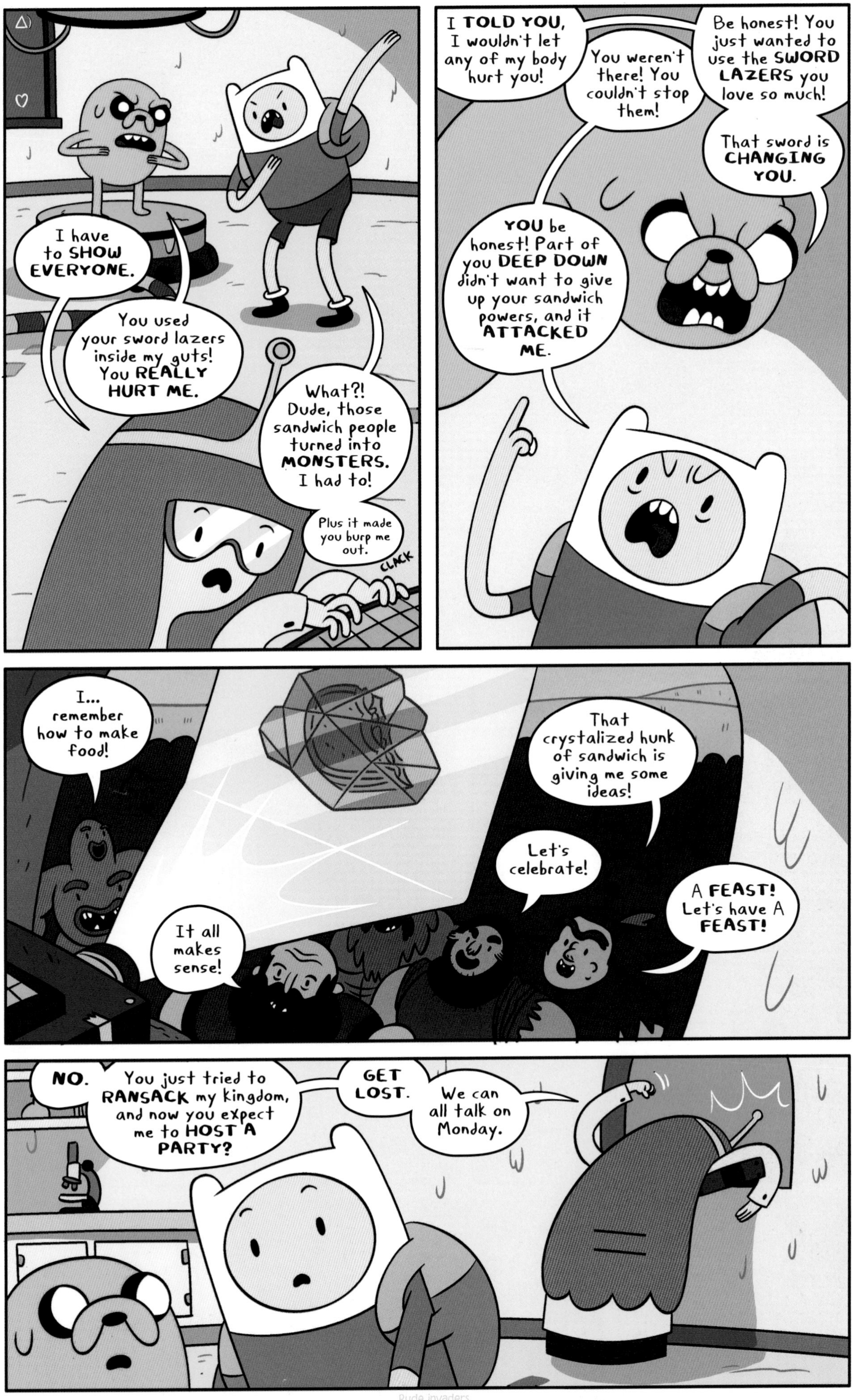
I have to SHOW EVERYONE.
You used your sword lazers inside my guts! You REALLY HURT ME.
What?! Dude, those sandwich people turned into MONSTERS. I had to!
Plus it made you burp me out.
CLACK
I TOLD YOU, I wouldn't let any of my body hurt you!
You weren't there! You couldn't stop them!
Be honest! You just wanted to use the SWORD LAZERS you love so much!
That sword is CHANGING YOU.
YOU be honest! Part of you DEEP DOWN didn't want to give up your sandwich powers, and it ATTACKED ME.
I... remember how to make food!
That crystalized hunk of sandwich is giving me some ideas!
Let's celebrate!
It all makes sense!
A FEAST! Let's have A FEAST!
NO.
You just tried to RANSACK my kingdom, and now you expect me to HOST A PARTY?
GET LOST.
We can all talk on Monday.

Rude invaders.

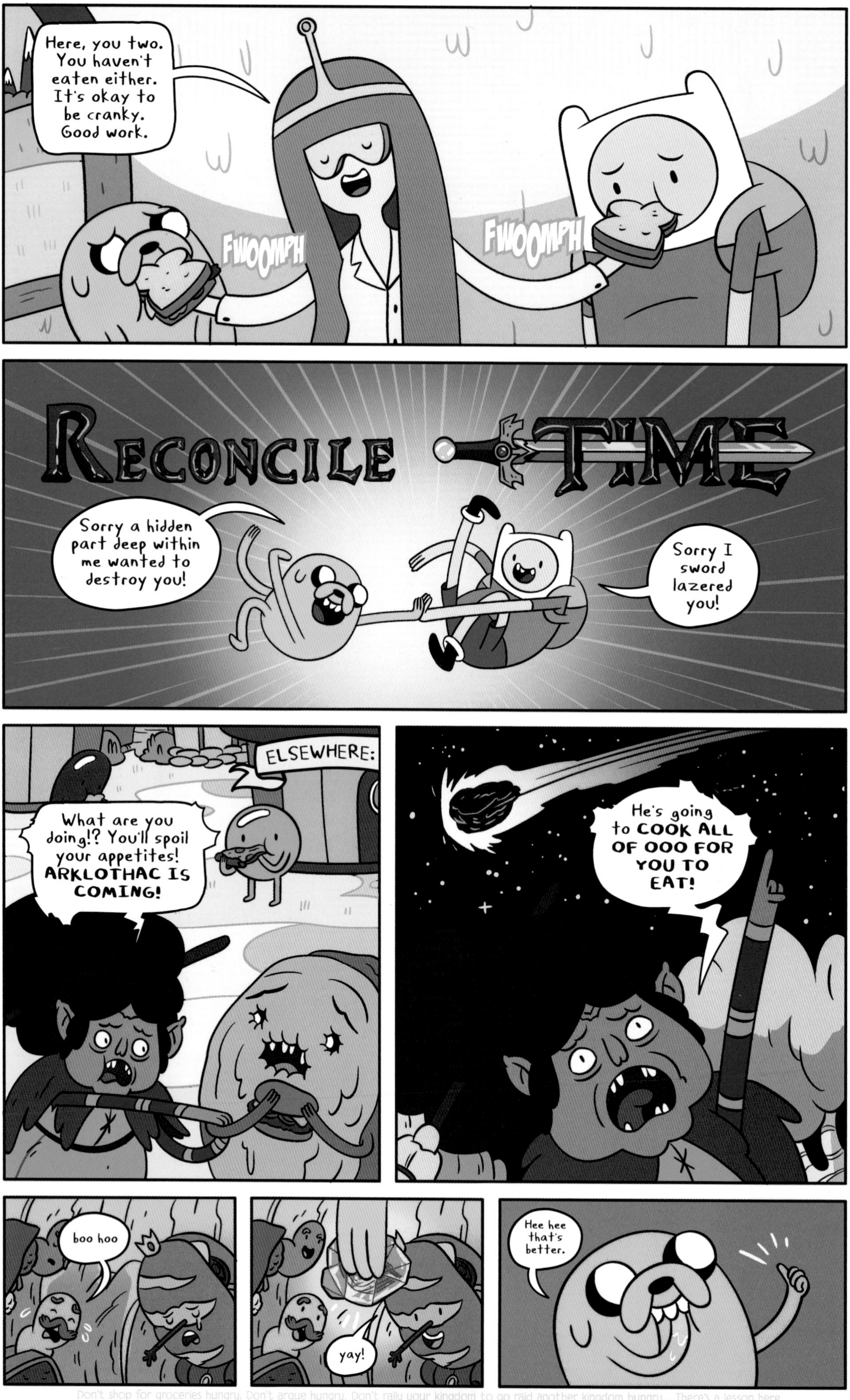
Here, you two. You haven't eaten either. It's okay to be cranky. Good work.
FWOOMPH
FWOOMPH
RECONCILE TIME
Sorry a hidden part deep within me wanted to destroy you!
Sorry I sword lazered you!
ELSEWHERE:
What are you doing!? You'll spoil your appetites! ARKLOTHAC IS COMING!
He's going to COOK ALL OF OOO FOR YOU TO EAT!
boo hoo
yay!
Hee hee that's better.

Don't shop for groceries hungry. Don't argue hungry. Don't rally your kingdom to go raid another kingdom hungry... There's a lesson here.

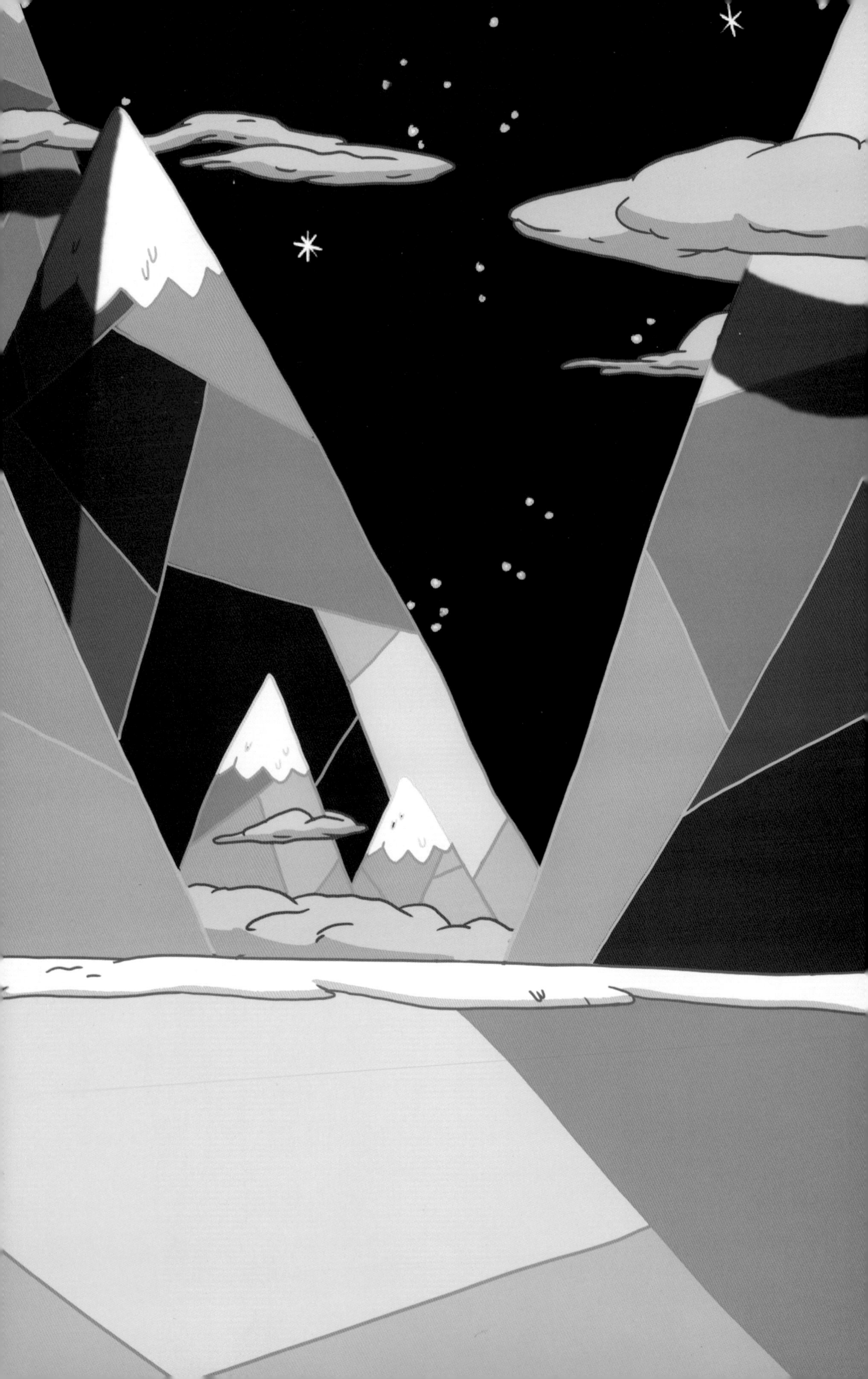

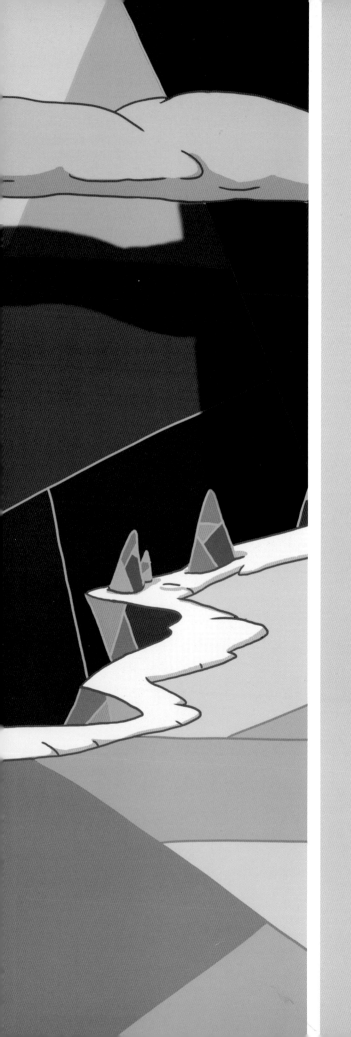

CHAPTER FIVE

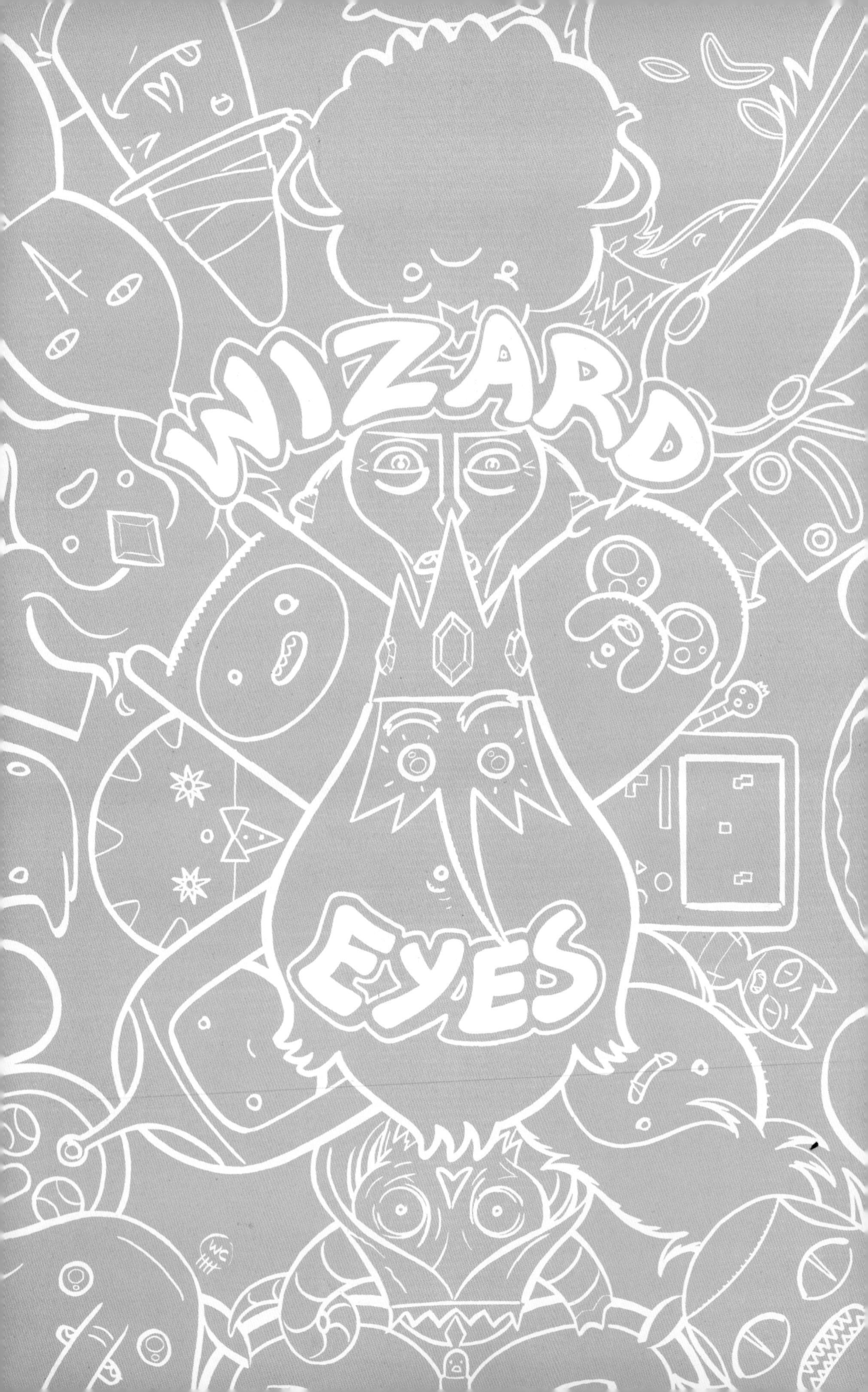
WIZARD
EYES

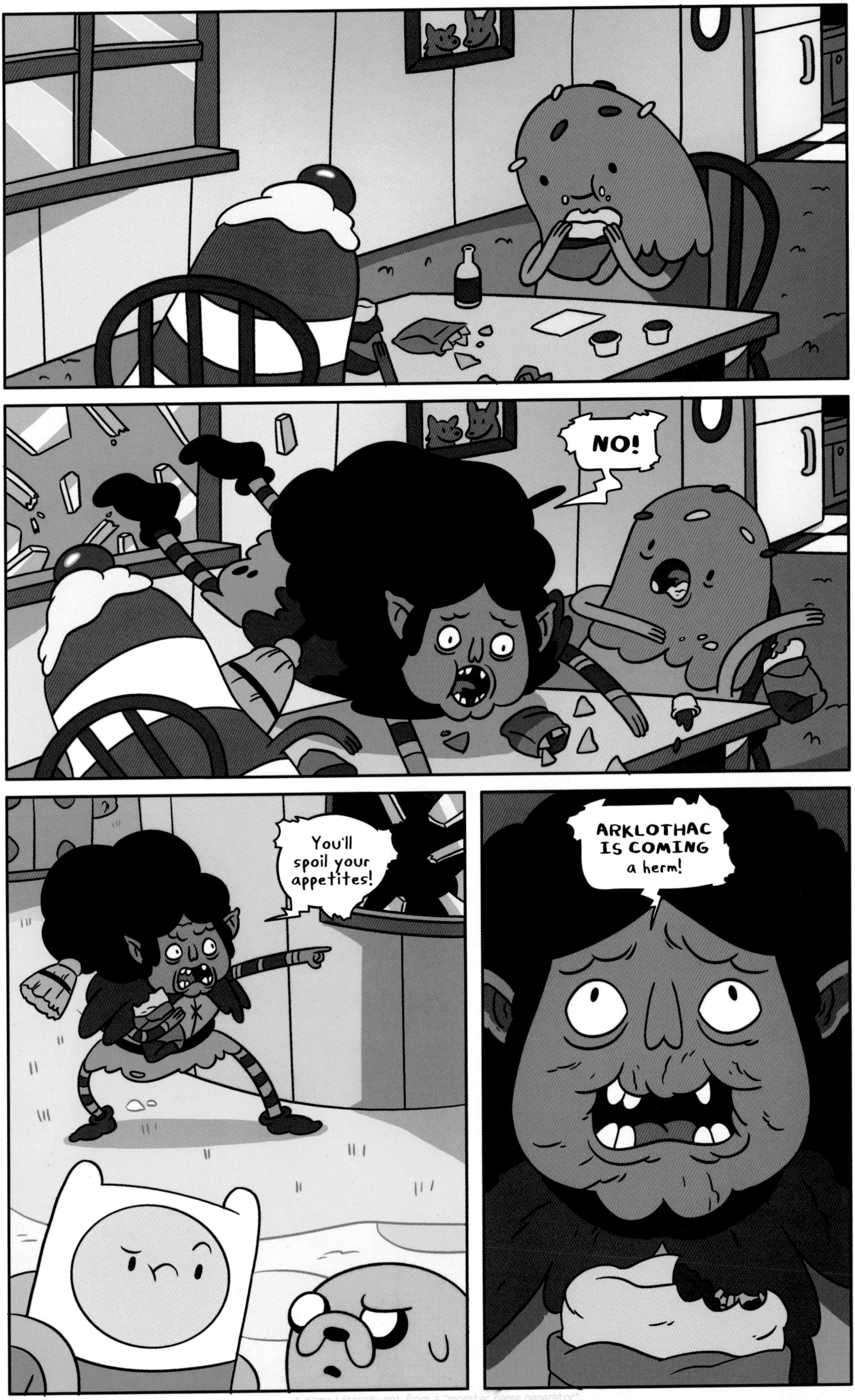
NO!
You'll spoil your appetites!
ARKLOTHAC IS COMING a herm!

A name I literally got from a "monster name generator".

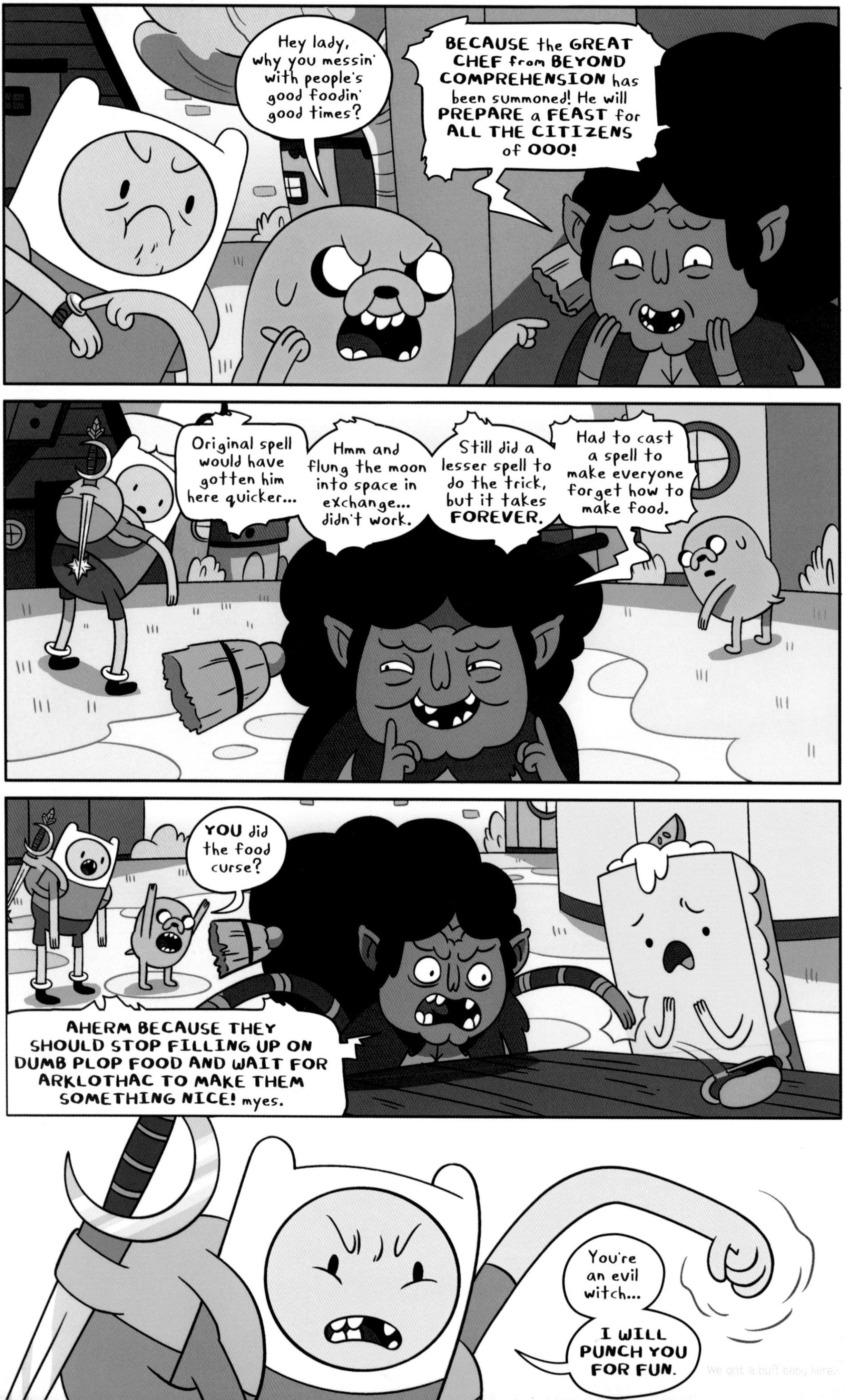
Hey lady, why you messin' with people's good foodin' good times?
BECAUSE the GREAT CHEF from BEYOND COMPREHENSION has been summoned! He will PREPARE a FEAST for ALL THE CITIZENS of OOO!
Had to cast a spell to make everyone forget how to make food.
Still did a lesser spell to do the trick, but it takes FOREVER.
Hmm and flung the moon into space in exchange... didn't work.
Original spell would have gotten him here quicker...
YOU did the food curse?
AHERM BECAUSE THEY SHOULD STOP FILLING UP ON DUMB PLOP FOOD AND WAIT FOR ARKLOTHAC TO MAKE THEM SOMETHING NICE! myes.
You're an evil witch...
I WILL PUNCH YOU FOR FUN.
We got a buff baby here.

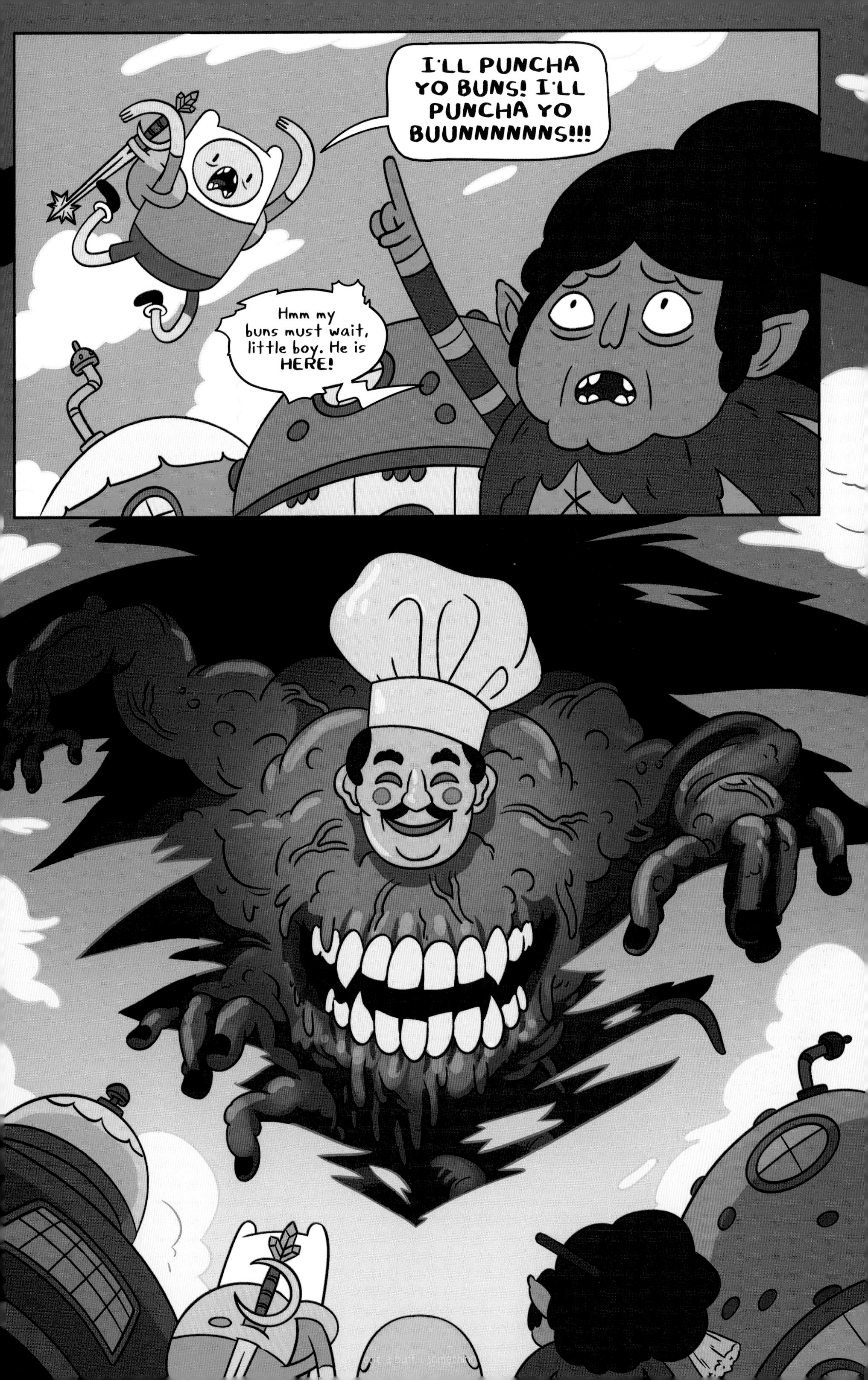
I'LL PUNCHA YO BUNS! I'LL PUNCHA YO BUUNNNNNNS!!!
Hmm my buns must wait, little boy. He is HERE!

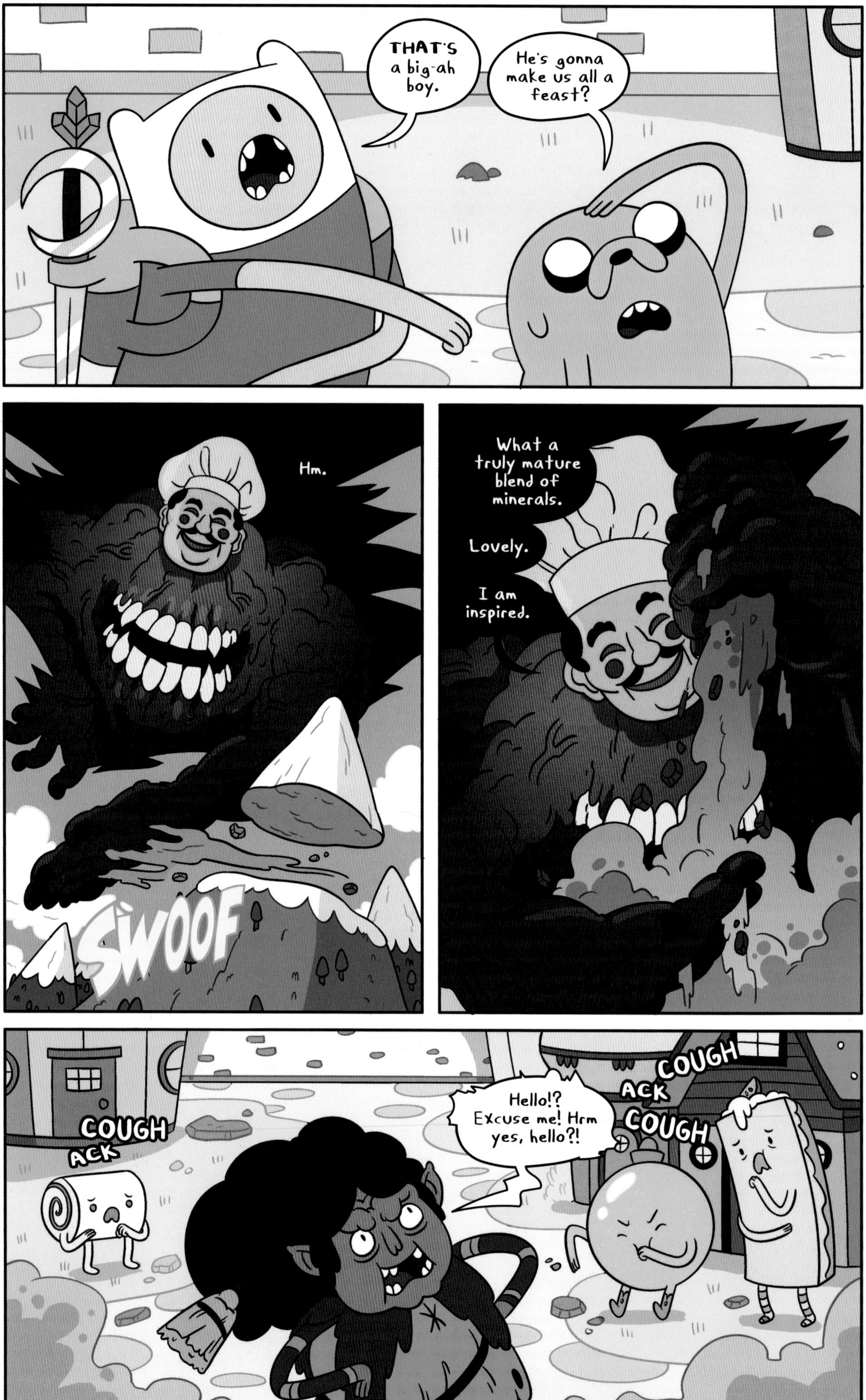
THAT'S a big-ah boy.
He's gonna make us all a feast?
Hm.
SWOOF
What a truly mature blend of minerals.
Lovely.
I am inspired.
COUGH
ACK
Hello!? Excuse me! Hrm yes, hello?!
COUGH
ACK
COUGH

Hello! Oh, you're not talking to me. You're talking to another character in the book. Carry on.

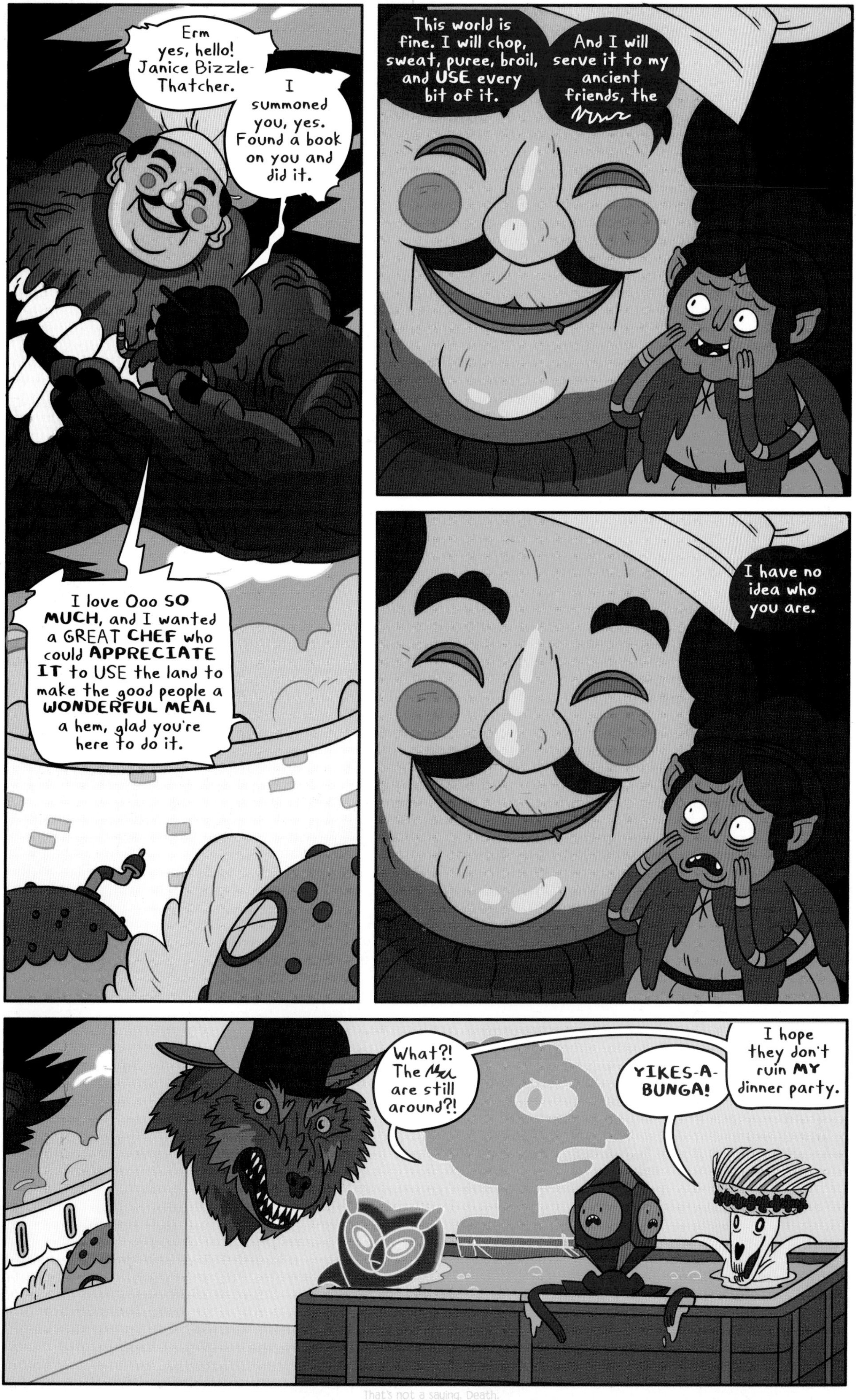
Erm yes, hello! Janice Bizzle-Thatcher.
I summoned you, yes. Found a book on you and did it.
I love Ooo SO MUCH, and I wanted a GREAT CHEF who could APPRECIATE IT to USE the land to make the good people a WONDERFUL MEAL a hem, glad you're here to do it.
This world is fine. I will chop, sweat, puree, broil, and USE every bit of it.
And I will serve it to my ancient friends, the
I have no idea who you are.
What?! The are still around?!
YIKES-A-BUNGA!
I hope they don't ruin MY dinner party.

That's not a saying, Death.

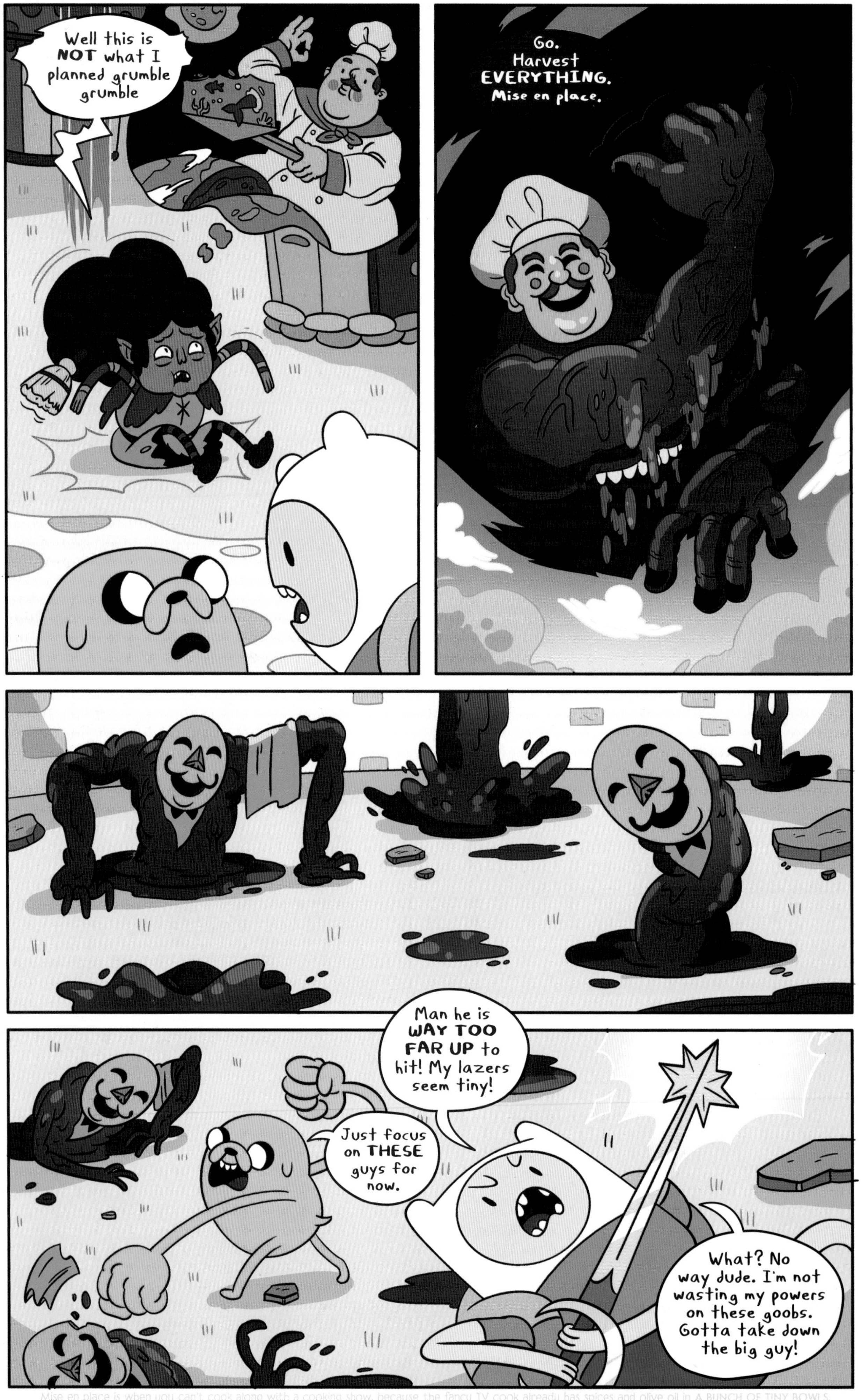
Well this is NOT what I planned grumble grumble
Go. Harvest EVERYTHING. Mise en place.
Man he is WAY TOO FAR UP to hit! My lazers seem tiny!
Just focus on THESE guys for now.
What? No way dude. I'm not wasting my powers on these goobs. Gotta take down the big guy!

Mise en place is when you can't cook along with a cooking show, because the fancy TV cook already has spices and olive oil in A BUNCH OF TINY BOWLS.

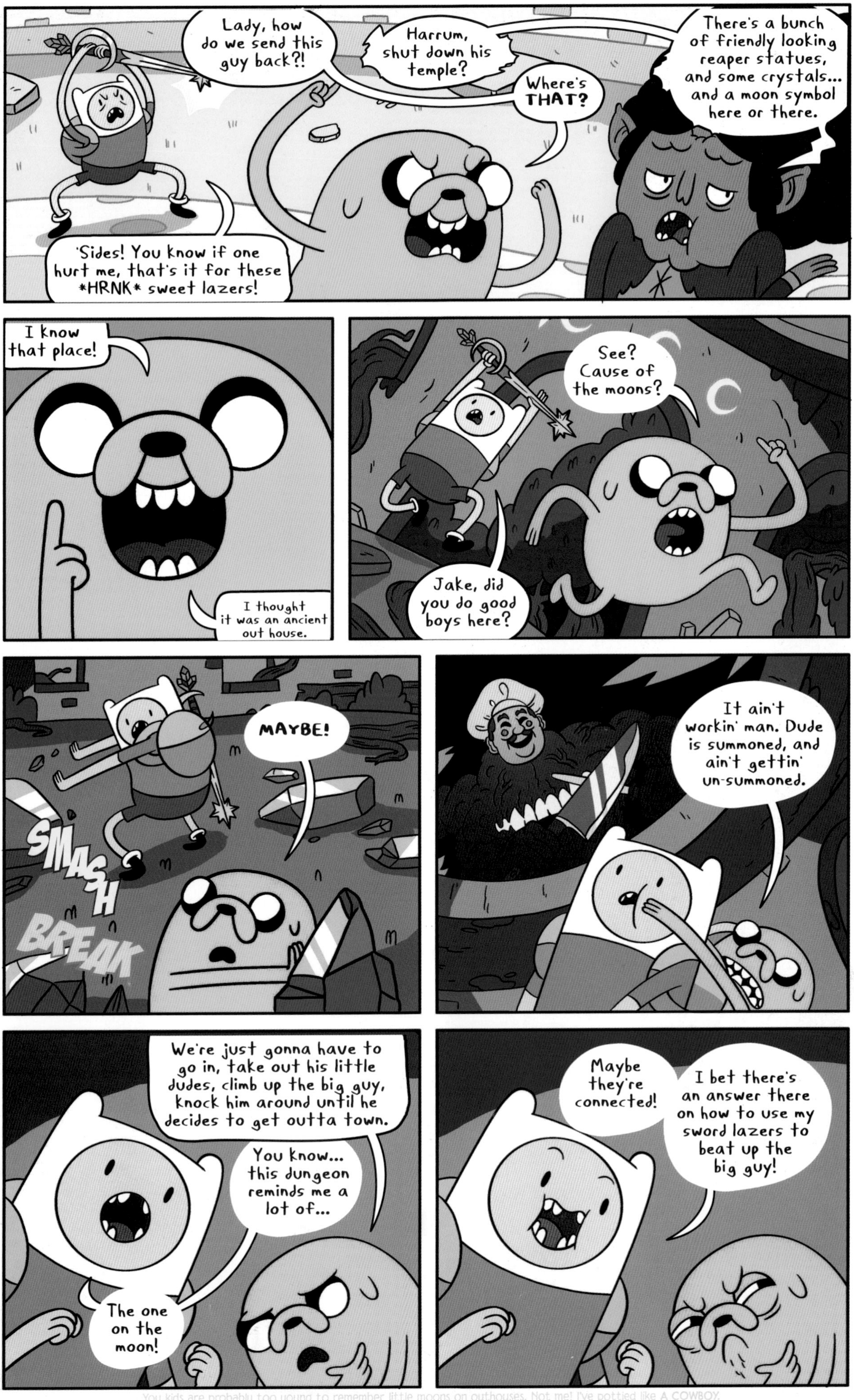
Lady, how do we send this guy back?!
Harrum, shut down his temple?
Where's THAT?
There's a bunch of friendly looking reaper statues, and some crystals... and a moon symbol here or there.
'Sides! You know if one hurt me, that's it for these *HRNK* sweet lazers!
I know that place!
I thought it was an ancient out house.
See? Cause of the moons?
Jake, did you do good boys here?
MAYBE!
SMASH
BREAK
It ain't workin' man. Dude is summoned, and ain't gettin' un-summoned.
We're just gonna have to go in, take out his little dudes, climb up the big guy, knock him around until he decides to get outta town.
You know... this dungeon reminds me a lot of...
The one on the moon!
Maybe they're connected!
I bet there's an answer there on how to use my sword lazers to beat up the big guy!

You kids are probably too young to remember little moons on outhouses. Not me! I've pottied like A COWBOY.

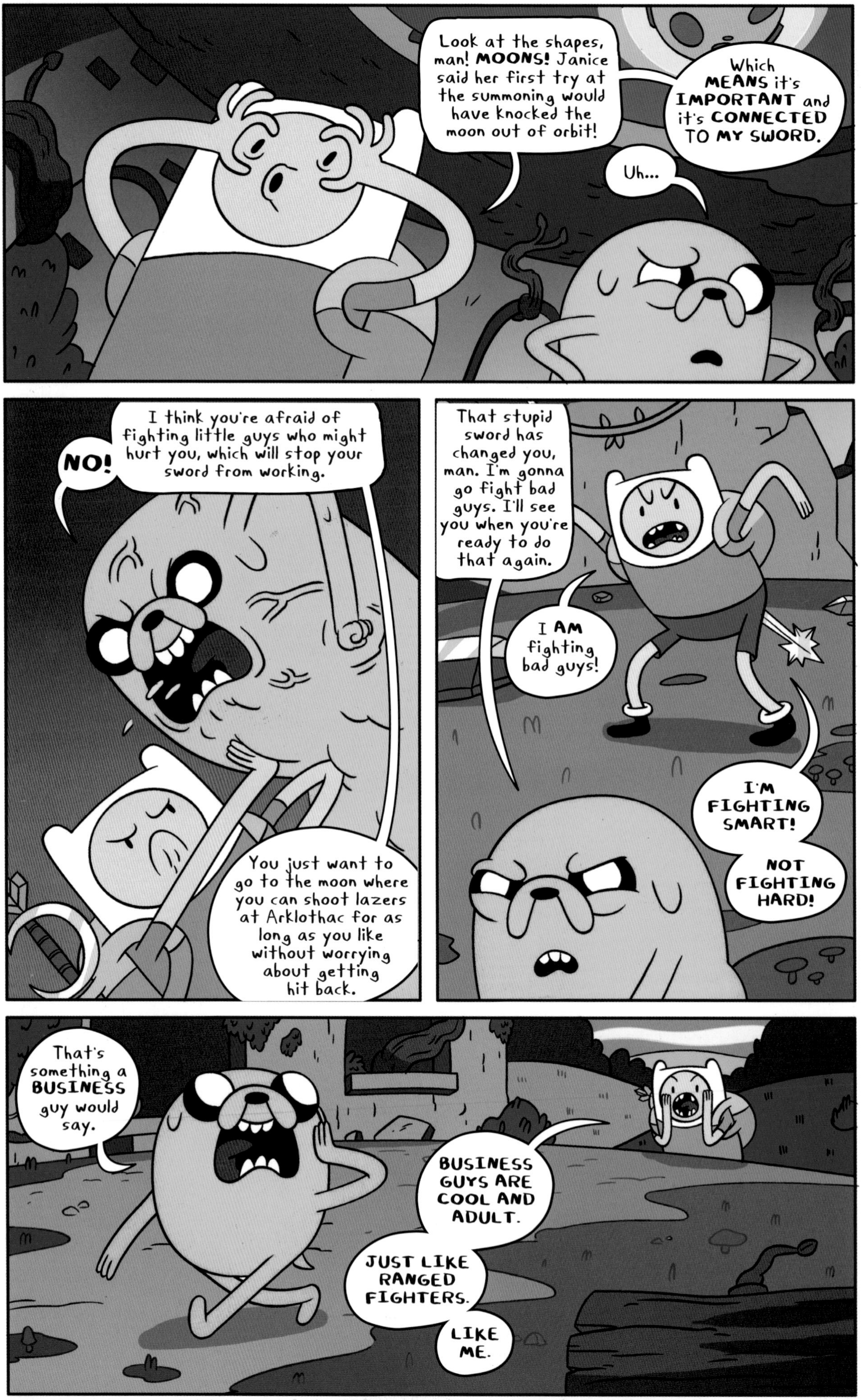
Look at the shapes, man! MOONS! Janice said her first try at the summoning would have knocked the moon out of orbit!
Which MEANS it's IMPORTANT and it's CONNECTED TO MY SWORD.
Uh...
I think you're afraid of fighting little guys who might hurt you, which will stop your sword from working.
NO!
You just want to go to the moon where you can shoot lazers at Arklothac for as long as you like without worrying about getting hit back.
That stupid sword has changed you, man. I'm gonna go fight bad guys. I'll see you when you're ready to do that again.
I AM fighting bad guys!
I'M FIGHTING SMART!
NOT FIGHTING HARD!
That's something a BUSINESS guy would say.
BUSINESS GUYS ARE COOL AND ADULT.
JUST LIKE RANGED FIGHTERS.
LIKE ME.

I'm just picturing an elf archer, kick-flipping on a calculator skateboard, saying "BUDGETS ARE DOPE"

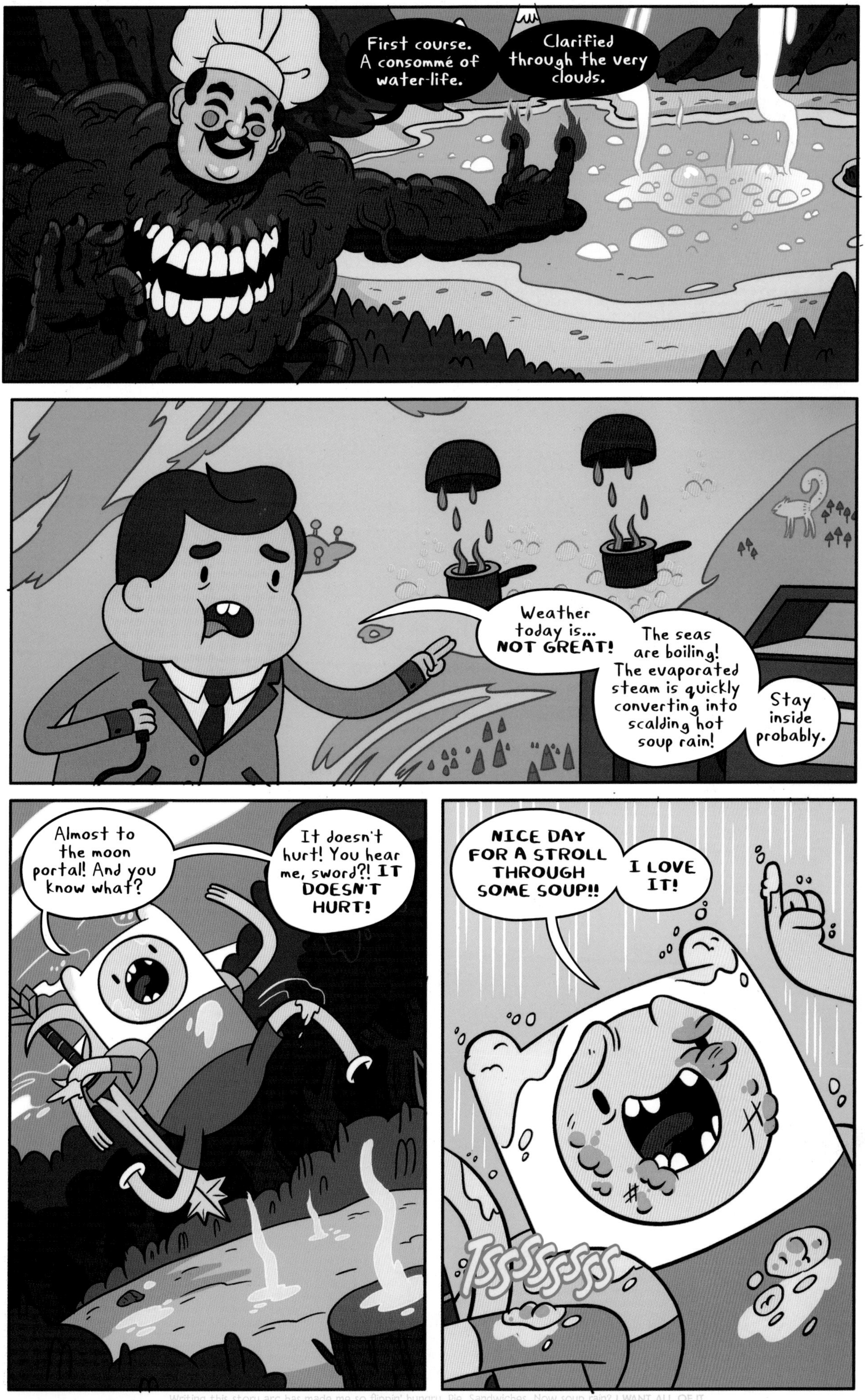
First course. A consommé of water-life.
Clarified through the very clouds.
Weather today is... NOT GREAT!
The seas are boiling! The evaporated steam is quickly converting into scalding hot soup rain!
Stay inside probably.
Almost to the moon portal! And you know what?
It doesn't hurt! You hear me, sword?! IT DOESN'T HURT!
NICE DAY FOR A STROLL THROUGH SOME SOUP!!
I LOVE IT!
TSSSSSSS

Writing this story arc has made me so flippin' hungry. Pie. Sandwiches. Now soup rain? I WANT ALL OF IT.

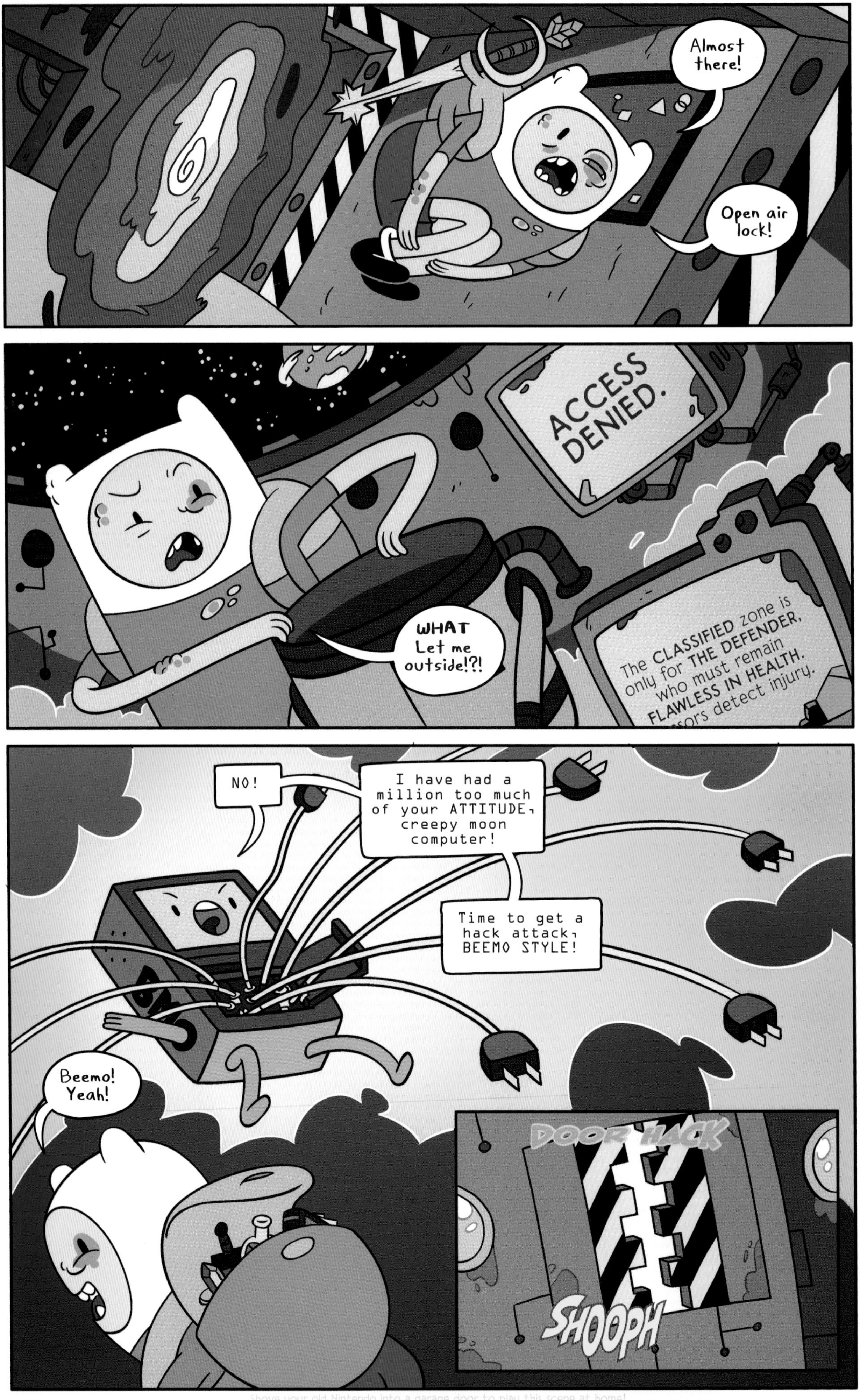
Almost there!
Open air lock!
ACCESS DENIED.
The CLASSIFIED zone is only for THE DEFENDER, who must remain FLAWLESS IN HEALTH.
sors detect injury.
WHAT Let me outside!?!
NO!
I have had a million too much of your ATTITUDE, creepy moon computer!
Time to get a hack attack, BEEMO STYLE!
Beemo! Yeah!
DOOR HACK
SHOOPH

Shove your old Nintendo into a garage door to play this scene at home!

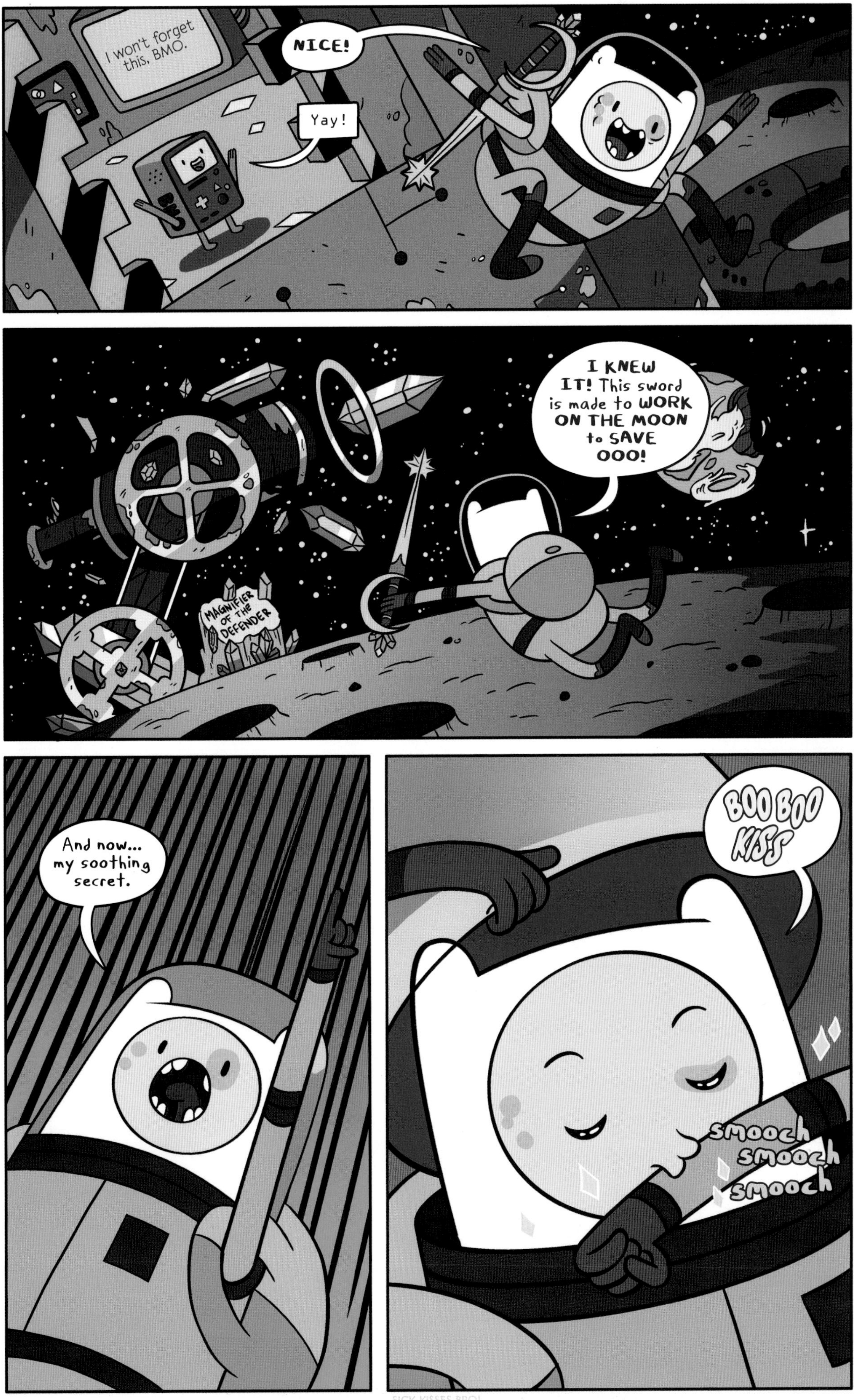
I won't forget this, BMO.
NICE!
Yay!
I KNEW IT! This sword is made to WORK ON THE MOON to SAVE OOO!
MAGNIFIER OF THE DEFENDER
And now... my soothing secret.
BOO BOO KISS
smooch smooch smooch

Uhh...
Why... isn't my sword health meter filling up?
BOO BOO KISS
BOO BOO KISS
It's NOT WORKING!
Beemo will kiss your boo boos, Finn!
Sorry, Beemo. Robot lips don't have enough healing love power in them for something THIS bad...
Just like mine I guess.
Oh.
I know something you can do, Beemo!
What is it?!
Is it video games?! Is it kisses?!
IS IT VIDEO GAMES?!
Hack into that MOON-A-PAULT.

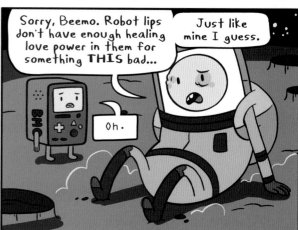

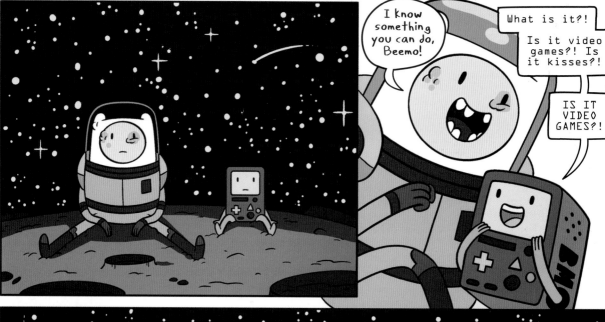

It's... kind of video games.

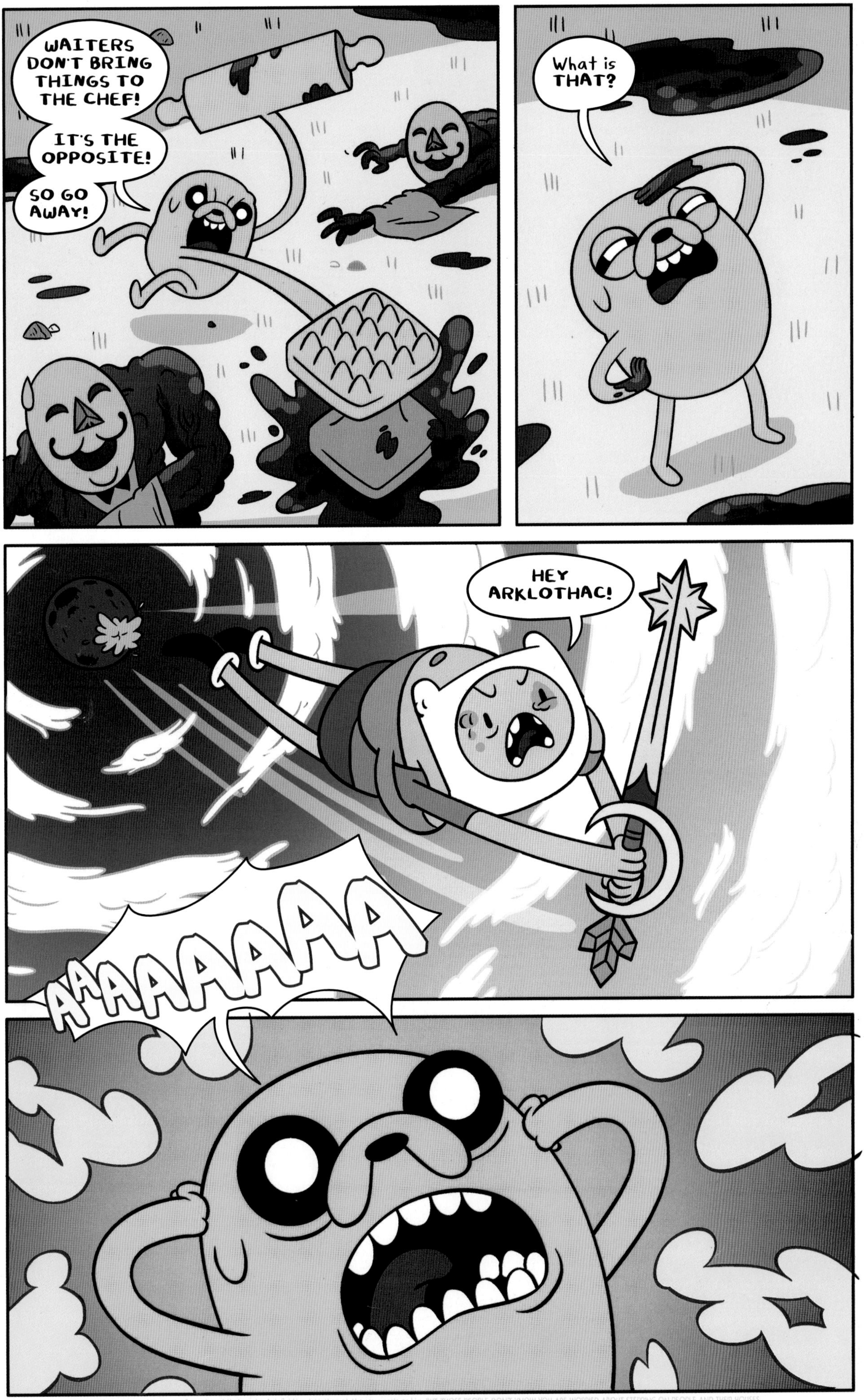

WAITERS DON'T BRING THINGS TO THE CHEF!
IT'S THE OPPOSITE!
SO GO AWAY!
What is THAT?
HEY ARKLOTHAC!
AAAAAAAAA

Jake, you're making a lot of people sad that you're not fighting Arklothac at the same scale as him. BUT THOSE PEOPLE DON'T KNOW YOU ARE WORRIED ABOUT STEPPING ON PEOPLE AND THEIR HOUSES..

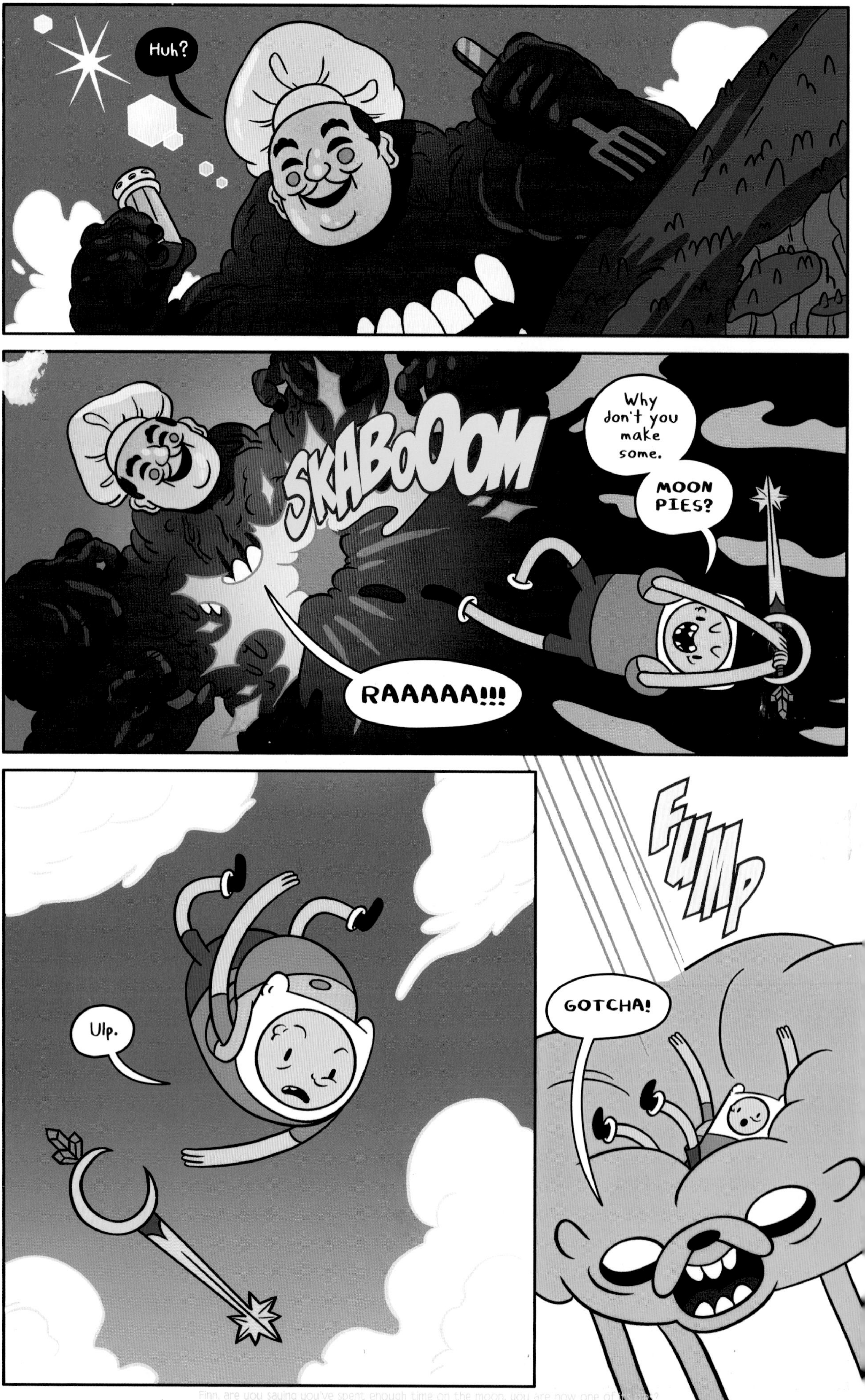
Huh?
SKABOOOM
Why don't you make some.
MOON PIES?
RAAAAA!!!
Ulp.
FUMP
GOTCHA!

Finn, are you saying you've spent enough time on the moon, you are now one of its pies?

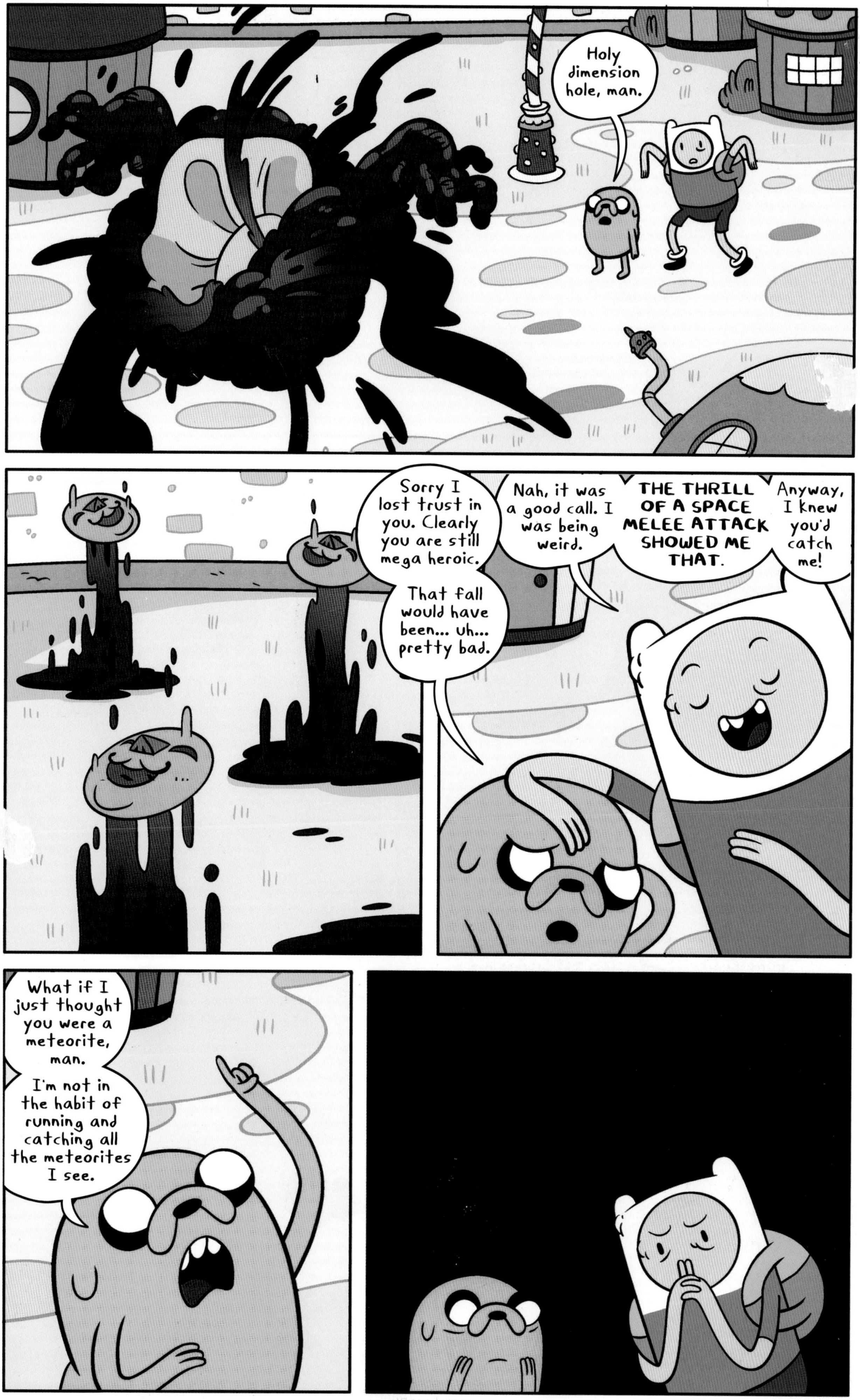

Holy dimension hole, man.
...
Sorry I lost trust in you. Clearly you are still mega heroic.
That fall would have been... uh... pretty bad.
Nah, it was a good call. I was being weird.
THE THRILL OF A SPACE MELEE ATTACK SHOWED ME THAT.
Anyway, I knew you'd catch me!
What if I just thought you were a meteorite, man.
I'm not in the habit of running and catching all the meteorites I see.

Yikes-a-bunga.

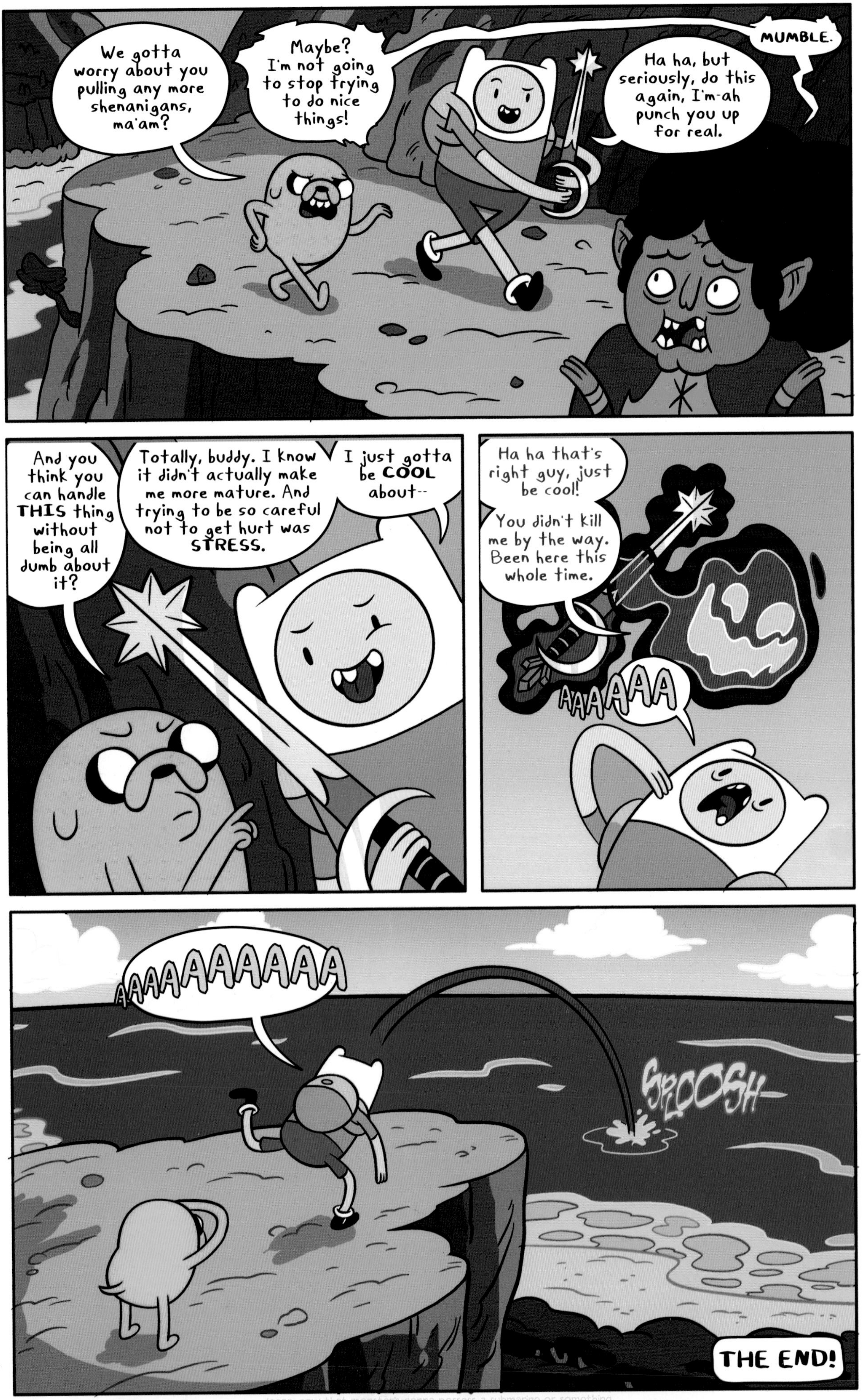
We gotta worry about you pulling any more shenanigans, ma'am?
Maybe? I'm not going to stop trying to do nice things!
MUMBLE.
Ha ha, but seriously, do this again, I'm-ah punch you up for real.
And you think you can handle THIS thing without being all dumb about it?
Totally, buddy. I know it didn't actually make me more mature. And trying to be so careful not to get hurt was STRESS.
I just gotta be COOL about--
Ha ha that's right guy, just be cool!
You didn't kill me by the way. Been here this whole time.
AAAAAAA
AAAAAAAAAAAA
SPLOOSH
THE END!

Jeeze, now that monster's gonna possess a submarine or something.

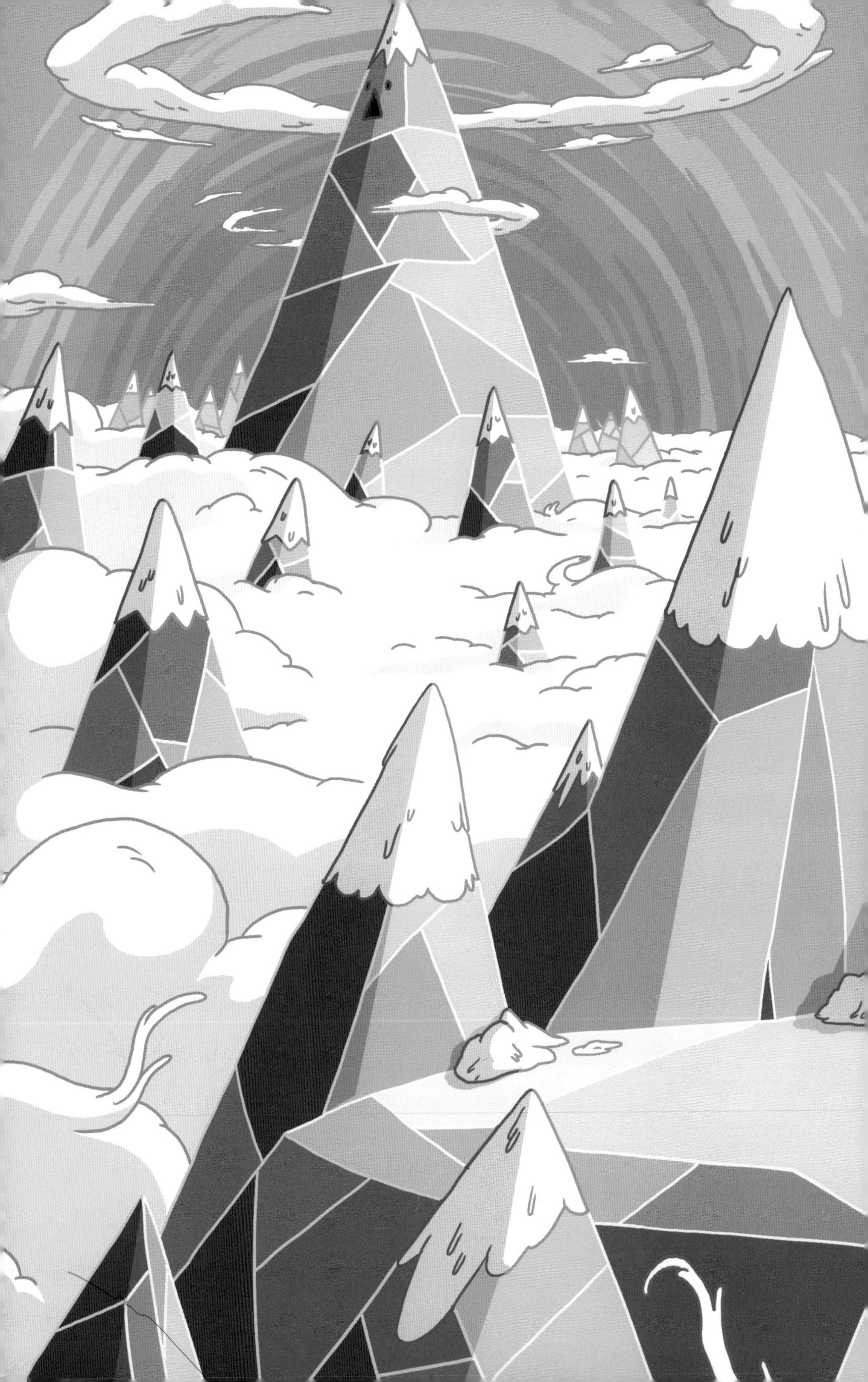

COVER GALLERY

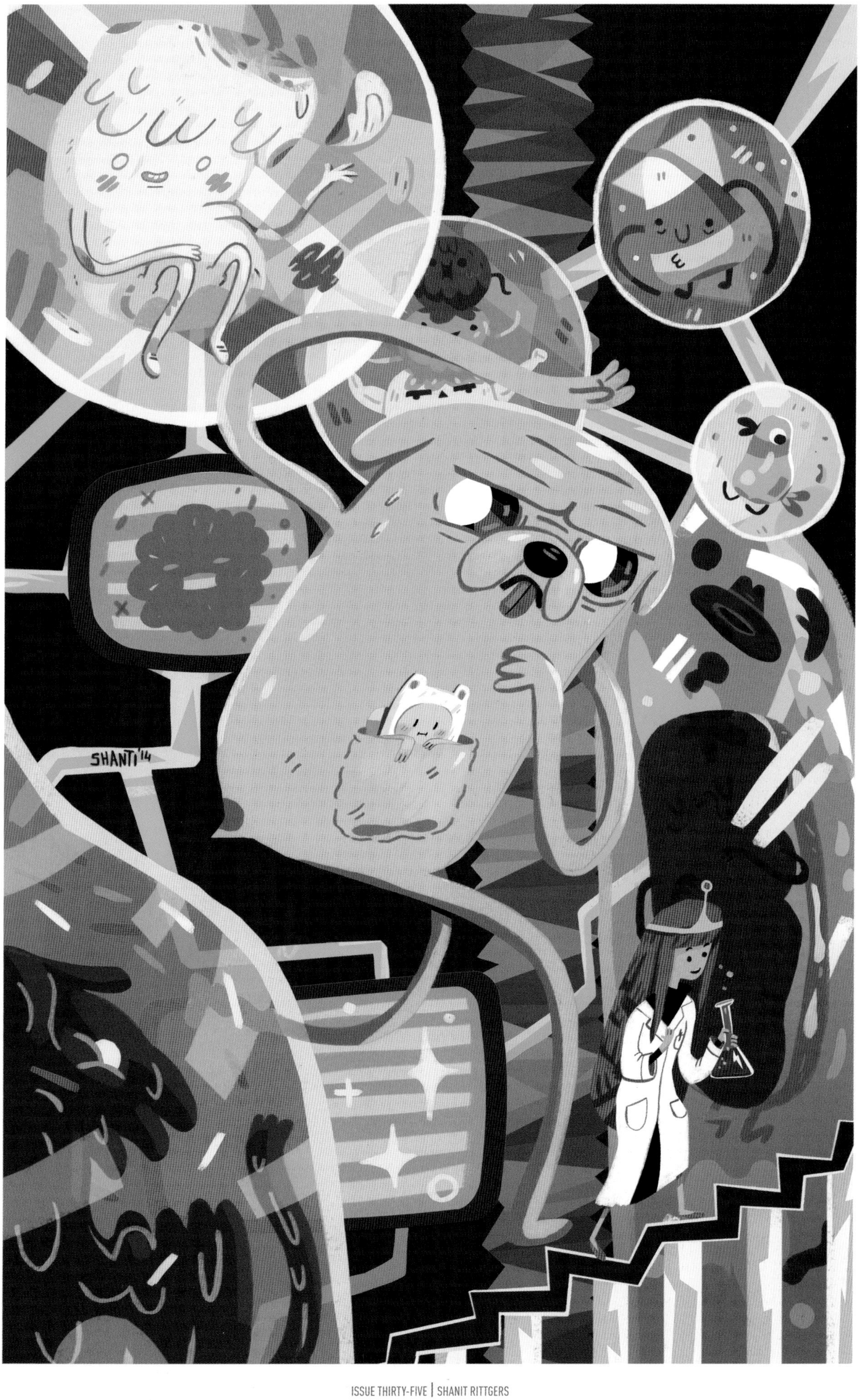
SHANTI'14

ISSUE THIRTY-FIVE | SHANIT RITTGERS

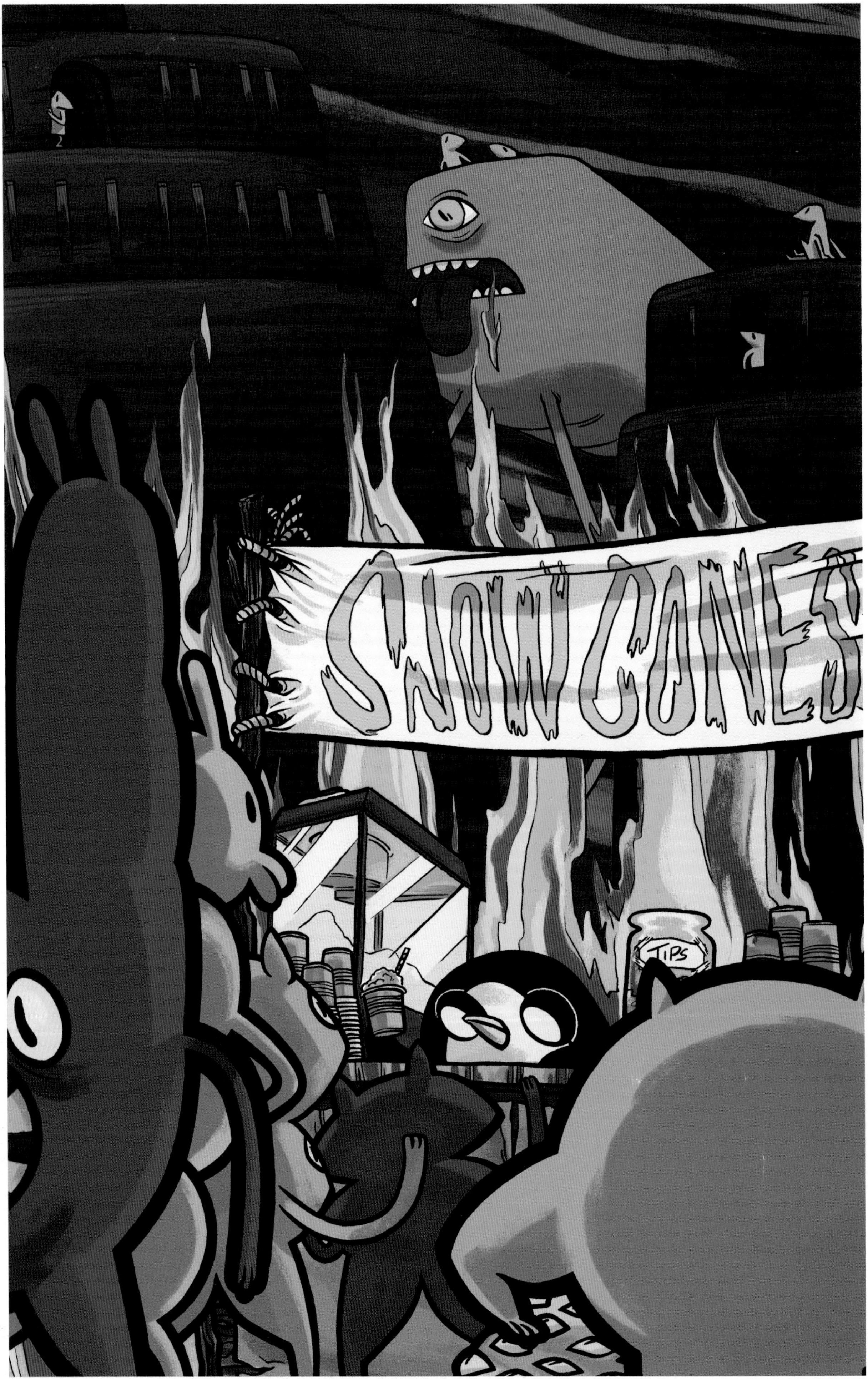
SNOW CONES
TIPS

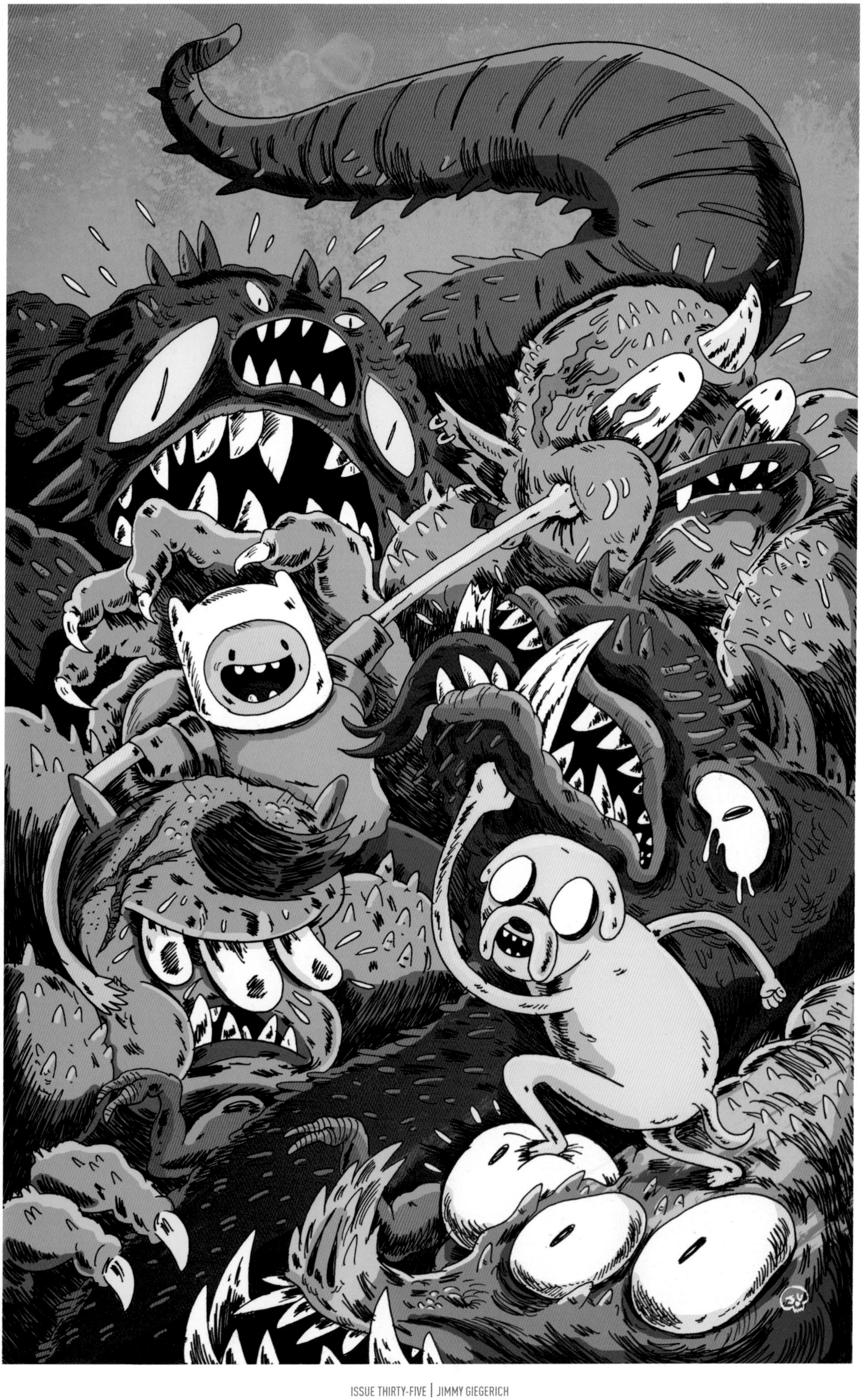

ISSUE THIRTY-FIVE | JIMMY GIEGERICH

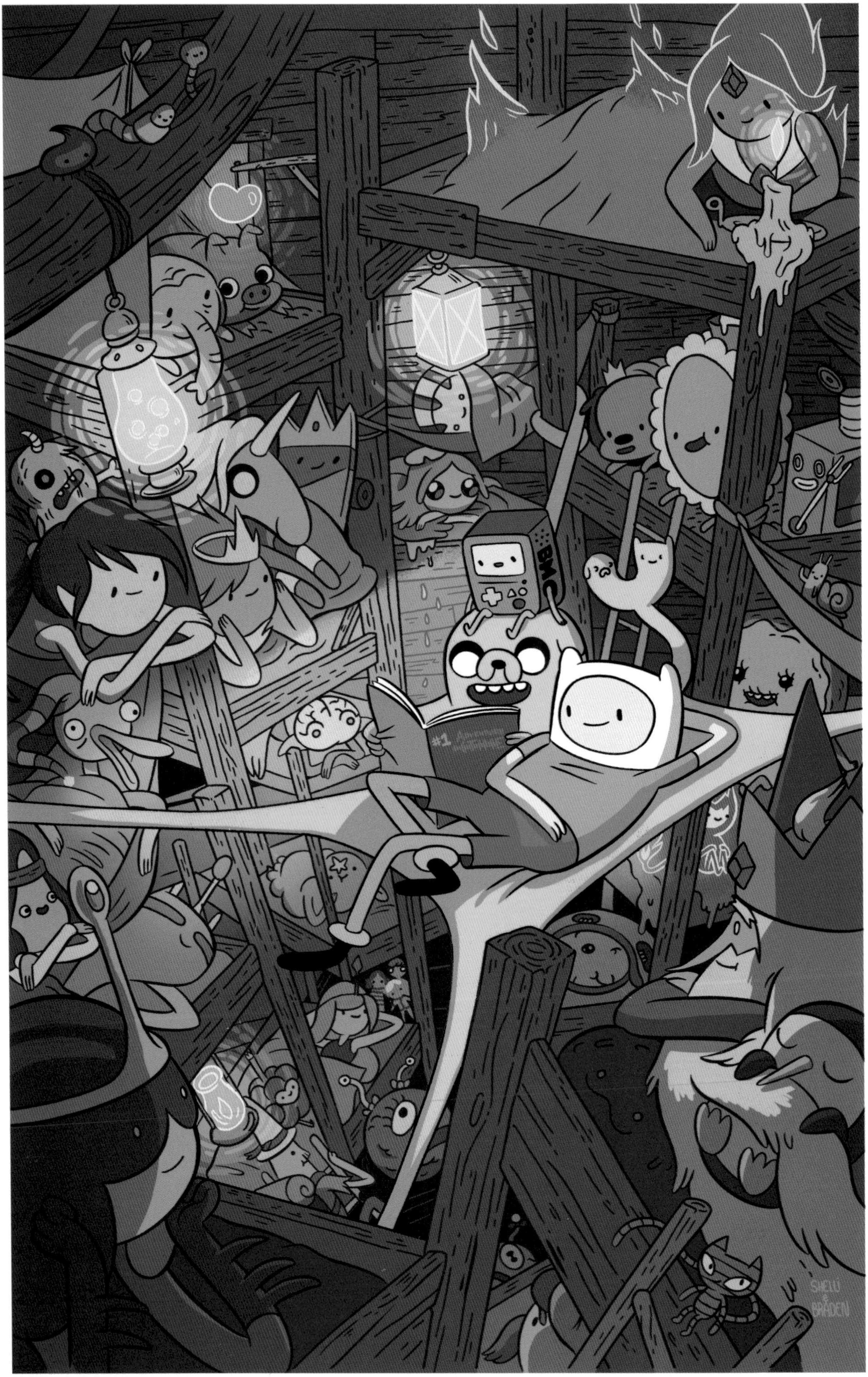
BMO
#1
SHELLI
&
BRADEN

ISSUE THIRTY-FIVE FOC VARIANT | SHELLI PAROLINE & BRADEN LAMB

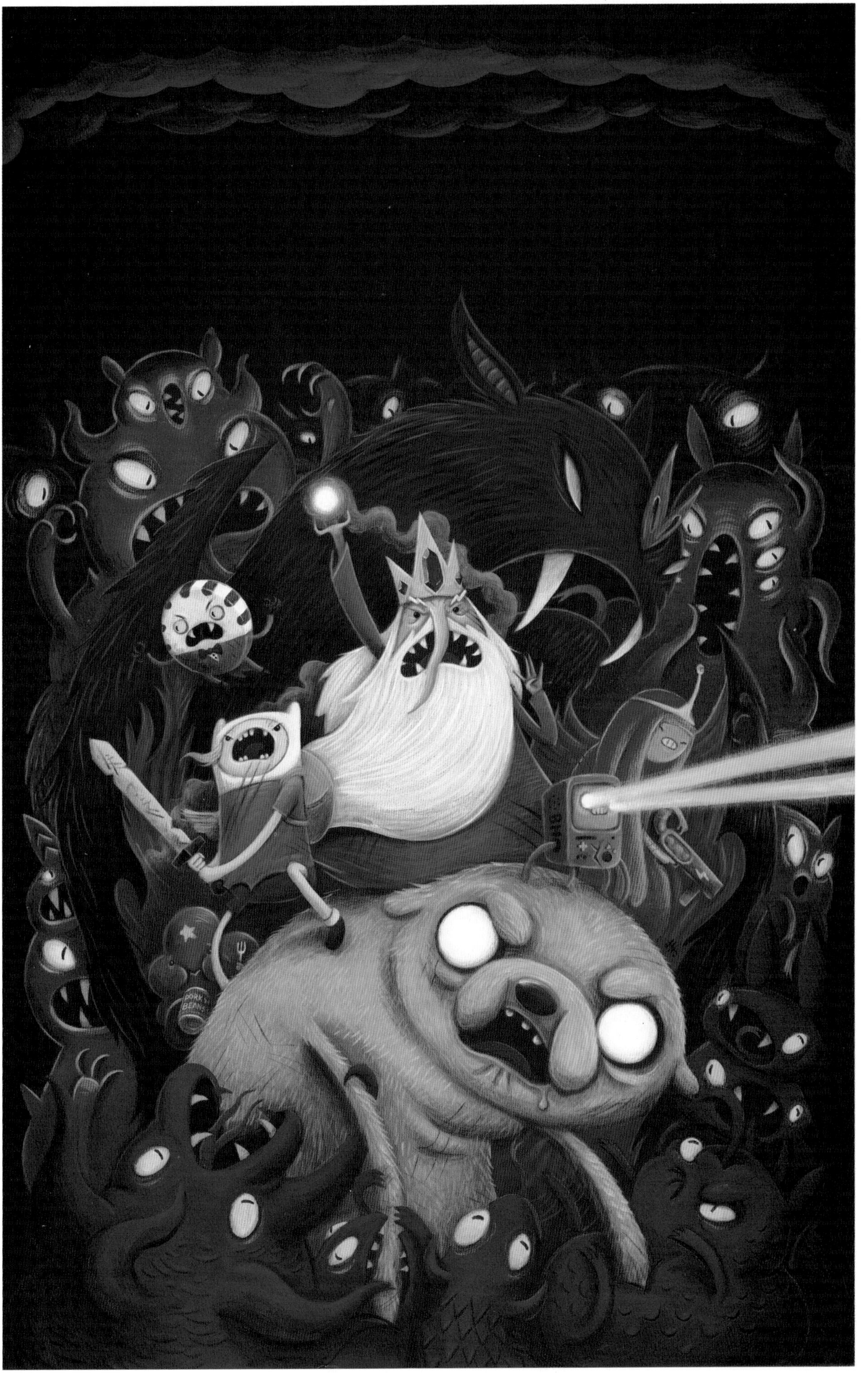

ISSUE THIRTY-SIX | JUSTIN HILLGROVE

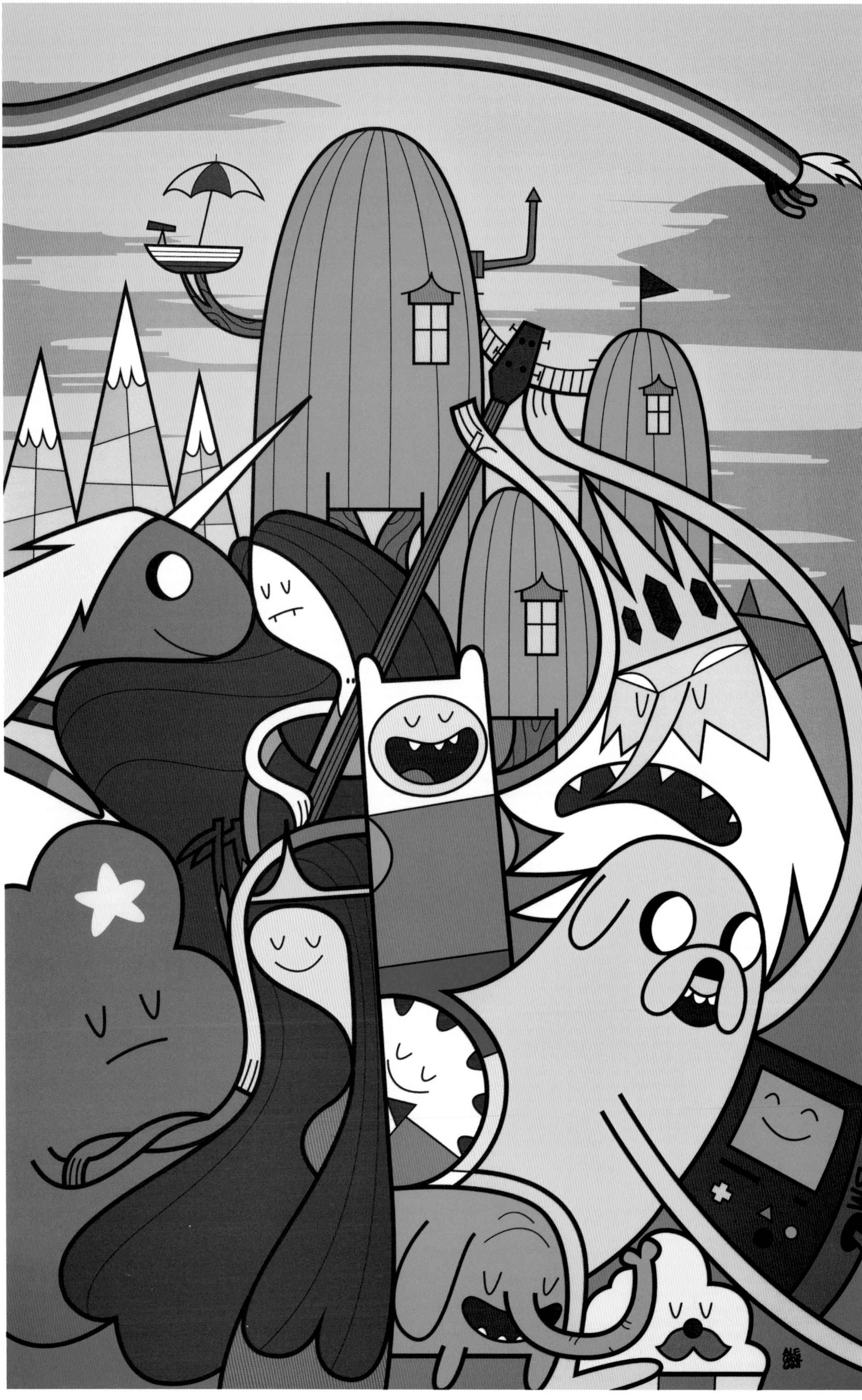

ISSUE THIRTY-SIX SUBSCRIPTION | ALE GIORGINI

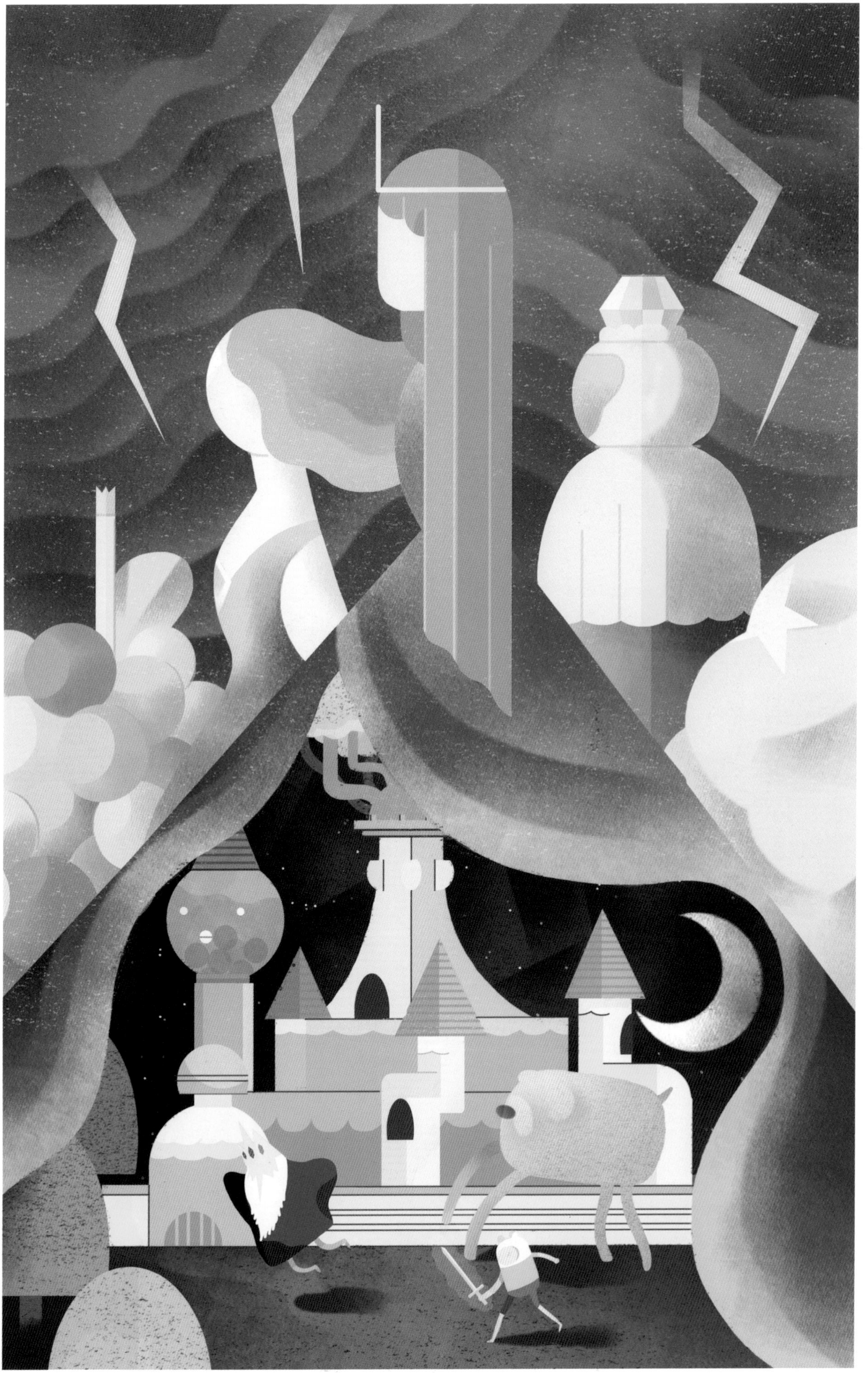

ISSUE THIRTY-SIX VARIANT | REBEKKA DUNLAP

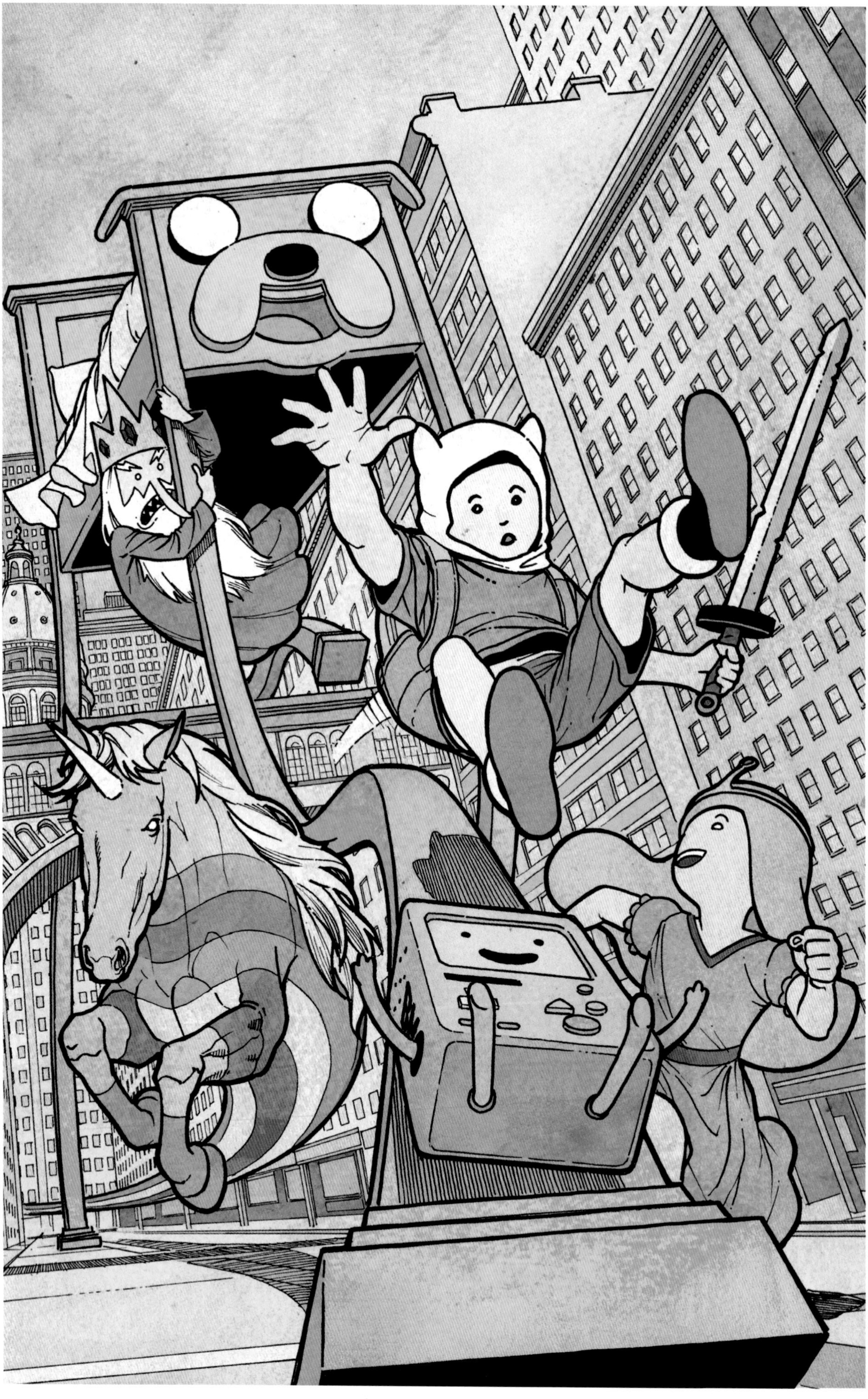

ISSUE THIRTY-SIX COMICS PRO VARIANT | SEAN CHEN WITH COLORS BY WHITNEY COGAR

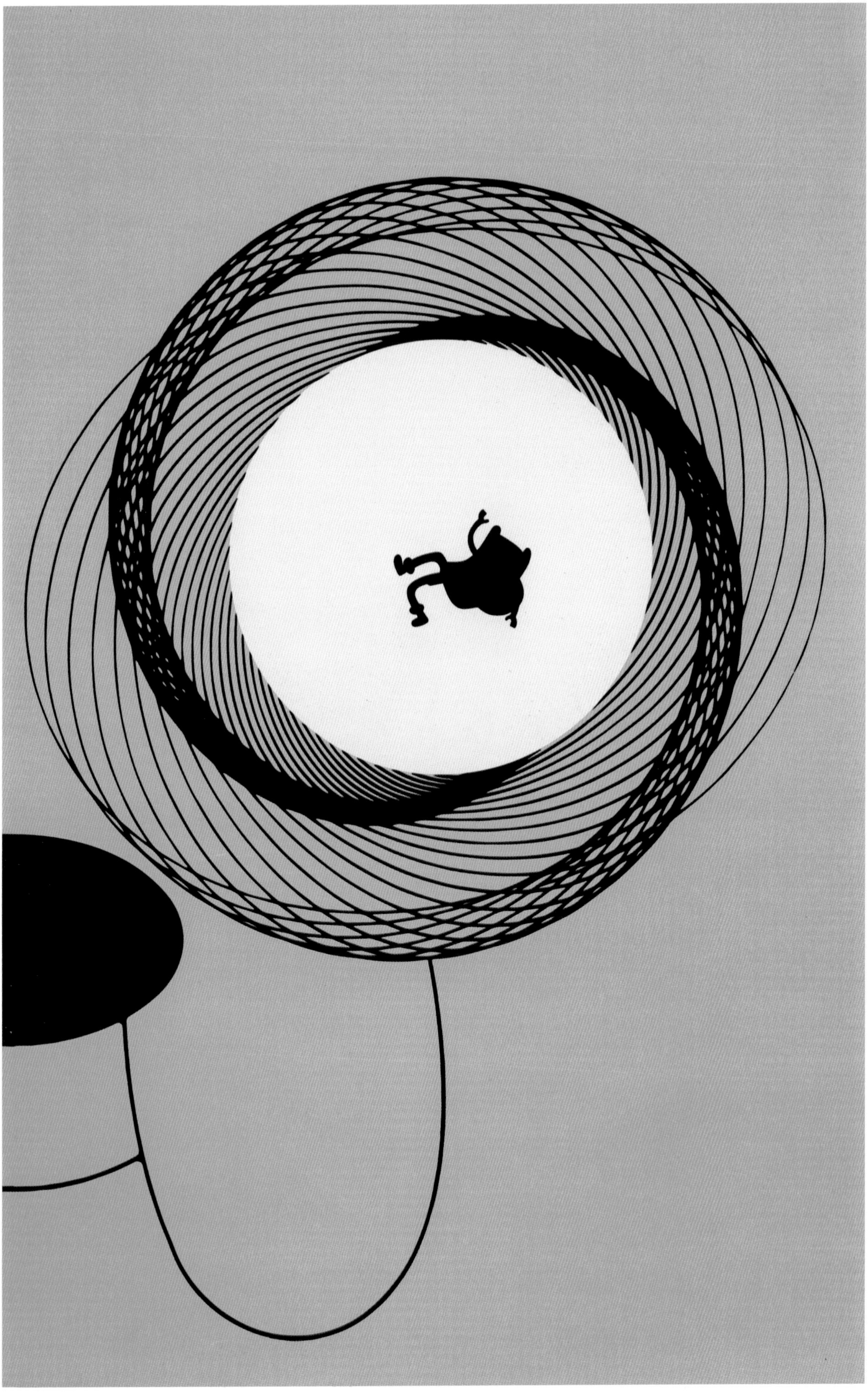

ISSUE THIRTY-SIX SECOND PRINT | JAY SHAW

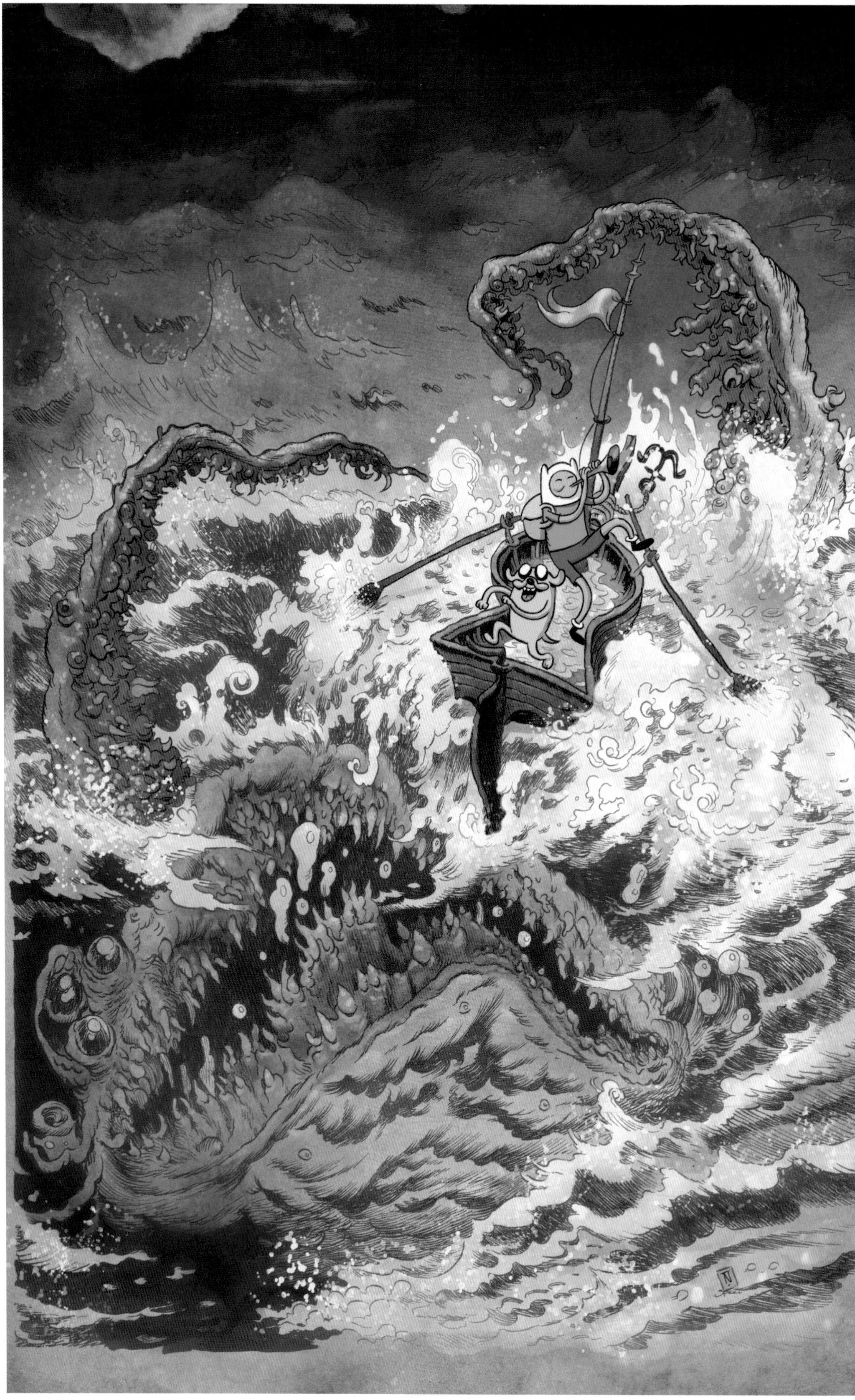

ISSUE THIRTY-SEVEN | TROY NIXEY WITH COLORS BY MICHAEL SPICER

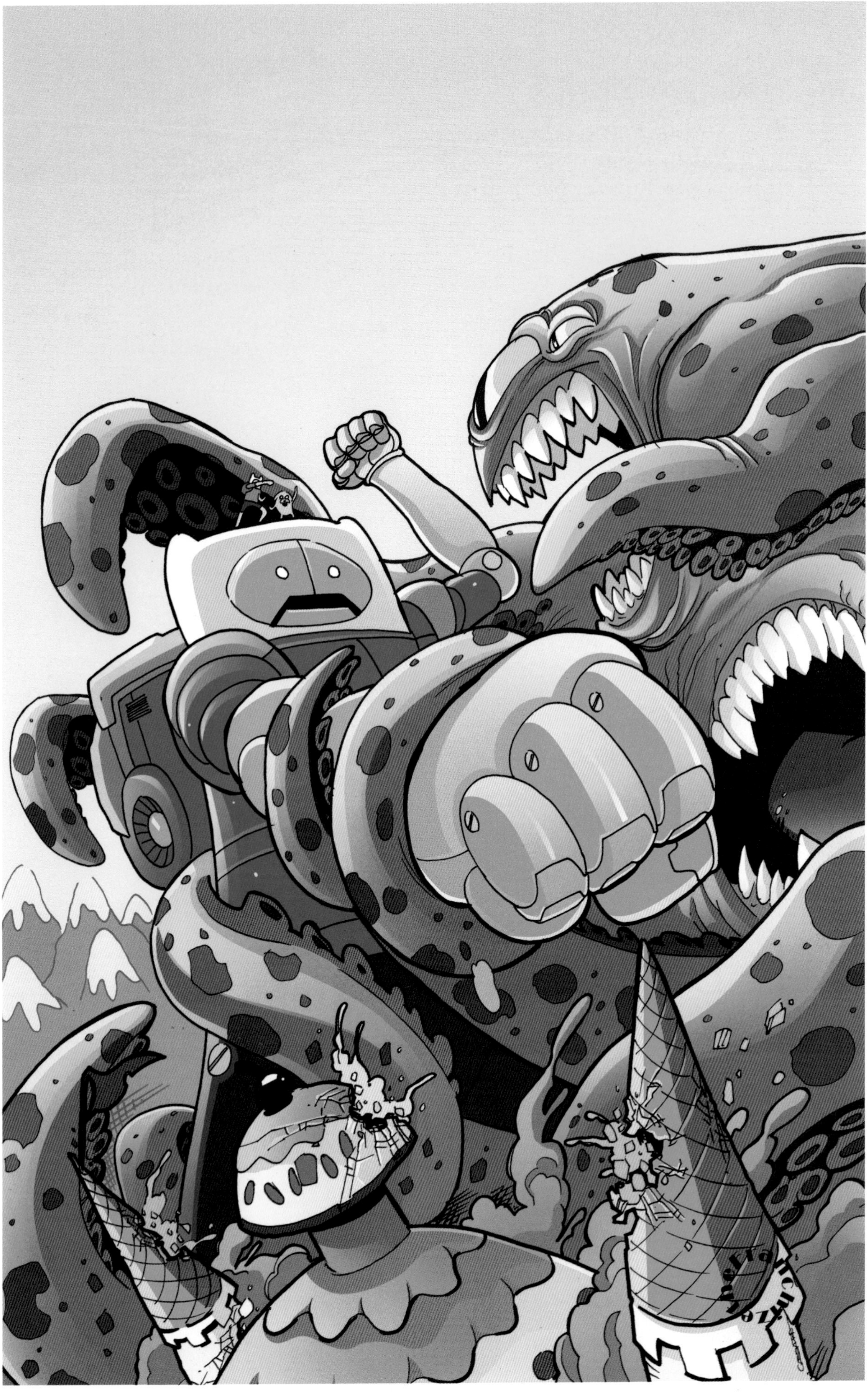

ISSUE THIRTY-SEVEN SUBSCRIPTION | JERRY GAYLORD

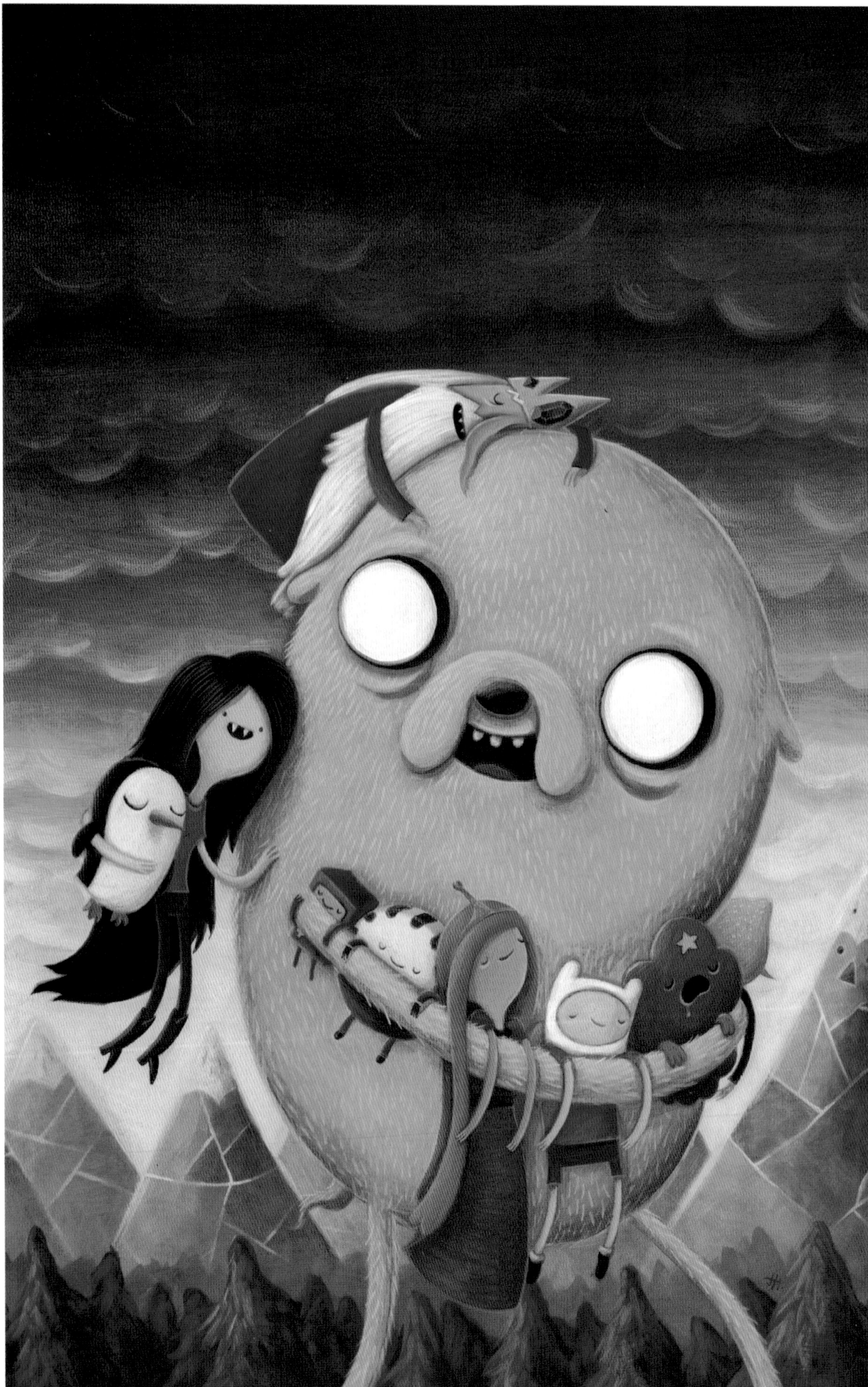

ISSUE THIRTY-SEVEN VARIANT | JUSTIN HILLGROVE

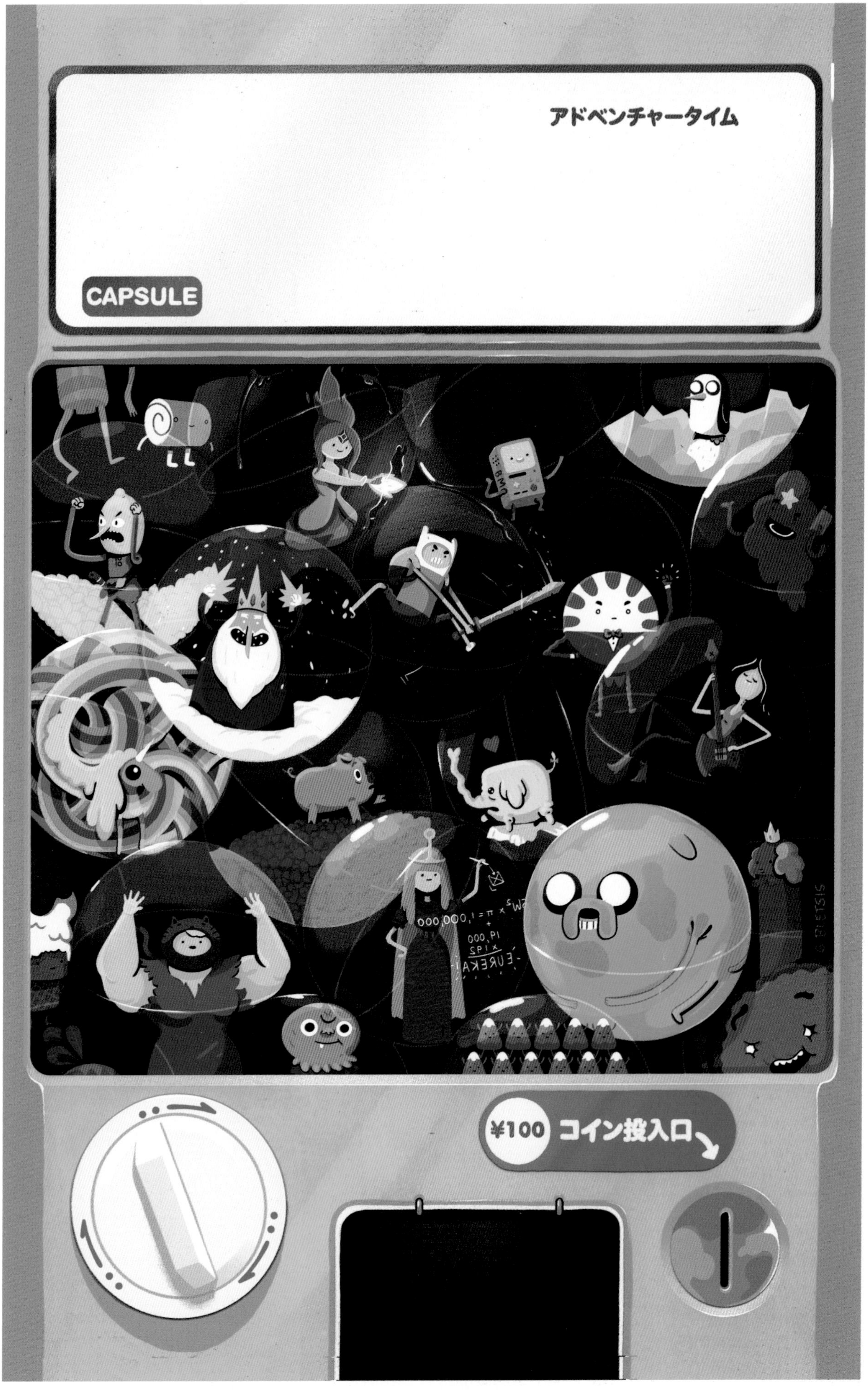
アドベンチャータイム
CAPSULE
BMO
¥100
コイン投入口

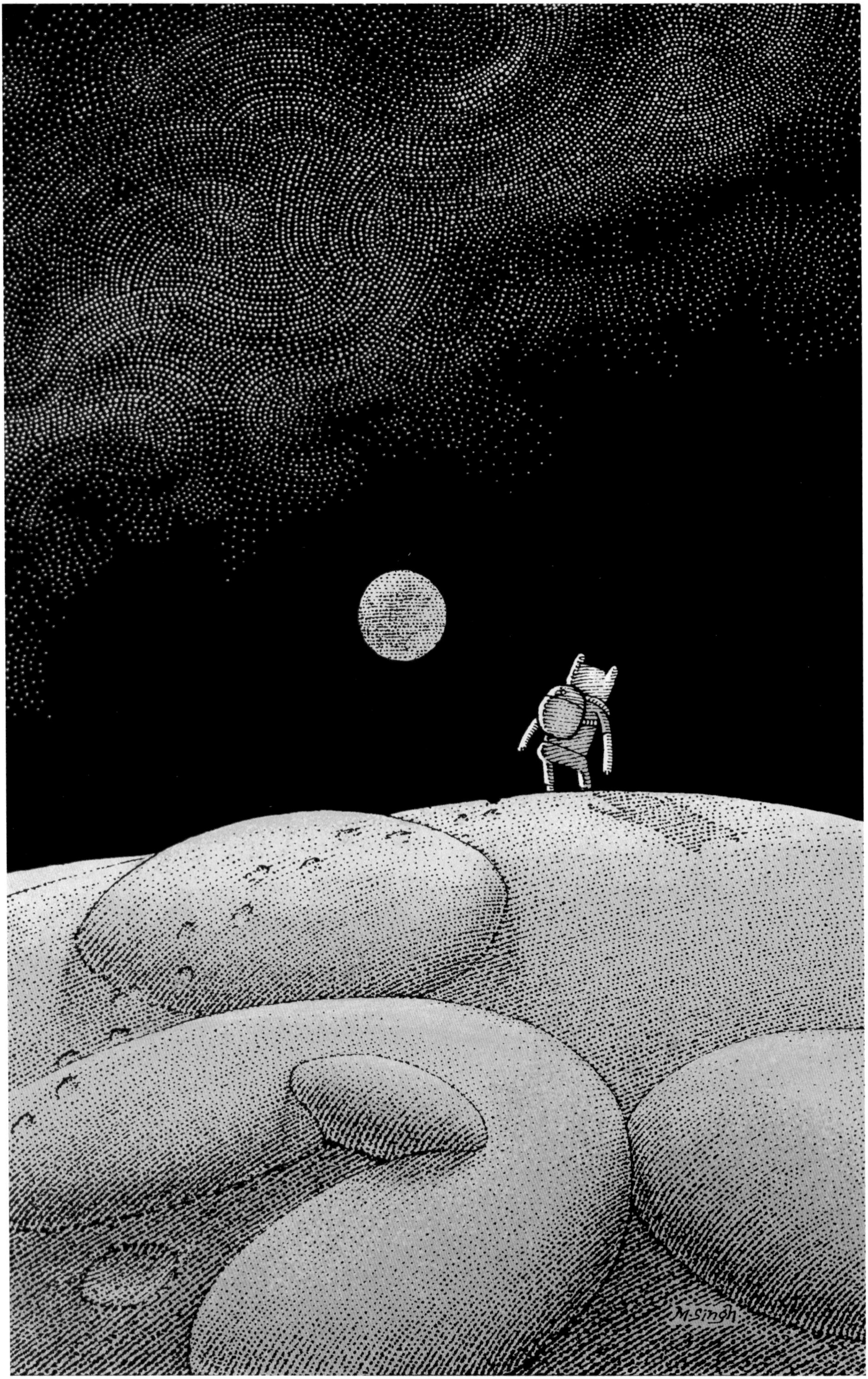
M.Singh

ISSUE THIRTY-EIGHT SUBSCRIPTION | MAHENDRA SINGH

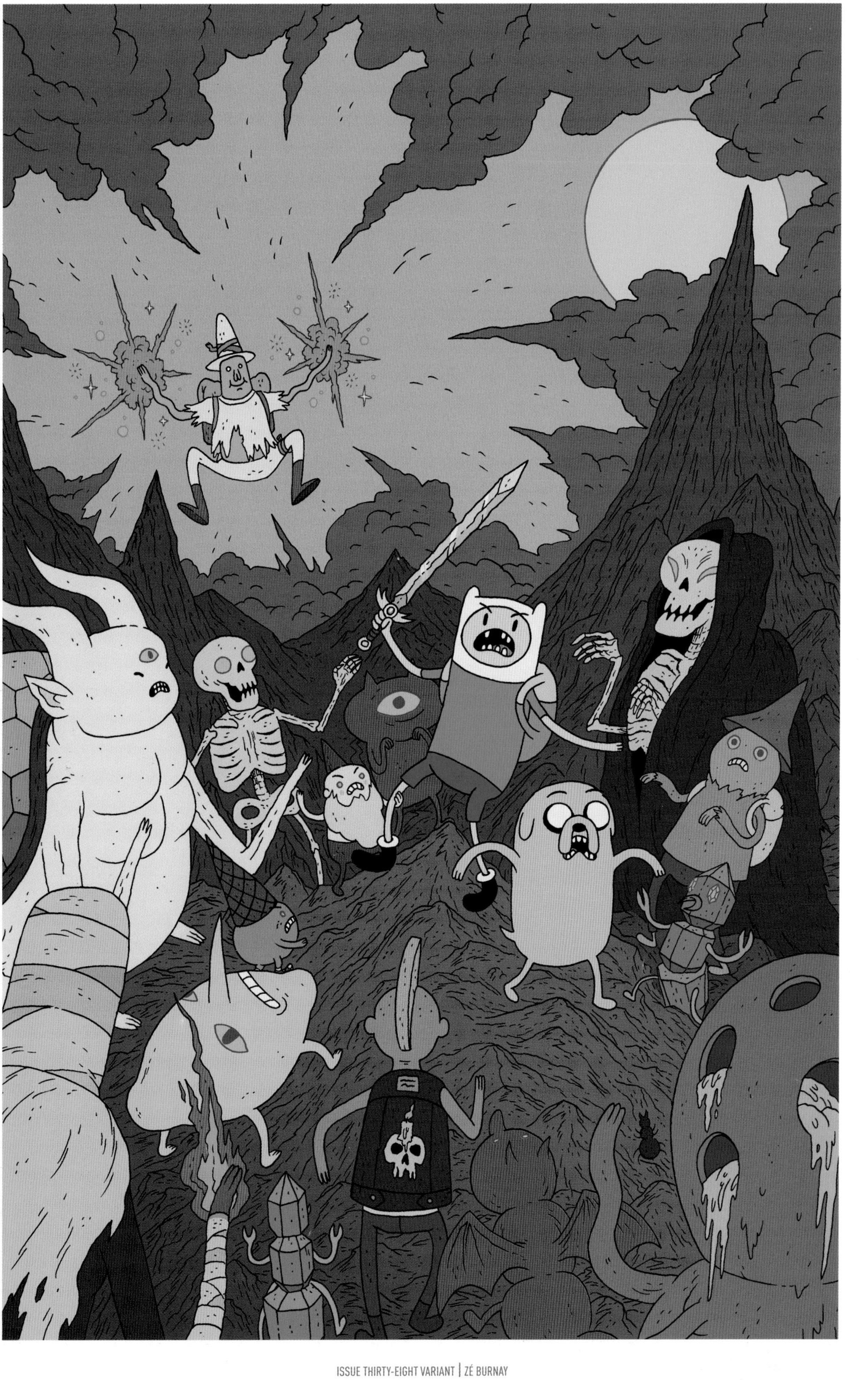

ISSUE THIRTY-EIGHT VARIANT | ZÉ BURNAY

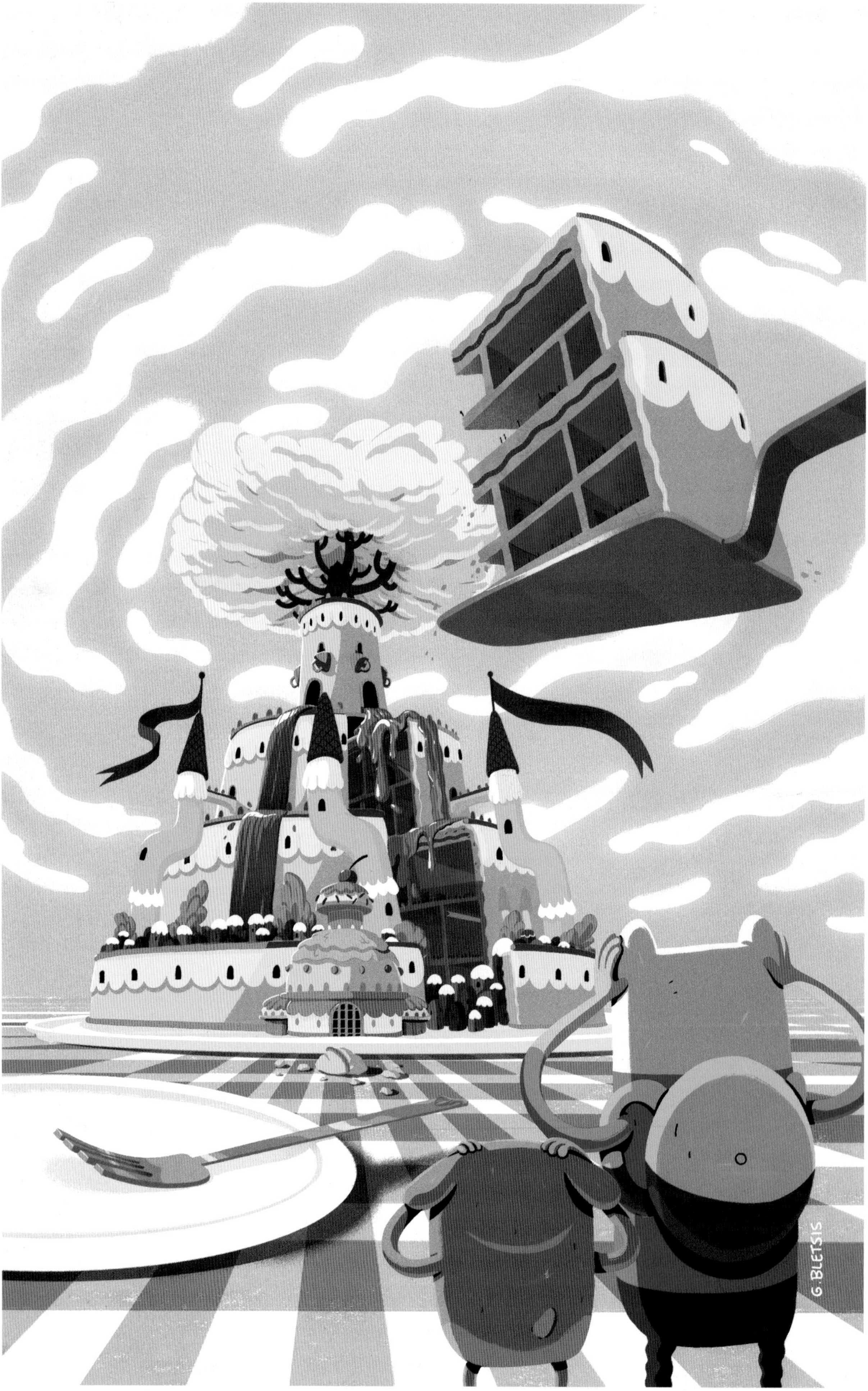
G.BLETSIS

ISSUE THIRTY-NINE | GEORGE BLETSIS

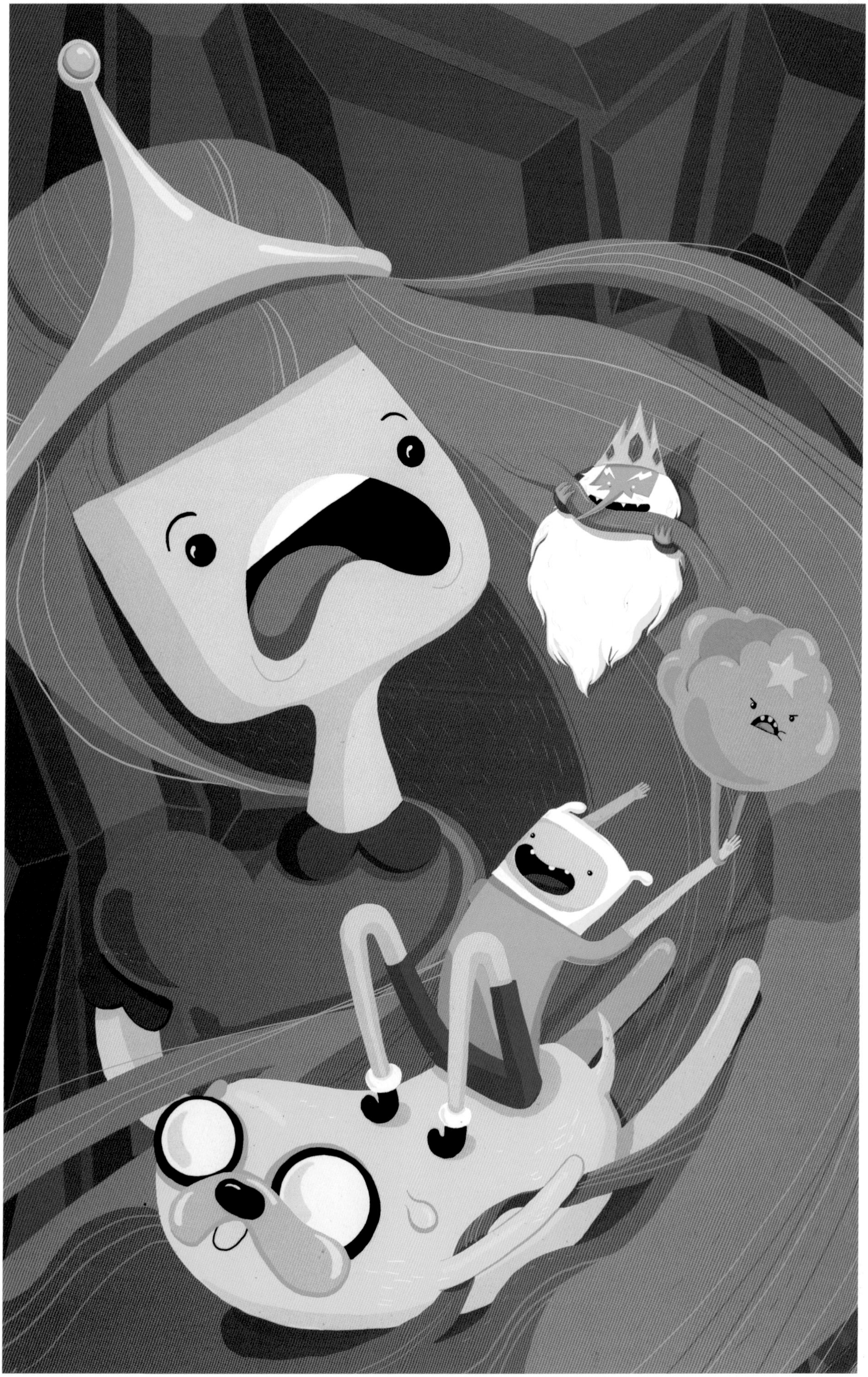

ISSUE THIRTY-NINE SUBSCRIPTION | ANNA STRAIN

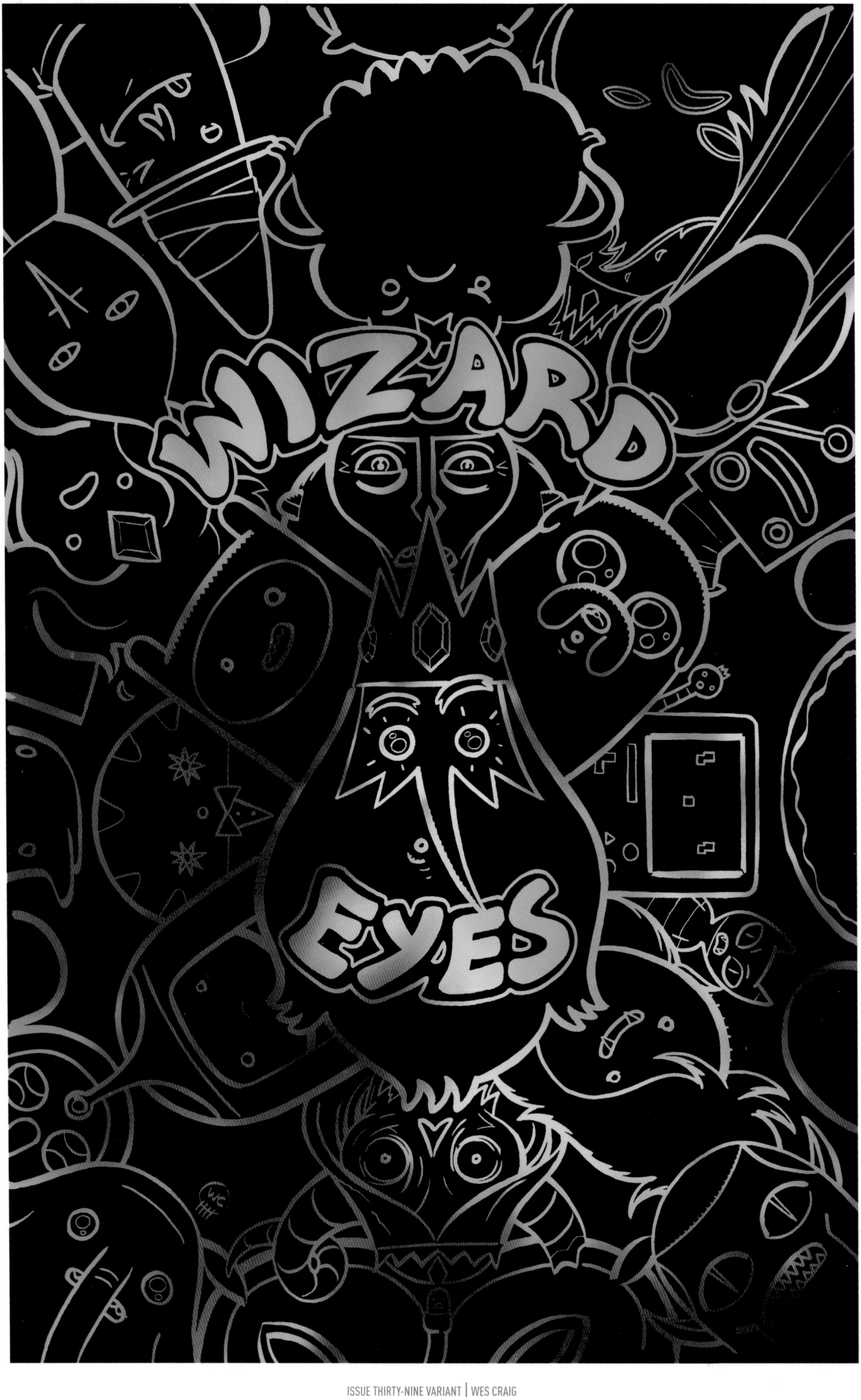
WIZARD
EYES

ISSUE THIRTY-NINE VARIANT | WES CRAIG

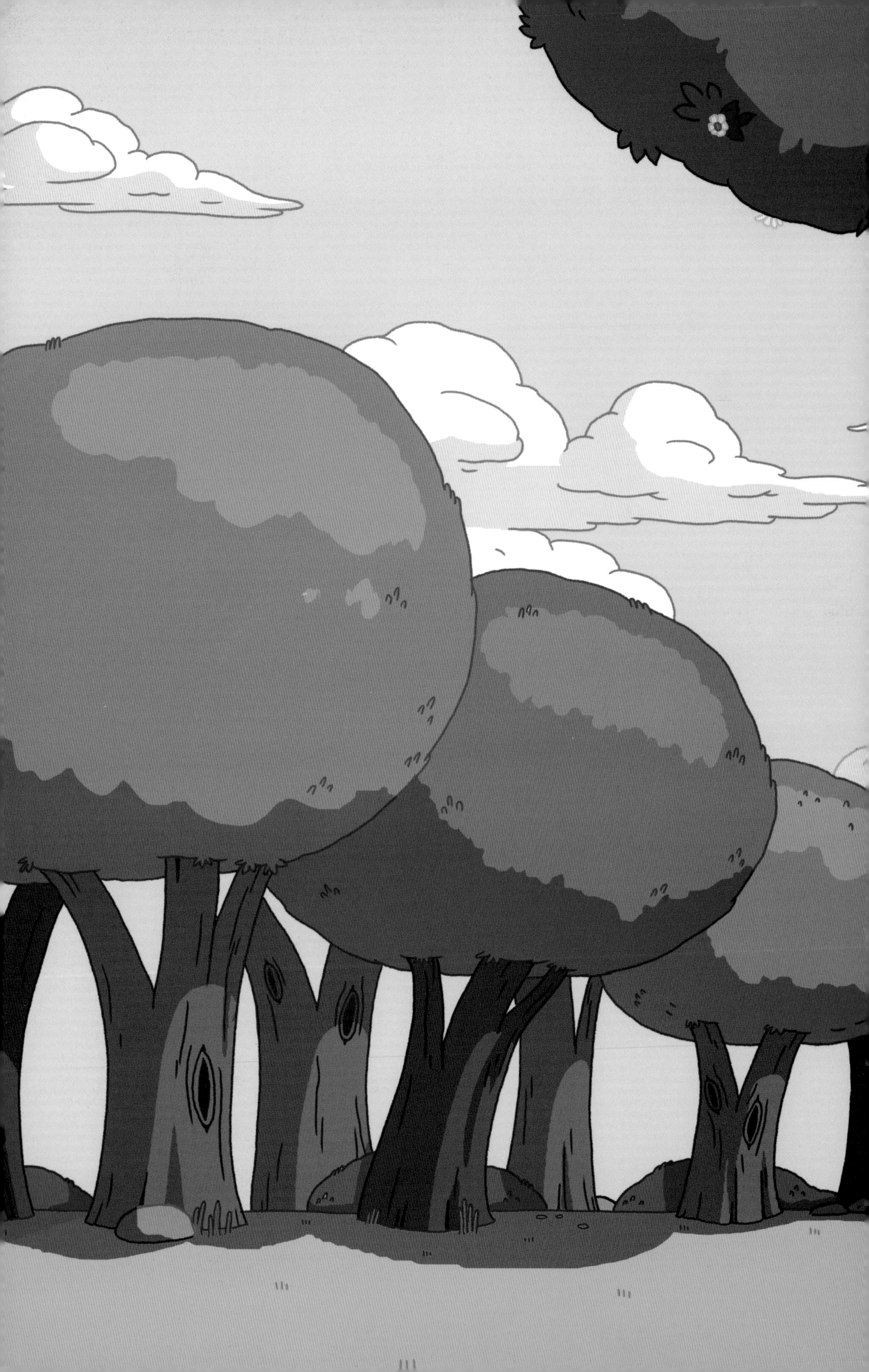

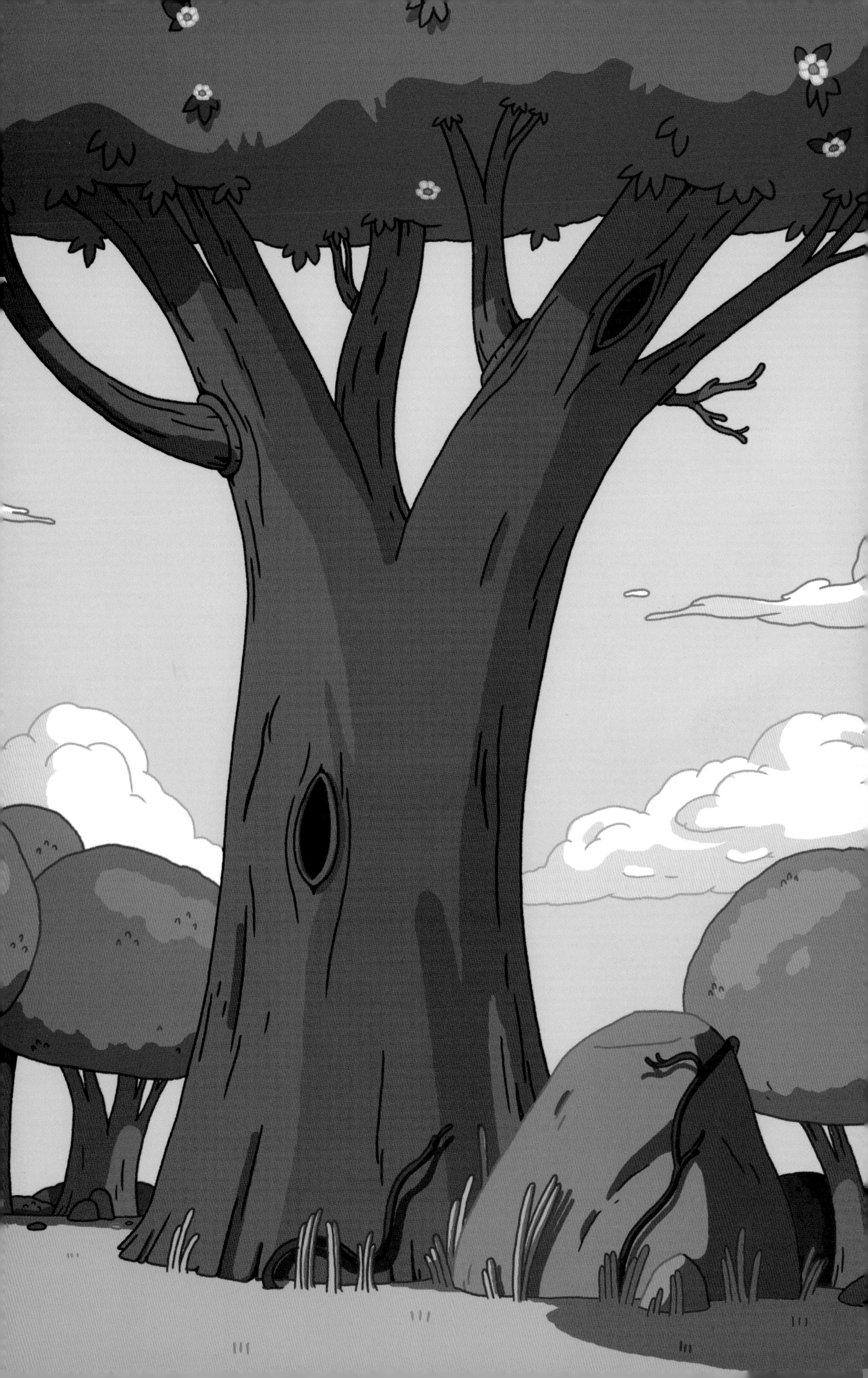

BEHIND THE SCENES

BEHIND THE SCENES

by Ryan North

LSP'S MISSING STAR (#35)

This was the last *Adventure Time* that me, Braden, and Shelli would be working on together before we handed the book off to some new artists (and friends!) to run with it. So we wanted to do something special! We'd already seen Finn's (altered) future in the last arc, so this one was a chance to hang out with these characters one last time. And of course the first page opens up with a riff on the ending credits of the show, just as the first page of our very first issue opens up with a riff on the opening credits. Symmetry! It's great! Humans love it!

Here is the secret to writing BMO's noir dialogue: put on the noirest possible music, and say everything you write out loud in the graveliest possible voice you can muster. If you follow these steps, you will produce insanely noir dialogue that is amazing. Use this secret well, my friends.

The last page is a fold-in, features some of our favourite characters (Lamprey Princess! I LOVE YOU, LAMPREY PRINCESS) and reveals our last message to you guys at the top and bottom of the page when it's folded together. Thank you for going on this journey with us, and I know you're gonna love what comes next. Remember: the adventure never ends!!

Thank you *so much* for reading our comics.

MY VERY FIRST ARC! (#36-39)

So, Ryan North has just wrapped up an Eisner Award winning arc on *Adventure Time*, and hands it off to his old pal, Christopher. (That is me. Hello.) What the heck do I do to FOLLOW UP FROM THAT?! WHAT A TERRIBLE THING HE HAS DONE TO HIS FRIEND! WHAT DO I DO?! *ADVENTURE TIME* IS SO GOOD! I LOVE IT, AND I AM PANICKING I AM GOING TO MESS THIS WHOLE THING UP!

First thing I did was rewatch every single episode of the show, and then watched my favorite ones a second time. I read all the previous comics. I literally interviewed Ryan on the phone, promising I wouldn't publish his answers. I started writing notes, thinking about what I liked, what I noticed we hadn't seen.

And I'll tell you where I landed. Finn and Jake on the moon. I love the moon. I love that there is a giant rock that hangs above our planet, just floating there, and we can look at the giant rock, glowing at night, and we can go visit it if we want. Go walk around, play golf on it, stick a flag on it, grab some of it, bring it back. So... let's put a labyrinth or dungeon up there, and pump up the mystery even more. I love the ruins that hint at life before the Adventure Time characters came around. So it was fun to have an abandoned moon base up there with skeletons and such.

And then Finn finds a SWORD up there. It can shoot lasers, but ONLY if the wielder is in perfect health. Sound familiar? Sound like one of your favorite VIDEO GAME swords? That is exactly what that is. I liked thinking about when I am armed with such a weapon, I'm maybe OVERLY cautious in my video game adventures, because I want to hang onto that laser power, and then when I get a little bit dinged up and the lasers don't work anymore, the whole experience seems... tainted. I wanted to see that explored by our good adventuring boy, Finn.

That lead to a couple of themes, the main one being the idea of "saving it for later." What is "it?" Well that depended on what was going on throughout the arc. The main thing is Finn, running away from battles, so that he could preserve his laser powers for bigger theoretical threats down the road. The sword drove him a little bit nutty in that regard. There's the cultist witch, Janice, who thought she could summon the ancient, powerful chef, Arklothac to cook up the best meal for all of Ooo that all of Ooo has ever known. But she wanted everyone to SAVE their APPETITES, so she cast a spell that made everyone forget how to prepare food.

We go into Ice King's freezer where he's been SAVING frozen food his whole life, until we find he's actually run out of it. Crazy old Ice King's been relying on that giant freezer for so long,

now that it's empty, it's a moment of true crisis. It's a bit like the danger of procrastinating. If you have 3 months to do your paper, you can put it off every single day up until the end, and it's not a big deal, until that final night before it's due, your printer is out of ink and Ye Olde Ink Shoppe is closed. It suddenly becomes a crisis.

From there, we find that a tiny crystallized chunk of Perfect Sandwich has been SAVED in Jake's guts. So perfect and magical, it actually created a little society of sandwich worshippers created from Jake's shifting flesh. This story created a bit of a problem for me, because when I first jumped on the comic, I knew it was very important to do things in the comic that weren't being done in the show. Why read the comic if it's just rehashing stuff in the show? Well as I was writing this one about a society of people formed from Jake INSIDE of Jake, WHICH episode should air? Of course it's the one about all the Jake people inside of Jake. Thankfully the episode ended up being pretty different from what happened on the show, and all I had to do was have Jake say something like "Never been inside THIS part of me before" and there we go.

By the way, want to know what my predecessor, Ryan's advice was when I told him about this situation? "Oh, that's my worst nightmare. I'm glad it never happened to me."

Anyway, everyone in Ooo learns how to cook again, because Jake's magic sandwich gem had the knowledge to make sandwiches and that unlocks the whole curse. But it's too late. Arklothac shows up and Finn and Jake must send him away. They finally have the confrontation over how weird Finn has been with his sword, and we get into the second major theme, which is maturity. The issue of Finn's maturity is something we go back to many times over the course of my time writing Adventure Time, but we have to start somewhere, so here in the beginning, well... Finn isn't very mature at all, and even has some very wrong ideas about what it means to be mature.

As you read further volumes, you'll see Finn finding out more and more what true maturity means. Right now he seems to think it's just about ranged attacks. Thankfully he gives up on that idea, and does a sweet move shooting himself and his sword flying toward Ooo from the moon like an awesome Finn-Spear, taking down Arklothac and saving Ooo for another day.

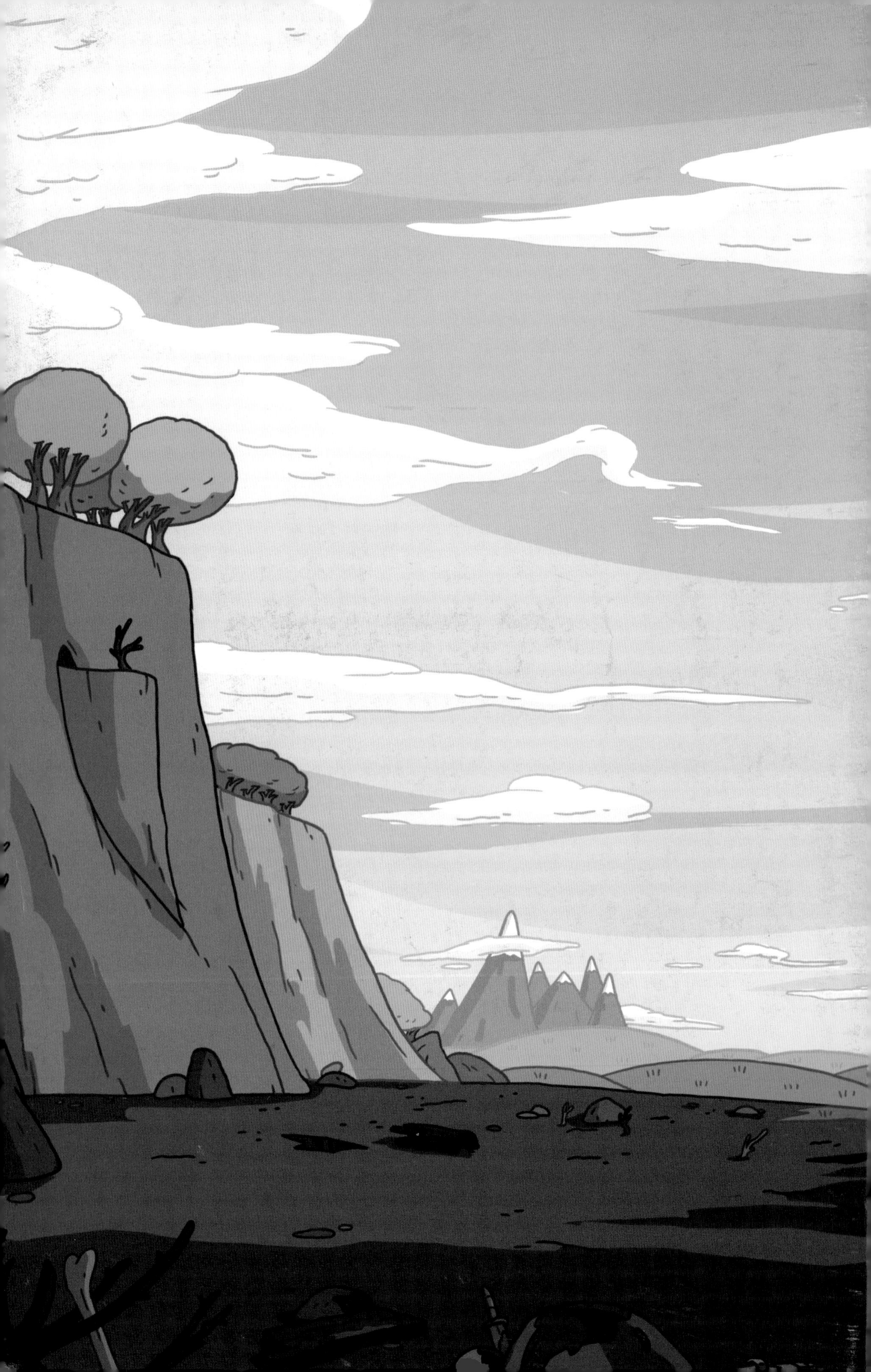

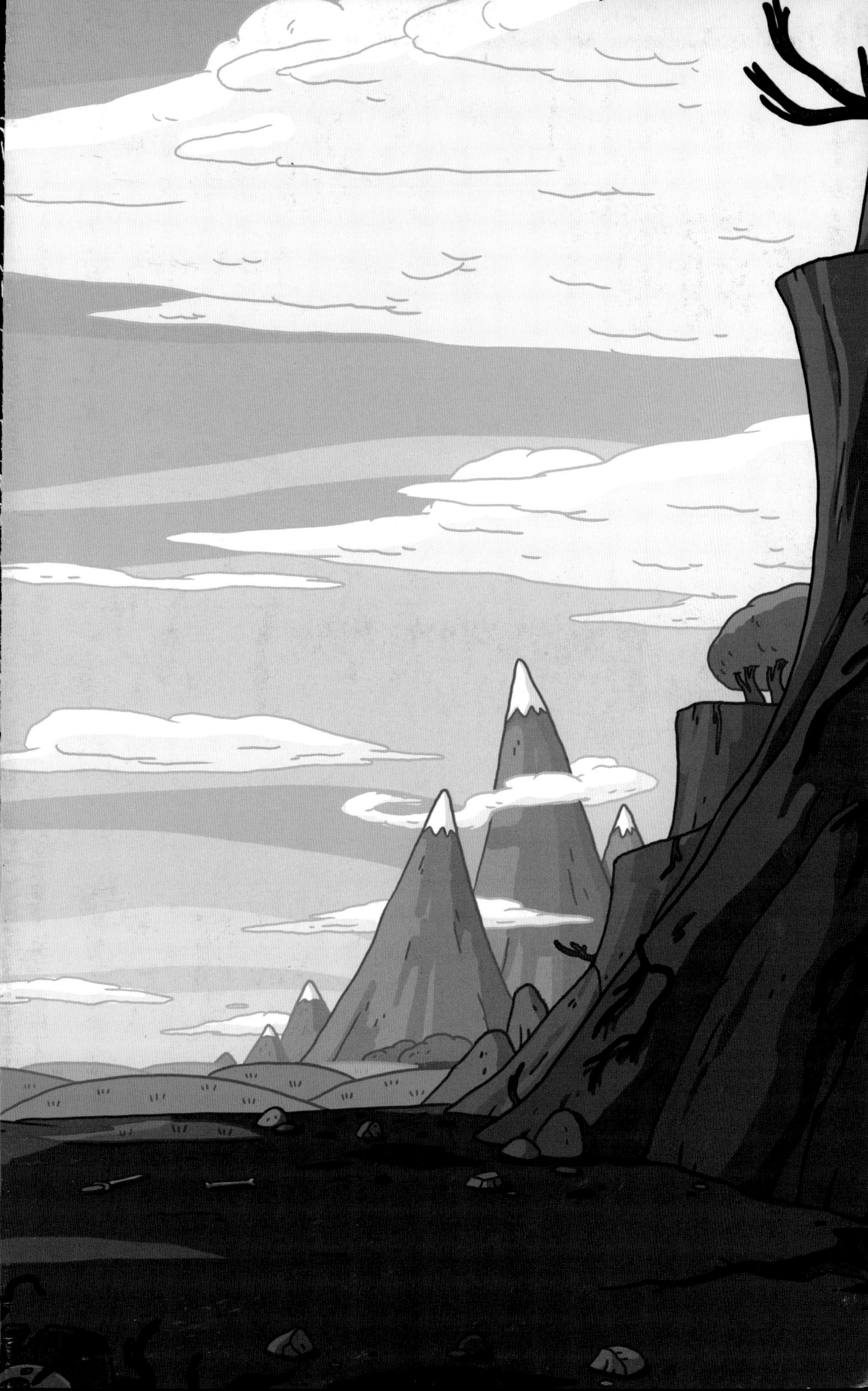

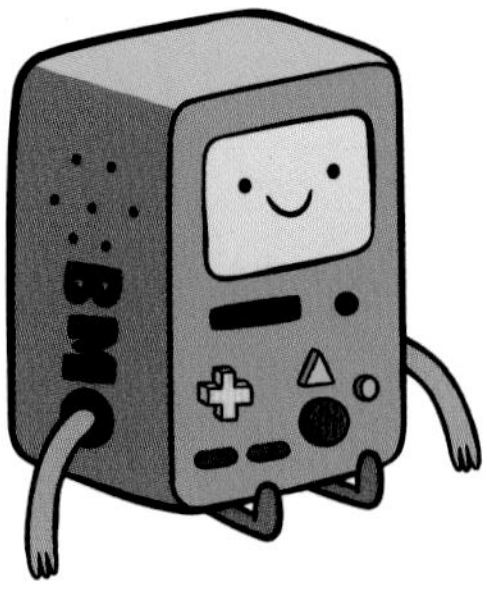
BMO

Ryan North lives in Toronto with his rad wife and sweet dog. He writes comics at dinosaurcomics.com every day. His interests include skateboarding, being a good friend, and eating tasty things. He really hopes you like the comics!

Christopher Hastings is a writer who mostly works in comic books. He is the author of *The Adventures of Dr. McNinja*, a continuing online comic series with book collections available from Dark Horse Comics. He also writes the ongoing *Adventure Time* comic series, and the *Unbelievable Gwenpool*, which he co-created. Christopher has also written *Vote Loki*, *Longshot Saves the Marvel Universe*, and a smattering of *Deadpool* comics.

Shelli Paroline escaped early on into the world of comics, cartoons, and science fiction. She has now returned to the Boston area, where she works as an unassuming illustrator and designer.

Braden Lamb grew up in Seattle, studied film in upstate New York, learned about vikings in Iceland and Norway, and established an art career in Boston. Now he draws and colors comics, and wouldn't have it any other way.

Zachary Sterling is a New York Times Best-Selling illustrator, designer and sequential artist based in Portland, OR. Best known as the artist on BOOM! Studio's *Adventure Time* comic and prop designer on the *Bee & PuppyCat* cartoon. He studied at *The Pacific Northwest College of Art*, *Art Insitute of Portland* and interned at *Periscope Studio.*